THE SORORITY

Books by Tamara Thorne

HAUNTED

MOONFALL

ETERNITY

CANDLE BAY

BAD THINGS

THE FORGOTTEN

THUNDER ROAD

THE SORORITY

Published by Kensington Publishing Corporation

TAMARA THORNE

The SORORITY

KENSINGTON BOOKS
www.kensingtonbooks.com

KENSINGTON BOOKS are published by

Kensington Publishing Corp.
119 West 40th Street
New York, NY 10018

All Kensington titles, imprints, and distributed lines are available at special quantity discounts for bulk purchases for sales promotion, premiums, fund-raising, and educational or institutional use.

Special book excerpts or customized printings can also be created to fit specific needs. For details, write or phone the office of the Kensington Special Sales Manager: Kensington Publishing Corp., 119 West 40th Street, New York, NY 10018. Attn. Special Sales Department. Phone: 1-800-221-2647.

ISBN-13: 978-0-7582-8551-5
ISBN-10: 0-7582-8551-5
First Kensington Trade Paperback Printing: September 2013

eISBN-13: 978-0-7582-9164-6
eISBN-10: 0-7582-9164-7
First Kensington Electronic Edition: September 2013

10 9 8 7 6 5 4 3 2 1

Printed in the United States of America

To the memory of my mother
Who told me stories of a real town
drowned beneath a lake;
Of what it was like to live there before,
and to swim above it, after.

For Q.L. Pearce
Purveyor of magical mystery tours
Thanks for all the rides
Past, present, and future.

For Bill Gagliani,
Boon Companion
and
Keeper of Rare Stories

Acknowledgments

Thanks go to:
My darling Damien, provider of the necessities of life, no
matter how kinky they may be.
John Scognamiglio, for faith, patience, and making
order out of chaos.
Kay McCauley, for taking care of business.
Heather Locke, for making my Web a site to behold.
Q.L. Pearce, for books and fun.
Chelsea Quinn Yarbro, for advice and fun.
Bill Gagliani, for always knowing weird things.
Brian and Leah, for understanding and doing the cooking.
Michele Santelices, Gerina Dunwich, Adam Contreas,
Jim Beusse, Eric Hoheisele, and Brett Boyd for aid
and inspiration in a rainbow of ranges.
The Orange Boys for applying decorative
ginger fur to all my clothes.
Secret Societies for being so secretive.
The New World Order for providing so much basic
horror material.
Monty Python and the National Lampoon for
helping shape my adolescent view of Arthurian
lore and Greek college societies.
And to the little handfuls of sorority girls and
cheerleaders who alienated everyone, even their
own squads and sisterhoods, with their shameless arrogance.
This one's on you, babes!

Contents

Eve

Applehead Lake Cheerleading Camp

Eight Years Ago

1

"They say she's still down there." Merilynn Morris trailed her fingers through the cool summer water as Samantha and Eve dipped their oars, slowly paddling toward the little island in the center of the lake. "She's still down there, trapped. Waiting."

"Waiting for what?" asked Sam. "Prince Charming?"

Merilynn looked up at Samantha Penrose and Eve Camlan with eyes so green that when they first met, Eve thought she wore colored contact lenses. But she didn't, and contacts couldn't do what Merilynn's eyes could do. Now they appeared to change from the deep shades of the shadowy forest to that of brilliant emeralds. At the sight, even scared-of-nothing Sam stopped giggling.

Merilynn looked far older than her eight years as she regarded them. "Prince Charming's for little kids—" she said archly.

"I kno-ow," Sam interrupted. "I was joking. Who cares about dumb old Prince Charming, anyway?"

Eve did, but she didn't say so. She'd already figured out that Sam, who was pretty much a tomboy, and almost a whole year older, would think she was a wimp if she talked about handsome princes and beautiful princesses, about dragons and knights and true love. And Merilynn? She wouldn't tease, probably, but she'd do that weird, serene smile of hers, like in those paintings by the Old Misters.

In fact, Eve had no idea what went on in the green-eyed girl's mind, but it was something mysterious, interesting, and a little spooky. Like the way she could change the color of her eyes. Eve thought it was magic, but when she said so, Merilynn had a giggle fit. For an instant, Eve thought she was going to make fun of her, but instead she said thank you and kissed her forehead, which was another weird but kind of nice thing Merilynn did sometimes.

"Holly Gayle," Merilynn said, sitting up straight in the little boat but looking down into the dark water, "is waiting to smite the evildoers who drowned her town and murdered her for her treasure."

"Smite?" asked Eve. "What's 'smite'?"

"It's something God does," Sam said. "It's like squishing a bug."

"Eww."

Samantha grinned, somberness all gone. "Yeah, Evie, this giant hand comes down out of the clouds thumb first, and starts squashing people." She demonstrated on her knee. "But that's not real and neither is any old treasure. I've been hearing this story since the first night of camp, and there's no treasure. That's just a fairy tale. Probably, Holly Gayle wasn't ever real either."

"It's all true," Merilynn said solemnly. "Holly Gayle was real. She's at the bottom of the lake. She's waiting." Late afternoon sun reflected on the lake water and blazed through her red hair.

"Merilynn, you're giving me the creeps," Eve said, glancing at the sky, involuntarily shivering as a cloud edged in front of the sun. "Maybe we should get back. It might rain and we need to practice our cheers."

Sam rolled her eyes to the sky. "It's not going to rain and we're almost there. Paddle faster. I want to see the island—we might not get another chance."

Eve nodded and did as Samantha ordered. She couldn't let spooky stories stop her now. The three had planned this trip to Applehead Island for two days, and now, while just about everybody was on a field trip to Greenbriar University, on the other side of the lake, was the only time they could get away with it.

"Why do you think the island is off-limits?" Eve asked as

they drew near the rocky tree-topped oasis. They were close enough that she could make out misshapen apples on a few of the ancient, arthritic trees. Years ago, there were orchards here. Now the rest of the trees were under the lake. Could they still grow apples? *Dark orchard, tree limbs reaching in vain toward the sun as they drown.* She shivered. "The counselors sounded really serious when they said we couldn't come out here."

"It's haunted," Merilynn said, staring past Eve at the island.

"Shut up!" Samantha said, laughing. "You'll scare her. Eve, it's off-limits because it's a make-out spot. Our counselors meet the counselors from the football camp out here at night." She giggled. "We'll probably find all sorts of nasty things up there."

"Nasty?" Eve asked, delighted, her fears forgotten.

"Yep. Like blankets and underwear and stuff."

"And condoms," Merilynn added sagely.

"Huh?" Eve asked as Sam cracked up.

"You don't know what condoms are?" She pushed long titian hair from her face.

"I know," Sam said. "My parents have them in the bottom drawer of my mom's nightstand." She giggled some more. "They have all kinds of weird stuff in that drawer. I think it's sex stuff."

"But what are condoms?" Eve asked, pleased that know-it-all Sam didn't really know after all. "Come on, Merilynn."

Laughter tinkled down the scale and the girl's green eyes glowed with mischief. "They're for *sex,*" she said.

"And?" Sam urged.

"Guys stick 'em on their thingies so they don't get girls pregnant when they stick it in."

"When they *what?*" Eve gasped.

"Stick it in." Merilynn was controlling her giggles, but just barely. "Eve, don't you know what sexual intercourse is?"

Eve shook her head.

Samantha cleared her throat. "You know those boring cartoons they show us about how guys' sperms go in and look for your egg so they can make a baby?"

Eve remembered the stupid drawings, all right. What a snore. "So?"

"What do you think those cartoons are supposed to be?"

"Bodies," Eve said slowly. She shook blond hair out of her face.

"*Whose* bodies?" Merilynn asked.

"'Toons' bodies, how should I know?" Eve glanced at Sam, who was red-faced, shaking, and just about ready to explode. "What's so funny? Whose bodies, Sam?"

"Grown-ups." Sam snorted and started giggling again.

"You guys don't know anything, do you?" Merilynn said. "After you get your period and your boobies grow, you want boys to stick it in you. They have to wear condoms so that you don't make babies."

"Ewwwww!" Sam and Eve cried in unison.

"Your parents *do it*, Sam," Merilynn said happily. "They have condoms. That's proof. Both your parents did it and didn't use condoms, because if they did you wouldn't have gotten made."

"So our counselors are doing it on the island?" Sam asked. "With *boys?*"

"Well, if they're not doing with boys, we won't find any condoms. And you know what that means?" Merilynn twinkled.

"What?" Sam asked.

"They're lezzies."

"Oh, gross!" Eve wasn't positive what lezzies were, but was pretty sure it was disgusting.

"We should spy on them," Sam said.

"We can't," Eve said. Sam wanted to spy on everybody. She always wanted to know everything about everyone, which was kind of fun, but no way did Eve want to be on Applehead Island after dark. "They'd know the boat was gone when they go to come out here."

"No," Sam said. "I mean, let's look in the counselors' cabin after they go to bed and see what they're doing."

"Okay," Merilynn said, carefully standing. "We're here." She jumped out of the boat into thigh-deep water. "Woo! Cold!" She walked to the pointy end and yanked it forward, onto the narrow beach. "Help me!"

The others got out and together they pulled the rowboat up far enough to be sure it wouldn't float away.

"We need to hurry," Eve said.

"Why?" Sam asked. "It's only about four o'clock. They won't be back from the field trip until five-thirty, at least."

"Look at the sky," Merilynn said.

Overhead, clouds dotted the sky now, puffy white on top but gray and flat on the bottom. "Where'd those come from?" Eve asked. "A few minutes ago, there was only one."

Merilynn giggled. "Maybe it had babies."

"Come on, you guys." Sam had already hiked up the little hill and was looking back down at them. "Follow me." She turned and started walking.

Merilynn glanced at Eve and stepped forward, but Eve put her hand out and touched her arm. "Can I ask you a question?"

"Sure." Merilynn looked into her eyes. "Anything."

"How come you're here? I mean, you said your father is, well, a Father."

"A priest," Merilynn said. "That's right."

"So, he doesn't have sex."

"Well, he's really my uncle Martin. He adopted me when I was a baby after his brother—my dad and my mom—got killed in a car accident."

"But you call him 'Father,'" Eve said.

Merilynn's nose crinkled in a pixyish grin. "Everybody calls him 'Father' because he's a priest. I do too because I think of him as my real father, but I could call him Uncle Martin if I wanted."

"But he's a priest. Isn't that wrong or something, calling him Father?"

Merilynn shrugged. "I don't think so. He doesn't mind. He says he gets the best of both worlds because he's a Father *and* a father."

"Are you guys coming or what?" Sam's voice called from somewhere above.

"In a second," Merilynn yelled. "Listen, Eve, I'll tell you a secret, but you have to promise not to tell."

"Even Sam?"

"Yes, even Sam, because she'd start playing Lois Lane or something and snooping too much, and this is private. It's probably not even true, but I think it is. I have a hunch it is."

"What?" Eve's hand tightened on her friend's arm. "Cross my heart, I won't tell."

"Okay. I think Father isn't my uncle. I think he's my real father. As in, once he had sex and didn't use a condom."

"But he's a priest," Eve protested, shocked. "You mean he had you before he was a priest?"

"No. He's been a priest for like twelve or thirteen years."

"Then he couldn't be your father. He can't have sex."

Merilynn bent forward and kissed Eve's forehead again. "No, Evie. He *could* have sex, he's just not supposed to. I think some beautiful fairy queen made love to him when he was asleep."

"You mean like an angel?"

Merilynn nodded somberly. "Yes, only I think angels don't have anything, you know, *down there,* so it was a fairy queen. They've got lady parts and so she got pregnant and had me, but couldn't take care of me in the fairy kingdom, so she left me with him. And he made up the story about my real mother and father dying when I was only a few days old to cover it all up. Because they probably wouldn't let him be a priest anymore if they knew the truth."

"But—"

"But nothing, Evie. I looked everywhere. On the Net and in Father's pictures from when he was little. He had a brother just a couple years younger than him that's in the photos up until Father was about ten, but then there's no sign of him. No more pictures. I think maybe he died a really long time ago."

"Do you have a grandma you can ask?"

"No. Nobody but Father." She started walking, Eve beside her. "It's just a theory of mine."

"It's nice," Eve said. "I see why you don't want Sam to know, besides the snooping part."

Merilynn paused. "Why?"

"She'd think the fairy goddess mother was silly."

Merilynn nodded and took Eve's hand as they reached the top of the hill. "She would think it was silly. But she'd be wrong."

"Yes," Eve said, squeezing Merilynn's hand. "She'd be wrong."

2

Applehead Island was so named because it was a lump of land shaped kind of like an ugly head poking out of the water. It rose maybe a total of twenty feet out of the lake at its peak, and scraggly old half-dead apple trees stuck out of the upper reaches like spiky hair. From the lake's edge, at times of day when the sun hit it just right, it really looked like a face, from the nose up. A jetty of land at water's edge stuck out like a nose on the side facing the cheerleading camp, and above it, two rocky hollows peered, eyelike, toward shore. Then, a little above, the trees poked up like bristly hair. From shore, Eve, Sam, Merilynn, and some of the other campers loved telling ghost stories about the face, like how it was the head of a giant and he'd walk to shore at three in the morning and peep into the cabins (that part, the peeping part, was Sam's idea of course). If you were foolish enough to be outside when he came ashore, he'd snatch you and take you back to his underwater town and keep you there with Holly Gayle and the treasure forever. Or maybe eat you, if you preferred Sam's version of the story.

But from here, standing between gnarled old trees with their litter of puny greenish apples, the island wasn't all that spooky. But the water was. The sky, filling with gray-bottomed clouds, made the lake look black and fathomless. Here and there sunlight still hit the water in little lightninglike flashes, but that didn't make it any cheerier. Pretty much the opposite, Eve thought, shivering. "There's a whole town down there," she said.

"Yes," Merilynn said softly. "It's still there. It's been there forever."

"And lots of trees." Sam jumped down from a boulder behind them. "It's only been there since 1906," she said. "I looked it up. They flooded the valley to make this reservoir that year."

"And killed all the people," Eve sighed, feeling a delicious little tremor run through her.

"No, they didn't. That's just made-up stuff," Sam said. "Everyone had already moved out. Most of the people went to settle in Caledonia, and some moved to the other side, near the university, and created a new town and named it Greenbriar, after the university."

"Some town," Eve said. "A gas station, a dinky store with a post office inside it, and a motel. Bor-ring."

"There're some houses and stuff," Merilynn said. "But you're right, Evie. It's pretty dinky."

"There used to be more stuff there," Sam told them. "More people and more businesses. There was even a church."

"The church is still there," Merilynn said, pointing toward the far side of the lake. "In the woods behind the university. It's a ruin now, haunted by the green ghost. The Forest Knight. There are still some old deserted cottages in the woods, too. They say the people just disappeared from them. Left their food on the table and fires in the hearths and just—pop!—vanished into thin air. Maybe the green ghost took them. Or the people who trapped Holly Gayle. They're still here, too. Their ghosts, or maybe even the actual people. Maybe they were Druids and they never die. No one knows for sure."

Sam rolled her eyes. "That's nonsense, Merilynn, old silly stories. But there really was a church. And a school, too."

"Greenbriar University is a school," Eve said, glad that Sam thought Merilynn's stories were made up.

"I mean a regular kids' school, not a college. A public school."

"Where'd all the people go?" Merilynn prodded, with a slight smile. "I mean if they didn't mysteriously disappear in the forest."

"Nobody 'mysteriously disappeared' unless maybe bears ate them or they murdered each other," Sam said. "They left because it's nicer on the coast. It's easier to get to, on a main road, and there are more places to work. And Caledonia's pretty; probably most of them went there, or down to Red Cay to start fishing businesses. Some must have gone to live in San Francisco."

"It's nice *here*," Merilynn countered, gesturing around. "A lake, forests all around, ancient oak trees, pine trees, squirrels—"

"Nuts." Sam laughed.

Sam was pretty for a tomboy, with sable-brown eyes and thick dark hair that would look really good if she'd let Eve style it for her.

"Samantha," Eve said firmly, "Merilynn's right. It's nice here. Maybe the people moved away because of a curse."

"The curse of Holly Gayle," Merilynn added.

"You two." Sam shook her head. "Okay. There was *maybe* a coed at the university named Holly Gayle, and *maybe* she drowned—"

"Was murdered," said Merilynn.

"*Maybe*. Whatever, the records that far back were mostly destroyed in a fire in the administration building. There's no proof."

"She's down there," Merilynn said calmly. "Sometimes, late at night, you can hear her calling for help from the old drowned ghost town under the lake, where they imprisoned her forever."

"Or until somebody can set her free," Eve added, trying to make the idea more appealing to no-nonsense Sam. It didn't help.

"Who captured her?" Sam asked, grinning. "Satanists?"

Merilynn made a face. "Of course not. Satanists are, like, *sooo* boring. The people that captured her were Druids or something. They worshipped the old gods."

"Older-than-God gods?" Eve asked.

Merilynn nodded, eyes sparkling. "The day Holly Gayle is released from bondage, all these old trees will grow leaves like crazy and make a ton of big sweet fruit. The green ghost in the chapel in the woods will make all the flowers bloom again and kill all the old icky Druids who are still around here, hiding. Only I don't think they're Druids exactly. Father says old-time Druids sacrificed people and animals all the time for the old gods, so I guess they were bad, but Christians were always slaughtering lambs and stuff, and that one guy killed his kid for God—"

"And God let people kill Jesus, his very own kid," Sam added. "I think that's just as bad. I think it's just the same, in fact. No offense, Merilynn, but religion is creepy."

Merilynn nodded slowly. "Yeah, I know. Well, whatever they were, the ones who caught Holly Gayle, they worshipped old gods and the green ghost is going to kill them."

Sam snorted. "Why? I thought old gods liked Druids. Why would he kill them? Isn't he supposed to be an old god?"

"Is he?" asked Eve. "An old god?"

"I don't know. Maybe. He was a magical knight, I think. I never thought about it." Merilynn looked thoughtful. "Besides, maybe they aren't Druids. Or maybe they're *evil* Druids."

"You're Catholic," Sam said. "What do you know about Druids and stuff? Isn't that a sin or something, to know that stuff?"

Merilynn looked solemn. "Father studies lots of things like that and he tells me about them. He says knowledge isn't a sin unless you use it to do bad things."

"He's one weird priest," said Sam.

"Yeah," Merilynn agreed. "Isn't that great?"

Eve was watching the sky darken with clouds. "We should go soon. I want to practice my cheers."

"Come on, let's just see what's around over there." Sam

pointed at some rocky outcroppings that hid more of the little island. "Real quick, I promise."

"There's supposed to be a cave," Merilynn said.

"Cool." Sam started hiking and the other two followed.

"Look!" Eve pointed at a dark grotto twenty feet beyond the rocky projection.

"The cave," Merilynn said, scrambling forward.

Eve followed the other two, hoping it wasn't really a cave. Sort of hoping, anyway. Black lake water gleamed darkly and she thought about the town below. How many houses had there been? Were there farms and orchards and stores and a schoolhouse, like on *Little House* reruns? Were there ghosts?

"Merilynn, don't go too close," Sam said.

Eve turned to look at the cave thingy. It looked like a ring of rocks sticking up from the ground against the hill, which hung over it like a little cliff, twisted apple tree roots hanging down like skeletal fingers. Merilynn was leaning over the rocks, looking down. "I don't think it's very deep," she said. "But I can't see because it's really dark in there. Stupid clouds. I wish we'd brought a flashlight." She wiggled up higher, her feet leaving the ground as she tilted herself down to get a better look.

"Well, we didn't bring one," Sam said as she and Eve both looked into the fissure. "Don't go falling in there, Merilynn. You'll land in old panties and condoms and stuff."

That worked; Merilynn stood up and stepped back. "Yuck. But maybe it's a cave. Maybe Holly Gayle's down there somewhere. We'll have to come back."

Wind gusted, blowing their hair into their eyes, making sparse leaves on old apple trees sputter. And a long, low wail rose from within the dark grotto. It seemed to spiral up and out, until it built into a banshee scream. Eve and Merilynn scuttled backward, and even Sam jumped away from the hole. "It's just the wind," she said, but she didn't sound too convinced. "Let's get back before it rains." She pushed her fingers against Eve's shoulder. "Get going!"

Without another word, Eve took off, scrambling back around the rocks, spurred on by the wailing sound that grew even louder behind them. She moved quickly, earth trickling down the hillside under her sneakers. Suddenly, her foot caught under an exposed tree root and she went down, landing hard on her knees and hands. "Ow!"

Sam nearly fell over her but managed to leap to the right, barely touching her. Instantly, she turned and crouched. "Are you okay?"

Eve looked up at her and nodded; then Sam stood and offered her hand. Eve slapped her own together, brushing off twigs and dirt, then took Sam's to help her stand up. "Ouch," she said, becoming aware of stinging pain in one knee. She put her foot on a rock and checked out the damage.

"Now *that's* what I call a skinned knee," Sam said admiringly.

"Oh, eww. It's ugly and it hurts." Her stomach twisted—the knee was nasty and bloody, pocked with dirt and debris. Cringing, but determined not to get all shaky in front of Sam, Eve started to pick pebbles and leaves out of the wound, but then she saw something moving. "Oh, God," she whispered. "Oh, God, oh God, oh God. Sam, get it off me!"

"What?"

"That!" She pointed at the thing. "Hurry! I think I'm going to faint!"

Sam bent, then reached out and plucked the thing off, held it out. "It's just an earthworm," she said. "You're not going to faint."

"Get it away from me. I don't want to see it!"

"Jeez, Evie, it's not even a whole worm, just part of one. See?"

"Oh, gross! *Please* get rid of it! Now!"

Sam put the worm down in some leaves by the tree root while Eve picked more gunk off her knee, gravel and bits of leaves. "I hope it doesn't scar," she said.

"It's not going to scar. It's just your stupid knee!" Sam looked around. "Where's Merilynn?"

"I don't know!" Another banshee howl suddenly tore the air.

Eve forgot about the injury and hugged herself tightly. "Merilynn!" she yelled, but her voice was stolen by the wind.

"Stay put," Sam told her and started back toward the rocks. "I'll get her." Eve nodded, happy to stay behind.

Long minutes passed, and the howling rose and fell as the tree branches whipped up and the sky turned a uniform steel gray. The lake shimmered, a black mirror cracked with low-ridged whitecaps. Across the water, a mist was rising in the dark, haunted woods. She could barely see the camp's short dock, and the tall flagpole was invisible except for the American flag at the top. The green and gold camp flag blended in with the trees. They had to row all the way back across the black lake, and the thought terrified her as much as the howls of wind that echoed all around now, calling across the water like hungry wolves. *Stop it! You can't be scared! Sam'll make fun of you. She might tell the others and then they'll all make fun of you!*

"Samantha?" she called, suddenly. "Merilynn? Hurry up!" Shivering from both cold and fear, she took tentative steps back toward the cave. A heavy raindrop splatted on her forearm, followed a few seconds later by another. "You guys? Are you okay?"

She thought she heard Sam's voice, but wasn't positive. "You guys? Sam? It's starting to rain!" She climbed around the outcropping and saw Samantha, well, saw everything but her head and shoulders because she was bending over, looking down into the rock-lined hole or cave or whatever it was.

"Sam?" she called from a dozen feet away.

"Eve! Get over here!"

Eve barely heard her since Sam didn't look up, but she rushed to join her, instantly positive Merilynn had fallen into the hole and Sam was trying to rescue her. But as she arrived, she saw the other girl had only been hidden in the shadows of dangling roots on the far side of the opening. She, too, was looking down into the darkness, bent so far over that none of her coppery hair was visible.

A dozen raindrops spattered on Eve's face. "What are you doing, you guys? We have to get back. Hurry up! It's raining!"

Sam raised her head and looked at Eve. "Look!" She turned back. "Look!"

The howling wind still came from all around, from the forest across the lake, from the trees on the island; if it had been the banshee shriek from the grotto, Eve couldn't have made herself look into that dark hole again. Swallowing hard, she gripped the rocky edge. Across from her, Merilynn glanced up and smiled, eyes dancing with emerald light.

The sun is gone. How can her eyes do that?

It had only lasted an instant; already, Merilynn had dipped her head back down. Deciding she'd imagined the light, Eve closed her eyes and held her breath, as if she were diving into the lake, then tilted her neck down, her face to the darkness.

And opened her eyes.

The perfect darkness was broken only by two tiny sparkling dabs of green deep, deep down. Eve stared. "What are those lights?" she murmured, too fascinated to be afraid.

"I don't know," Sam said softly. "Lights. Maybe glowing rocks?"

"No." Merilynn spoke in a near whisper.

The emerald chips winked out for a split second, then came back on.

"It's an animal," Sam said. "Like a mountain lion or a bob-cat. Cats' eyes glow in the dark."

"It's trapped down there?" Concern washed over Eve. "We have to tell someone and get it rescued. Poor kitty."

"It's not trapped," Sam said. I'm sure there's an entrance lower down, probably on the other side of the island."

"Then it's dangerous to be here if it's a mountain lion," Eve said.

"Shh!" Merilynn looked up, the green sparks in her eyes the same shade as the green dabs far below. "It's not a mountain lion. It's not an animal."

"What is it, then?" Sam asked.

"Look," Merilynn replied. "Look at them."

And Eve realized that the twin green lights were slowly but surely growing larger.

Coming closer. "Sam, we should leave *right* now." She clutched her wrist, but both of them continued to watch the lights' slow movement.

"What is it, Merilynn?" Sam asked.

"I'm not sure. The green ghost? Holly Gayle?"

Not six feet below them now, the glowing orbs blinked slowly, once, twice, then moved slightly, and suddenly Eve knew beyond all doubt that they were eyes and they were looking right at her. "Run!" she screamed, dragging Sam with her. She glimpsed Merilynn bringing up the rear just as the banshee shriek spiraled up behind them, so loud and ragged that it hurt her ears.

The rain pelted her face, but Eve didn't notice, and each time any one of the girls tripped, the other two would scoop the third to her feet, barely missing a stride. Soaked with rain, legs sheathed in mud and leaves, they skidded the last few feet down the hillside to the rowboat and, wordless, pushed it into the water, turning it around as soon as it was afloat. They climbed in, Eve and Sam both grabbing oars and sitting so that they faced the land across the lake. They began paddling, and Eve quickly copied Sam's sure, deep strokes that moved them rapidly away from the island despite the wind. The banshee shriek receded, mingling with the howls of the storm. Thunder cracked.

Merilynn sat in the prow, facing the island, her green gaze dark and unwavering. Even a flash of lightning didn't spark them.

"What do you see?" Sam asked when they were a quarter of the way across the lake.

Merilynn squinted toward Applehead Island. Rain swatted the onyx surface, oars sluiced up freshets of lake water to mix and fall back down with the rain. "I don't know," she said after a long moment. "I don't know what I saw."

Steadily, they continued to row. To Eve, Merilynn looked like a solemn lady in a medieval painting. Beside her, Sam sat straight, her chin set, her entire profile showing determination. Eve copied her, and although her arms were beginning to ache, she didn't complain at all, but just kept rowing. It was almost as dark as night, the forest swathed in dark green-grays. Once, she looked down at the water, watching it move under the oars and, deep, deep below, thought she saw little lights winking on. Yellow-white and dim, like the lights of a town glimpsed from an airplane window on a stormy night.

"Something wrong, Evie?" Sam asked as she rowed.

"No." Telling herself it was only reflected lightning, Eve kept her eyes on the shoreline because she knew that if she looked down and the lights were still there, she'd start screaming and wouldn't be able to stop.

TODAY

3

Eve Camlan, dressed only in her pink cotton baby-doll pj's, the ones with the little white rabbits printed all over them, fought down the urge to huddle up and try to keep her bunnies hidden. She hadn't even had a robe handy when the rush committee from Gamma Eta Pi pounded on her dorm room door and snatched her from her bed. Most of the other girls sitting on the sofas and chairs in the big, high-ceilinged common room of Gamma House had chosen their sleepwear with the rush in mind. They wore neat satin pajamas or long silky nightgowns with matching robes. A few wore sleep T-shirts, the shortest still providing more leg coverage than Eve's idiotic bunny outfit.

Some of the girls even looked like they'd gone to bed with lipstick on, just in case. At least there weren't many positive fashion statements in the hair department; evidently no one had managed to grab a brush as they were pulled out of their doors. Eve's hair was pulled back in a low ponytail and now she reached up and removed the pink scrunchie. Slipping it onto her wrist like a bracelet, she quickly combed her fingers through the golden mane, encouraging the natural curls to spring to life. *Thank heaven for the waves.* When she was younger, she straightened it most days, but now she knew the loose waves she'd inherited from her mother let her look fashionably tousled when straight-haired girls looked as if they had limp spaghetti stuck on their heads.

Still, she wished she had a robe, a mirror, and some lipstick. *Look confident,* she reminded herself. Looking confident was the key to everything. She'd learned that years and years ago, back in the cheerleader camp run by sisters of this very sorority to which she hoped to pledge. She'd really learned about confidence more from Samantha Penrose than the college-age counselors, but that was beside the point. *I'm sitting here in pink rabbit baby-dolls, waiting to be judged worthy of the best house on campus. The only house if I really want to be a cheerleader. The only house I ever wanted to join. Stupid, stupid, stupid!*

And she'd wanted to get into Gamma since that first summer at cheerleader camp. At the end of her ninth summer, she'd gone back to school and practiced on her own, then returned to the camp to learn more, back and forth, two more summers, until she reached junior high, aced the tryouts, and made the cheerleading squad. She'd soon made captain, then, in high school, been chosen for the varsity squad on her first try. She worked her way up to second-in-command of the squad and prom queen in her junior year, and in her senior, she was captain *and* homecoming queen. And in the annual, she was voted Most Likely to Be a Movie Star, which gave her a little thrill even though she didn't want to be a movie star. That year she graduated with honors after *lots* of hard studying and was accepted to Greenbriar University, even garnering a small scholarship, which added to the college fund her parents had saved for her. She could study and practice cheering full-time without having to flip burgers. She would have time to do volunteer work too, but she hadn't started yet. School had barely begun and she wanted to volunteer for one of the Gamma charities if she got in. *I'm in. They wouldn't have rushed me tonight if I wasn't in. . . .*

Still, she had doubts, which was silly, since she had accomplished everything she'd set out to do in her life so far. Next on her list was this—being accepted as a sister of Gamma Eta Pi, making the varsity cheerleader squad, eventually becoming captain and the president of the sorority, and finding true love along the way. She'd never thought out her plans for after college since it seemed so far away, but if her true love hadn't yet appeared, maybe she'd tryout to be a cheerleader for a pro football team. She had the figure for it even if she wasn't as tall as most of the pros. Or maybe she'd become a junior high school teacher and coach the beginning cheerleading squad for the school. Or, if her true love happened to be well-to-do or good at making money, she wouldn't have to work for other people at all. Maybe she could start her own cheerleading school. She smiled to herself, liking the idea. A lot.

"Hi, I'm Kendra," said the girl next to her on the overstuffed cabbage rose-covered sofa. Her sparkling smile was infectious.

Eve smiled back, wishing she'd popped a breath mint. "Hi. I'm Eve Camlan. Aren't you in Professor Piccolo's English 101 with me?"

"Eleven A.M.? Yeah. That's where I thought I recognized you from. I hate those stupid journals we're supposed to keep, don't you?"

"Yeah. Like I'm going to tell some ancient guy in his forties my private thoughts."

"I know, isn't that disgusting to even *think* about?"

Eve laughed softly. "You know what I do? I look up the soap opera plots for the week in *TV Guide*, and write down things I see there like it's from my life. You know, 'I think my aunt is having an affair with her husband's brother's uncle,' or 'I think the mailman may be the real father of my neighbors' new baby.'"

"Mr. Mailman's making deliveries, huh?" Kendra chuckled warmly. "I love it. Do you want to know what I do?"

"Yes. What?"

"Pretty much the same thing, only worse."

"What do you mean?"

"I make up rumors about students for him."

"Who?"

She laughed again. "Don't worry, not about anybody real. I say stuff about how I was way deep in the library stacks and saw a couple doing the dirty on the floor in front of the paleontology books."

"I saw that on *Friends*."

"Me too." Kendra beamed at her. "See? We're doing the same thing. When I can't think of anything, I turn on *The Brady*

Bunch and tell some story from Marcia's—I mean *my*—child-hood."

"That's more fun than what I do. You're so creative!"

"Well, I don't know about that. I just take modern folklore and spice it up a little more. You could too." She snickered. "You should say you saw the couple in the anthropology stacks too. I bet Piccolo would start hanging around there to see if it's true. I bet he likes to watch!"

"You're bad," Eve said happily.

"Thanks. And isn't *this* exciting?" Kendra nodded toward the other side of the room where the rush committee, wearing daytime clothes, sat huddled together around an ornate antique desk, conferring.

"Yes. I wish I'd dressed better."

Kendra, in a black satin pajama set—shorts and a short-sleeved button-down top, both trimmed with neat bronze piping—checked her out. "You look fine."

"I feel naked."

"Why? You wearing crotchless panties or something?"

Eve burst into restrained giggles. "No, of course not."

"Well, you don't look naked to me. Can't see a thing through those bunnies."

Eve rolled her eyes. "These make me look like I'm ten years old. I have nice pajamas, but I got superstitious and thought that if I put them on, I wouldn't be chosen." She felt her cheeks heat up. "You know what I mean? Pretty stupid, huh?"

"I know. It's silly, but not stupid. My granny's like that. She throws salt over her shoulder and won't walk under ladders."

"Oh, well, I'm not that bad. Not that that's bad—I mean—"

"Oh, hush up," the dark-haired girl said, smiling. "That's okay. I know what you mean. My granny isn't totally supersti-tious; she's not afraid of black cats. She has one named Luthor and he crosses her path all the time. He's got the biggest green eyes you ever saw. Sometimes, the way he stares at you, I think he should be named Lucifer, not Luthor." She paused. "What's wrong? You afraid of cats?"

"No, I love cats," Eve said. "I love all animals."

"Well, you look like somebody just walked over your grave." Another brilliant grin. "At least that's what my granny would say."

"The thing you said about big green eyes made me remember once, when I was little, seeing green eyes glowing in a cave. It was a mountain lion, I think. It scared me half to death. Sometimes I still have nightmares."

"A mountain lion?"

Eve nodded.

"But you don't *know* it was a mountain lion? You just *think* it was?"

"My friends and I ran." That stormy afternoon on the island didn't come back to her very often—she didn't allow it—but when it did, she felt as if it were happening all over again. "One of the girls I was with, this kind of brainiac tomboy, she said it had to be a mountain lion."

"Wow. Where'd that happen?"

Eve clasped her hands together to stop a tremble from coming on. "You know Applehead Lake?"

"Sure. It's like, what, a mile's walk through the woods behind the campus?"

"Yeah. We were at the cheerleader camp on the far side of the lake. We stole a boat and rowed out to the island. That's where we saw it. The mountain lion. A storm was coming up and the wind was howling and we scared ourselves half to death."

"You've gone all white on white," Kendra said, touching her hand. "It's still scary for you, isn't it?"

"A little, I guess."

"Have you ever heard the stories about the green ghost or the Forest Knight? They're really the same thing."

Eve's smile was wry. "Yes. The other girl I was with thought that's what we saw. She didn't think it was a mountain lion. She said it was either the green ghost or Holly Gayle. Do you know about her?"

"Who doesn't?" Kendra said. "That girl's supposed to haunt *this* house."

Eve glanced around the room, taking in everything from the

crystal vases of fresh roses to the ornate molding on the high ceilings, the dark wainscoting, and the floral wallpaper, heavy forest green blotched with big reddish roses trailing ivy. The room was filled with roses in every form. She could smell them, a cloying sweetness that seemed old and stale, not fresh. She glanced at the cabbage rose slipcovers. Way too many roses, and it made the room spooky and Gothic-looking. "Holly haunts this house? Back at camp, I heard she was trapped under the lake. It involved some sort of story about treasure and sacrifices. Silly kid stuff."

"My granny's granny worked here when Holly Gayle disappeared in 1909. She was a cleaning lady, right here in this very house, from the time she was just fourteen years old. And Holly Gayle was a sorority sister." Kendra leaned closer and whispered, "Part of the secret sorority."

"Secret sorority?"

"Shh. You don't know about that?"

Eve shook her head.

"Don't ask. I'll tell you later, when we're not here. Anyway, listen. Holly disappeared and they said she killed herself or was murdered, drowned in the lake. Granny's granny said she saw her ghost walking along the lake shore once, and that she looked real at first, but then just sort of faded away. Later, they started seeing her walking around in the house sometimes. Maybe they still do."

"They never found her body?"

Kendra shook her head. "Never."

Eve hid her nervousness. "Maybe she just ran away. Maybe she wasn't killed on purpose and maybe she didn't commit suicide. Maybe she eloped. Maybe she fell in love with some prince and went to Europe to live in a castle. Or maybe she wanted to go to New York and be an actress. Maybe—"

"No," Kendra said firmly. "Granny's granny recognized her."

"But how did she know she died in the lake?"

"That's easy, girl. She wore this old-fashioned long white dress and it was soaking wet from her being drowned. And sometimes, even when Granny's granny couldn't see her, she *smelled* her. Granny's mama saw her once, too, and smelled her lots of times. She said she heard her screaming and crying a few times. And Granny even saw her *and* smelled her, both, just once, when she went in one of the rooms upstairs. Holly's ghost was in there, looking out the window. Granny thought she was a student and said hello, and the girl turned and Granny saw her eyes even though the room was pretty dark. And then she just faded away and Granny heard a scream as this big old whoosh of wind passed over her. She smelled the smell and Granny knew it was the ghost. She said it was the devil's business, and she left and never came back. She said the smell scared her more than her eyes, and the eyes *glowed. Green.*"

"Perfume?" Eve asked, purposely ignoring the part about the green eyes. "I've heard stories about ghosts who trail perfume in old castles in England and Scotland."

"You've got castles on the brain. And, no, it wasn't perfume. She smelled like the lake. You know that smell. That cold, dark, watery smell."

"Yes, I know that smell." She paused, pushing away memories, getting herself together. "Was your granny a student here?"

Kendra laughed lightly. "Are you serious or are you just trying to be politically correct?"

"I'm serious."

Kendra studied her, then smiled. "No, but when she was a girl, she worked here for a while, with her mama. *My* mama was the first woman in our family to go to college."

"Here?"

"No. Granny wouldn't let her. She said this was a bad place. Mama went to Cal Poly in San Luis Obispo."

"So why are you here?"

"Because I wanted to go here in honor of all the people in my family who worked at Greenbriar over the years." She grinned. "And I wanted to join Gamma House because this is where my three grannies worked."

"What does your granny think of you going here?"

"She tried to talk me out of it. Said if I had to come here, to stay away from this house. Said it was evil. Isn't that funny?"

"Um, is it? I mean, she must hate that you're here at Gamma. What did she say when you told her you wanted to pledge?"

"You kidding? I didn't tell her."

"What about your mother? Does she know?"

Kendra's smile faded. "Not exactly. I told her I'm thinking about it. She doesn't want me to, not really, but she's conflicted, too. You know, she thinks Granny's silly about the ghost stories, but she's not so sure about some of the other stuff."

"What other stuff?"

"Hush." Kendra glanced around, then bent closer to Eve. "The secret stuff. I'll tell you later." She relaxed. "My mom's good about my coming to Greenbriar for my degree. She kinda likes it, in fact. She couldn't afford to rebel and come here, so I'm doing it for her, you know?" She tilted her head. "So, why did *you* choose Greenbriar?"

"Cheerleading camp. The counselors were cheerleaders from Gamma."

"You're kidding."

"No. Why would you think that?"

"This is West Coast Ivy League. People come here for the name 'Greenbriar' on their diplomas. So, come on, what's your major?"

Eve flushed, suddenly ashamed. "I haven't declared yet."

Kendra patted her hand. "Lots of people don't choose for a couple years. You've got plenty of time."

"What's your major?"

"Sociology or anthropology or psychology. I don't know, exactly. I want to study cultures and folklore, you know, do the Joseph Campbell thing."

Eve grinned. "So part of the reason you want to be in Gamma is to check out the ghost stories?"

Kendra studied her nails briefly. "Of course, but I didn't tell my family."

"You aren't afraid of ghosts?"

"No. They're just stories."

"Come on. If you thought that, you wouldn't be here looking for them."

Kendra shrugged, one side of her mouth crooked up. "See? I knew you were too smart to just be a pom-pom girl. I've seen a few strange things, but they're nothing to be frightened of. The stories are scarier than reality."

"What—"

Two sharp hand claps interrupted Eve's question.

4

"May I have your attention, please?"

Eve looked up at the exotic raven-haired young woman who now stood before the huge fireplace at the end of the room. The hearth was dark this warm September night. Instead of fire, between the andirons lay—what else?—a huge spray of dried roses, their tints faded false flames of apricot, red, and yellow.

"I'm Malory Thomas, president of Gamma Eta Pi."

Her teeth flashed brilliant and white as her dark eyes flickered over the pajama-clad girls in the room. Briefly, she caught Eve's gaze and held it. Eve tried to smile back, but her lip barely trembled before the eyes moved on to their next target. She had met Malory on rush night and had been just as intimidated by her then as now. The Gamma president, with her regal bearing, implacable features, and milk-white skin, was an ice goddess, maybe the Snow Queen herself. Eve glanced at Kendra, who replied with a hint of a smile. Eve felt better; she could tell that Kendra didn't like Malory either.

"Welcome," Malory continued. "As I'm sure you all suspect, you have been selected as pledges for Gamma Eta Pi, the oldest, most prestigious sorority on Greenbriar's campus. In fact,

Gamma maintains chapters at the most exclusive universities not only nationwide, but around the world. Our sisterhood is small but it is the best."

She paused, letting her eyes graze the room. "You have rigorous times ahead of you, pledges, in order to prove yourselves worthy of Gamma. Some of you won't make it—in fact, probably fewer than half of you will."

The room seemed to chill ten degrees. Eve hugged herself.

"All of you will be required to swear an oath never to repeat what you see or hear in this house, whether you make it to full sisterhood or not."

Someone cleared her throat. Malory turned toward the sound. "Do you have a question?"

"No," a Chinese girl said softly. She looked embarrassed. "I just had a frog in my—"

"Throat," Malory finished briskly. "Are you *sure* you don't have a question?"

"Yes."

"Maybe you're just a little nervous? You don't need to be nervous. You may ask whatever you wish."

The girl shook her head. "No questions."

"I have a question," Kendra said.

Eve tried to disappear as Malory turned in their direction. "Yes? And you are?"

"Kendra Phillips."

"What's your question, Kendra?"

"Say a pledge washes out and then she talks about what happens here. What will happen to her?"

Malory smiled with her mouth but not her eyes, nodding as she glanced around to include the other pledges in her answer. "Congratulations, Kendra. I'm sure all your sisters-to-be are wondering the same thing, but none of them had the courage to ask."

Casting withering glances at the new girls, she paced the length of the room, from the fireplace to the room entrance. The double doors were wide open, and beyond the room the large foyer twinkled with quavery light cast from a crystal chandelier Eve had admired the first time she visited the house.

"I can't tell you what will happen to a pledge who breaks her vows until you take the vows," Malory said, moving toward the center of the room again. "But I can tell you that those who have broken them generally end up leaving Greenbriar University and won't be welcomed at any other learning institution where a Gamma chapter exists." She approached Kendra. "Does that answer your question?"

Kendra met her gaze. "I guess it does. Thank you."

Malory addressed the room. "Any of you who wish to, may leave now or after this meeting without any repercussions. If you are uncomfortable with the idea of secrecy within our sisterhood or feel that you can't maintain our trust, we ask that you not return.

"Those of you who wish to proceed with pledging are asked to return to the house tomorrow afternoon between three and six o'clock to sign in as official pledges. After six, we will convene to get better acquainted and begin your initiations into the sisterhood."

A girl sitting on a pillow on the floor almost out of Eve's view raised her hand. Eve craned her head to see her, but only saw some long red hair and the sleeve of a forest-green pajama top.

"Yes?" said Malory.

"Are initiations allowed?" the young woman asked quickly.

She sounded familiar to Eve, but Malory laughed. "Of course initiations are allowed. Miss?"

"Morris."

Morris, thought Eve. *It couldn't be . . .*

"Miss Morris, I think you're referring to hazings." She looked around the room. "Hazings are beneath us and, no, *they* aren't allowed. You all know what hazings are, don't you?"

No one replied, though a general murmur arose.

"Fraternities, especially jock fraternities, are notorious for hazing, a practice long banned here at Greenbriar. Years ago, however, one of the fraternities here routinely stripped their pledges, blindfolded them, and took them out on Applehead Lake, then dropped them from a rowboat into the water. They did this at night, during the dark of the moon so when a pledge tore his blindfold off, he still couldn't see where he was. He had to swim to shore. If he couldn't make it—if the brothers in the boat had to rescue him—he was rejected. The practice ended in 1972, when a pledge drowned." She paced back to the fireplace. "You will be put to the test, ladies, no doubt about that. But we will not humiliate you in public. You have my promise of that."

Eve wondered if they would humiliate her in private instead. *Stop thinking like that. The other sisters look nice. And there's nothing wrong with Malory. She's just not your kind of person.* She watched Malory turn and nod at the Gamma sisters seated at the desk. Two of them rose and came to join her in front of the fireplace.

"This is our rush chairman, Heather Horner." Malory indicated the girl to her right. She had curly shoulder-length chestnut hair and when she smiled her eyes crinkled with humor. Eve instantly decided she liked her. "If you decide to go ahead with your pledging, Heather will be at the desk tomorrow afternoon with the papers for you to sign."

"Excuse me," Eve heard herself say.

"Yes?" Malory answered. "You are?"

"Eve—Genevieve Camlan. Are the papers we sign tomorrow our oaths?" *God, I sound so stupid!* "I mean, is that all there is to becoming a pledge?" *Kill me now. Just kill me now!*

Heather answered in a warm voice. "The papers just make you an official pledge."

"And as an official pledge, you are sworn to forever keep the secrets of our sisterhood," Malory added darkly, "whether you make it into full sisterhood or not."

"Th-thank you."

Cocking an eyebrow, Malory gestured at the sister on her left, a shiny blonde in a short scoop-necked top and designer jeans. She had a small yellow bag of Peanut M&Ms in her hand and appeared to have one or two of the candies stuffed in one cheek. A belly button ring glittered gold against her stomach and Eve spied part of a small tattoo of a red rose blooming on her left hipbone, just above her jeans. "This is the sorority's vice president, Brittany Woodcock."

"Hi, pledges!" she chirped, then popped another M&M in her glossy-painted mouth and crunched.

Kendra stifled a giggle. Eve elbowed her but didn't look her way, knowing that if they made eye contact, she'd laugh too. Vice President Brittany sounded like a dumb blond chipmunk.

"Welcome to Gamma Eta Pi House," she chirped. "From the looks of some of you, it'll be Gamma Eta *Cherry* Pi House! How many of you are virgins?"

Only Malory's glacial glare silenced the unesteemed vice president, who blinked and backed up a step as the president spoke. "Attention, please, everyone. Still seated at the desk are our other senior officers, Treasurer Michele Marano and Secretary Teri Knolls."

The duo nodded greetings. They were both attractive, but not particularly memorable; Eve wasn't sure if they'd actually talked before.

"The tradition of the sisters of Gamma is long and distinguished," Malory continued. "If you become one of us, you will be among the most powerful women on earth. You will share your lives with your sisters, now and forever. You will always have friends. You will have the best careers in whatever fields you choose. As long as you have your sisters, you will never have enemies—or if you do, you won't have to worry about them. As sisters, and later as alumni of Gamma Eta Pi, you will help change the world." She flashed her predatory smile. "Any questions?"

There weren't.

"Go back to your beds now and think about your decision. It may be the most important one of your life. We hope to see you tomorrow afternoon. Good night."

Malory Thomas turned on her heel and walked briskly toward the side of the room, Brittany right behind her. Just as Eve started to look forward to her slamming into the wall, a panel slid open. They disappeared into darkness.

The panel slid closed again so quickly and silently that Eve almost wondered if she had really seen the opening at all.

The two sisters manning the desk, Michele and Teri, rose and left the room the old-fashioned way—through the open doors—but not one of the pajama-clad pledges made a move. Heather Horner, still standing before the fireplace, grinned. "Our president has a flair for drama, kids," she said, walking forward. "See you all tomorrow!"

The pledges responded this time, getting up and leaving singly and in groups of two or three. As Eve and Kendra stood up, Heather said, "Eve? Just a minute."

Eve turned, surprised. "Yes?"

Heather smiled and crooked her finger. Eve stepped forward while Kendra hung back.

"I'm the captain of the varsity cheerleading team," Heather told her. "I hope you're intending to join the squad."

Eve beamed. "Well, I sure want to try out!"

"Trying out is just a formality for you. If you want it, you're in, as long as you pledge the sorority. You *are* pledging, right?"

"Yes!" All lingering doubts fled in that instant.

The girl smiled warmly. "You've got so many awards, you're like the star quarterback all the colleges want for their team. We want you for our squad!"

"I—thanks, but I just have a few little high school awards," Eve began, but she couldn't stand pretending to be humble and bubbled, "And it's why I came here! I want to be on your squad more than anything!"

Heather laughed, then leaned forward and hugged her. "I know. I read your letter and your recommendations from your high school coach. Welcome to the squad," she said softly. "To keep it fair, we can't just announce you're already in, you know—"

"I know. Thank you so much for telling me, though!"

"Is your friend trying out?" Heather glanced Kendra's way.

"My friend? Oh, I don't know. We just met. I don't think so, though. Why?"

"I just wondered. I think this should be our little secret for now, either way."

"Sure." She started to reach for Heather's hand, but the other girl bypassed it and gave her a warm hug instead. "Welcome, Sister."

Eve just grinned.

5

Eve and Kendra walked out of Gamma House together, and neither spoke until they were well away from the huge old southern-style mansion. "A transplanted plantation house," Eve observed.

"Sure is," Kendra murmured as they continued to walk. "Kind of creepy."

The house was set far back on a long greensward, Applehead Forest dark behind it. Before it, the wide veranda met the low stairway down to an elderly cracked sidewalk edged with rose-bushes. It led straight across twenty yards of manicured lawn before reaching a long rectangular reflecting pool where it divided into two walkways, one leading along either side of the pool. Unseen frogs croaked on dark lily pads floating in patches on the still water.

"All this place needs is some moss hanging from the trees and fireflies blinking around, and I'd think we were at Tara with Rhett and Scarlett."

"Don't forget the kudzu vine and big-ass mosquitoes," Kendra said.

"You've been there?"

"My father's family still lives down there. Sometimes we'd visit during summer vacation. Trust me, it's a lot nicer here." Kendra stopped walking and glanced back at the mansion. "I'm not too sure I want to live in that old house."

"Why? It's so big and beautiful and cool!"

Kendra chuckled. "You're really stoked about this place, aren't you?"

"Yes!"

"It doesn't spook you or give you any funny feelings?"

"You mean because of the ghost stories?"

Kendra shrugged.

"Of course not. I don't believe in ghosts." Eve shivered despite her words and the late summer heat, imagining green eyes glowing out at her from the forest behind the house. "Let's go. I've got early classes."

They reached the road and crossed it, then followed a much newer walkway across the campus, past darkened Gothic buildings and up through a tree-filled garden area, finally arriving at their dorm rooms, which turned out to be located on different floors of the same big square building. The faceless multistoried dormitory looked like it had been built in the sixties or seventies and much of its unadorned ugliness was blessedly hidden by pines and oaks. The dorm didn't fit in with the older main buildings of the college any more than the Gammas' plantation house did. The whole campus was, Eve thought, a decorator's nightmare.

Even at midnight, the September air was warm enough that Eve didn't feel chilled in her horrible rabbit nightie. "Kendra?" she asked as the other girl reached for the glass door to let them into the building.

"Yes?"

"That secret stuff you were talking about. When will you tell me about it?"

Kendra studied her. "I don't know if I should. Judging by the hug you got, I think maybe you're on the fast track right into the secret stuff."

"That wasn't anything." Eve grinned. "Don't tell, but I think I'm in the varsity cheerleading squad. Heather's the captain."

"Well . . ." Kendra paused as a girl in forest green pajamas and a matching robe approached. "Hi."

"Hi." The girl smiled. She had beautiful long straight red hair and eyes so green that even in the bad light, they shone.

Oh, my God. "Hi," Eve managed. *It is her.*

"Have we met?" the redhead asked.

"Uh, I don't think so."

"You look familiar. What's your name?"

"Eve."

"Right. You asked a question at the meeting. I think we've met somewhere before. You look familiar and your name fits you. I mean, if I had to guess your name, I'd guess Eve."

"Maybe you met at the rush party," Kendra said, watching the two of them.

"I'm Merilynn Morris. Do you recognize my name?" She pinned Eve with her eyes.

"I—I'm not sure. Maybe. You said it at the meeting. That's probably why it sounds a little familiar."

Merilynn gazed at her steadily. "That must be it. Well, good night." She pushed open the door and disappeared inside.

"What was all that about?" Kendra asked.

"Nothing."

"You want me to tell you the secret stuff, you don't lie to me. What was that? Where do you know her from?"

"You know the mountain lion story from when I was a kid at cheer camp?"

"Yes."

"She was one of the girls I was with."

Kendra considered. "So what's the problem? Why didn't you say so?"

"I don't know." She looked at Kendra and shrugged. "I really don't know."

"Come on." Kendra opened the door and held it for her. "We'll talk later. Let's get some sleep."

6

Professor Piccolo's English 101 class was filled to bursting with young women, and young women were exactly what the good professor loved most. They came in all shapes and sizes, in all colors and fragrances, and with nary an exception, Timothy Piccolo worshipped them all.

Women were his reason for being, his sum, his all. He lived for the scent of a woman's skin, for the silky touch of feminine flesh. He knew the soft warm fragrance of the nape of a woman's neck that had been hidden beneath a curtain of long hair, and eyes closed, he could tell the scent of the back of a feminine knee from that of an elbow. He could tell a delicate blonde from a luxurious brunette and could identify the special spice of a redhead.

Piccolo looked across the sea of young women and as he spoke of Shakespeare and Bacon, he studied a slender gamine and thought of the taste of her lightly freckled sun-warmed skin. He drank in the beauty of a feminine Othello in the first row, her long legs stretching endlessly from nearly-not-there sandals and enameled maroon toenails to the shadowed triangle under her desk. He couldn't tell if she wore a skirt or shorts, but it didn't matter; in his mind, his face was buried in that triangle, nose inhaling, tongue exploring the treasures folded within. Musk, he thought, and spice. *A hint of cinnamon? Perhaps.*

A fresh-faced blonde sat at the desk next to the lady Moor's and he saw them exchange glances as he spoke. *Ah, to be the meat in that sandwich.* He had noticed them both before, just as he noticed all women, but had never seen any sign that they knew one another until now. The pairing excited him. The blonde was a blushing peach, but a California peach, not a Georgian. An all-American girl full of enthusiasm and bouncy friendliness. He could tell these things by looks and body language without ever hearing her speak. She was a true blonde with unblemished clear skin and thick waves of golden hair grazing her collarbone. Nordic-blue eyes gazed at him from above perfect lips painted a delicate shade of pink. Her fingernail enamel matched her lipstick, but her toes were a mystery, hidden in bright white Reeboks and short pink socks.

Her denim cutoffs were short, but not too short; she gave off innocent sexuality, sun-kissed fruit hanging ripe and ready to be plucked. Her legs were very lightly tanned, as were her arms. She wore a pale pink and blue plaid camp shirt open over a light blue tank top that revealed a luscious hint of cleavage. He spoke of blank verse as he imagined being smothered between those perfect globes. If he were to move forward now and kneel to gently roll up her tank top to reveal her breasts, he knew he would find nipples the color of pink roses and, if he were to oh-so-carefully cup one breast and lift it so that his tongue could taste the sweat beneath it, he knew he would die of pleasure.

A giggle startled him. A soft musical giggle, just two syllables. Another, a trio of titters, followed from somewhere else in the classroom and Timothy Piccolo realized his participle was no longer dangling. Quickly, he moved behind his desk and continued his lecture, his eyes alighting briefly on girl after girl, passing over the males as if they didn't exist.

Eyes of all colors returned his looks, most of them smiling eyes. A few lips were licked and, unable to resist, he paused and picked up his bottle of Evian. Unscrewing the lid, he said, "Any questions?" then drank.

For just an instant, he allowed his tongue to lave the bottle's opening. He flipped a water drop onto his upper lip as he lowered the bottle and reattached the lid. Then his tongue, a snake wishing to hide in bush, flickered out and cleaned the stray drop of water away.

The proverbial pin might have dropped in that bare instant; if it had it would have been as loud as a rock smashing into a wall. They were watching him. They had heard about his tongue. His wonderful, talented tongue.

Fresh giggles interrupted the silence. Professor Tongue cleared his throat and returned to his lecture.

Few of his admirers ever met his tongue, for he was a man of honor, and did not allow himself to indulge in any relations with students under twenty-one. In fact, he never touched less than a senior and really preferred graduate students. There were female teachers and professors who tempted him almost daily, but he rarely allowed himself to be seduced since he knew from experience that jealousies among the ladies were inevitable. That was the joy of the senior student: she would graduate and be off instead of becoming a problem. And, as an instructor, he always hoped that each of his loves would teach her future beaus a little about the art of the tongue. They were all wonderful girls, wonderful women, and they deserved the best.

Professor Piccolo smiled at the class, ending his lecture so that the bell rang as a coda. He beamed from his desk as a handful of young ladies rushed up with trumped-up excuses to talk to him, to flirt, to test the waters. To perhaps see him lick his lips. They loved to see his tongue—it was a legend in his own mouth. A warm tingly feeling shot through his groin. There was a reason his egghead buddies called him the Cunning Linguist.

7

Eve and Kendra sat on an ornate wooden bench in the shade of a gnarled oak on a broad lawn dotted with other lunching students. Both starving, they'd bought take-out food from the student cafeteria and now, unwrapping it, they looked at each other and giggled. Well, Eve giggled. Kendra was more the sophisticated chuckle type. The type, Eve knew, that rarely had any interest in cheerleaders.

"What?" Kendra opened a container of not-quite-fresh-looking fresh fruit chunks and stuck two forks in unidentifiable orange-colored pieces. "What do you think these are? Peaches or mangos? And what are you looking at me like that for?"

Eve took the speared fruit and popped it in her mouth, chewed, and swallowed. "Mango. Probably. It's hard to tell. Whatever it is, it's not awful."

Kendra tried a piece, then went back for a chunk of pineapple. "Now, tell me about that look you were giving me."

"'Well, in high school, girls like you didn't usually like girls like me."

"What? Explain that a little more."

"Well, you're into studying."

"You think I'm a nerd?"

"No! No! That's not what I meant. Nerds don't look like you do. They don't know how to dress or do their hair. They don't even care, most of the time."

Kendra chuckled and handed Eve half of a chicken salad sandwich. "I don't care like you do. You look so perfect, it's hard to tell you have makeup on, but you do."

"Sure."

"I'm not wearing any."

"I could show you—"

"No. I know how." Kendra grinned. "Like you said, I'm not a nerd. I'm just not into doing all that primping if I don't have to."

"That's what I mean," Eve said, pointing the corner of her sandwich at the other girl. "You're sort of beyond it all. I mean, you're smart and beautiful, and you don't care about cheerleading, right?"

"No, I don't care about cheerleading. I've noticed a few football players that look like they're worth cheering, though. This chicken salad doesn't have any celery in it. That's not right."

"It isn't?"

"Nope. I think I'll complain."

"Really? It's just a sandwich."

"Maybe they'll put celery in it if I complain— that means ask nicely. They sure won't if I don't say anything."

"See? That's what I mean. You think things through. You're, um, mature. You were probably born mature."

Kendra laughed. "Thanks, I think. And what about you? Were you born to be perky?"

Eve hesitated. "Usually, if a girl like you asked me that, I'd know I was being put down. I don't think you're doing that though. Are you?"

"Of course not. So, were you born perky or did you learn it?"

"I don't know. A little bit of both, probably. My mother was a beauty queen. She started in pageants when she was eight years old." Eve shook her head. "She was Little Miss Annie's Baton School, Little Miss Caledonia, Miss Caledonia Dairy Products, and even Miss Central California. She always did flaming batons, and boy, was she good!" Eve giggled. "Sometimes, if she has too much to drink at Christmas, she wants to do her old act, but Daddy always stops her because he's afraid she'll catch herself on fire."

"That's nice."

"Huh?"

"He worries that *she'll* catch on fire, not that the house will. So do you do beauty pageants?"

"She kind of tried to get me to, but I didn't like it. I only did one, when I was little, and she stopped trying to get me to do any more after that little girl was murdered in Colorado and the news started doing exposés on kid pageants."

"So how are you with flaming batons?"

Eve had a long sip of Diet Coke. "Fire scares me. Daddy said that once, when I was about two, my mother had too much eggnog and managed to get her batons lit before he could stop her. I kind of remember, but not really. She threw the batons up and they hit the ceiling, of course, and came down hard. He said one landed a foot from me and that I just stood there and stared at it and wouldn't talk for a couple days. I had nightmares for a long time."

"About the batons?"

"Yeah, but not exactly. I kept dreaming that clouds would gather for a storm and then instead of water, it would rain drops of fire." She didn't add that the dreams only went away after the incident at Applehead Lake, to be replaced by nightmares about glowing green eyes and black lake water pounded by real rain.

"So, was your mother a cheerleader?"

"A twirler." Eve made her voice as serious as she could. "Me, I'm a pom-pom woman."

It worked. Kendra snorted laughter. "How'd they meet? Your parents, I mean?"

"Mom was Miss Central Coast. Daddy was one of the judges." She cocked an eyebrow. "And it's not what you're probably thinking. No funny business—Hi, Heather!"

"Hi, you two!" The captain of the cheerleading squad approached quickly, chestnut curls bouncing in the sun. She wore a short-skirted cheering uniform, green trimmed in gold and white. It was gorgeous. Even more gorgeous with the pair of guys flanking her. They were big, clean-cut young men, one light, one dark, both with gleaming smiles. They weren't in uniform, but Eve knew they were football players.

"I want you to meet Art Caliburn and Spencer Lake. Art is the Knights' captain and star quarterback, and Spence is a wide receiver." Heather smiled. "They're both being scouted by the majors."

The blond stepped forward and extended his hand. "I'm Art."

Kendra took it and introduced herself; then Eve did the same. She could feel herself blushing as the hunky football player looked into her eyes. Sparks seemed to tingle between their hands. Then Spence stepped in, speaking first to Kendra, then breaking the grip between Art and Eve, replacing the QB's hand with his own.

More sparks flew. Maybe even bigger sparks.

"Can't wait to see you two cheering on our team," Art said, breaking the spell.

Kendra laughingly declined but Eve just kept blushing. College was going to be even more fun than she'd expected.

8

Signing the pledge agreement had been anticlimactic, to say the least. Now Eve dawdled in the big main room of the house, studying old paintings, old wallpaper, and various antiques. The room smelled old, centuries old, and roses, fresh and dried lay above the ancient background scent, like flowers in a mausoleum.

She wanted to check out the house, but nobody else seemed to be taking self-guided tours. If Kendra showed up soon, maybe they could take a look around together. She glanced at her watch; it was only a little after four o'clock and not too many pledges or sisters were here yet. Heather was the only person she knew, and she was busy at the sign-up table doing her thing as rush chairman. Her Majesty Malory had yet to make an appearance and that was half the reason Eve didn't want to go wandering by herself—she might run into her.

She walked out into the huge foyer. The floor was covered with white marble tile streaked in browns ranging from tan to russet. Sheer curtains covered tall narrow sidelights on each side of the door, the thick old glass casting odd prisms across the floor. The distance from the front entrance to the central grand staircase was about twice the width of her small dorm room. It was breathtaking. The broad staircase went up a dozen steps, then swept into two separate normal-width stairways, one to the west wing, one to the east. They disappeared from view at the first-floor landing, which appeared to run along the length of the old mansion. As she watched, Eve heard a door above open and close. Feminine voices echoed from above and two of the sisters came into view. They saw her staring at them.

"Hello!" Eve said with all the cheer she could muster.

"Hi," said one, an Asian girl with blond streaks in her hair. The other girl, pale with smooth glossy dark hair curling under an inch below her firm jawline, looked at her and nodded, then looked again.

Eve didn't like the look, though it wasn't mean or cold. It was just curious. "Have we met?" the girl asked.

It can't be Sam Penrose. She'd never join a sorority. Or wear makeup. Or a dress. Never a dress. "I don't think so. Maybe at the rush party?"

The girl—*it's not Sam Penrose, I haven't seen her since camp, she's just the same type*—opened her mouth to say something, then paused, looking behind Eve. Eve turned to see one of the entrance doors opening. "Kendra! I was afraid you might not come after all."

"I told you I would. Did you already sign your life away?"

"Yep."

"Well, let's get this over with." Taking Eve's arm, she started toward the common room's open doorway.

Eve glanced up, but the dark-haired girl was nowhere to be seen.

"What?" Kendra asked as they entered the main room. "What's bugging you now?"

"Nothing. I just got caught staring at a couple of sisters. It was stupid."

Kendra laughed. "You sure are jumpy, but then I guess you're supposed to be."

"Huh?"

"You're a cheerleader. You jump. It's natural." She smiled. "Come on, relax."

9

Malory Thomas stretched like a cat, her perfect body momentarily sated and looking exquisite against the rumpled red satin sheets on Professor Tongue's water bed. It was king-sized and clunky, a watery throwback that bounced and jounced and exuded warmth from beneath. Malory had owned one once herself, back when it was cool to have one.

Timothy Piccolo's water bed wasn't cool, but then neither was the good—the *very* good—professor. But both were kitschy, she decided, feeling kind. She glanced up, hearing the shower running, when the bathroom door opened. Steam curled about the man with the golden tongue as he peered out. "Care to join me in a hot shower?" he asked.

He was naked, a shortish sturdy man with moderate love handles and a dinky penis. It didn't matter much—the tongue was what made the man in this case. Some men couldn't reach a cervix with their dicks, the professor included; but he could hit it with that snake he hid in his mouth. And he was an artist. He could tap. He could rap. He could play Reveille.

He was so good at it that she thought it might be worth performing a little magic to keep him around, to keep him from aging further. Then again, men could become so boring so easily, even ones with special talents. Perhaps just a short extension . . .

"Well?" he asked.

"Start without me. I'll be in in a minute." No, she decided, when she was done here, she'd probably leave him behind when she moved on.

When he started singing in the shower, she smiled and knew it.

She rose from the bed and opened the window. Professor Tongue's little house was an old favorite of hers. A small craftsman-style cottage owned by the university, the century-old abode was only a brisk five-minute walk from Gamma House. Near the edge of the woods, its privacy was ensured by well-tended gardens, lots of trees and bushes. The university spent a fortune on gardeners; briefly she wondered if any of the administrators ever wondered why the place was so green, why the grass grew faster than theirs did at their homes. Probably not. The ones who lived in Greenbriar wouldn't realize it and the ones who commuted from Caledonia and farther places probably just thought it was the type of grass, or something in the soil. *And they'd be right.* . . .

Malory smiled at the chipmunk that chirped at her from the branch of a young oak near the window. Whenever she spent time at Greenbriar, Malory ensconced her lovers in this cottage. When she discovered Professor Tongue's talents two years ago, she had promptly decided his off-campus excuse for an apartment wouldn't do; it was much too far away.

Fortunately, in no time at all, elderly Professor Higgins, a stuffy old English instructor who was then living here, one who had taught at the college for thirty years and looked at her oddly now and then, as if he might remember her from long ago, suffered a stroke that rendered him unable to speak a coherent sentence. He'd babbled like an idiot, but the university took pity on him and let him remain, so Malory had taken more drastic measures. More permanent ones. Higgins ceased his babbling for all time.

And Professor Tongue had been moved in before the old man was cold in the ground.

"Malory?"

Malory looked out at the tree and caught her breath as Brittany popped up from beneath the window, right in her face. She hid her annoyance. "Were you watching?"

Brittany nodded and produced a Peanut M&M from her pocket. "Yes." *Crunch, crunch.*

"Jealous?"

"You know it. Can I come in?"

"Are you forgetting something?"

Brittany looked cute and stupid. She was good at that. "What?"

"How's the pledge sign-up going?"

"Fine. Can I come in?"

Malory glanced at her watch. "It's five. I need to be there by six. I don't think it's a good idea."

Brittany dimpled up. "Please? Just for a few minutes."

"He's in the shower."

"So? Tell him to hurry up. I watched you guys for fifteen minutes. I *need* to come in."

Malory wanted to say no, but looking at that hopeful face, she just couldn't. Brittany was like a pet to her, but much more. She reached out and gently patted the girl's cheek. "Okay. Hurry up. I'll get Professor Tongue out of the shower. You get ready."

Leaving Brittany to climb in the window, Malory left to retrieve the professor. The good thing about tongues compared to cocks was that a good athletic one didn't need any downtime. She smiled. *Hmmm. Maybe I should keep him around.*

10

Professor Daniel S. McCobb, emeritus in age but not in practice, stood under an old-fashioned street lamp on the sidewalk across the campus road from Gamma House. He'd gone for a stroll after his last cultural anthropology class and the perfect weather had inspired him to walk farther than usual.

Once each year, usually in late September, as tonight, a marvelous harbinger occurred. On a night still warm with late summer, the first hint of autumn would appear. This was such a night. He loved it; the cool tang of fall riding the breeze, singing to him of fluttering golden leaves, the red glow of heat from a nearly finished fireplace log at midnight, of pumpkins on porches, Caledonia's Halloween parade, and hayrides along this very street at Greenbriar. In the old days, when the road was paved with cobblestones, the annual hayride was better. Asphalt just wasn't the same.

But the old sorority house, resting far back on its broad lawn across the way, hadn't changed a bit. It was a monstrous piece of genuine Greek Revivalist architecture. Six Ionic columns ran across the front of the house, edging the wide wraparound veranda. The house appeared to be two tall stories, but an attic was hidden in the wide cornices below the roof and behind the central pediment with its anthemia ornamentation. Golden light shone from the leaded entry-door sidelights and downstairs windows. Above, about a third of the windows were lit.

Something was going on at Gamma House tonight; McCobb caught snatches of feminine laughter on the autumn wind and saw figures moving on the veranda. Since it was a weeknight, it probably wasn't initiations, but that would come soon. *Bad stuff, that.* Initiation rituals were rough in every culture. Meant to draw together individual personalities into a cohesive whole, they served their purposes best in primitive cultures where villages depended on each member to ensure survival. Fraternity and sorority initiations, in McCobb's opinion, served little purpose. They ensured that young people would learn loyalty born of fear and humiliation. They created young adults who knew how to conform to the will of the majority, who would do as they were told. Those who didn't learn, who stayed but broke vows of secrecy, were punished.

You old fool. This stuff's been toned down, especially here at Greenbriar. Still, he felt a chill in his ancient bones, one having nothing to do with the slight hint of autumn. Fraternity hazings had stopped early in the seventies when a pledge drowned in the lake, and sororities were generally far gentler than the male societies.

Except for this one.

He had no proof, of course. But he'd been around a long time. He *knew* . . . He'd seen some things, researched others. He taught the only folklore classes on campus, and what would he be if he ignored the lore of Applehead Valley and Greenbriar University? *Not much, that's what.*

"Excuse me," said a woman's voice.

He stepped back as two girls approached from the path across the quad. "Pardon me, ladies."

The girls, a small blonde with all her curves on display and a taller, better-dressed girl with raven hair who exuded sexuality like perfume, passed him by; then the dark one paused and turned. The blonde pulled up short and turned as well, her eyes bright and cheeks flushed.

"Professor McCobb?" asked the dark one.

"Yes," he said, fascinated. A small trill of fear played up his spine, but at his age, it was easy to hide. "You know me," he said smoothly. "But I see so many students. I'm afraid you have the advantage, young lady."

Her dark eyes bored into him. He felt as if she could read his mind. "Malory Thomas," she said finally. "President of Gamma Eta Pi."

"Pleased to make your acquaintance," he said without offering his hand. "Are you in one of my classes?"

"No," she said. "I just know who you are. You're an author."

He smiled benignly. "Just some musty old papers."

"And a book of urban legends," Malory Thomas said. "I've read it."

He chuckled. "I'm still trying to live that down. I'm afraid that it amuses my colleagues to no end."

"It's cool," said the blonde. She wore so much lip gloss he was surprised it didn't drip.

"Thank you, Miss . . . ?" *What are you calling yourself these days?*

"Brittany Woodcock. Gamma VP!"

"Miss Woodcock. I'm glad you enjoyed my little effort."

"I read it because of the title. The title was cool. *Is That a Hook in Your Pocket or Are You Just Glad to See Me?* That's just so cool." She popped something in her mouth and crunched it up. "So was the book."

"That was the publisher's title, I'm afraid. Granted, it sold better than my title would have—"

"Nice talking to you, Professor," Malory Thomas cut in. "I have to get to the house."

"We're showing the pledges around," Brittany called as she chased after Malory.

Watching them leave, Daniel McCobb allowed himself a small sigh of relief. He'd passed the test. The woman calling herself Malory Thomas didn't know he remembered her.

She hadn't aged a day.

INITIATION

11

When Malory Thomas strutted into the drawing room, all the pledges stopped talking and stared at her. The sorority president silenced one stray giggle with the barest glance, and moved to stand in front of the huge fireplace. Brittany plopped her tight-jeaned butt down on a dusky rose floor pillow a few feet from her. She wore a green Gamma T-shirt with the Greek letters— ΓΗΠ—emblazoned in gold across her breasts. The letters were almost too stretched out to read and the shirt bottom had been tied in a knot below her bosom to show off her svelte waist and belly button ring.

Eve watched the little blonde stare adoringly at Malory and wondered if they were a couple. The girl seemed to stick to her like glue. Superglue. Meanwhile, Malory just stood there and gazed about the room, acting like royalty. She and the other officers wore the school and sorority colors in the form of long silky scarves with the Greek letters embroidered in gold thread prominently on the ends. They also wore enameled pins, delicate dark pink rosebuds on green stems. Each stem had two leaves and a few thorns, which seemed a little weird.

Watching Malory stand before the girls, Eve suspected she was basking in the pledges' terror and momentarily wondered why she wasn't feeling afraid herself, then decided the high-handed president pissed her off too much to scare her. *Who does she think she is?*

That's easy. She's the president of the most powerful sorority on campus. She has every right to act like an arrogant bitch. Eve quelled a burgeoning smile. Malory would never approve.

"Welcome to Gamma House," the president said, her voice

as regal as her stance. "Over the next few weeks, you will attempt to earn your status as full sisters. During this time, and forevermore, you are sworn to keep all of our traditions and secrets safe from outsiders, and to take them with you to your grave. Are there any questions?" Her black eyes flashed over the pledges, daring them to speak.

Eve's skin crawled and she realized she was properly terrorized again. None of that had been on the paper she'd signed. The wording had been much gentler, more businesslike, like the nondisclosure paper she'd signed when she'd done volunteer work at the hospital the summer before last, where she just had to promise not to discuss any patients' conditions.

She glanced at Kendra, beside her on the sofa. She was gazing down at her hands, her face serene, a hint of amusement curling up her lips. Eve realized her new friend wasn't intimidated at all and wondered why she didn't ask any questions. *For the same reason I'm not. She doesn't want to call that bitch's attention to herself.*

"Ladies," Malory said, "do you understand the gravity of the vows you are about to take? If you have any qualms, any notion that you might get drunk and tell a boyfriend or anyone else anything about the secrets of this sorority, I ask that you go to the desk, find your oath, and tear it in half, then leave. I am giving you this last chance to reconsider for your own good. To make this easier, we will take a five-minute break. I urge you all to get up and move around so that anyone who wishes to leave may do so without humiliation." Her smile was as cold as death. "Humiliating anyone is the last thing a Gamma sister wants to do."

12

Eve and Kendra glanced at each other and headed outside, coming to a halt on the veranda about twenty feet from the now-open entry doors. "What do you think?" Eve asked quietly.

Kendra shook her head. "I'm not sure what I think. It's probably the usual sorority nonsense, but you know that stuff I haven't told you about yet—the extra-secret stuff my granny told me about?"

Eve nodded. "What about it?"

"Not now and not here, Evie." She glanced around making sure no one had wandered close enough to hear her. "The thing is, it's probably all just hooey. Even Granny admitted that. But they could be serious about keeping secrets. You know about Skull and Bones?"

"Huh?"

"At Yale. It's a society that's super secret and really powerful. It grooms men for power positions. Both George and George Junior were members."

"The presidents? Of the United States?"

"Yes, those Georges. Other ones too, and all sorts of politicians and powerful types all over the world. It's really creepy."

"You're serious?" Eve asked. "I've heard of the Yale Lampoon—"

"Girl, that's the Harvard Lampoon and that's not what I'm talking about *at all*. That's funny stuff. Skull and Bones is *serious* stuff. And what might be going on here."

"But you're still going to pledge?" Eve asked in alarm.

"Sure. I don't think there're any secrets to worry about unless you get into that secret part."

"The Skull and Bones thing?"

"Yes, but don't say it anymore. If it's real, they're probably damned serious and you don't want to mess with that. You don't want them to know you even suspect unless they tell you about it."

"What if they tell?"

Kendra chuckled. "You're cute, you know that? They're not going to tell you anything, not now. Not until you're proven as a sister. But listen, the way that Heather fawned over you, you might be one of the ones they ask."

"What about you?"

Kendra shrugged. "I'm surprised they let me in at all. They check everybody out. You can be sure they know my granny's granny and the rest, right up the line, worked here."

"So they wouldn't want you because they worked here?"

Kendra opened her mouth, closed it, opened it again. "I don't mean because they *worked* here— because they were hired help. The one thing about Gamma that's good is that it isn't elitist." She laughed quietly. "I mean, it is, but only after you're in. The sorority itself is elite, but it chooses members from every income level and all kinds of backgrounds. Their thing is, they don't care what you were; they only care about what you become."

"Kind of like the army."

"Yeah. And that's a little scary too." She paused. "There's one girl here that's in my cultural iconography class."

"Your what?"

"It's one of Professor McCobb's classes. He's a folklore expert, among other things—the author of the urban legend book that's all over the student bookstore?"

"Sure. I know. So what about the girl?"

"Well, she's a really serious student. I don't really know her, I think she's six months or a year ahead of us—she's already a sister—but I think maybe she's snooping around."

"Why?"

"She's not the sorority type at all."

"And you are?" Eve grinned.

"Good point. Anyway, she's a journalism major, big time. And she's all over McCobb with questions. I think she's researching the sorority."

"Did you ask her?"

"Sort of. She just looked at me like I was nuts and said that being a sorority member is good for future career opportunities. That's why she's in. And I didn't ask any more questions. That girl has a stare that's as intense as Malory's."

"Eww."

"It's not mean, though. Just intense—and I sure knew I wasn't supposed to ask any more questions. Don't let on I said anything."

"Of course not. Who is she?"

Kendra looked upward, thinking. "I'm blanking. I know her name—I hate brain farts. It's on the tip of my tongue—"

The pair looked at each other and snickered. "Bad word choice," Kendra said. "God, if I'm this bad at eighteen, what'll I be like at Granny's age? What's that girl's name?"

The porch lights flicked off and on twice, like a theater calling back its patrons. "I'll introduce you later, or poke you if she speaks up. Okay?"

Eve nodded. "So, are you up for this, Kendra?"

"The mysteries await." Kendra took her arm and they went back into the house.

13

The vows sounded serious and solemn. As Eve and the other pledges took them simultaneously, she actually thought they were pretty silly. Full of hooey, as Kendra would say. They had to stand in a half circle facing the fireplace and the officers while they repeated the words Malory spoke. The oath was dramatic as hell and used the phrase "to the death," several times, which really was goofy for a bunch of girls just out of high school to say. It felt as if they were playing a game of pretend, and probably that's exactly what they were doing.

It was intimidating nonetheless, especially since, just before the vows began, many more Gammas arrived, along with a couple of pushcarts of folding chairs. Nice wooden ones with upholstered seats, not the usual gray metal things, Eve had noted approvingly. The sisters, perhaps two dozen of them, had set up their chairs at the far end of the room. Most wore jeans and green Gamma T-shirts, but a few wore the green silk scarves instead. Maybe pins too; Eve couldn't tell in the brief instant she'd looked at the audience of sisters.

"Time for introductions," Veep Brittany chirped. She sounded like Alvin the Chipmunk's sister. "Heather, are all the sisters here?"

Heather, standing before the fireplace with Malory, Brittany, and the other officers, Teri and Michele, nodded. "I believe everyone is here?" She raised her voice and her eyes, looking toward the other end of the room.

A murmur arose among the Gammas, then someone said, "Everyone is present and accounted for, Madam Chairman."

Eve glanced at Kendra, who turned out to already be looking her way. Both let their eyes start to roll, but stopped short.

"Pledges, please take your seats," Malory ordered. She waited for them to settle in, then spoke again. "I'd like you each to stand and introduce yourself, tell us your long-range goals and why you want to be a Gamma." She nodded at the nearest pledge, the Chinese girl Eve had noticed the day before.

"I'm Nicole Chang, from Santa Cruz, California. I'm a biophysics major and I'd like to work in nanotechnology."

A brain. Anything having to do with numbers turned Eve off, and she'd bet her mother's batons that nanotechnology was something that involved math.

"I wish to be a Gamma sister in order to enjoy the friendships that come with such a fine house, and of course to aid in my career, should I prove worthy. Thank you." The nervous girl sat down quickly.

And so it went. There were thirteen pledges and five more

spoke as Eve nervously awaited her turn. Each one said basically the same thing about wanting to make friends and improve her career chances, but their majors varied greatly. There was a lit major, a drama, two biologies, and a linguistics.

And then Malory's eyes were on Eve. She rose. "I'm Eve Camlan, from Caledonia. I want to join the sorority to make friends and to help my career someday." She started to sit.

"Your career and your major are?" Malory said archly.

Eve felt herself blushing as she came back into full upright position. *My major is—What do I say? They all have majors picked out already!*

"Liberal arts," Kendra whispered.

"Liberal arts," Eve said. "For now. I'm not sure, but I think I'd like to be a teacher."

"Elementary?" Malory said, an eyebrow up, no smile anywhere.

"No. Junior high or high school." *Let me die now.*

"Malory, everyone," said Heather, "Eve Camlan is an award-winning cheerleader and I sincerely hope she wants to try out for our squad. I think she'll outshine all of us."

Bless you. "Thanks. I'd like to try," she managed, then sank into her seat.

Kendra did much better. She didn't mention her interest in folklore, but said she wanted to be a cultural anthropologist. Eve smiled at her as she sat down.

Two more girls introduced themselves. One was in premed, the other an English major. And then came the girl with the fiery hair and intense green eyes.

"I'm Merilynn Morris."

Eve's stomach dropped. She had hoped the girl wouldn't come back. The lake, the storm, the eyes came rushing back.

"I'm from Santo Verde, California, and I haven't decided on my major yet."

"Any clues, dear?" Malory asked.

"Not yet," Merilynn said, obviously not intimidated. "I'm a dabbler."

"You must have some long-term goals. I'm sure you listed something on your application."

The girl paused, then said serenely, "Chemistry. I might become a chemist."

"The kind that cures cancer or makes perfume?" the president inquired.

"Maybe I'll make perfume that cures cancer," Merilynn replied. "I wanted to join Gamma because I'm told my mother was a sister."

"You were *told?*" Malory actually smiled. It was hideous.

"She died shortly after I was born, so yes, I was told."

"I don't remember seeing any mention of this on your application."

"Well, Malory, I wanted to get in on my own, not as a legacy."

The president nodded, evidently satisfied by the answer. Merilynn sat down and Eve relaxed slightly.

The final two pledges—a poly sci and another English major—spoke; then Malory asked the sisters in the audience to introduce themselves. Eve listened, but not as well as she might have. Exhaustion was overtaking her. Then Kendra poked her as one of the sisters rose. It was the one with shortish dark hair that she'd seen on the landing earlier.

"My name is Samantha Penrose. I'm going to be a journalist."

Eve felt dizzy as more memories swept over her. She'd never expected to see either of these girls again. She hadn't seen them in years and years. She didn't want to see them. And here they were. Both of them.

"Hey, are you all right?" Kendra whispered, touching her hand.

Eve nodded.

"What's wrong?" Kendra mouthed.

Eve bent slightly and whispered in her ear, "Déjà vu."

14

"You want to meet her?" Kendra asked as they began a half hour of mingling, new sisters and old, after the ceremony.

"Who?"

"The girl I told you about from my cultural iconography class. Sam Penrose. I poked you when she spoke. You felt that, right?"

"Yes." Eve was having trouble concentrating. Knowing that both her old acquaintances from cheer camp, the two that had shared the nightmarish adventures, were in the same room with her now, was upsetting, even though she knew it shouldn't be, even though she had known it would probably happen. *You should say hello, long time no see, and be done with it. They probably don't want to hash over old times any more than you do.*

"Evie, come on," Kendra said, hauling her to a corner in the rear where a crystal punch bowl sat on a long narrow tapestry runner on an antique sideboard. Plates of munchies—cookies, chips, dip, veggies—surrounded it. She ladled punch into a crystal cup and handed it to Eve, then made one for herself. "What's up with you?" she asked.

Eve studied the punch cup. "This looks like real crystal. But that would be nuts."

"Speaking of nuts, check it out." Kendra nodded toward another small table where Brittany was scooping up peanuts from a bowl and putting them in her pockets. It was hard work; those skintight pockets didn't hold much. The veep glanced up, saw them looking at her, and a black look flashed through her eyes. Eve could almost feel the anger in it—but it was gone quickly, replaced with a smile, wide and cheerful. She took more nuts and popped them in her mouth and wandered off without a word. Not that she could say anything with so many nuts in her mouth. "How does she keep her figure?" Kendra said with a chuckle.

"I don't know. She must have the metabolism of a humming-bird. She's always eating." Eve sipped her drink thirstily.

Kendra grinned. "Your punch pleases you?"

"It does." Eve refilled her cup and snagged a carrot stick.

"Okay, so are you going to tell me what's scaring you?"

"Nothing."

"Come on. You're one of those social butterflies. Don't try and deny it—I know your type."

"I'm not—"

"Come on, I'm teasing you. Where's your sense of humor? You're a cheerleader but your perkiness is missing. What's bugging you?"

"It's stupid."

"Tell me anyway."

"Samantha Penrose?"

"What about her?"

"She was the other girl on Applehead Island with me—she and Merilynn Morris were both there."

"Really? Sam's the brainiac you talked about?"

Eve nodded.

"I believe you. So what's the problem?"

"I don't know. I just don't want to talk to her. Or Merilynn. I don't want them to be here. I wish they weren't."

"Did you guys fight or something?"

"No. I just don't want to have to talk about old times."

Kendra studied her a long moment. "That was some scary stuff."

"It was."

15

"Excuse me!"

As Heather Horner approached, the central point in a V of seven girls, Kendra smiled, amused by their Barbie-ness; even though they came in several colors, they were all cast from the same mold. *Cheerleaders.* She glanced at Eve; she was beaming. *She recognizes her own kind.* Kendra smiled. Eve had the same look, but maybe because she'd gotten to know her, she could see more than the Barbie-doll mask. She could see vulnerability and sensitivity behind the bright smile and she hoped that it wouldn't disappear under the influences of this gaggle of giggling airheads. *You don't know they're airheads. Don't be such a snob. At least for Evie's sake.*

"Hi, Eve, hi, Kendra," Heather said. Kendra saw her glance at her name tag, but not at Eve's. *She's a cheerleader. She's mentally incapable of remembering everyone's name.*

"What?" Heather asked, seeing Kendra's smile.

"Nothing. Just happy to be here."

Heather nodded. "I wanted to introduce you to my squad. You've met our secretary and treasurer, Teri and Michele, already, right?"

The two shook hands with Eve, then Kendra. "Are you a cheerleader?" Michele asked, obviously being polite.

"No, just an onlooker."

"Meet the rest of the squad," Heather said, gesturing. "This is Julie, this is Jeannie, this is Jenny, and last but not least, this is Ginny."

What, no Joanie? The cookie-cutout girls, giggling greetings, were all over Eve, hugging her like old friends, barely sparing nods for Kendra. *Maybe this is the secret society. A secret society of cheerleaders. Now* there's *a scary thought!*

"So, guess what, Eve!" Heather bubbled.

"What?"

"Normally, anyone chosen this weekend for tryouts would be a substitute only until next year, but this time, whoever's the very best of the newbies will get to join the squad immediately. It'll be lots of hard work." Heather winked. "But we need a replacement right away."

"One of you is leaving?"

"She already left." The squad cast their eyes down as one. "She died. It was terrible."

"That's awful! I'm so sorry. May I ask . . . what happened? Have I met her?"

"I don't think you met her," Heather said. "I think she went missing the night of the rush. We thought maybe she'd just run off for a while—we *prayed* she had—but they found Mulva's body just a few hours ago." She glanced around furtively. "We didn't want to bring it up and spoil the evening."

"Will there be services?"

"Just a little memorial among ourselves. Frankly, nobody liked her very much."

"That's pretty cold," Kendra said.

Heather shot her a harsh glance. "You didn't know her. I won't speak ill of the dead, but she had us all fooled. She wasn't what she appeared to be."

"What happened?" Kendra couldn't stop herself. "Did she tell some sorority secrets?"

Heather was a statue for a second; then she reanimated, all warmth and understanding. "Of course not. You don't think—" She paused dramatically, then put her arm around Kendra, giving her a quick squeeze. "Sweetie, that stuff is just talk, you know that. And I guess that did sound cold. It's just that, well, Mulva had problems."

"What kind of problems?" Eve asked.

"Heroin, for one thing. Can you imagine a Gamma Eta Pi with a *drug* problem? Especially a cheerleader? It's against everything we stand for. And she knew she could come to her sisters to help solve the problem, but she didn't. Instead, she even tried to talk Jenny into getting high with her."

"She did," one of the J-clones said solemnly.

"That's still cold," Kendra said. "Maybe she was embarrassed."

"When Jenny wouldn't take heroin with her, she tried to give it to her while she was asleep."

"What?" Kendra asked. "How?"

"She put some in her mouth."

"She tried to put it under my tongue," the clone said, "but I woke up."

"What happened?"

"I got really sick."

"But that's not all," Heather said.

"What else?" Kendra asked.

Instead of replying, Heather nodded at the other girls. "Tell her."

"She tried to give it to me," said one.

"And me," said another.

"And me," the third said, her eyes like saucers.

"She was trying to turn *my* squad into *drug addicts*. Can you imagine?"

"That's pretty bad," Kendra said. *And it sounds like bullshit.*

"Once, she even approached Teri and Michele, *officers* of the *sorority!* Can you *imagine?*"

"It's pretty hard to imagine."

"And that's not all," Heather said yet again.

"What else?" Kendra asked, thinking they were being fed a whole silo of shit.

"She peed in Malory's lemonade."

Eve giggled nervously.

"How do you know that?" Kendra asked.

"Malory caught her. Malory loves lemonade. Our housekeeper, Mildred, makes a special batch just for her. It's in a different container."

"That's weird," Kendra said.

"No. Malory likes it without any sweetener."

"Oh." *Why doesn't that surprise me?*

"And—"

"That's not all," Kendra finished, crossing her arms. "So, what are the other reasons that you aren't mourning her death?"

"Ex-Lax in the hot chocolate."

"Old trick. Not a biggie."

"On Parent Night?"

"Okay, that's pretty nasty."

"You're not kidding," said either Michele or Teri, the officer-clones. "Housekeeper wouldn't clean the toilets."

"You didn't make Mulva clean them?" Kendra asked.

"She took off. We couldn't leave them dirty until she came back," Heather explained.

"They were really, really dirty," said one of the J-clones.

"She used *a lot* of Ex-Lax!" added another.

"It was like really stinky modern art," said one more.

"Stinky," added the forth J-clone, sounding a little like Homer Simpson thinking about chili burgers.

"Why did you accept her as a member if she was like this?"

"Like I said, she fooled everyone. We had no idea. She was a champion cheerleader back at her high school in French Lick."

"In what?"

"French Lick," Heather said, all seriousness. "It's in Indiana."

A J-clone started to giggle. Heather shot her a look worthy of Malory. The giggle stopped. "You can look it up."

"I've heard of it," Kendra said.

"She was a farm girl," Teri or Michele said. "She must have been on the edge and we think that moving to a place like this probably put her over the top."

"A place like this?"

"You know, with mountains and the ocean. She was used to the plains."

"Flatland," said the other Michele or Teri.

"Not used to the big city," Kendra said. She added a slight smile, deciding at the last instant not to bait them further. She'd play along.

Heather smiled back. "That's funny."

"Maybe it's true," Eve said. "If she ever went to a big place like San Francisco, maybe it freaked her out."

Eve obviously thought that Indiana was something out of a corn-fed musical. No cities. Maybe no airports. Kendra had a sudden desire to drag Eve kicking and screaming out of the sorority house before she turned into one of *them. The Stepford Cheerleaders.*

Maybe you should just drag yourself out of here. Maybe you're the one who doesn't belong here.

"Attention, attention!" Malory stood in the entryway and clapped her hands sharply. "Quiet, please." She only had to wait a few seconds before silence reigned.

"We're going to take you pledges on house tours now. Heather, Michele, and Brittany will escort you." She beckoned at the girls and they went to join her, leaving Kendra and Eve alone among the J-clones.

"Please divide yourselves up into groups."

"Come on," Eve said to Kendra and headed straight for Heather. Kendra followed.

16

"Okay," Heather told Eve, Kendra, and two other pledges. "Stay with me. No dawdling or wandering off on your own."

With that, she led them through the first floor. "Everyone stay together," Heather Horner repeated. "No wandering off on your own. First of all, the room you've spent all your time in so far, we call the drawing room."

"Why?" asked a short pledge. She had golden brown hair and glasses and according to her name tag, she answered to "Lou."

Heather smiled. "Why not? That's what it's always been called. Now come along." She led them into the hall and turned right, showing them the parlor, which was a room like the drawing room but about half the size. The furniture was older and less pristine. Chairs and two couches were arranged informally around coffee and side tables near the smaller fireplace. Several of the sisters were already curled up on the furniture, their books and notepads scattered across the nearest low table. "Let's let them study," said their guide, then led them on.

"When it was built, the house had all the modern conveniences," Heather told them. "The wall sconces used to be gas lamps. Today, of course, they've been wired for electricity. Until a few years ago, all of the power lines were in pipes running along the outside of the walls." She smiled as she led them down a connecting hall with tall double-hung windows sheathed in sheer eggshell curtain panels. Paintings of Greenbriar and environs punctuated the wall space between the windows. One painting of Applehead Lake gave Eve a shiver. It was dark with a storm-clouded sky and black water, the island with its skeletal trees a dark silhouette.

"Gamma House was very quaint," Heather continued. "Fortunately, our alumni have helped fund continuing renovations and modernizations. It's very expensive keeping up a house like this. Far more expensive than tearing it down and rebuilding, but it's worth it. The house has such history. Here's the kitchen."

She took them down a short flight of steps and into a cavernous room. "What do you think?"

"It's amazing," Kendra said. The others ah'd their agreements.

"The refrigerators and dishwashers are modern, of course. The stoves date from the thirties."

"The microwave doesn't look too new either," Kendra said.

Heather laughed. "It's at least ten years old. We keep it because it still works and it's huge. There are three new ones over there, on the long counter under the glass-fronted cabinets."

Eve took her eyes off the three old stoves and looked at the long counter, cabinets above and below. The glass inserts in the upper doors were thick and wavy-looking, sort of art deco, she thought. The lower cabinets' contents were hidden behind simple painted wooden doors.

"The kitchen was redone in the thirties, new cabinets and everything," Heather verified. "Of course, it's pretty quaint now too. We may work on a fund to remodel it—new cabinets and all."

"I love it as it is," Eve said.

"Me too." Kendra looked around. "Before it was redone, most of the cabinets were open. The top ones. Everything was painted white."

"You've been reading up on the house?" Heather asked.

"No. Several generations of my family worked here."

She said it nonchalantly, but Eve could see defiance in her eyes as she waited for rude remarks, or maybe just rude looks. None appeared.

"You must know some stories about the old days," Heather said. "Maybe you can tell some sometime."

"I doubt I know any stories you don't," Kendra replied, gazing steadily at the other girl.

"Oh? Okay. You guys want to see the dumbwaiter?"

17

Kendra knew there was a passage from a door in the corner of the kitchen that led deeper into the ground into a root cellar, and another that led across the rear yard to an old smokehouse, but Heather had mentioned neither one. The tunnel would be all blocked off, probably damaged by earthquakes over the years. The smokehouse's roof could be seen among the trees, but it wasn't in use even when Granny worked there, so Kendra guessed it was locked up tight now. It was one of the places the ghost of Holly Gayle was supposed to appear. Kendra said nothing, but quietly let herself be led into the cellar where a monstrous old boiler sat in summer dormancy. It would come into use again soon, Heather said, explaining that the heating had yet to be upgraded. Another fund-raising project down the road. They hoped to get rid of the window air conditioners scattered throughout the house as well, but it would require plenty of effort and Gamma spirit. Kendra managed not to roll her eyes over that phrase. *What am I doing here?*

They climbed the stairs to the second floor, Kendra admiring the banister and rails gleaming darkly, the patina of age polished to a high shine. "No wonder your housekeeper wouldn't clean the bathrooms. She must spend all her time waxing the woodwork."

"Mildred has enough to do without polishing everything. I'm afraid that's the job of our new sisters," Heather said, showing dimples. "That means you guys take it over as soon as you move in."

"For how long?" Kendra was fuming, feeling used, but could see the other girls were barely dismayed at the idea.

"Until next year. We all have jobs helping around the house, but as newbies, you get the worst. You also divvy up the non-carpeted floors with the sophomores."

"What do the other girls do?" asked Neelie, the other pledge, a willowy studious type, the poly sci major.

"Sophomores do windows and floors. Juniors vacuum. Seniors supervise."

"I guess so," Kendra muttered.

"What?"

"So, I guess all the bedrooms are on this floor?" She smiled, something warning her not to piss off Heather.

"Yes, they are, except for the two guest and/or broken-leg bedrooms downstairs. I forgot to show you those. You can see them later. Okay, this is important. Listen up: never, ever go into the east wing on this floor. It's off-limits. Totally, absolutely off-limits."

"Why?" Lou asked.

"Is it unsafe?" Neelie chimed in.

"A lot of it is uninhabited at this point—the rooms need to be restored. The rest makes up the senior section." She looked at Eve. "And some cheerleaders also get to room there. We have separate rooms there and only two girls to a bathroom. But that's all you need to know about that. You'll be sharing rooms in the west wing. Come on. There are thirteen of you and five available rooms. Three rooms have three beds each and the other two are doubles. Your roommates are your choice, of course."

Kendra glanced at Eve, wondering if she really wanted to room with a cheerleader. Eve saw her look, misread it, and squeezed her hand. "Roomie?" she asked silently. Kendra nodded. It was fate.

18

"*I love* this room!" Eve cried as she dragged Kendra back to a two-bed room after the tour. "Do you love it?"

Kendra looked around. It was beautiful if you liked pastels. The ceilings—normal height on this floor—were white with decorative molding. The walls were painted a light delicate color that Kendra wanted to believe was peach. They were nearly peach. Pinkish peach. She didn't like the idea of a pink room.

"Don't you love the color scheme?"

"Not really my colors, Eve, but it will do."

"You don't like it?" Eve asked, stricken. "We can take that other room, the blue one."

"No, this is fine. I really didn't like that blue one anyway. It seemed cold."

"I love the bedspreads. Do you?"

Kendra looked at the dainty floral pattern and tried not to wince. "I can live with them. What I like is this window." She reached across the small desk beneath it and drew the curtain back—*too frilly*—and looked out at the fifty feet of back lawn, the gardens, a tiny pond, and the old smokehouse, at the edge of the forest. From here, she could see more of it—the top half. The windows were shuttered. Undoubtedly, the door was locked. It fascinated her, maybe because of Granny's stories. She wanted to see inside. "Eve, look." She pointed out the smokehouse.

Eve joined her at the window. "The forest is spooky. I didn't think about that. Do you like looking at it?"

"Sure. And the smokehouse. That's what I wanted to show you."

Eve looked some more. "I don't think I like it either. It's forbidding." She paused. "Do you want the bed by the window? The desk under the window?"

"You bet. You're okay with that?"

"Am I ever!" Eve left the window and went to the other side of the room, plopping down on the windowless bed, by the windowless desk. "You're sure?'

"Absolutely. I love the view."

19

Eve sailed through the cheerleading tryouts. She was good at all the positions, topper, bottom, and her kicks and splits went perfectly. She tried out with cheers based on ones she'd made up for other tryouts, gearing them now to the Greenbriar Knights football team. At first nervous, she soon forgot her fears in the excitement of the moment; cheering took her to another place, a place where she never lacked confidence, a place where she felt at her best and most alive. Eight other girls, four of them Gammas, including little Lou from last night's tour, tried out as well, and only the Gamma members made the cut, even though a couple of the other girls, in Eve's opinion, were more talented. One Gamma member didn't make it either.

"You'll serve as substitutes for the rest of the year," Heather told the four after the others left the gym. "All but one of you, that is. The girl with the top score becomes part of the squad immediately and will have to practice really hard because she'll be cheering in tomorrow night's game against the Fort Charles Dragons. Who feels up to that?"

Eve shot her hand up without thinking twice, and she would have even if she hadn't already known she was the chosen one. The others put their hands up haltingly. What Heather was asking—learning routines in a day—was nearly impossible. *Unless you're almost a pro,* Eve thought proudly.

"Eve, I'm glad you're eager to do it because you outscored everyone today. You're the new full member of the squad. Congratulations!"

"Thank you! Thank you so much!" Eve bubbled, happily enduring a round of hugs and congratulations.

"Thank you, Eve! We're proud to have you," Heather said at last. "The rest of you will practice, too. As subs, you have to know the routines. You will all be called upon to fill in this year. Are you ready?"

The girls agreed happily.

"You never know," Heather said. "We may need a sub tomorrow night, so I want you all to practice like mad."

"What about uniforms?" Eve asked.

"Don't worry, we have them ready for you all. Now, you girls go into the locker room and do whatever you need to do to get ready to work your asses off. We," she said, gesturing at the six cheerleaders behind her, "will work with you individually and together for a couple of hours. We'll have a dinner break, and then more practice. Okay. Any questions?"

Lou raised her hand.

"Yes?"

"I was just wondering . . . Did you begin the year without any substitutes?"

"Good question. Yes, we did. Jenny and Ginny were our newest graduates from subbing. We had two more, but they didn't come back after summer vacation. We had intended to bring them on and expand the squad size by two, but it didn't work out. And then, as you may know, we lost Mulva Delacourt, an experienced cheerleader, which is why we have to bring one of you right onto the squad."

"Excuse me," Eve said.

"Yes?"

"I just wondered what happened to her? You said someone found her body? Does that mean she was murdered? If it's okay to ask."

Heather studied her so long that Eve's stomach was in knots by the time the other girl replied. "We don't know what happened to her. We probably never will, not for sure, but she probably went off into the woods, overdosed, and got lost. I'm afraid that there wasn't much left—just some bones. Animals got to the body. There's not much to autopsy." She shook her head regretfully. "We don't know for sure, but it will probably be ruled death by misadventure." She paused. "We do ask that none of you talk about the incident to outsiders."

"What does that mean exactly?" Eve asked.

"It means you don't answer any questions or ask any. It's terrible that it happened, but we can't let it ruin our school spirit. As cheerleaders, ladies, it's our job to keep morale tiptop. Got it?"

"Got it," Eve murmured.

"Could she have been murdered?" Lou asked. "I heard there was a serial killer in the woods."

"That serial killer story has been around for a century, so the killer would have to be pretty old by now." Heather smiled. "I wouldn't worry about that. But, girls, it's not a good idea to wander around the forest. Things do happen. In the woods."

"Then she could be a murder victim," Lou persisted.

"No. She was just another victim of drug abuse. Now, go get ready for a real practice!"

With that, the new girls cheered and dashed off to the lockers, Eve in the lead. She pushed the dead girl from her mind, deciding to ask Kendra about legends of killers and rapists later.

20

"Brittany," Malory said, rubbing her gently behind one ear. The blonde looked up into Malory's dark eyes. "Huh?"

"What do you think of Eve Camlan?"

Brittany nestled her head comfortably in Mal's lap. "I think she'll be perfect. You made an excellent choice. Don't stop."

Malory renewed her petting, now moving her hand to Brittany's forehead, smoothing away the hair. If the girl had been a cat, she'd purr. Instead, she reached, eyes closed, for a handful of sunflower seeds from a package resting against her side.

"Do you think she's full of juice, Brittany?"

"Very full. She's ripe and ready. She'll be perfect." The girl opened her eyes and gazed into her mistress's. "Feed me?"

"You're spoiled," Malory said, but she took the seeds from Brittany's palm and started feeding her one at a time. "I don't know why I do this for you. You don't deserve it."

"Sure I deserve it. I always deserve it. What would you do without me?"

"I have no idea, you little brat. I have no idea."

They stayed as they were for a long time, Malory sitting on the overstuffed green velvet sofa in her room, Brittany sprawled across it, Malory's lap her pillow. They drew energy from one another and in doing so, strengthened their individual and combined power.

Malory could live without her; at one time, many, many years ago, she had. But when she cast out a call for a familiar, a companion, here in this very wood, long before it was called Applehead, Brittany had answered. It happened one warm summer night. After performing her sorcery, Malory had gone to sleep near the spot where the deserted chapel now stood, barely a mile from here, hidden among the oak and pine in a very old place of power. When she awoke, Brittany was there beside her, watching her with those bright, inquisitive eyes. She had been alone longer than Malory, waiting long years for the right mistress to call her. They were meant to be together.

And that, Malory knew, was why she put up with the girl's constant demands and need for attention. Sometimes she wanted to boot her across the room—and had, occasionally, when she truly deserved it—but they always made up. They were two powerful beings entwined to make one far more powerful one. And they loved each other loyally, always sharing everything, from plates of food to lovers. Often, Brittany left her adjoining bedroom and slept with Malory. There was sex, but not often unless a man joined them; their desire to be together was born of their need for one another. Their love was pure.

And that was just about the only pure thing about either of them.

Malory smiled sleepily as Brittany nibbled the last sunflower seed from her fingers, then pulled the hand down between her breasts. She loved to have her belly rubbed.

"Mmmm, harder."

Malory scratched Brittany's side gently with her fingernails. One of the girl's legs wiggled a little in time with the scratching. "Brittany?"

"Hmmm?"

"What do you think of Professor Tongue?"

"I think he's an arrogant nerd, but I don't care because of what he can do."

"Do you mind his small penis?"

"Why?" Her eyes opened. "Could you put a spell on it, make it bigger?"

"We've tried that before, my sweet. It doesn't work too well, remember? It's too hard to control the size."

"Remember that man who lived in Applehead Valley? That big blond farmer?" Brittany laughed sleepily.

"That's exactly who I was thinking of." Jake Vanderdickens had been a handsome, strapping man, tall with broad shoulders and a full beard of gold spun with red. He reminded Malory of her brother, dead so many years, but that didn't diminish her ardor; after all, she had seduced him as well. The poor idiot had nearly killed himself when he found out he had fucked his sister while under a glamour that made him mistake her for his wife. Malory chuckled. Jake excited her partly because of that forbidden night of lust with her own brother. And she excited Jake, who often left his family on moonlit nights to meet her in the forest and make love on a fragrant bed of pine needles and ferns, on the place of power.

Jake was a skilled lover, or was once Malory had taught him the art. He, like Timothy Piccolo, had a long tongue and used it masterfully. It wasn't as long or as talented as the professor's, but it was a fine instrument nonetheless. Unfortunately, like Piccolo, he had a bantam-sized cock. And one day Malory, with Brittany's help, tried to change its dimensions.

The next night, when he came to her, what hung between his legs was a monster; the width of his strong arm, it hung almost to his knees at rest and resembled a baseball bat once aroused. At the same time, his tongue nearly disappeared, shrinking to a nubbin of its former size. Malory knew she had broken some law of nature, something to do with balance and power. She'd sent him home unsatisfied and that night, while she was trying to figure out how to fix what she had damaged, Jake accidentally fucked his wife, Moira, to death. Moira was the daughter of the Applehead Valley police chief and the next morning, when he came by and found Jake crying by the body, he arrested him. Filled with grief and fury, the chief paid some roughs to spirit Jake from his jail cell the next night and see that the man, whose only crime was being too well hung, was well hung by the neck, from the limb of an old oak.

Intrigued, Malory had since tried variations on the spell on men who didn't really matter to her, men who matched the criteria of long tongue and small genitalia. It was always the same. She'd also tried it on women, casting spells to increase breast size, but it always resulted in shrinkage that made their asses look like old men with stoved-in cheeks. It was, she thought, something to do with distribution of mass. You couldn't really change the physicality of a mere human, one lacking any magical capability, without consequences. Humans were no different from other animals; they were made of simple stuff. She smiled, thinking about her long-ago mentor's story about how he'd accidentally created the platypus. "Sometime," she told Brittany softly, "it might be fun to find a man with a huge nose, a normal tongue, and a small cock. That might work better."

"Give him a nose job?" She giggled merrily.

"Um-hmm. And a dick enlargement."

"Noses are different from tongues and cocks though," her familiar cautioned, giving Malory a glimpse of the old wisdom she usually kept hidden. "Those are similar in texture. Noses are full of cartilage. You might get something monstrous."

"Like a cock that never softened?"

Brittany smiled. "If you're lucky." She stretched and turned on her side, burrowing her nose into Malory's navel, her warm breath tickling her abdomen. "So why were you thinking about Professor Tongue?"

Malory understood the muffled words only because of long practice. "I was thinking of giving him an extension. Keeping him at the age he is now."

"For how long?"

"I don't know. We have to switch locations next year. If I magicked him, we could take him with us. If we want to leave him behind, well, it would be a pity to come back here in twenty years and have him be old and decrepit. What do you think? Should I do it?"

"How much would it cost?"

"For two decades without any aging? The life of a mindless loser ought to do the trick. I wouldn't need much power."

"It doesn't have to be a virgin or anything?"

"Not at all. It can be a chicken fucker with an IQ of twenty-three."

"Well, then, Malory, I think you should think about it. There's plenty of time to decide." She turned her face up to her mistress, a slow wicked smile on her lips. "I think you should spend that time testing his stamina and skill and that you should let me help you."

Malory bent and brushed her lips lightly against Brittany's. "Of course. Don't I always?"

21

Standing on the Greenbriar football field, waiting for a cue from Heather to begin another cheer, Eve knew that if she hadn't been so excited about cheering for the first time, she would have dropped from exhaustion. Heather and the other girls had pushed all the newbies to the limit and beyond and Eve received the biggest push of all. It had been like a cheerleader boot camp, drilling and drilling and then drilling some more. She was glad she'd kept up with her aerobics and dancercise; it had kept her from collapsing.

Today, she awoke with stiff burning muscles and spent twenty minutes in the dorm showers easing the soreness away with hot water. By the time she hit her morning classes she felt good despite her muscular exhaustion. At noon, she'd gone to join the other girls for more practice, feeling only a little wicked at skipping out on her afternoon classes. The practice went on until four o'clock and by then, Eve felt pretty confident. The new subs fared decently except for little Lou, who had to sit out the last hour. Eve felt sorry for her, knowing the girl felt humiliated and weak even though she'd withstood far more than any average coed could.

After practice, they showered and had a picnic at a table in a little patio area outside the gym brought to them by Mildred McArthur, the housekeeper and cook, who didn't polish wood or clean windows or bathrooms. The woman was a glaring troll, tall and broad with a Neanderthal brow and dark steel-gray hair, the color of clouds ready to burst. She reminded Eve of Mrs. Van Dyke, a nightmarish PE teacher in tenth grade.

She wore a very dated dress the same stern color as her tightly bunned hair. Almost military, the shirtwaisted statement of non-fashion had long sleeves neatly folded up to just below her elbows, shoulder pads, and a breast pocket holding a small note-book and pen. Mildred had buttoned it over her massive bosom, all the way up to her chin. Blackish hose and black leather clunker shoes—the sensible old-fashioned kind that couldn't be as com-fortable as modern ones—completed the outfit.

Eve shrunk back as the woman approached, bearing a mas-sive wicker picnic basket. Heather introduced the subs to her and she stared each one down in turn, never saying a word or even nodding. She just set the basket on the table and stalked off.

"You'll get used to her," Heather said as a couple of the J-clones opened the basket and began setting out paper plates, cups, utensils, and finally an array of food fit for a king's feast. Heather opened a purple jug and poured equally purple liquid from it into the cups. "This is Mildred's special energy drink. We don't quite know what she puts in it, but it's good once you're used to it, and it'll bring you all back to life. Everybody drink up before you eat. We have Gatorade and bottles of water to have with your food."

Eve thought it was grape juice until she put the cup to her lips. It was more like blackberries, raspberries, and blueberries, all mixed up together, very tasty except for a peculiar herby undertaste. She drank quickly, her eyes on the food containers.

Roast chicken pieces, strips of turkey breast, and bloody-looking paper-thin slices of rare roast beef were revealed. A lit-tle pot of horseradish wafted deliciously, making Eve zero in on the beef that went with it even though she usually skipped red meat. There were thin slices of cucumber and red onion, flow-ered radishes, perfect lettuce leaves. Tomatoes, shredded bell peppers in three colors, and pots of fresh salsa completed the vegetable menu. Carbs were less abundant—there was pita bread, very thin pumpernickel slices, and a container of hot steaming flour tortillas. Fresh pineapple, kiwi, papaya, and mango chunks served as dessert.

And as Eve ate, she understood why they put up with the dour Mildred McArthur. The woman was a wizard with food.

When they were done, they talked and planned, then finally went to dress for the game. Eve's green and gold uniform fit perfectly, which wasn't too surprising since there was a lot of Spandex involved. The bottom—a short skirt with attached panties—was simple, the hem and navel-revealing waistline edged in gold. The cropped midriff top was sleeveless and had the Knight's insignia, a golden shield, emblazoned on it.

"You look great, Eve," Heather said, catching her admiring herself in the mirror.

Eve blushed. She'd never worn a uniform so sexy and revealing. "So do you."

Behind Heather, the rest of the squad gathered and Eve saw that each of the regulars had a red rosebud tattooed on her hip. The green stems disappeared under the uniform bottom.

"Uh, the roses—" Eve began.

Heather smiled. "Cute, aren't they? She linked her arm in Eve's. "We'll talk later. Right now we have football players to cheer to a big win! Let's go, girls!"

22

Professor Daniel McCobb had stayed late grading papers, and leaving for Caledonia just before the game began, had to wait for streams and trickles of students crossing the campus road as they made their way to the bright lights of the stadium. Everything had looked right and he felt a little of the old thrill. He hadn't gone to a game in years but at that moment, with the scent of fall spurring his sense of nostalgia, he was briefly tempted to look in.

And he might have done it, but Vera had phoned to tell him their son, Dennis, had arrived for the weekend and that they and her pot roast with mashed potatoes, gravy, and baby glazed carrots were waiting for his arrival. *And baked apples. Don't forget those!*

His stomach growled an order to hurry home. He complied. Exiting the campus grounds, he turned left onto Greenbriar Road, then took a quick right on the old road that bypassed the tiny town itself. Applehead Road ran just inside the edge of the forest, passing only trees and a few crumbling stone buildings left over from Greenbriar's brief halcyon years. It curved along the hillside past the road leading into the cheer-leading camp on the lake, and then another mile where it again joined with Greenbriar Road and the cutoff for the Pacific Coast Highway and Caledonia. Applehead Road ran him a mile out of the way, but it was generally much faster than braving the town's overly civilized route. One could only stand so many stop signs in one's lifetime.

Even though it was not yet fully dark, McCobb turned on his high beams as soon as the last campus light was hidden behind the trees. Applehead Road was gloomy on all but the sunniest days, the tall thick pines looming over the road, the oaks, still green, filling in spaces where the sun might dare to cast a ray.

A deer ran onto the road and paused, caught in the headlights. McCobb, unsurprised, tapped the brakes to slow and honked the deer back into action. Its white tail disappeared into the trees as he passed.

He slowed again as the road became a squiggle. His headlights flashed over the ruins of an old Wells Fargo office from the days of the Pony Express, half-walls of stone, a few old timbers on the ground. The mild switchback then caused illumination of the other side of the road, the deep forest side.

Somewhere beyond those trees lay the old Greenbriar Chapel, a place rumored to be the home of various unholy (at least to Christians) beings, the primary one being the Greenbriar Ghost or "green ghost" as it was usually called. At one time, it was also referred to as the "forest knight," but few knew that name anymore.

McCobb realized he'd slowed to a bare crawl as he peered into the forest. He thought he saw a flickering light moving among the trees. *Idiot students.* The young never learned. They loved to go to the chapel ruins to drink and grope one another; it didn't matter that another dead coed had been found out here, that many bodies—too many for coincidence—had littered the woods over the years. No, the excitement of the stories of the Greenbriar Ghost—which wasn't even a ghost but really a nature elemental according to the older myths—compelled them to seek out the place. And even more compelling to the college kids were the ghost stories concerning the long-ago coed, Holly Gayle. He smiled slightly, remembering how he loved to scare Vera with his own ghostly tales back when they were students at Stanford. They'd park in woods not so different from these, and he'd put his arm around her, making her giggle with delight over the dangers of The Hook, that hoariest of urban legends, before reeling her in with more believable tales.

But here . . . Somehow it seemed more dangerous here in these woods than it had where he'd done his wooing. *Is it really, or am I just an old man, too close to death to enjoy its threat anymore?*

He rolled the passenger-side window halfway down, to see better. Yes, there was definitely a light, deep in the woods. Greenish, probably due to refractions of light on leaves. *The Greenbriar Ghost is green.* He tried to be amused by the thought, but felt a chill instead. Still, he idled, watching and wondering if he should warn the kids away.

The light winked out. He watched a little longer, one second, two. Silence enveloped him. He realized no crickets chirped, no birds sang. Something had disturbed them—

Suddenly, a dark head appeared, the eyes glowing green pinpricks of light looking at him above the open glass. He gasped as the eyes grew brighter, larger, illuminating the face so that he could see a hint of leaves, a yawn of shadows.

Preternaturally calm, Daniel McCobb was aware of his hand flipping the window switch, rolling it closed, his foot punching the gas pedal. As he drove off, he laughed in delight and disbelief.

23

The Greenbriar Knights were ahead of the Fort Charles Dragons by three points at halftime and Eve's enthusiasm gave her the energy she needed to perform the sets she had learned in the last twenty-four hours. Carried along by the more experienced girls and boosted by her years of practice, she felt confident, even during the tricky Rolling Pyramid routine, which she'd had a terrible time even semimastering in such a small amount of time.

As they came out of it, Heather caught her eye and nodded, giving her a thumbs-up. Eve felt elated as they moved to the side of the field in preparation for the return of the team. The only thing that bothered her was the tattoo. She kept noticing the rose on the rest of the squad's hipbones. *They can't force me to get a tattoo, can they? I won't do it. I can do a decal. Some of those must be decals.*

The Knights, in green tunics, gold pants with green stripes, and golden helmets with green and black shields emblazoned upon them, trotted proudly onto the field. Art Caliban was in the lead, flanked by the other team stars, wide receiver Spencer Lake and Ron Spears, the running back. Eve's eyes danced over their tall broad-shouldered forms and then Art looked her way, grinned, and half waved, half pointed at her. She felt a thrill.

Don't be conceited. Maybe he was looking at somebody else. After all, he was a senior and she was a lowly freshman. Still, that look in his eye . . . She tingled. *Genevieve Camlan, you're imagining things. You can't really even see his eyes under that helmet.*

She didn't care. She *knew*—well, *almost* knew— that he had signaled her.

24

"**I** kid you not," Daniel McCobb told his wife and son. "I saw the Greenbriar Ghost. In the flesh as it were." He chuckled as he wiped his lips in preparation for a second slice of Vera's succulent pot roast.

"In the flesh, Dad?" Dennis, with his mother's once-auburn hair and the same dark blue eyes, raised an eyebrow, a more paternal trait.

"Yes, in the flesh. I'm sure now that it was a student holding a false head or wearing a mask. There were batteries involved." He shook his head, smiling. "The eyes glowed green and the intensity increased. This wasn't a ten-dollar Halloween mask. This was superb. Why, I nearly wet myself!"

Vera laughed and Dennis, as usual, looked vaguely confused. How they'd had such a straight-arrow boy, Daniel didn't know. Dennis was thirty-two now and still hadn't figured them out. "Son," Daniel said, "it's funny. Laugh! Your old man fell for a college prank. A sophomoric one at that!"

"You sound happy about it, Dad."

"Well, I suppose I am. It makes me feel young and naive. Vera, remember the story about the Mt. Sutro phantom I'd tell you about when we were in college?"

His wife blushed. Her laughter tinkled, still music to his ears. "You were such a devil, Danny. Scaring me like that."

Dennis half smiled. "Why'd he scare you?"

"To get into my pants, of course." Vera crinkled up. "More potatoes, honey?"

"Mom, I don't want to hear about that." He held out his plate and she piled on a fresh load.

"You asked," she told him, then passed the gravy and winked at Daniel. "Your father was so good at scaring me, I'm surprised you weren't conceived before we got married."

"Mom! Stop it. That's disgusting."

"All right, Dennis." She looked at Daniel. "Are you sure it was a prank?"

"If it wasn't, I'm either hallucinating or I really did see our mysterious forest elemental."

Vera clapped her hands together. "Oh, Danny, wouldn't that be wonderful, to actually see it after all these years?"

"Doll, it doesn't exist. It's just folklore. Legend."

"You used to think it might be real. You aren't getting all old and stuffy on me, are you, Danny?"

Instead of answering her, he put beef in his mouth and shut his eyes as he chewed. "Heaven on earth, my doll. How you do it, I don't know, but every time you make this delectable dish, it's better than the last."

"Bosh, you're just easy to please, isn't he, Dennis?"

This, their son understood. "No, Mom. I can't believe how good this is. I miss it."

"You should visit more often. It's only a five-hour drive up from Santo Verde."

"Six, at least. And Jordan hates it when I go away for the weekend."

"She's so jealous!"

"She gets lonely, rambling around in that big house, all alone, all weekend."

"You can bring her."

"You know she hates to travel."

"Bosh, she'd be fine once she got used to it. She's welcome here. And she and Roxie would get along just fine."

"Jordan's a *cat*, Mom."

"I know. Cats and dogs are often friends."

"She's five years old and she's never seen one. They wouldn't get along."

"Nonsense. Roxie would be very nice to her."

"I know. But Jordan's bigger than your little wiener dog. She'd terrorize her."

"You can bring her anyway. She can stay in the guest room with you. I'll make a nice little litter box and she can borrow some of Roxie's dishes."

"I'll think about it." He looked at Daniel. "Dad? Did you really think that the Greenbriar Ghost might exist? Really?"

"I just try to keep an open mind, Dennis. Most legends are based on something real, no matter how far from reality they've strayed."

"What's this one based on?"

"Nature elementals. The green man, primarily. It's also tied in ways to that damned sorority. Their secret society."

"That's still in existence, Danny?" Vera asked. "You haven't mentioned it in years."

"I try not to think about them. But yes, it still exists." *Fata Morgana*. He didn't say the words aloud. "The Gamma sorority president, who is, allegedly, always the leader of the secret society, threw me for a loop when I ran into her the other day. She was nearly a ringer for a president from twenty, twenty-five years ago. Only the hair color didn't match." He felt the chill again, thinking of that young woman.

"Maybe she's the daughter of the former president."

"Could be." Daniel forked food into his mouth, but it had lost some of its flavor. He might tell Vera, but never Dennis, that

Malory Thomas and the past president were one in the same. The creature didn't age, and that was how the sorority was tied to the forest elemental. There were sacrifices involved as well. *All legend. It's all just legend.*

He pushed his plate back, and rose. "I'll go make us some coffee."

Vera opened her mouth to tell him she'd do it, then saw his expression and simply nodded.

25

"Ten seconds left on the clock and Art Caliban hands off to Ron Spears. Look at him go! Five seconds as Knights' QB Spencer Lake clears the way—three seconds, two—and touchdown! The Greenbriar Knights win twenty-seven to twenty-one. A great night for some great Knights!"

The cries of the crowd nearly drowned out the announcer and as the squad went into the winning cheers, Eve heard no more. With renewed energy, she picked up her pom-poms and yelled and jumped as the team congratulated itself on the center of the field.

"Okay," Heather said, signaling the squad to stop. "You guys did great! Eve, you were amazing!"

Male voices, laughing and whooping, approached and then the girls were surrounded by big, happy, sweaty men. It was great. "Hey," Art Caliban said, laying a surprisingly gentle hand on her shoulder. She looked up, met his eyes, and smiled, melting inside.

"Hi, Art. Congratulations."

"You want to go get a Coke with me after I clean up?"

"Sure!"

"No, Art," Heather said, appearing suddenly. "Not tonight. We're taking Eve out ourselves. It's her first night as one of us."

"Heather, you're a mother hen. You can have her some other time. You wouldn't begrudge a returning hero a soda with such a fair maiden, would you?"

A look of displeasure crossed Heather's face so quickly that Eve wasn't sure if she'd imagined it or not. "I guess we should leave it up to Eve. What do you want to do?"

Eve knew exactly what she wanted to do, but was afraid to say so. She looked into Art Caliban's eyes and melted some more, then glanced at Heather and knew she had to go with her sisters. "I'm sorry, Art. Can I have a rain check?"

"You're strong-arming her, Heather, and you know it." Art crossed his arms. He meant business.

Eve felt even more attracted to him, but made herself choose her sisters. "I'm sorry. It's my first night. You know. . . ."

"I know." He put his big arm across her shoulders and gave her a little squeeze. "Go with them tonight. Tomorrow night, we'll go out on a real date. How's that?"

"Sure," Eve agreed, purposely not looking at Heather. "That sounds like fun."

"I'll pick you up at six."

"Great!"

"Where?"

"Where what?"

"Where will I find you?"

"Oh, sorry. At my dorm—"

"No," Heather said. "She'll be all moved into Gamma House by then. You can pick her up there."

"Is that okay?" He smiled.

"It's great!"

"Hi!" Spencer Lake, the quarterback arrived and slapped Art on the back. "Are you moving in on this lady before anyone else has a chance, buddy?"

He smiled at Eve and she felt another warm shiver as a short, obscene vision flashed through her mind. She almost shocked herself with the thought.

"I sure am," Art said, his gaze on Eve. "Better luck next time."

26

The way Heather had acted, Eve half expected that the squad would have some big blowout of a party when they returned to Gamma, still in their uniforms. Instead, two of the subs were sent into the kitchen to fetch glasses and a monstrous pitcher of sweet lemonade. The rest sprawled out on the old comfy furniture in the parlor, sitting up only when the girls returned with the refreshments. Heather had them set the trays on a buffet behind the sofas, then told them to sit down while she did the pouring and serving herself.

Eve thought that was a nice gesture and gratefully took her icy glass, trying to force herself to sip, not chug, the liquid. Her adrenaline had deserted her and now she was glad she hadn't gone out with Art—she was exhausted. She was also relieved when the J-clones drifted upstairs to shower and change. Two had late dates, two were going to bed.

Bed was sounding better by the second. Eve's muscles were beginning to ache and the long hours of practice, combined with the cheering at the game, had drained her last ounce of energy. "I'm going to sleep for a week," she announced. The subs, who had been stationed at either end of the home team's side to lead the crowd in simpler cheers, murmured agreement. Heather and the officers, Teri and Michele, just smiled.

"You'll move in tomorrow," Heather said. "So go back to

your dorms and sleep in. We'll expect to see you all tomorrow, with luggage." She rose and walked them out onto the veranda. "Stick together on the walk back to your rooms. Good night."

The night was dark and clear as they set off across the road and started down the sidewalk across the big manicured lawn. There were few students out, considering that it was a Friday night and only half past eleven. "I wonder why Heather told us to stick together," Eve said.

"Maybe because of that dead girl?" little Lou suggested.

"I don't care what they say," chimed in Jelly, who was really Angelica. "I think there's a serial killer in the woods. The trees are close," she added, glancing west, toward the dark forest. "He could be watching us."

"Do you really think so?" Lou asked, picking up her pace.

"Maybe it's the green ghost," suggested Nancy, the other sub.

"Come on," Eve said as they walked even faster. "That's just an old kids' story. I heard it when I was at cheer camp."

"Yeah," Lou said. "It's silly."

"Okay," Nancy said, "then what about the Gamma ghost? Holly Gayle?"

Eve shivered. "You know about that?"

"My sister was a Gamma. She saw her once."

"Yeah, right," said Jelly.

"Where?" Eve asked.

"In the house. She was just sort of gliding along the second-floor landing. Her feet didn't quite touch the ground. She was dressed in this old-fashioned white dress and her hair looked wet."

"And you believed your sister?" Jelly asked.

"I don't know. I guess not," Nancy admitted. "If I really did believe there was a ghost in Gamma House, I sure as hell wouldn't want to live there."

They crossed another road, nearly at the dorms. "Eve?" Nancy asked.

"Yes?"

"What do you know about the Gamma ghost?"

"Nothing."

"You sounded like you knew something—you seemed surprised I did."

"Well, yeah. I thought that story was pretty obscure. I heard it at camp. Holly was supposed to haunt the lake." She told the truth, simply leaving out what Kendra had told her. It didn't seem like a good idea to repeat all that stuff. *Maybe I'm just afraid to talk about it.* "Here we are," she said as they approached her dorm.

Lou was also in this dorm, while Jelly and Nancy were in a much smaller one next door. They said good night.

Eve entered her room and changed into her robe and slippers, grabbed her pjs and toiletry bag, and headed for the showers down the hall. Every move, now that the adrenaline brought back by the ghost talk had once again deserted her, was forced. She could barely force herself to go through with it; she wanted to turn around and flop on the bed, sweat and all. But she kept going.

The showers were deserted and the large white room with its little stalls echoed her every move, making her nervous. Still, she finally forgot herself under the pounding pulse of the hot water. By the time she dried and dressed for bed, she could barely keep her eyes open, but she didn't ache so much.

It was well after midnight when she finally slipped between cool sheets and set her alarm clock for nine A.M., mere seconds before falling into a deep, dreamless sleep.

27

"Where have you been?" Malory asked when Brittany finally straggled into the windowless ritual room on the second floor of the east wing of Gamma House.

"Sorr-rry!" the girl said, tugging off her clothes unselfconsciously and tossing them against the wall. Nude, Brittany was catnip to cats and bones to dogs, strawberries to cream. Her elemental essence vibrated unfettered throughout the room and harsh words over her tardiness turned mild. Other than masking her true form, Brittany had little magic of her own. Magnetism was her only active art. Animal magnetism—only it wasn't really animal, it was elemental. No one except Malory, and perhaps Heather, really understood the difference. Teri and Michele knew but were too young to comprehend; the rest had no idea she wasn't exactly human.

All of them, even Malory, also not entirely human, were susceptible to her charm if Brittany was nude. Clothing acted like a force field, keeping her charisma from oozing from her pores, preventing people from falling into her thrall.

Humans would interpret what she possessed as a scent, pheromones probably, but it was far more than that. It was beyond definition, part of a sense that had yet to be recognized. It was literally a magnetism, tied to the power of the earth. She was magnetism incarnate and, naked, irresistible.

Naked but for this flesh she had made her own and habitually worn since first teaming with her mistress, she stretched, showing off to the other eleven in the room. All but Malory wore black velvet robes lined with soft forest-green silk; Malory's was green with black silk lining.

Beneath the robes, Brittany knew, they wore nothing. Power was always strongest unencumbered by restrictive clothing; that was true even for humans. The loose robes constricted not at all and actually served to help build up power, holding it in, gathering it, like insulation until the time came to unleash whatever sorcery they were engaged in.

"Where were you?" Malory asked again, trying to refuse the charm. If anyone could, she could.

Brittany smiled, thinking of approaching her, but decided against it; once in Malory's grasp, what power she had was not her own to control anymore. "I was out for a walk in the woods," she lied.

"Really." Malory wasn't buying it. "Did you see him?"

"Him?" Brittany panicked briefly, thinking she meant Professor Tongue. *Guilty, madam.* Then she realized to whom Malory was referring. "No, I didn't see him."

"He's out tonight," her mistress said. "I can feel him. He's impatient. He's hungry."

"I know." Brittany touched her nipples, hardening them. She heard Jenny gasp, looked with amusement at all the younger members of Fata Morgana. Cow eyes, the lot of them, practically drooling, their eyes glued to her. With her charm, her magnetism, she could have any or all of them, even though none but Jenny was gay—and Jenny didn't even know it yet. And Brittany, though genderless when out of body, was now so accustomed to her female flesh that she preferred men most of the time.

"Put your robe on," Malory ordered.

Brittany continued to hesitate.

"I know you weren't in the woods tonight," Malory said. "I was there."

"At the Green Chapel?" Brittany asked innocently.

"Of course."

"I didn't go there."

"You? You can't stay away from the chapel."

"Sure I can. I went for a romp in the woods, to run and climb and look for pine nuts. Only that and nothing more."

Malory eyed her in the way that told Brittany she'd give her no more trouble, so she took her robe off one of the thirteen hooks on the wall and slipped it over her body, then joined the circle of sisters.

"We have three things to discuss. One is initiation rites for Gamma Eta Pi. Since that's not directly Fata Morgana–related and can wait, it shall. Tomorrow, we'll meet here to finalize those plans. No robes necessary for that; we won't be doing magick.

"The two items we must deal with tonight are, of course, preparation of the sacrifice to the Forest Knight, and replacing that bitch Mulva. We need our full circle of thirteen to be at our best." Malory looked from face to face. "I'll take any suggestions you have now."

Brittany knew this was nothing but a game. Malory already had her circle member chosen; there could be no other.

"What about Petra Mills?" Michele said. "She's worthy of sisterhood."

"Yes," Teri agreed.

Malory appeared to consider the idea. "I'm not quite sure about her," she said finally. "You know she takes Prozac. That will dampen any natural power she possesses, and without it, I'm afraid she'd be too depressing to deal with. Any other ideas?"

"Kathryn Whitt?"

"She was raised in a military family. She may have other loyalties that would pop up at inconvenient times. Anyone else?"

She waited a long moment, but no one spoke up. Even the newest members of the circle sensed a decision coming.

"Merilynn Morris," Brittany said. She just couldn't resist.

"Yes. Merilynn Morris," Malory affirmed.

"But she's just a freshman pledge," Heather said.

"Yes, but she holds great power. Haven't you sensed it?" She looked at the others with an expression that seemed to betray amazement at their lack of observational skills.

"She does?" Heather asked. Heather was the ballsiest human here, third in command behind Brittany and Malory herself. "Granted, her eyes seem to show a tie to the forest, but what makes you think she's powerful?"

"Am I ever wrong?"

"No. Well, Mulva disappointed us. You chose her."

"Actually, no, I didn't. She was Brittany's idea. Right, Britt?"

"I'm afraid so," Brittany said smoothly. It was a lie, but that was part of her function as a familiar—to protect her mistress.

"You'll just have to trust me on this, ladies," Malory said. "She's the one."

"But . . ." Michele began.

"But what? Go ahead, you're among friends. I know you're looking out for the welfare of the Fata Morgana."

"Well, the thing is, her uncle raised her from infancy and the man is a Catholic priest."

Malory smiled, eyes sparking merrily. "Yes, that just makes it all the better, don't you think?" She paused. "The girl is not Catholic; she's widely read and, in fact, the priest taught her about all sorts of religions and philosophies. He's not your average pope worshipper."

"And if she doesn't work out, we can always sacrifice her, right, Mal?" Brittany said cheerfully.

Malory looked her up and down. "If it came to that, she'd make a fine sacrifice. And none of you need to worry. I know what I'm doing. I always know."

"So how do we do this?" Michele asked. "She's not even completely initiated into Gamma yet."

"We do that first, of course. Then we'll initiate her into Fata Morgana."

"How do you know she'll want to be a member?"

"Who wouldn't want immortality?"

No one replied; none had been around long enough to be tired of eternal youth yet.

"Very well. Time to perform the rites of sacrifice. Please join hands." She paused. "Tonight we will visit Genevieve Camlan to begin preparing her as a gift to the Forest Knight."

"Does it really have to be Eve?" Heather asked. "I know we agreed, but she's an absolutely fantastic cheerleader. None of the subs can touch her, and I really hate to lose her."

The other cheerleaders murmured agreement.

"Heather, I know," Malory consoled. "And I'm sorry, but it must be. She has the right vibrations, she has power of a sort, and she's a virgin. That old green goat insists on a virgin."

Heather and the pom-pom pushers looked forlorn.

"Don't worry. The fact that she is so dear to you will make her an even better sacrifice. We shall receive many years of grace in exchange for her life. Okay?"

Heather nodded, eyes downcast.

"Good." Malory looked at each girl in turn. "Now, everyone concentrate on sending your power to me so that I can show her the first dream."

Everyone but Malory and Brittany, directly across from her, closed their eyes. Malory began to chant, never breaking the power-inducing gaze she shared with Brittany. After a few moments, the static electricity in the room grew so strong that Brittany could feel her hair trying to lift away from her arms and scalp.

Suddenly, there was an audible *snap* of electricity and all their robes fell from their shoulders. The room swirled with energy; Brittany basked in it, orgasmic with it. She could see the hair rising on the other girls and slowly, she felt gravity lose its grip. Her heels, then toes, left the ground.

"Genevieve," Malory said. "What scares you, Genevieve?"

She closed her eyes and Brittany saw that her mistress had already divined the answer to that question.

28

Eve awoke in blackness, the dark wet smell of the lake over-whelming her senses. She lay paralyzed, suffocated by si-lence.

I'm dead.

No. You're dreaming.

She tried to reach for the bedside lamp, but her arms wouldn't obey. She squinted into the darkness but discerned nothing except a slight cool breeze on her cheek, a breeze scented by lake water, an odor of wet stones and moss, a vague scent of violets beneath it, like musty old cologne.

Where am I?

Her tiny dorm room had a window and normally she could see the yellow glow of one of the tall sodium lights that guarded the entrances to the building. But now it was blotted out; every-thing was lost to perfect blackness, so thick she could feel it pressing against her.

And then a voice, a murmur so soft it seemed almost to be within her head. "Genevieve."

Who's there?

It's me, Eve. Remember me?

It was a feminine voice, but Eve didn't recognize it. She strained to move, but invisible ropes seemed to hold her to the bed. Still, she could not speak. *No. I don't remember you. Who are you? What do you want?*

High-pitched laughter tinkled down the scale. *We met a long time ago.*

Where? Terror filled Eve; she felt as if her heart would stop.

You've hurt my feelings. You know me. You've seen me.

Then tell me who you are.

You saw me on Applehead Island a long time ago.

Eve suddenly wished to die; she couldn't take the terror she felt now. *The green ghost,* she thought.

There was a pause.

"Damn," Malory murmured, "I thought she was afraid of Holly Gayle." She smiled. "This is better."

So you remember me now?

As she heard the words, the voice began to deepen.

Eve saw a pair of glowing green eyes blink to life. Slowly, they moved closer to the bed.

Genevieve, you remember me now, don't you?

Eve told herself it was a dream. Just a dream. The paralysis wouldn't break. She tried to scream, but she couldn't open her mouth; it seemed sewed shut.

It's not a dream, Eve. I'm here, to visit you.

Go away! Please, go away!

The eyes stared down at her, right at the bedside now. *You're afraid, aren't you, little Eve? Afraid of me?*

Lake water seemed to drench her. *Please go away! You're not real!*

The laugh came again, now masculine. *Here's how real I am, Eve.*

The eyes lowered toward her. Eve tried to shut her own, but nothing happened. She couldn't look away. *It's a dream. It's a dream. Wake up! Wake up right now!*

The eyes moved until they were directly in front of her face, only inches from her own. Emerald-green fire with slitted pupils, they blinked slowly. *Genevieve, you're mine.*

She felt cold breath from the mouth she couldn't see. It was dank and icy against her face. *Go away!*

A cold, slimy tongue touched her chin, then licked upward, over her left cheek, across her forehead, slowly, so slowly, and then down her right cheek, back to her chin. It left a cold snail trail in its wake.

No!

Yes! The tongue wiggled across her lips, probing, entering her mouth, licking the insides of her lips, tasting her teeth.

Saliva, cold thick gel, tasting of lake water and earth, oozed into her mouth. She opened her mouth to scream and though there was no sound, her teeth parted. The tongue, like a piece of raw chicken cold from the refrigerator, pushed into her mouth, examining her tongue, her molars, running along her gums.

Stop it!

"Damn it!" Malory said again, this time breaking the spell.

Gravity pulled at their toes, drawing them back down an inch, so that their feet were solidly on the floor. Electric hair settled. Tension left the room.

"What happened?" Heather asked.

Malory laughed lightly. "The bad news is, I lost her. The good news is that she was so frightened, she fainted."

29

Eve first awoke to darkness, confused and afraid, unable to remember what happened. *A nightmare? I must have had a nightmare.*

She turned her head and looked toward the window, vague relief flooding her as she spied the outline of the frame, the Roman shade left half up. Beyond the glass, the street lamp cast an amber glow. Then she noticed the funny taste in her mouth.

No, not a funny taste. A bad taste. A *horrible* taste.

She reached out and touched the bedside lamp. It glowed dimly. She tapped it again to bring more light, then sat up, moving her tongue against the roof of her mouth, touching her teeth. *Disgusting.* The dream came back, a harsh jolt. The tongue licking her face, invading her mouth, leaving snail trails of cold slime behind.

She jumped out of bed, gagging, fumbled with the chain lock, and opened her door. The dimly lit hall was deserted. She raced to the closest rest room and paused in front of the sinks and mirrors just long enough to see the sticky glistening tracks on her face. "Dear God," she whispered. "It really happened!"

She barely made it into a stall before she lost the contents of her stomach. There wasn't much to throw up, but she couldn't stop. The harsh acidic dregs of lemonade burned her throat with every heave.

Gasping, she finally stood up, flushed, and left the toilet. At the sink she used her hands as a cup, repeatedly swishing water through her mouth and spitting it out. Finally, she scrubbed her face in water too hot to be good for her complexion, but she didn't care; all she wanted to do was get the feeling of filth off her skin.

Back in her room, she turned on the overhead light and sat on her bed, trying to figure out what happened. It felt like a dream—but that slime on her face, in her mouth. It must have been real. Had someone broken in?

The alarm clock read four-thirty. She rose and began searching the room for signs of an intruder. She stopped, her eyes on the door. The chain latch. She'd slipped it in place when she came home and she'd undone it when she ran to the rest room. No one could have been in the room. *Unless . . .*

Remembering the hidden panel Malory had used at Gamma House, she examined the walls of her room, but there was nothing to find in the little shoe box of a bedroom. The building was modern and the off-white plaster walls weren't capable of hiding any mysteries.

So it had to be a dream. What else could it be?

Slightly less nervous, but leaving the overhead light on, Eve slipped back into bed and turned on her side to keep the light from shining directly in her eyes. Staring in the direction of the door, she thought more about what could have happened and eventually decided that something she ate had disagreed with her digestive system, causing her to produce lots of nasty saliva herself. That made sense. *I was so tired that when I got nauseated, I didn't even wake up. Instead it made me dream.*

Slowly, her eyes closed and the next time she woke up, the sun was up, the sky clear and blue outside her window.

30

"I know what you showed Eve last night," Brittany said as she painted her toenails.

"Of course you do," Malory replied, brushing her dark hair in long, even strokes. "What else is new?"

Brittany paused, looking at her mistress. "The dream you sent her was very interesting. That astral form of the Forest Knight was something else."

"It really drew a lot of energy," Malory replied. "Almost more than the girls could handle. We have to get our thirteenth member installed right away."

"Yes, I know. But, Malory, what about the astral form? You added a new twist."

Malory blinked slowly. "What was a new twist?"

"Don't tease me. You know. Do I have to say it?"

"Of course you do."

"The tongue. I want to know the inspiration for it."

Malory half smiled. "You know the inspiration for it. Intimately. Frankly, what made me think of it was your tardiness."

"What?"

"I know where you were last night. Under Piccolo's tongue. Shame on you."

"I never—"

"Oh, don't bother. We both know you did."

"Why is it all right for you to visit him alone, but not me?"

"Those are the rules."

"I'm tired of the rules."

"You shouldn't be. You break them often enough."

Was she bluffing? Brittany couldn't tell, but she had thought that Malory rarely realized what she was up to. She capped her nail polish and stretched out on her mistress's wide bed.

"Brittany? Haven't you anything to say?"

"I do *not* break the rules. Hardly ever. I wouldn't lie to you."

Malory whirled and crossed the room so quickly that even Brittany, as quick as she was, couldn't avoid being pinned against the bed. "You lie frequently," Malory said, her face only inches above Brittany's.

"Watch out—you'll smear my nail polish." She lifted her head and planted a quick kiss on Malory's lips. "I'm your most faithful companion," she said softly. "You know that."

"You're also my most horny companion."

"Thank you."

"That wasn't a compliment."

"It felt like one." She kissed her again, trying to charm her. *Damned clothes, always getting in the way.*

Malory's nostrils flared, her voice softened, and she brought her face closer to Brittany's, traveling down to her neck, then up by one ear, taking in her scent. "I know what you're doing."

It's working. "I'm not doing anything, mistress. You're the one on top."

"Yes, I am. Remember that. I'm always on top. Don't play with my toys behind my back. That includes Professor Tongue." She sat up, keeping Brittany pinned beneath her. "Promise."

"I promise." Brittany reached up to touch Malory's breasts.

"None of that. You're off the hook and we have work to do.

It's moving day. The pledges will start showing up soon." She swung away, freeing Brittany. "Get up and get busy."

"What do you want me to do?"

"Make sure all the sisters in the west wing have clean rooms. We want the pledges to be impressed."

"Okay." Brittany got up and slipped her feet into sandals, then grabbed a half-empty yellow bag of Peanut M&Ms and headed for the door.

"Britt?"

She turned, her hand on the knob. "Yes?"

"Be good. Maybe later I'll take you to the professor's house with me."

Brittany smiled and blew her a kiss, then left Malory's room. The biggest in the east wing, it was more like a hotel suite, with a small living area, walk-in closets, and a luxurious bathroom. It had been luxurious before they returned to Greenbriar after their stint running a Gamma House in Vermont, but Malory had it remodeled three years ago to include a whirlpool and all new furniture, paint, and fixtures. Only Brittany was allowed extended visits. The other Fata Morganas had seen the room occasionally, but never the ordinary sisters.

She crossed the stair landing and walked into the west wing and knocked on the first door.

"Come in," called a sister.

Brittany entered, chirped a greeting around the M&M she sucked on. The room was nice, a single, but it was only a bedroom glorified with nice furniture. This sister shared an adjoining bath with the next single room, which seemed pretty great if you didn't know that Malory's digs took up at least five times the space, not counting her private bathroom and walk-in closet. And the Fata Morganas' single rooms were all twice the size of this one, each with its own private bathroom. Malory was right about not letting the simpler sisters see how they lived in the east wing.

This sister, the newest one, barely out of pledgehood, looked at Brittany questioningly. "What's up?"

What's her damned name? "You have a nice room," she said, glancing around. Her eyes landed on the girl's desk. A copy of the school paper, the *Greenbriar Herald,* lay on top, open to a story about a possible food poisoning incident in the school cafeteria. The byline told her what she needed to know. *Samantha Penrose.*

"Samantha, I just wanted to let you know that the pledges will start drifting in soon."

"Just Sam, please." Just Sam stared at her expectantly. "Is there something I should do?"

"Do? No. Just answer questions if you're around, okay?"

"No problem. Maybe I'll ask some too."

"What? What do you mean?"

"You know I write for the *Herald.* I saw you got my name off the paper."

"No—"

"It's all right. You have to remember a lot of names." She smiled. "Maybe I'll see if I can get some good comments and do a story about the pledges' moving day."

"Oh, sure, I guess. Maybe you should check with Malory."

"Why?"

Brittany didn't like the look in this one's eye. "She's in charge," she said. "Everybody checks everything with Malory."

"I see."

"Okay, see you later."

"See you."

Brittany left the room, closing the door behind her. How had Sam Penrose become a Gamma? *A brain, destined to edit the paper. We could use a good journalist on our side. Now and in the future.* She nodded to herself, remembering Malory's words. It made sense, but it didn't make her like the girl any better. Still, Malory knew best. Usually.

She knocked on the next door. No one replied, so she let herself in—regular sisters didn't get to lock their doors; it was part of the trust-and-loyalty thing Malory kept beating into them. Brittany rifled through the absent sister's desk and dresser. Of course, the lack of locks was for Malory's benefit. *And mine.*

She fished a shiny red thong from the drawer. It looked to be her size. Quickly, she checked the crotch. *Doesn't look dirty.* She sniffed it. *Doesn't smell dirty.* In fact, it smelled brand-new. She tucked it into her jeans, closed the drawer, and went on about her appointed rounds.

31

Kendra Phillips set her computer monitor on her desk. "There," she said. "That's the last of my stuff. I'm officially out of the dorm, I guess."

"You *guess?*" Eve asked. "This room is huge! It's probably five times the size of my dorm room. That was nothing but a walk-in closet. This is so nice and airy!"

"I had a roommate at the dorm, and I'll tell you, a double over there was just a one-and-a-half. I could barely breathe. My roommate was an idiot. And she snored. She'd wake me up sometimes making these funny little 'wee-wee-wee' snorts. 'Wee-wee-wee, all the way home.'" She shook her head. "I sure won't miss that."

Eve smiled, but didn't speak. She seemed to be concentrating on neatly placing pair after pair of underwear in her chest of drawers.

"So, do you snore?" Kendra prodded.

"What? Oh, no! I mean, I don't think so. Oh—"

"Eve, don't be so serious. I'm teasing you."

"I don't think I snore."

"I don't think I do either, but if I do, you just poke me and tell me to turn over." She watched Eve. "I can't read you. You're overjoyed to be moving in here, but you're all weird and serious. What's up? And is there any color of panties that you *don't* have?"

Eve smiled again. "I don't have red ones."

"Why not?"

"I don't like red underwear."

"I know what you mean. Reminds you of your first period, doesn't it?"

Eve's jaw dropped. "No! Ewww! Gross!"

Kendra collapsed onto a small empty spot on her bed, laughing helplessly.

"What?" Eve asked.

Kendra couldn't answer.

Eve watched her. "You were kidding? That was a joke?"

"Yes, I was joking." Her words sputtered among her laughs. "Girl, you are the most gullible thing I've ever met."

"No, I'm not. I mean, it was logical."

"Spotty."

"What?"

"Spotty. That's what I got called for the last half of my freshman year. Fortunately, those girls in gym class didn't remember to start calling me that again the next year."

"They called you that? Because—"

"Because of a couple little spots. I didn't realize I wasn't, well, protected as well as I should have been. I didn't know until they started yelling it at me in the locker room."

"That's awful. Like *Carrie*."

"Evie, you don't know how right you are. They'd seen that movie and they pelted me with tampons." She smiled. "At least they weren't used!"

"Gross." Eve hesitated. "Were you—did you have a hard time in high school? I mean—"

"Was I a loser, a nerd? No, not really. It just happened that the girls I shared a locker room with were a bunch of cliquey bitches. They all had nicknames for each other. Spice, Sugar, Brown Sugar, Vanilla, Nutmeg, and Limey. I'll never forget those nicknames."

"*Limey?*" Eve gasped. "What was wrong with her? Jaundice?"

"Sweetie, it's not *all* about color! She was British."

"Oh."

"Actually, most of the names were about color, now that I think about it. But not like you think. Brown Sugar was white and spent all her free time in a tanning bed. Sugar was Latina, Vanilla was African-American but thought she was white. She was an Oreo."

"What do you mean?"

"Vanilla loved country music. And no self-respecting black girl does the Texas two-step, except Vanilla. She did. She even got them to do some cowboy-style cheerleading. It was hysterical, but everybody loved it."

"Wait a minute," Eve said. "You mean the girls that called you that awful name were *cheerleaders?*"

"I'm afraid so." She smiled. "You won't call me 'Spotty' though, will you?"

"Of course not!"

Kendra grinned.

"You're teasing again," Eve said firmly. "You know I wouldn't ever call you that. I think it's awful. I feel like I should apologize to you on behalf of good cheerleaders everywhere."

"As opposed to evil cheerleaders?"

Eve hesitated, then smiled broadly. "Yeah, why not?"

"To be completely fair, that clique wasn't evil, even if most of them were airheads. They nicknamed everybody they liked. Some of their friends had names just as bad as 'Spotty.' It was probably a compliment."

"If it was, it was a bad one. I have to admit that some cheerleaders really are major airheads, totally full of themselves."

"Hanging all over the football players." Kendra started to chuckle, then stopped herself, seeing the look on Eve's face. "What did I just say? You're as red as a radish."

"I have a date tonight," Eve said softly. "With the captain of the Greenbriar Knights."

"Oh! Lord, I stuck my foot in my mouth so far they'll need the jaws of life to get it out again. I didn't mean—"

"Of course not." Gradually, Eve began smiling. "I know the girls you mean. The power freaks. They're only interested in a guy they can show off. They don't care anything about the guy. They only care about what he looks like and what his rep around school is."

"He's a trophy," Kendra added, to spur Eve on, to bring her out of whatever had put her in a funk.

"Exactly. And there are girls who are twice as bad."

"Which ones are those?"

"The ones who steal your boyfriend. Those bitches only want a guy because he's spoken for . . . and because he's a big deal on campus."

"Sounds like you've experienced one of those bitches."

"Yes. More than once."

"Let me guess. You were head cheerleader?"

Eve nodded.

"And your boyfriend was on the football team?"

"Yes. One was the captain." Her lips crooked up wryly.

"Shit, Evie," Kendra said. "Then you were just asking for it."

Finally, Eve chuckled with her. "I guess so. You know, I didn't think about it when I accepted the date with Art—I hope he doesn't have a girlfriend."

"You didn't get here early enough to hear the local gossip. Art Caliburn has never been ensnared in any romances, nor has his buddy the running back—"

"Spencer Lake."

"Yeah. Spencer." Kendra licked her upper lip suggestively. "You know, Spence looked pretty tasty. For a jock. Think you can fix me up—okay, what did I say now?"

"Nothing. You didn't say anything wrong."

"Do you just turn colors for no reason? Now you're doing your ghost impression again. What'd I do? Are you crying?" Not waiting for a reply, she crossed to the door and shut it, then put an arm around Eve and led her to the bed, sat her down, then made room for herself next to her.

"Okay, Evie," she said, taking one of her hands in both her own. "Look at me. Are you crying?"

"No."

"Then why are you shaking?"

"I'm not."

"You're lying. I can *feel* you shaking."

Eve tried to pull her hand away, but Kendra wouldn't allow it. "Look, we're stuck with each other for the duration, Evie, and you have to tell me how I upset you, or I'll never stop. You'll be turning all sorts of colors every time I open my mouth, and I'll just keep making you cry—"

"I'm not crying." Eve finally met her gaze.

"Well, then, what's that stuff running down your face if it's not tears? Oh, shit. *Now* what did I do?"

"You didn't *do* anything. You said something this time. God, I'm acting like such an idiot!" Eve's voice trembled, but there was a giggly tone to it that belied the fresh crop of tears.

Kendra switched from hand-holding to a hug, a hard one. "Eve, listen to me. You're going to get hysterical if you don't get a grip right now."

Eve sobbed a giggle.

Kendra decided slapping her face would be a bad idea. Instead, she took her shoulders in both hands and forced her to turn toward her. "Control yourself. If you don't, you'll attract attention and that gossip group I told you about will be gossiping about *you*. Now, take a deep breath. Good. Exhale. Another breath. Hold it. Exhale."

The fourth deep inhalation did the trick. Kendra handed her a tissue and Eve wiped away the tears from her cheeks and the hysteria from her eyes. A small giggle escaped, but it sounded normal.

"So, are you one of those high-maintenance girls, Evie?"

"No. I'm so sorry. I can just imagine what you think of me. I was being so stupid—"

"Stop calling yourself stupid. Do you know how often you do that?"

"No."

"You do it a lot. You're not stupid."

"I do lots of stupid things."

"No. You're not stupid and I don't ever want to hear you saying that again. I'm going to interrupt you if you say it until you learn not to. Evie, you're smart. And you're gullible as hell, but you've got me now."

"What do you mean?"

"I'll teach you to be a first-class bullshit detective."

For a second, she thought Eve was going to cry again, but the girl sat up straighter and quickly dashed away the tears welling in her eyes. "That's the sweetest thing anyone ever said to me, Kendra. Thank you." With that, she hugged back, long and warm.

What have *I gotten myself into?* Kendra felt a little teary herself, mired in all this warm sentimental goo that she herself had somehow stirred up. She stroked Eve's hair, then pulled gently from the hug. *An egghead and a cheerleader, who would've thought?*

"Okay. Now, tell me what I did and what I said. Leave nothing out."

"It's stupid—"

"What'd I tell you?"

"Sorry. But, well, okay. It's embarrassing. I had a nightmare. . . ."

32

At three o'clock, all the sisters, old and new, of Gamma Eta Pi met in the drawing room, and this time, the pledges were assigned to wheel in the extra chairs and set them up. And this time, Brittany informed them in her chirpy little voice, they got the cheap seats while the more senior sisters took the upholstered furniture.

Eve unfolded several chairs, very aware of Kendra sticking close, like a mama lion. She'd never experienced the kind of understanding that her new roommate offered her, nor the warmth. After she told her the details of the horrible dream about the slimy tongue, Kendra told her about a tribe of Australian aboriginals who taught their children to control their dreams, to call their parents into their dreams for help, then invited Eve to call on her the same way.

No one had ever treated her this way, not her friends or even her parents. They were great parents, but they tended to worry a lot about what other people thought of their family, of their home, their career status. Eve never would have dared repeat the dream to her mother or any of the friends she'd made since she became a cheerleader long before high school. Her mother would have told her not to let her imagination run away with her, her friends would have laughed.

"Eve?" someone asked.

She turned and came eye to eye with Merilynn Morris. "Hi."

"Do you remember me now?" Merilynn asked.

"Uh, from camp, right?" She forced herself to maintain eye contact. Sensing Kendra standing slightly behind her left shoulder gave her an added boost.

"Yes, from camp. Don't tell me you've forgotten about our adventures."

Eve hesitated. Merilynn, slender and smaller in every way, was still beautiful in a Renaissance painting sort of way. The brilliant green eyes, long and slightly hooded, pinned her, but they were nothing like the monster eyes she'd dreamed up the previous night. They were friendly, but faraway, as if their owner always had one foot in the clouds—and as far as Eve could recall, that was accurate.

Her face was more round than oval, but on her it looked good. Her mouth was long, like her eyes, the lips neither narrow nor full. The corners tilted up, by genetic design or habit, Eve didn't know, but either way, it worked. As she studied her, she kept thinking of a painting she'd seen prints of several times. It was a portrait of a woman with long tendrils of bright auburn hair and she wore a gown shaded in golds and fiery oranges. Her eyes were green and she appeared serene yet amused, much like the Mona Lisa, but prettier and happier and far more colorful. Eve had always been drawn to the painting, though looking at it made her slightly uneasy. Seeing Merilynn now, she finally understood why. They were nearly twins, though Merilynn's eyes were more startling and a faint spray of freckles over her nose and cheeks gave her an impish look.

"Hello," Kendra said, extending her hand. "I'm Eve's roommate, Kendra Phillips."

"Merilynn Morris. I'm pleased to meet you. Eve? Have you forgotten our adventures?"

Eve told herself to smile. "I'm sorry. I really don't remember all that much—I haven't thought of it in years. I mean, well, I went to Applehead every year, not just once, so there are lots of things to remember."

Merilynn smiled widely and dimples appeared. Eve had forgotten she had them. She looked more elfin than ever. "Of course. I liked Applehead—I loved being there, on that lake—but I didn't have any talent for cheerleading. Father just thought I might like to try it. He told me all those old ghost stories." Eyes twinkling, she added, "I didn't know the ghost of Holly Gayle is supposed to walk the halls of Gamma though. I thought she was a lake spirit."

Eve swallowed panic. Merilynn was doing exactly what she feared she'd do: dredging up old nightmares. "So, how's your father these days?"

"He's great. Aging beautifully. Too bad he's celibate. He'd be a real chick magnet."

"Your father is celibate?" Kendra asked.

"He's a Catholic priest," Eve said.

"See, you remember me!"

"Not everybody has a priest for a dad."

"How did *that* happen?" Kendra moved closer.

"My parents died when I was a baby. Father is really my uncle Martin. My father's brother."

"I remember you said you thought he might be your real dad. Do you still think so?"

Merilynn shrugged. "I was just a kid. You know how kids are. So how come you remember all that stuff but not our trip out to the island?"

"I remember we did it." Eve shifted uncomfortably, hoping the meeting would be called to order. "It rained. We barely got back before everybody got back from the field trip." She glanced at Kendra and knew she didn't have to worry about her spilling the story about the island she'd told her when they first met.

"Do you remember what we saw?"

"We spooked ourselves, making up stories."

Merilynn paused, then barely nodded. "We sure did. Have you talked to Sam Penrose yet?"

"No."

"You remember her though?"

"Sure. She always made me nervous."

"Really?" Merilynn smiled at Kendra. "Sam went on our adventures too. She's already a full sister here. Can you imagine *her* joining a sorority?"

I can't imagine you joining a sorority. Or why you had to choose this one. "Gamma's really good for careers, and she was the most driven person I've ever met."

"She still is. She's going to be a journalist. The serious kind. I guarantee you that girl will bust open government scandals in the future. Or maybe she'll be a war correspondent."

"She'll probably do both," Eve said. "I've never met anybody braver."

"Sam Penrose sounds very imposing." Kendra chuckled. "I don't know if I want to meet her or not."

"Too late," Merilynn said, waving at someone who just came into the room. "Sam, come here!"

"Hello, Merilynn."

"Sam Penrose, meet Kendra Phillips, and I think you already know Eve Camlan."

Sam shook hands with both of them, then looked Eve up and down. "You're drop-dead gorgeous. I always thought you would be."

"Thanks. You look great too." Great but scary. She was of average size, but somehow she came off as tall and imposing. She still had her straight-backed, square-shouldered posture, her figure hidden beneath a black tank top and an oversize blue broadcloth shirt, the sleeves rolled up to her elbows. Her face was strong, with dark, perfectly arched eyebrows over dark eyes. Prominent cheekbones offset her square chin. Her sable hair was much better kept now, sleek with a biometric cut that let it shape naturally into a below–the–chin bob. The youthful Sam had had no interest in hair, but puberty must have tamed the tomboy within. "I love your hair," Eve said with complete sincerity.

"Thanks." Sam's left eyebrow shot up in a question mark. Eve had forgotten about that too. It was the "you are an alien, please explain" look she'd seen back at camp so many times. It made her think of Mr. Spock.

"Where do you get it cut?"

"That place in Caledonia on Main Street."

"Everything's on Main Street in Caledonia," Kendra noted.

"The little place between Java the Hut and the dildo store. Has a cute name."

"Everything in Caledonia—" Kendra began.

"—has a cute name," they finished in unison. Eve was amused, mainly because the smile that passed between the two young women made her a little jealous. She knew it was silly. Kendra was just the sort of person Sam would get along with. Another brain with balls.

"The dildo store?" Merilynn asked.

"The Marital Aide Museum and Emporium," Kendra explained.

"That's the name." Sam rubbed the faint cleft in her chin and peered briefly at the ceiling. "It's something like Hair Today, Gone Tomorrow."

Kendra cracked up, which signaled Eve that the serious journalist had made a joke. She hadn't known Sam had a sense of humor and because of that, she hadn't zoned in on the goofy name. She'd taken it seriously. Maybe Sam wasn't as bad as she'd thought.

"Sam, Eve doesn't remember much about our adventures."

"Which adventures?"

"At Applehead Island, for one."

"We rowed out there, goofed off, and rowed back in a rainstorm. We nearly got caught. It was fun."

"What, you don't remember what we saw?" Merilynn asked, eyes wide.

Up went the eyebrow. Sam glanced toward the fireplace. "The meeting is starting. We'll talk more later." She left the pledges to sit with the full sisters.

"Hmmph," Merilynn said. "I guess you're both in denial."

"The meeting will come to order," called out Malory Thomas.

Eve sat down, grateful to Kendra for deftly maneuvering herself into a chair that would separate her from Merilynn.

33

"I hope all the Gamma meetings won't be that long and boring," Kendra told Eve as soon as they got back to their room and shut the door.

Eve rolled her eyes. "It was awful!" She tossed the booklet of Gamma House rules and history on her desk. "I don't know what pisses me off most. That we have to be in before eleven tonight or that we have to practically memorize that rule book because they're going to test us. I *hate* tests. I freeze."

"We'll study together. We'll make it fun."

"You like to study?"

"Not this stupid book." Kendra tossed hers on her bed. "I've got enough real studying to do. Way too much. I shouldn't have taken so many credits this semester. It's just too much. Look at that stack of books on my desk." She indicated a solid foot and a half of texts. "I have to write two papers and read chapters out of every book in that stack. Before Monday."

"Why don't you drop a class or two?" Eve slid her closet open and started looking through her wardrobe for something to wear on her date.

"Are you kidding? I wouldn't know what to drop. I managed to get into ones I didn't think I would. I can't drop those— they're interesting."

"What about Piccolo's class?"

"It's easy, and I'd have to pick it up again later if I dropped it now. I'd rather get it over with. Besides, we have it together three days a week and it's just before lunch."

Eve laughed. "Don't drop it." She pulled a cobalt-blue dress from the closet and held it up. "What do you think?"

"It's gorgeous. A little dressy, probably."

"You're right." Eve replaced the dress and continued searching. "So what do you know about Professor Piccolo? Something's going on with him."

"You mean all those girls who are moony for him?"

"Yeah. I mean, he's *old,* but not all that good looking. He's just average."

"I think he's not average in *one* department."

Eve whirled around, holding up a lavender dress with a ruffled neckline.

"Too floofy. Way too floofy. I'd throw that one out if I were you."

"What's floofy mean?"

"You know—puffy and too sweet. Stuff that makes you look like you should be working in the Enchanted Castle at Disneyland."

"Oh." Eve looked the dress over. She loved it, but Kendra

was right. She hung it up at the far end of the closet, then turned back to Kendra. "So Piccolo's packing a giant dingus?" She giggled.

"Is there anything that doesn't make you blush?" Kendra asked in mock annoyance. "Actually, I don't think they're talking penis, but where did you ever get a word like 'dingus'?"

"That's not a regular word?"

"I never heard it used that way before."

"Oh? That's what my mother calls them." She snickered and blushed again. "Dinguses. There's some old movie called *Dirty Dingus McGee* and my mother would just fall apart when she heard the title. My dad said it a lot. I asked her why it was funny, but she didn't tell me until I was thirteen. Her mother called it a 'dingus' too." She laughed. "So I guess it's a family heirloom."

"Dingus. It's growing on me."

"Eww!" Eve giggled, blushing madly.

"So, little Miss Innocence, you get the nasty jokes fast."

Eve grinned and held up a summery white halter-topped dress.

"Nope. Way too Marilyn Monroe. People will think you're a drag queen."

"Hey!"

"Not really."

"Thank you."

"You don't have an Adam's apple."

"You're messing with me."

"Yep." Kendra joined her at the closet and started pawing through the clothes.

"I don't have a fourth as much in my wardrobe as you do. This is amazing. I'm surprised they all fit in here."

"You can borrow whatever you want."

"That's sweet of you."

"So what isn't average about Piccolo if it isn't his dingus?"

"Well, I haven't heard much yet, but rumor has it he can lick his own forehead. Of course, if he could do that, he'd be a freak of nature." She laughed. "And being a guy, he'd probably spend all his time licking himself."

Eve's giggles faded after a few seconds. "You mean he has a huge *tongue?*"

Kendra looked her in the eye. "Yeah. I purposely didn't use that word. Because of your nightmare."

"It's a pretty weird coincidence."

"But that's all it is."

"I know. And I'm pretty much over the tongue dream. Telling you got it out of my system."

"Good. So I'll tell you the rest. He has a nickname."

"What is it?"

"Professor Tongue. And I don't know if it's true or not, but I heard he's currently servicing President Malory."

"Really?"

Kendra nodded as she pulled forth a sleek pair of black pants. "Wear these."

"With what?"

"Depends. Are you a first-timer?"

"How'd you know?"

"I didn't. I didn't really think you'd say yes. I mean, with all that blushing and words like 'dingus,' and all, I was starting to think you're a virgin."

"I am. That's not what you meant?"

"Lord, no. I meant, do you ever have sex on a first date?"

Eve's eyes widened. "Of course not! I've never gone all the way!"

"Saving it for your wedding night?"

"No, just for the right guy."

"Okay, so, how do we dress a virgin for a first date?"

"Don't tell anyone!"

"Of course not. Did you hear me ratting you out to Merilynn about that island adventure you pretended not to remember?"

"I'm sorry. I'm not used to trusting other females."

"But you're a cheerleader. You have all those bonds with other women."

"Which is why I don't usually trust them."

"I'm curious. Do you trust Merilynn? I know you don't want to be around her, but would you trust her?"

"Honestly? No. She's a little scary."

"She and Sam Penrose both scare you?"

"Totally different scaries," Eve explained. "Sam is like royalty or something. She commands. She keeps people together. I doubt we'd have gotten off that island in that storm without her. She never loses her head." She paused. "Of course, we probably wouldn't have gotten there without her, either. She figured out when and how to do it without getting caught. She made it happen."

"So she doesn't actually *frighten* you?"

"No. But I don't like being around her—she's just so intense. Actually, she's a lot like you, but without a personality."

"Is that a compliment?"

"Yes."

"I thought so. She's got a personality, but you're right. She intimidates people. I doubt if she even realizes it consciously. She'll have to figure it out to make it as a journalist. She'll have to learn to tone it down when she needs to."

"At least Gamma's the right place to do it."

"Yeah. All that stuff about teaching us all about reading body language and decoding the way people use words—that's going to be cool. Lessons like that are hard to come by."

"No wonder this sorority has so many successful alumni."

"Here." Kendra handed her a black tank top. "Wear this."

"All black? It's hot out. And I'm not really the all-black type. Or do you mean I should just wear the pants and top, nothing over it?"

"Nope." Kendra returned to the closet. "I saw the perfect thing in here somewhere. Tell me how Merilynn is scary."

"She's impetuous. She thinks of something and runs off and does it without thinking about consequences. And she's probably still into all that witchy stuff."

"I wouldn't trust her either—she seems a little flaky. But she's into witchcraft? Wicca?"

"I don't know. She always knew about all sorts of occult things. She liked to mess with herbs and hold séances and things like that."

"Well, that doesn't make her flaky. A lot of that stuff is pretty legitimate. I think her flakiness is probably just an inborn trait. Like Sam should be an army general. Or maybe a conductor."

"On a train?"

Kendra laughed. "No, no! I mean an orchestra conductor."

Eve smiled. "So I guess being a cheerleader is my inborn trait. What's yours?"

Kendra had never thought about it before, but she instantly answered. "I'm a storyteller. Old stories, not new ones. Aha. Here." She took a lightweight pale pink jacket from its hanger and handed it to Eve. "I assume you have jewelry of some sort that has pink in it."

"I do. It's a pendant. A heart carved out of pink crystal."

"Perfect. You'll look great." She paused, watching Eve look over the outfit she'd picked out. "You don't have to wear that. I mean, you probably know lots more about clothes than I do."

"Probably, but this is interesting. I've never worn this jacket with black before. I always wear pastels with it."

"You should wear whatever makes you feel good."

"I think this might make me feel good," Eve said, kicking off her shoes.

Kendra sat down at her desk and started picking through the textbooks. "Well, while you're out having a good time, I'm going to work on my paper for Professor McCobb's class. At least it's interesting. It's on modern American iconography."

"Translation?" Eve's voice was muffled behind her clothing.

"The immortality of Elvis Presley, for instance. He was a real person, but he's turning into a modern folk hero."

"That *is* interesting. Okay. How's this look?"

Kendra turned. Eve had completely dressed, right down to the pendant, in under a minute. "Amazing."

"You like it, then."

"I love it. It makes you look more mature, which is good

when you're dating a senior. But what's amazing is how fast you changed clothes."

"Being a cheerleader teaches you to be a quick-change artist." She moved to the mirror of the dresser they shared, quickly brushing her hair and applying makeup.

Kendra watched in fascination. "You've got to teach me how to do that."

"Do what?" Eve asked, dropping her lipstick in a small black shoulder bag.

"Put on makeup that fast. It takes me forever."

Someone knocked on the door.

"Art," Kendra said.

Eve smiled and opened the door, but it wasn't Art Caliban.

Heather smiled at her. "Art's waiting for you in the foyer. And guess what?"

"What?"

"He's taking you to Thai Gonzales. My date and I are going there too, so we're going to double-date. Won't that be fun?"

Eve shot a grimace to Kendra that spoke of slow death and torture. "What is Thai Gonzales?" she asked brightly.

"It's a nice little restaurant in Greenbriar. Since we have to be back early, it's the perfect choice."

"Oh?"

"They serve Thai and Mexican food. You can get just one or a combo. The cuisines use some of the same spices. Cilantro. Red pepper. Cumin. They're really good mixed. You'll love it." Heather flashed her teeth. "You ready? Let's go!"

"Have fun, kids," Kendra called. *Poor Eve.*

34

"They're gone," Brittany told Malory as soon as Heather and Eve left with their dates.

Malory stood in front of the open refrigerator drinking her private reserve of sour lemonade directly from the pitcher. "Good. Heather will make sure Caliban doesn't ruin our virgin." She put the pitcher back and shut the door. "Is everything ready for tonight?"

"Yes. Everything's ready. Michele and Teri are finishing up. So . . ."

"So, what?" Malory smiled.

"Can I go with you to visit Professor Tongue?"

"Yes. He even knows you're coming along this time."

"Really? You decided not to surprise him?"

"He's cooking. I had to tell him."

"We're getting sex *and* dinner?"

"We are. He's not a bad chef, either."

"What's he making?"

"Something Italian." Malory opened a cabinet above the counter and took something out. "We'll bring the nibbles."

"Honey-roasted peanuts!" Brittany exclaimed, stomach growling. "My favorite."

"I know. Come on, let's get out of here." She handed Brittany the nuts. "You can't open them until we get there."

"Okay. Malory? Why are you being so pleasant tonight?"

"I'm always pleasant when a sacrifice is coming up."

Brittany gave the can of nuts a quick shake. She loved the sound. "So, do you think Holly Gayle will come around?"

"That damned ghost. Of course she'll come around. She always does when we're sacrificing one of her own. The stupid, dead bitch!"

35

Around eight, Kendra finished her paper for McCobb. By nine she had read three of the four chapters assigned from other classes and written the beginning of a simple essay on government for a required and detested course. The professor could put sharks to sleep. She got up from the desk and did a few stretches, thought about going downstairs and socializing, but decided she'd rather have some downtime. Seeing the Gamma rule book on her bed, she fluffed up the bed's two pillows—*a definite improvement on the dorm room*—and arranged them to shield herself from the curving brass headboard, then plopped down and picked up the book. Looking at it— *assigned reading for a sorority!*—she wondered if joining Gamma was a bad move.

She wasn't a joiner, but it was something she'd always planned to do, ever since she first heard the stories about Granny's granny. It sounded like such a grand thing when Granny told the stories; grand despite the mysteries and the ghost stories. Even now, she wasn't sure why joining this sorority was important. She suspected she was just proving some point about how, in the old days, her grannies worked for the girls in the sorority, but now times had changed and she was one of the chosen ones. *Whatever. No experience is ever a waste.* Granny's words. She wanted to tell her grandmother she had been accepted into the sorority, but knew Granny wouldn't be impressed. She'd ask her if she had lost her mind.

Maybe I have. But she'd met interesting people. Eve was a delightful revelation, an eye-opener, and she knew she was the same for Eve. She thought about the hysterics that were barely fended off and hoped that wasn't a sign of things to come. Eve had seemed a little neurotic all along, but that was normal.

Everybody had quirks and rarely were they aware of them. She and Eve were going to have quite a ride, finding out each other's eccentricities and making compromises. They'd moved in so quickly, they hadn't discussed anything important about rooming together. Music could be a problem; she had no idea what Eve listened to and vice versa, but since neither brought more than a small radio/CD player with them, chances were it wouldn't matter much. *What if Eve had hauled in a bunch of boy band CDs? But she didn't. Don't look for trouble.*

Granny always said that too, but just moving into this house was looking for trouble. She thought of Holly Gayle. A haunt could be real trouble, especially if someone as sensitive as Eve was exposed. *I wonder where that room is that Granny saw Holly in?* She couldn't ask her directly; the old lady had a knack for seeing through things and she'd know something was up. *Maybe Mom knows.* She was unsure about asking her, though, as well since she wasn't happy about Gamma either and if Kendra brought up ghost stories, her oh-so-rational mother might let Granny's stories get to her. After all, she'd been raised on them.

"Oh, well," Kendra sighed. She opened the book and started reading.

Just after ten, there was a knock on the door. "Who's there?" Kendra called.

"It's me."

"Get in here, Eve!"

Her roommate came in. Closing the door behind her, she felt for a lock, then bent, looking for one.

"It's no use. There isn't a lock."

"Well, we should put one on right away. Anyone could just walk in on us."

"That's the idea." Kendra held up the rule book. "No locks. It's to teach us to have no secrets from our sisters and to respect one another's privacy, not because we have to, but because we *want* to. It's all in here." She rolled her eyes.

"Well, that's ridiculous. We have to have a lock."

"Grounds for expulsion, the book says."

Eve dropped her purse on her bureau, then picked up the wooden desk chair and carried it to the door. "I'm not sleeping in an unlocked room."

"Well, a chair isn't technically a lock. But wait—I think they're going to hit us with the real initiation tonight. That's why they wanted everyone in early."

"We already took the oath."

"But we haven't been put through hell yet."

"True." Eve hung her jacket up and started undressing. "Do you think they'll come after we're asleep?"

"I don't know. But I sure wouldn't wear pj's to bed tonight. I'm wearing my jeans and this Henley all night. My running shoes are staying on."

"Don't worry." Eve picked up the pair of jeans she'd worn while moving in and pulled them back on. She pulled a fresh short-sleeved pink T-shirt over her head, then grabbed her socks and Reeboks and put them on.

"You sure love pink."

"Sorry."

"Don't be sorry. I wasn't criticizing, just observing. How'd you feel in your sophisticated outfit tonight?"

"I'm so glad I wore it. I felt more confident than I usually do."

"You're a cheerleader. That's supposed to be the embodiment of self-confidence."

"It is—when I'm on the field. Otherwise, not that confident."

"You'll get there. How was the date?"

"What date? I really liked Heather until now. Tonight, she was like a bloodhound or something. She followed me to the bathroom."

"That's normal."

Eve tilted her head. "I know it's normal, but she didn't do it the normal way."

"What? She tried to wipe your ass for you?"

Eve snickered. "That's not what I mean. She just kept watching me. Staring at me."

"Maybe she likes you."

"Stop it. It was creepy. And when we were at the table, she

just kept talking. Art and I hardly even got to talk, let alone get to know each other."

"So is he worth knowing?"

"I think so. It was hard to tell. Heather's date was a talker too. Between them, we just sat there and listened."

"What did they talk about?"

"School. Competitions. Football. The sorority." She sat back on her bed. "You know, I should have found that a lot more interesting than I did. I think you're influencing me."

"And is that a good thing or a bad thing?"

"Listen!"

"What?" Even as Kendra asked, she heard footsteps approaching. Someone pounded on the door to the next room. "Quick, put the chair back where it belongs! They're coming for us!"

36

First there were blindfolds. The four girls who pounded on their door and rushed in uninvited were hidden within green cowled robes. Eve saw them briefly, a flash of rich gold satin edging the sleeves and hood. Then two of them jumped her, and the other two descended on Kendra. While one tied her hands behind her back, the other blindfolded her.

"Kendra?" she called as they rushed her forward, her feet stumbling.

"Hang tight, Evie!" Kendra called after her. "You'll be okay!"

They pulled her down the hall and didn't even attempt to let her stay on her feet as they descended to the first floor. Her toes thumped over the risers, her captors grasping her arms tightly.

They reached the first floor and silently let her gain her feet, then started moving again.

"Please slow down a little. You're hurting my arms! Please!"

No reply came, but the grips grew tighter and the pace sped up until she tripped more than she walked. She decided to try logic. "I have to cheer at the football game next week. I can't have bruises all over my arms! Please be—ow!"

She shut her mouth and tried to keep up. She didn't know the house very well, but was pretty sure they'd taken her past the main rooms and into the echoey kitchen. Abruptly, they halted. Eve heard a door open, felt cold dank air on her face.

On the move again, down a short narrow flight of stairs. The air seemed close and wet. It smelled of damp earth. They pulled her along and she did her best to keep up. Finally, they came to another set of stairs. These led upward. They pushed her ahead of them, never speaking.

A dozen steps up, the sisters once again moved up beside her and took her elbows. Here, she could smell a hint of long-gone wood smoke, a pleasant scent if it weren't for the very faint whiff of decayed flesh that laced it. Panic rose in her throat. She forced it back.

They marched her through the room, stopping again to open a door. This one creaked; old wood on rusty hinges. They took her through the doorway and she tripped on something covering the floor. From the smell, it was old straw. And something had died on it a long time ago.

Eve's captors undid the bindings on her hands. Just as she began rubbing them to get the blood flowing, they took them again and pulled them above her head. She heard chains. A key in a padlock. The lock snapping open.

"Please, no," she cried as they fitted the manacles over her wrists and locked them down. "You're not going to leave me in the dark, are you? Please! Please don't leave me." Chains moved, pulling her arms up until her elbows couldn't bend. Eve fought back terror. Silent tears soaked the blindfold. "Please don't leave me here in the dark. Please don't leave me alone."

Unbidden, images from her nightmare shot through her mind. Suddenly, she was certain that thing from her nightmare—*the green ghost*— had been real and that it would return as soon as they left her. It would choke her with its tongue. It would do worse, too. *Stop thinking like that. This is just an initiation. Just college girls. Don't be afraid. It'll be over soon!*

Someone undid the blindfold. "Thank you!" she gasped before the soft material left her face. "Thank you!"

The cloth was gone. She opened her eyes slowly, so the light wouldn't hurt them. But there was nothing except darkness so thick it nearly smothered her, only that and her captors.

A click. Suddenly, a face appeared, inches away, illuminated from below by a small flashlight. "Malory!"

Malory smiled her cold, cold smile.

A second click. "Don't forget me."

It was Brittany, grinning madly. "Are you comfortable?"

"No."

"I'm glad you told the truth," Malory said. "If you hadn't, I'd have to pull your arms up until you squeak."

37

"You are here to pledge as a sister of Gamma Eta Pi," a feminine voice intoned for at least the third time. And, for the third time since Kendra, still blindfolded, had been hustled into whatever place they'd chosen for the initiation rites, the voice droned on about honor and loyalty and the spirit of sisterhood. She could hear the other pledges shifting and breathing around her.

Standing in darkness, draped in a cowled robe and forbidden

to speak, she wondered if either of the girls flanking her was Eve. She doubted it; she thought she would probably sense the presence of her new roommate.

"Everyone, kneel," the voice commanded.

Carefully, Kendra got to her knees. The voice didn't belong to Malory or Brittany, which was surprising; she thought Malory would delight in doing the ordering. Instead, Kendra was almost certain it was Heather who was commanding the new sisters. Maybe that was logical, since she was the rush chairman.

Someone coughed.

"Silence!" the voice thundered. "Silence, or suffer the consequences!"

"Excuse me," some brave soul said softly. "Could you tell us what the consequences are?"

"Tell you?" the voice asked. "No, we won't tell you. But we'll show you."

Mocking laughter came from all around. Kendra realized one of the sisters who laughed stood directly behind her.

"No pledges shall move. We will now remove your blindfolds."

Kendra heard the rustle of robes and then hands roughly untied the cloth covering her eyes.

All she had known about the room was that it had to be on the second floor. Now her eyes told her a little more. It was neither small nor large. Lit only by flickering candles, the octagonal walls appeared to be covered entirely in velvety dark green draperies. The pledges, faces shadowed by their cowls, knelt in a circle. Kendra tried to spot Eve, but it was impossible in the dim light. The full sisters, their identities also hidden by their robes, stood behind them, an outer circle. Three sisters stood farther back, one behind an elevated podium, the others on either side, arms crossed.

"Who spoke?" the one—*Heather*—behind the podium asked.

"I did."

"Rise."

The girl did.

"You were told not to speak. You disobeyed. What say you?"

"It was a reasonable question," the shadowed pledge replied.

"And so it was. Come forward and receive your answer."

The girl stepped up to the podium. The two sisters flanking the speaker moved quickly, pulling her robe from her.

It was little Lou, the new substitute cheerleader.

"Strip." Heather's words were ice.

"What?"

"More punishment will be received for each word you speak. Strip."

Reluctantly, Lou pulled off her pajama top. Candle light flickered over her small breasts.

"Strip."

"But—I'm not wearing underwear."

"Strip or suffer further punishment if the sisters must do it for you."

Lou's lower lip started trembling. Seeing a silent tear on run down her cheek as she bent to remove her pajama bottoms, Kendra looked away, embarrassed for her.

"Everyone keep your eyes on your sister!" Heather ordered. Whoever stood behind Kendra roughly yanked her head back up.

Finally, Lou stood naked before them all. After an excruciatingly long pause, Heather stepped down from behind the podium. "Bend over and hold your ankles," she ordered.

The girl whimpered, but did as she was told.

Nothing happened. No one moved. Finally, Heather held out one hand and one of her helpers turned and took something from the podium and handed it to her.

It was a paddle. *A goddamned stupid paddle. The oldest initiation trick in the book.*

"You will receive your punishment silently," Heather said, raising the wooden paddle. "Every time you cry out, you will receive one more hit."

And so it began.

The swats were firm but not cruel; the only cruelty was the humiliation, and that was very cruel indeed. *What the hell am I doing here?* Kendra, aware of the sisters looming around them, reluctantly kept her mouth shut and her eyes on the scene before her. She felt like she was in the Nazi Youth fraternity scene from *Animal House.*

38

"How can I cheer if you hurt me?" Eve asked, fighting back tears. Her arms, stretched above her, hurt so much she could hardly stand it. But the darkness was even worse. *I won't let them see me cry! I won't!* "My muscles are sore from practice. They're cramping. I won't be able to cheer!"

"Genevieve," Malory said, her voice deepening to the depths of the voice in her nightmare. "You're all done cheering."

"You had your night of glory." Brittany chittered, a vile sound that hurt Eve's ears.

"I don't understand." *I won't cry! I won't!*

And then hands ran over her breasts, pinching and prodding. They moved lower, undid her jeans. Eve braced herself as the hands—they had to be Brittany's since Malory's face remained unmoving before her—slipped inside her jeans.

"How'd you like me to do you with a dildo so big you'll think you're going to be split open?" Brittany's fingers pushed lower, invading, probing.

"Please stop! I'm a virgin!"

Brittany cackled, but Malory's deep laugh was pure malevolence.

"Exactly the reason you're here, Genevieve. Brittany, stop it right now. If you break her maidenhead, I'll have your sweet little ass on a platter for my dinner."

The hand withdrew. Brittany sighed.

A darkness speckled with woozy dots of light swirled before Eve's eyes as she felt herself trying to slip away in a faint. She welcomed the relief, but Malory wafted something acrid under her nose, bringing Eve fully back to consciousness.

"No, no," Malory said, the voice deepening again. "I know that trick, my dear. You spoiled my fun last night. I barely got to explore you before your little mind ran away and tried to hide from me."

"That was you? How?" Eve bit her lip, trying not to cry, trying to think of a way out of this.

The light clicked out. "I thought you'd have known it was me by the sound of my voice." Pinprick green eyes began to glow in the darkness before her, growing quickly, the demonic slitted pupils taking form. She smelled the lake, the forest, all the dead things in the woods on its breath.

The eyes moved closer. The slimy cold tongue touched her lips, tried to work its way between her clenched teeth.

It's real. Eve's mind, trapped, whirled, filled with horror and repulsion. She couldn't think, couldn't breathe; all she could do was feel that fetid sticky tongue coating her with stinking mucous and saliva. She could almost feel her brain starting to crack, to break like an egg. It would happen soon. *Please, God, let it happen now! Let me go!*

It wouldn't be long before everything broke apart, and it would be sheer relief. She prayed for it.

39

The initiation seemed endless to Kendra.

After the paddling, each pledge was made to take communion while still on her knees. Kendra had been first and, in retrospect, was glad of it because she was one of the few who didn't know what was being put in her mouth.

She had nearly gagged when a small object was placed on her tongue and, before she swallowed, felt tiny legs moving on her taste buds. An insect, a small roach, probably, ran blindly down her throat, saving her the horror of crunching it. The sister who fed it to her gave her a sip of fruity wine as a chaser, and after that, the worst was over.

There were recitations in some corrupted form of Latin, each girl had to lift her robe and drop panties for a ceremonial *thank-you-ma'am-may-I-have-another?* paddling, but no one else's face was revealed. Kendra kept herself from losing her temper by telling herself stories about initiations in other cultures; this one, in comparison, was a walk in the park.

At last, blindfolds were reapplied. Kendra sensed lights coming on and smelled candles being extinguished. After being twirled a few times to make her lose her sense of direction, she—and the others, she could tell by the sounds—were given another drink. This one began to take effect even as the elder sisters led her back to her bedroom. By the time she was laid out on the bed, she was beyond speaking. She wanted to say good night to Eve, but she couldn't find the energy. Instead, she drifted off into dreamless sleep.

40

"She's here!" Brittany spat the words in her chipmunk voice.

Something seemed different to Eve, something lightened the syrupy thick atmosphere. The tongue withdrew and Eve opened her eyes, her thoughts abruptly coherent. *Rescue!* "Help!" she cried. "Help!"

"I told you she'd show up," Malory said. "That bitch."

"You were right," Brittany replied. "As usual."

A greenish white glow behind Malory shimmered and began to shift, wavering slowly until it began to take human form. Eve stared hard, not understanding until the form completed transformation into a wet-haired girl in a soggy old-fashioned white dress. The flashlights went out. Malory turned her horrible greenish visage toward the apparition.

"Holly Gayle," Eve whispered.

She looked utterly real, lit by an inner light so that she was like a photo cut out and placed on black paper. She smiled sadly at Eve and glided forward.

Eve. Sister, I will help—

Malory began to chant, Brittany replying in unintelligible counterpoint. The voice in Eve's head silenced and the ghost of Holly Gayle stopped advancing.

"No," Eve cried as the image began to retreat slightly. "Please help me, Holly! Please!"

The ghost disappeared an instant later.

"She gave up pretty easily," Brittany said.

"The old bitch."

"Please," Eve began.

"'Please, please, please.' Are you always this polite?" Malory spat, turning on her. "Or is that all you know how to say?"

"Why are you doing this?" Eve shut her eyes as Malory's phantom face loomed before her.

"You're the one, Genevieve. You will soon be with the real Forest Knight. He will do far more to you than my tongue will. He will take your virginity and then I will take your life and your soul and I will give it to him. And he will give me everything I need."

The tongue flicked over one closed eyelid, then the other, leaving sticky slime that acted almost like glue. Eve slowly forced her eyes open as the tongue moved down, exploring her neck, tasting behind her ear. "Get away from me," she ordered.

The demonic face came up. The tongue touched her lips, then withdrew. "You dare to order me around, you little bitch?"

"Yes." Eve felt her mind cracking as she faced the eyes, unflinching now. "Yes, I dare. Who the hell do you think you are?"

"I'll show you."

And she did.

Eve's brain short-circuited, a broken toy. She floated up, fearless now, fearless and free. She saw her body sagging in its shackles, saw Malory and Brittany. Malory cursed, kicking Brittany, kicking Eve's lifeless body.

Eve! Leave that place while you can.

Holly Gayle's voice called to her to come outside. She hesitated just a few seconds longer, listening to the creatures below, then let herself drift toward the voice calling her name. She seeped through the walls of the old smokehouse and saw Holly Gayle standing in front of her.

Take my hand, Eve. We'll go to the lake and I'll tell you a story. Would you like that?

Yes.

Together, they drifted into the woods.

41

*K*endra?

She awoke slowly, her head thick, her mind muddy. The room was in darkness, the window over her desk open so that the filmy curtains fluttered in the breeze, ghosts on the wind.

Kendra?

The initiation. *They drugged me.* It started to come back.

And then the voice again, calling her.

Kendra.

"Eve?" she said, sitting up slowly. "Evie?"

Feeling for the beside lamp switch but not finding it, she looked toward the door of their room. Eve stood there solemnly, still dressed in jeans and the pink T-shirt. "Evie, did you just come in?"

Kendra.

She heard Eve's voice but the girl's lips didn't move as she glided toward her.

Kendra. Help me!

Kendra felt icy air as Eve neared her; she felt the hairs on the back of her neck lift, full of static electricity. The room was dark. She could barely see the curtains fluttering. But Eve was as plain as day. Eve, whose mouth didn't move, who glided instead of walked.

Kendra!

Kendra screamed.

MERILYNN

Applehead Lake Cheerleading Camp

Eight Years Ago

1

"A long time ago, the town of Applehead was located right there under the lake." Counselor Allie Mayhew pointed toward the lake, its black water slowly rippling with silver moonlight.

Merilynn Morris, sitting on a log across the crackling campfire from Allie, shivered with delight and anticipation, then glanced at the other campers gathered on the circle of logs. Most of the preteen girls were saucer-eyed with pleasurable terror, though a few, like Eve Camlan, looked honestly afraid. And then there was Sam Penrose, beside Merilynn. Sam looked—well, she looked bored.

But Merilynn knew that was just a facade, Sam's usual nothing-bothers-me attitude. After yesterday's trip to the island, how could it be anything else? She hadn't been able to talk to Sam or Eve today, to find out what they were really thinking about the previous day's adventures, but she didn't have to be a genius to know that both of them were avoiding her. They didn't want to talk about it. *Chickens!*

"Everyone knew the town was going to be flooded," Allie Mayhew went on. "And even though most people were a little sorry about losing their orchards and their old homes, they understood that their valley was the only logical place for a reservoir and that because of the drought that had plagued them for four years already, their trees would die of thirst anyway.

"So they moved, leaving their homes and apple trees behind. Many left and helped found the little village of Crackle Hill—"

"That's Caledonia now," some camper blurted.

"That's right, Megan," Allie said, nodding. "Others went farther north or south, but the people who really loved the valley and this forest, they stayed right here."

"*Right* here?" Merilynn asked. *Get to the ghost stories already!*

"Yes, some did. The main house where we have our meals and indoor meetings here at camp once belonged to a family named Gayle. Mr. and Mrs. Gayle had just one daughter and after she died, they moved away and willed the property to Greenbriar University."

"How did Holly Gayle die?" Merilynn prompted.

"You're a glutton for ghost stories, Merilynn," Allie said, smiling. "We've already told the story of Holly. She drowned."

"You've only told it twice." Merilynn looked around for support from her fellow campers. "Have *you* ever seen her ghost?"

Girls murmured, titillated.

"Me?" Allie asked.

Merilynn nodded.

Everyone stared at the counselor, who looked around, as if checking to make sure no one else was listening. Many of the girls turned their heads, too, nervously, probably more worried about Holly's ghost than eavesdropping counselors. In absolute heaven, Merilynn asked, "Have you, Allie? Have *you* seen her?"

"Well . . . maybe."

Hushed gasps hissed through the air. The firelight wavered.

"No," Allie added. "I can't really say I saw her. I just imagined it, I'm sure."

"Oh, come on, Allie," Merilynn urged. "Tell us anyway."

"Well . . ." She looked at the girls appraisingly. "It was last summer."

Tell! Tell! Tell! Merilynn could barely sit still.

"It was early September, the day after the last campers left for home. Only we—the counselors— were still here, cleaning up and closing things up for the season. That last night, we had the guys—the counselors from the football camp across the lake,"—she pointed—"over for our annual party. They drove over. It was still light out, only about six o'clock, when they arrived, but you know how these woods are. It seemed dark."

Allie paused dramatically, then glanced at her wristwatch. "It's late. Maybe I should finish the story tomorrow night—"

Girls moaned and begged, which Merilynn knew was just what she wanted. Allie was her favorite counselor because she loved telling stories.

"Okay. There were nearly two dozen of us altogether, us and the guys. We had a barbecue and then we all sat right here and toasted marshmallows over the campfire."

"Did you drink?" Sam Penrose asked, doing her Spocky-eyebrow thing.

"Drink?" Allie asked. Then, shocked, "You mean alcohol?"

"Yes."

"Of course not! That's not allowed!"

Bull puckies, thought Merilynn, trying not to grin too much. She knew right where they hid the beer and wine coolers. So did Sam. They'd found the treasure trove together, hidden in an old hollow log. She launched an elbow into Sam's arm to keep her from saying so. It might be fun to see Allie's reaction, but it would ruin the ghost story.

Sam returned the poke so hard that Merilynn had to stifle a yelp. They exchanged a look. Merilynn knew the other girl wouldn't tell.

"So, what happened?" Sam asked. "Did someone pretend to be a ghost while you were toasting your marshmallows?"

Merilynn poked her again, glared at her. "Don't spoil this," she whispered.

Sam crossed her eyes at her, but nodded acquiescence.

"It wasn't while we were around the campfire," Allie said at last. "It was later. Down by the dock."

Everyone turned their heads toward the little dock poking out into the lake, rowboats leashed to it like puppy dogs. There was a small boathouse too, right up against the far side of the dock, but it was rarely used during camping season. At the moment, it was nothing but a dark smudge on the narrow beach.

"It was probably ten or eleven o'clock and we'd split up, you know, to walk around and talk. Hold hands."

A couple of more knowledgeable girls giggled. Allie Mayhew silenced them with silence.

"Nothing bad was going on," she said. Merilynn knew she had to say that; then Sam leaned over and whispered, "Condoms" in her ear.

Merilynn just about lost it. To keep from laughing, she pinched the back of her hand until tears sprung into her eyes. She was going to have to get Sam back later. She was definitely messing with her.

"One of the guys and I were walking along the shore and we decided to go sit on the pier. We walked to the end, then sat down and took off our shoes so we could dangle our feet in the water."

Crickets chirped. Fire crackled.

"It was really dark. Darker than it is now. We were just talking and kind of looking down into the water. Way, way out, I saw a light come on under the water. One, then another."

Oohs and ahs, hushed, almost reverent, punctuated her pause.

"The other counselor saw them too. We looked at each other and he said, 'You know what that means?' and I said, 'What?'"

"What?" several girls murmured.

"He said the town was coming to life." Allie looked from girl to girl before adding, "'When the town starts coming to life,' he told me, 'that means Holly Gayle is taking a walk.'"

Merilynn saw Eve Camlan draw into herself, hugging herself with her arms. Merilynn felt sorry for her, being so afraid. But not that sorry. "And then you saw the ghost?" she asked Allie.

"Not yet. I got nervous. I mean, who wouldn't?"

Campers nodded enthusiastically.

"So I told Mark—the guy I was with—that we were just seeing starlight reflected on the water. He said maybe so.

"I stood up and said I was cold, you know, to get him to get off the dock." Flames glittered in Allie's wide eyes. "I mean, it was late, and those lights looked real, even if they weren't. I just

couldn't stand having my feet in the water then, because I just
knew one of Holly Gayle's cold, dead-white hands was going to
reach out of the water and grab my ankle and pull me in!"

A lot of girls looked frightened now, but Merilynn leaned forward, enthralled. "What happened? What did you see?"

"Well, I pulled my sandals on and Mark got up. He teased me
a little, but was pretty quick putting his own shoes back on. We
turned around to walk back down the dock." Allie smiled for
an instant, cut it off abruptly. "And then it happened. We saw
her."

Shocked inhalations, breaths held.

"And?" Merilynn said impatiently.

"She came out of the boathouse at the shoreline, right where
we'd have to pass to get off the dock. For a minute, I thought
she was just one of the other counselors. But she was wearing a
long white dress. *Holly,* I thought. Mark stopped walking and
just stared. Me too. And then I realized it was just one of the
counselors pretending to be Holly to scare us. I mean, isn't that
what you'd think?" She looked right at Merilynn.

"No," Merilynn said, throwing Allie off, loving that she
could. *"I'd* think it was the ghost."

"Well, Merilynn," Allie said, fear actually showing in her
eyes now, "you might have been right. It wasn't a counselor. The
girl in white *seemed* to be walking— but too smoothly, like
maybe she wasn't quite touching the ground. She was coming
toward us, very slowly, but didn't seem to be walking on the
dock exactly. I mean, really, she looked like she was *on the lake,*
but that's impossible."

"If it was a ghost, it's not impossible," Merilynn said.

Girls giggled, clutching one another now.

"Well, Mark and I still thought it had to be a joke, so we just
made ourselves head right toward her. You know, to get off the
pier. As we approached the boathouse, though, the girl just vanished. Faded away into thin air. But before she was gone, I saw
her face and hair. She was wet, her hair just hung around her
face like she'd been in the lake. Her dress, too. I could see water
dripping off her fingertips. And her face?"

Silence.

"It wasn't one of the counselors. I'd never seen her before. Her eyes seemed normal; then in the last second they seemed to be just dark smudges. Her face wasn't all there anymore."

Campers jabbered in soft tones, telling each other what they wanted to hear. Merilynn briefly caught Eve Camlan's gaze, saw the horror in her eyes, and sent her the gentlest smile she could muster. Then she rose and stretched, nonchalantly leaving the campfire circle to saunter—at least she hoped it looked like sauntering—twenty feet to the lake's edge.

The dark water rippled with silver moonlight. It was hard to be sure, but she thought she caught brief glimmers of deep golden light far out beneath the surface.

"Holly?" she whispered. "Holly, where are you?"

2

"This isn't a very bright idea," Sam Penrose whispered to Merilynn after they successfully sneaked out of the little cabin full of sleeping girls. It was just past midnight as she rubbed sleep from her eyes, then bent to tie the laces on her Nikes. "I don't know why I let you talk me into this. We're really pushing our luck."

"We're fine, but hurry up," Merilynn whispered, drowning in impatience. "We have to get away from the cabins or they really will hear us and we'll be caught. And you know what that means!"

Sam stood up straight, zipped her windbreaker, and made a face. "Yeah. They'll make us practice cheers for a couple extra hours."

"Or expel us!" Merilynn suggested.

"Nah, they'd only do that if they found out about our trip to the island," Sam said. "Hmm. That wouldn't be a bad thing, would it? Not as bad as extra practice. God, this place is *so* stupid. I think I'd like to get expelled!"

Merilynn studied Sam's expression, but in the moonlight she couldn't quite decide if the girl was joking or serious. Joking, probably, but she couldn't take a chance. Though she didn't give a rat's butt about the cheering either, Merilynn sure as heck didn't want to get sent home early. "They can't find out about yesterday unless one of us tells them. And then they'd find out about Eve too, and she loves this place. We have to keep it a total secret for her sake."

"We wouldn't have to mention her." As she spoke, Sam started leading the way toward the boathouse, walking quietly, keeping to the shadows.

Merilynn followed, pleased. Despite all her griping, there was no way Sam Penrose could resist an adventure. "If you hate cheering, why'd you come to this camp?" she asked as soon as they were away from the cabins.

"To find out what makes girls want to be cheerleaders."

"What do you mean?"

Sam halted in the shadows of an old oak tree. "Well, I want to know if cheerleaders are born that way or brainwashed."

"What way?" Merilynn grinned.

"You know, all stupid and bouncy and wanting to, well, cheer. I mean, *where* does that come from?" Sam leaned forward, peering intently at Merilynn, as if she really expected an answer. "Well?" she said after a few seconds of silence. "Where does that cheery stuff come from?"

Merilynn shrugged. "I dunno."

"You're not one of them."

"No." Merilynn put her hand over her mouth to quell incipient giggles. "But then why am I here?"

Sam's eyebrow twitched. "That's obvious. You're here for the ghost stories. You'll put up with anything for a stupid ghost story."

"Ghost stories aren't stupid. Some of them are, sure, but the ones around here are great!"

Sam smiled. "Yeah, I understand. You're pursuing an interest. I mean one that involves your brain."

"Kinda."

"You're more like me. I mean, that's why we're here, right? We're both researching things. Come on," Sam added, starting to walk again. "Let's get this over with."

Merilynn hurried to catch up. "Maybe they're born that way."

"Huh?"

"The cheerleaders."

Sam nodded, leading them toward the boathouse. "I guess they must be. Have you noticed, though, there's more than one kind? At least three kinds."

"No. Tell me."

"Okay, first you've got all these airheads who are wearing makeup and padded bras and spray hair spray all over the place. They talk about boys nonstop, and all they want is to be popular. They snipe at each other a lot. They don't read, they don't think."

"That describes most of them," Merilynn admitted. "But the counselors are all cheerleaders."

"*College* cheerleaders. Smart, cream of the crop. Most of the girls here won't ever get past high school."

"What other kinds are there?"

"The rare kind is Eve. She's *such* a mystery."

"How is she a mystery? She doesn't snipe, she reads."

"That's what I mean. She has values; she's better than them. But she wants to be a cheerleader so bad it hurts."

"Eve is pure," Merilynn said. "She's real, and she's nice. I think she'll be a counselor here someday."

Sam's smile flashed in the moonlight. "Yeah. I don't know why she wants to waste her brain yelling rhymes. She's not like most of them."

"Who says she's wasting her brain?"

"Come on. You know how stupid all that jumping around and talking about 'team spirit' is. It's hokey."

"To you, it is." Merilynn hesitated. "And to me. But my ghost story thing probably seems hokey to you, and I can think of a lot less goofy things to do than study cheerleaders."

"Yeah, okay. Different strokes."

"Father says sometimes you just have to accept that things exist or that things happen, and accept you'll never know why."

"I disagree."

"Of course you do. You're going to be a detective when you grow up. You'll solve mysteries and catch criminals."

"Investigative reporter," Sam corrected.

"Okay."

"You know the difference, don't you, between a cop and a reporter?" she asked as they reached the boathouse and dock.

"You're such a snob, Sam. Of course I know the difference. Probably most of the airheads do too."

Up went the eyebrow. Down again. Sam nodded. "Okay, but say it again and I'll punch you."

All in all, a good reaction. "What's the third kind of cheerleader?"

They stepped onto the dock and approached a rowboat. Sam climbed down, then held her hand out to help Merilynn into the bobbing vessel before sitting down. "The third type is the alpha cheerleader."

"Alpha?" Merilynn undid the tie to the dock, then sat and took an oar before turning to look at Sam, on the bench behind her. "What do you mean?"

"Alpha is what they call the leader of a pack of dogs. Every group has alphas. They're dominant."

Merilynn nodded. "The super-bitches. The ones all the airheads want to impress."

"Exactly. It's like they're cloned or something. They all do their makeup just alike, and you never see them do it. It's as if they have it tattooed on. And if any of them are stuffing their bras, I haven't been able to tell."

Merilynn giggled. "You're checking out their boobs?"

"Not like *that!*" She paused. "The alphas give me the creeps."

"The Stepford Cheerleaders," Merilynn said, shivering as a cold-water breeze fingered her hair. "They look all bubbly and friendly, but they're hard-core bitches."

"They're who the airheads want to be." Sam dipped her oar into the water. "I'll row from the left, you take the right."

"Okay, let's go."

"Where?"

"Out there." Merilynn stared across the dark water, trying to make out Applehead Island, thinking she saw the dark hulk of it, but not sure. Maybe she just imagined she could see it.

"We're *not* going to the island," Sam said. "That's not part of the plan."

Merilynn shook her head. "No." She pointed at the water west of the island, about halfway between it and the shore. "There. That's where the ghost lights are usually seen. I checked the maps. The center of town was about there."

"Okay," Sam said. "Start rowing."

3

Oars dipped and stirred, black water lapped at the sides of the boat. Merilynn listened for imaginary wolves, knowing she wouldn't hear any chorus of lonely howls, but hoping anyway because it would make everything even more fun. *Spookier! Mysterious!* Somewhere, not too far away, an owl hooted, and its call was answered by softer *hoo-hoos* from farther off. Merilynn thought she heard the flap of wings over the water sounds.

Beyond midnight, the moon too low to cast much light, the forest felt alive, full of eyes hidden in darkness, peering at them from between the limbs of pines and clusters of oaks leaves. The trees were too far away and too dark for her to see any detail, but she could call up images from hundreds of twilights spent in her yard sitting alone, or with Father, watching faces appear in the shrubs and bushes and trees, as sunlight drained away. She imagined them now, leafy green faces. Momentarily, her thoughts turned to the island and the green, green eyes she'd gazed into, and wondered if they belonged to the Green Ghost and if he was a nature god, a real Green Man.

"So, what'd you think of Allie's ghost story?" Sam asked, breaking Merilynn's reverie. "Do you think she saw Holly Gayle's ghost?"

She was trying to sound as if nothing was getting to her, not the story, not being alone on the haunted lake, but Merilynn could hear a faint quaver in her voice. She smiled to herself. "I don't know," she said, careful not to give the other girl any ammo; it was more fun to keep her nervous. "It was a pretty typical ghost story."

"What's *that* supposed to mean?" Sam feigned sarcasm.

"It means it's either more likely to be a made-up story, you know, like they saw some leaves blowing or a hunk of plastic or something and just *thought* it was a ghost. Or it means it's more likely true."

"Why?"

"Because Father says stories are patterned in truth. Real ghosts inspire the patterns in the stories. Allie's story fit just right." She paused, then added, "The clues are all there."

"Clues?" Sam's voice was suddenly a lot friendlier.

"Clues," Merilynn affirmed, feeling as if she'd caught a big fish, the word the hook.

"Such as?"

"Well, if somebody tells you a ghost talked to them, that's a clue that it's probably a fake story. Ghosts don't do that. I mean, they can talk, sort of, sometimes, but it's probably never personal. They don't call you by name, at least that's what Father says."

"They don't think."

"They? Oh, the ghosts?"

"Yeah."

"Father says they don't think, at least not much. They're always more like pictures or recordings than real people, he says."

"What do *you* think?"

"What's this? The third degree?"

"I'm investigating. So, tell me what you think."

"I think I don't know." Merilynn knew that was the only answer Sam would accept. If she told her the truth—that she thought, hoped maybe, that ghosts were sometimes real spirits, the other girl would go all sarcastic in a heartbeat. "I'm investigating too."

They paddled in silence for a few more minutes, slowly coming to verge upon the part of the lake Merilynn wanted to explore. She slowed her stroke, and Sam followed suit. "Start watching for lights."

Sam didn't say anything for several moments. Finally, she spoke. "You don't really expect to see anything, do you? I mean, the town's long gone. It can't light up. Back then, it wouldn't even have had electricity."

"They had candles and oil lamps." *Oops.* She regretted the words the moment she said them.

Sam snorted so loudly that the sound seemed to echo across the lake, silencing the crickets for half a minute. Merilynn hadn't even noticed them until they stopped, but when the seesaw chirping started again it seemed deafening.

"Candles and oil lamps don't light underwater," Sam remarked softly. She must have startled herself when she startled the crickets.

Eyes on the water, Merilynn said, "Lights can be ghosts, just like people can be ghosts."

"And lights can be reflections of stars or flashlights or the moon, just like a human ghost might be a plastic grocery bag flying in the wind. Or a piece of newspaper, or—"

"Look!" Lifting her oar from the water, Merilynn stared at a dim amber glow that seemed to emanate from far below. She heard Sam set her oar down in the boat. "Do you see it? Straight down on the right."

"I see it. It must be a reflection."

"Of what?"

"I don't know. A star?"

"That's stupid."

"What?"

"It's stupid. You want to solve the mystery so bad that you'd rather think it's a reflection of a star than admit you don't know what the heck it is."

"I suppose *you* do?"

"I know it's not a star . . . Look. There's another one!"

"Oh, wow. There're more coming on! Do you see them?"

"Yes." Merilynn felt delight and a shiver of fear as the dim lights began to come to life, mostly faint, but some growing brighter and larger. Some looked deeper down than others. There were a dozen now, all varying shades of amber.

And then, a larger, closer cluster of lights began to appear. They were multicolored. "The stained glass," she said.

"What?"

"The colored lights. I read about that. An old church down there had a stained-glass window. It's, like, the *ultimate* sighting. Samantha, we are *so* lucky to see it." As she spoke, the glow brightened. It was small and far away, but so brilliant in its jewel tones of ruby, sapphire, gold, and emerald that it looked like a beacon.

"Holy crap," Sam murmured.

"I wonder if I could dive deep enough to see it without gear."

When Sam didn't reply, Merilynn tore her eyes away from the ghost lights for just an instant. Sam was staring at her. "What?"

"You're serious." There was awe in her voice. "You really want to go down there?"

Eyes back on the lights, Merilynn said, "Yes."

"It even makes *me* a little nervous, thinking of going down there."

"A *little* nervous? You sound like you're ready to pee your pants."

"Pretty much," Sam said softly. "I can't believe they didn't salvage a stained-glass window," she added, trying to sound businesslike.

"They did. It's at Greenbriar University. They put it in a window there."

Silence, long. Lights bloomed, some tracing street-like patterns like a tiny town seen from an airplane window at night. "If there's no window," Sam asked, "why can we see it?"

"It's a ghost of the window. Even if the real one was still down there, we couldn't see it. I mean, no divers are down there holding a spotlight behind a window."

"I know, I know. Merilynn?"

"What?"

"Yesterday, when we were coming back from the island, did you see anything?"

"No. I kept forgetting to look. Eve thought she saw some lights though. She told me. Did you see some?"

"Maybe. I didn't think about it much."

"You were thinking about the eyes we saw on the island?"

"No. That was just an animal."

"If you say so. What were you thinking about?" Below, a few tiny pinpoints of light moved along the dead roads. *Ghosts carrying lanterns? Or just lanterns? God, I want to find out!* As soon as she got home, she'd start bugging Father to let her take diving lessons.

"I was thinking about rowing and getting back before the bus brought the cheerleaders back from the field trip."

"Not the eyes?"

"Not much. That was just silly, that eye thing. Sillier than ghosts."

"But the eyes are a kind of ghost too. A nature ghost."

"Mountain lion. Cats' eyes glow in the dark."

"If you say so. I can't believe what we're seeing. This is so great!"

Sam stayed silent. Minutes passed and Merilynn just took in

the lights, trying to memorize the positions, trying to see the pattern in the church window. Wind gusted, making her draw her coat closer and cross her arms for warmth. "Sam?"

Sam didn't answer.

"Sam?"

Hairs prickling up, Merilynn turned to look at Samantha. The girl was staring at something in the water on the other side of the boat. "What?" Merilynn asked, turning to face her. "What are you looking at?"

Sam didn't reply, just stared down.

Merilynn looked.

A girl, dead-white of face, dark hair waving in tendrils around her head, hovered just beneath the surface. Her mouth was open in a silent scream and her dark eyes bored into Samantha's.

Merilynn tilted forward for a better look, delicious tingles running up and down her spine. "When the ghost lights appear," she quoted, "it means Holly Gayle is going to walk again."

Sam bent farther over, farther and farther, until Merilynn could barely see Holly Gayle's face. Suddenly, she felt real fear. "Sam, be careful."

Sam didn't respond, but brought her hand up and over the side of the boat, letting her fingers touch the surface of the black water.

"Don't. It's a dead body!" Merilynn blurted, all the ghost talk chased away. Dead bodies scared her, not ghosts, so that's what this had to be.

A bloodless hand, blue white and delicate, suddenly snaked up, the fingers emerging from the lake, to slither between Sam's splayed fingers.

"No!" Merilynn cried as the dead fingers started to curl around Sam's. She reached out and yanked Sam away from the edge of the boat.

Both stared at the fingers as they uncurled, fingers that didn't shine but seemed lit from within, making them much too easy to see in the darkness. Just like the rest of Holly Gayle.

The hand, fingers upright, slowly, almost regally, slid beneath the water. The girls carefully peered over the side of the boat and watched the pale phantom turn and glide, eel-like, back into the depths, her white dress pluming out around her.

"That wasn't a dead body," Sam said.

"I know."

"It was her. Holly Gayle. Did you hear her?"

"No! She said something?"

"Maybe. In my head."

"What did she say?"

"She wanted me to go with her." Sam nodded toward the water. "Down there."

"Why?"

"She wanted to show me something."

"What?"

"I don't know. But if you hadn't pulled me back, well, I think maybe I would have gone overboard."

"That wouldn't be good."

"No. Thanks, Merilynn. Look, the lights are fading."

Merilynn looked. Even the stained-glass jewel was dimming. Smaller lights began to wink out, as if extinguished by unseen hands. "That was amazing!" Too elated to be afraid now, she giggled. "I can't wait to tell—"

"*No*. You can't tell. They'd think we were nuts— and we'd get in trouble, remember?"

"Not *them*. Father. I can't wait to tell him. And Eve. We can tell Eve."

"You can tell your father. I don't know about Eve. She might freak."

"She's part of this."

"Not anymore. She made that pretty clear when we got back to shore."

"True."

"Telling her will give her nightmares."

Merilynn nodded.

"You can't talk about this to anyone but me while you're here," Sam ordered.

Merilynn knew she was right, but it would be torture, keeping her mouth shut. "I know."

"And if you ever tell anyone what happened to me, you're dead. Got it?" She picked up her oar, ready to go.

"I know," Merilynn murmured. Sam was being tough because she was scared, and that didn't bother her. "I won't embarrass you." She turned around, once again facing the prow, and grabbed her own oar.

Silently, they dipped the paddles into the water and began to turn the boat back toward camp. Merilynn looked into the water one last time. As she did, the stained-glass light wavered, then blinked out. "That was great."

"Yeah, great. Let's get out of here. One. Two. Three. Row!"

GREENBRIAR UNIVERSITY
TODAY

4

In the rolling hills of this part of coastal central California, autumn had started to dye the leaves of *Liquidambar* trees shades of red, orange, and gold by mid-October. In Caledonia, on the coast, not so far away, green still ruled, but here, only fifteen miles inland, wrapped in small mountains, nature was already painting a scene that delighted Kendra Phillips. Sitting at her desk, looking out at the lawn and gardens behind Gamma House, she felt a small stir of pleasure at the sight. She was pleased that she had noticed at all. The death of Eve Camlan, her roommate, had been a sorry blow, one that knocked awareness of her own life right out of her. She had spent the few weeks since the memorial service deep in her books. Her new sisters tried to talk to her about it, but she didn't want to talk, and they understood. Or seemed to.

Below, she saw Heather working in the herb garden that edged one side of the lawn. A couple of the J-clone cheerleaders were having an impromptu practice, working on some sort of acrobatic move that involved tumbling and landing in the splits. It looked painful, and she turned away because watching them reminded her of Eve.

There had been a short, typed suicide note, but no body. There was talk that she'd left the note because she was running away. The girls all paid homage to this notion; it was what they said to Kendra most often. "You know, I'll bet she's just fine. I'll bet she decided to go to Europe for a year. Her parents wouldn't have approved. She couldn't tell them."

Bullshit. Kendra had seen her ghost. Genevieve Camlan had

neither run away nor committed suicide. Something had happened to her. She'd been murdered. Kendra felt it in her bones.

She said nothing to anyone about her suspicions— *they aren't suspicions, I know I'm right!*—everything had been so cut-and-dry. The police in Greenbriar weren't even real cops; they were campus cops, even in town. The university funded them. *Owned them.* Sure, they'd asked some questions about Eve's state of mind and other friends, all the stuff that cops were supposed to ask, but it was as if no one even wanted to suggest foul play. Maybe it was because so much of it seemed to go on around Greenbriar.

That stuff the sisters said about Eve's parents not wanting her to go to Europe turned out to have some truth to it. When they came to collect her things, Kendra had come right out and asked them about it. It turned out that Eve had talked about going, briefly, but her parents discouraged it—and Eve hadn't argued, mainly because she didn't want her cheerleading skills to atrophy.

So, that was a possibility. Except that Kendra had seen her ghost. She'd *felt* her, felt the cold, seen that she wasn't solid, seen the anguish in her eyes, heard it in the voice that she heard with her mind, not her ears. She couldn't remember the words. But tell anyone about that? Funny farm time. *Kendra believes the story about the Phantom Hitchhiker too. And maybe the Hook.* She'd almost talked to Sam Penrose, but the would-be journalist had been silent on the subject. Who knew where her loyalties lay? Granny always said never to take chances around people you didn't know. It was good advice.

Someone knocked on the door, three light raps.

"Come in." Kendra marked her place in the folklore text and turned in her chair as the door opened. "Merilynn?"

"Am I interrupting you?"

"No, of course not. I'm just surprised to see you."

The girl with long red hair and brilliant green eyes stepped into the room and closed the door behind her. "I understand. We've never really talked and, well, you seemed so tight with

Eve. You probably knew she didn't like me, so I've stayed away."

"Sit down."

"Thanks." Merilynn took the other chair. Eve's chair.

"She didn't dislike you, you know."

"She sure didn't want to be around me."

"No. You frightened her."

"I figured that was it. Back at camp, she was so frightened after we took a trip to the island."

"She told me about it."

Merilynn's eyes opened wide in surprise. "Really? I sort of thought she'd blocked the memory. Sam and I never even told her what we did the next night. I was going to, back then. I couldn't wait. Sam said it would freak her out, so I didn't."

She looked down at her hands, then back up at Kendra, her eyes sparkling with tears. One escaped, ran down her cheek, but she wiped it away as if it were nothing. Not at all like Eve. Merilynn looked fragile, but Eve had actually been the delicate one. "I'm so sorry she's dead. When I found out she joined this house, I had all these ideas about how I'd finally get to tell her about the ghost lights and seeing Holly and stuff." She paused. "You must think I'm nuts."

"Folklore's my thing. My family lived in Applehead, then Greenbriar before moving to civilization. Most of my relatives—ancestors, mostly—worked here. I know the stories."

"Do you believe in ghosts?"

Kendra hesitated. She didn't dare reveal much to a stranger. "Let's say I'm open-minded. I've seen some things that might be called ghosts."

"Have you ever seen the ghost lights? The town under the lake?"

"No. I've never been there at night."

"Why not?"

"Well, I didn't go to the camp, and I didn't grow up in town." Merilynn nodded. "They're amazing. I want to go back."

"Did you see Holly Gayle?"

The redhead nodded. "Sam and I both did." She giggled, putting her hand over her mouth. "But don't tell her I told you. The night we saw her, she swore me to secrecy." Another giggle. "She threatened to kill me if I ever dragged her name into any stories I decided I just had to tell."

Kendra smiled. "Well, I hope you'll tell me. Stories are my thing."

"I'd like to. I was wondering about something."

"What?"

"Well, just say no if you don't like the idea."

"What's the idea?"

"I'm in a room with two other girls. It's okay, but one's a cheerleader and the other just, well, sort of oozes sorority spirit. Know what I mean?"

Kendra nodded. "All too well."

"If you don't have a new roommate picked out, would I do? I'm pretty quiet. I don't take up much space." A slow, shy smile spread her face, revealing impish dimples. "I'm house-trained."

Kendra looked Merilynn up and down, mentally calling up Granny's rules. Though Merilynn struck her as offbeat, it was a good offbeat. She felt okay— Kendra wasn't picking up anything weird. Granny, she thought, would approve.

Standing up, she walked over to the other girl and held out her hand. "I think you'd make a great roommate. Welcome."

Merilynn rose, but ignored her hand; instead, putting her hands on her shoulders and leaning forward to plant a quick kiss on Kendra's forehead, she said, "What time is it?"

"Almost noon."

"Crap. I've gotta run or I'll be late for class. Will you still be here at one?"

"Sure."

"Because we should talk a little more before you say yes. You need to know more about me. I'm a little weird."

Kendra smiled. "I'll be expecting you."

"Thanks!" Merilynn called as she fled the room.

5

"There are four primary tastes," Malory Thomas said without consulting her index card of notes, "and four basic kinds of taste buds to taste them." She paused, glanced at Professor Tongue, then at the roomful of students. "The tastes are salty, sour, sweet, and"—another glance at Tongue—"spicy."

Girlish giggles erupted here and there.

"Since this is a public-speaking class," Professor Piccolo interrupted, "we won't criticize your alleged facts."

Malory batted her long black eyelashes. "I was joking. The fourth taste is bitter. I prefer spicy. Don't you, Professor?"

"A good point, as long as your talk is intended to be more amusing than instructional." Tongue looked flushed but managed a tight smile. "Continue, Ms. Thomas."

"Taste buds are little protuberances and you can see them with the"—pregnant pause, lower voice— "naked eye."

More giggles.

"How many of you have studied a tongue?" she asked throatily. "Your own, or your lover's?"

About half the women raised their hands, some tentatively, many giggling, a couple shooting shamelessly straight up. The dozen males were all leaning forward now, staring intently at Malory with big stupid grins on their faces and, undoubtedly, big throbbing boners in their shorts.

"Ms. Thomas—"

"Let's talk about tastes," she continued, cutting Piccolo off at the pass. "What does a banana taste like? Primarily sweet. How about a tongue? Who knows what a tongue tastes like? Some of you may be able to taste your own tongue, if you've inherited the ability to roll your tongue into different shapes like this." She opened her mouth in an O, then stuck her tongue out, curling it into a tube shape.

Just like the tubes forming in the jocks' Levi's.

She unrolled her tongue and let it fold in against itself, pivoting a little to make sure everyone, including the very good professor, could see. Then she stopped and said, as brightly as a young Mary Tyler Moore, "Okay, everybody, try it!"

"Ms. Thomas," Professor Tongue said in a voice just a little deeper and rougher than normal, "I think *your* demonstration is enough."

She smiled at him. "Please, you told us to get our audience involved, Professor P."

"Yes, but . . ."

"But what?" She opened her eyes wide, all false innocence, and batted the lashes some more. "Is there something wrong with my report? Does it bother you?"

Tongue, never rising from his desk in the right corner—she knew he was in no shape to stand up— looked uncomfortably at the class. All the females stared at him; most of the males were watching Malory in her carefully chosen black skirt and matching pullover sweater. Her enameled rose sorority pin showed prominently on one breast, pinned so that the pink bud would make people think of sex even though her clothing, as always, was tasteful. And they rarely were smart enough to figure the trick.

"I'm not sure how appropriate . . ." Again, the professor's words trailed off.

"Professor?" she asked sweetly. "I don't understand. What's wrong?"

"Nothing, nothing. Go on." He looked at his hands as he spoke.

"I'm just talking about something every one of us has in our mouths. It's there every day of our lives, but we never think about what an amazing organ it is." She smiled like Miss America.

"Go ahead, Ms. Thomas. You're quite right."

"Now, everyone, stick out your tongues." She caught the eye of big blond quarterback Art Caliburn and wouldn't give it back. "Let's see what you can do."

She never tired of the power that came to her when people obeyed her, and she basked in it now as two-thirds of the class had their tongues out, and half of that number were gleefully miming various forms of oral sex. Malory cast her gaze over the group, finally coming to Samantha Penrose, unwilling to show any tongue, but perfectly willing to look her in the eye. That was a rush; hardly anyone ever dared try it, but Samantha never failed. That was the primary reason Malory had let her into the sorority, despite the others' trepidation about the journalism major's loyalty.

Sam Penrose was special in many ways. A natural leader, she could go far in the world as an alumna of Fata Morgana. She would do great things for the sisterhood if she truly understood loyalty. And if not, she would probably make a fine sacrifice to the Forest Knight. Right after Eve Camlan escaped her fate, Malory had decided to use Sam as a replacement during All Hallows Eve, the next likely night for such a sacrifice. But in the weeks since Eve had left, Samantha had refrained from digging into the "suicide," and she'd made it clear to Malory that this was because of her loyalty to the Gamma sisters.

That was promising. Very promising. She nodded at Sam, Sam nodded back, almost imperceptibly. Sam was going to be fun. Later. One way or another.

Two seats over was Merilynn Morris, who was about to become a Fata Morgana, though she didn't know it yet. Merilynn, looking puckish yet angelic— *as she should*—was completely involved with her own tongue, looking cross-eyed at it. She had stuck it out as far as she could, curled the sides up, and was now trying to touch her nose. Malory smiled. Though the girl couldn't quite reach her goal, she definitely had latent talents.

Merilynn brought her tongue back down, still cross-eyed with interest, and stuck it straight out. It was a healthy shade of dark pink with a pointed tip.

Just like her mother's.

"Ms. Thomas," the King of Tongues said, "I think that's enough time for your demonstration."

"But, Professor Piccolo," she said, turning to him and wetting her lips, "I saw everyone but you try it. Can you curl *your* tongue?"

The classroom went silent. Twenty shades of red flashed over Piccolo's face before he spoke. "As your instructor, I respectfully decline."

"Please?" came a couple of girlish voices from somewhere in the sea of desks. Giggles erupted like brushfires.

"Finish your talk, please, Ms. Thomas. Class is almost over."

Malory nodded, seeing the time. She had barely begun to warm them up, hadn't even started to weave her spells over the room. "Professor, I need more time to finish my speech. You have to admit, I'm not getting my full thirty minutes today."

"I'd think you'd find that to be a relief, Ms. Thomas."

Students chuckled. Malory didn't like that a bit. "Professor, I want the best grade I'm capable of getting. I'd like another chance to excite you with my talk."

Now they giggled. That was more like it.

"We don't really have time." He hesitated. "You may finish your speech after class. I have a free period."

"Can we stay?" one of the guys asked. Others seconded the notion.

"Of course," Piccolo said quickly.

Malory smiled, knowing he preferred to have witnesses when dealing with any female student. It was a well-known fact that young ladies frequently made appointments for private discussions during his office hours. Though he kept his tongue hidden, and played down his reputation as rumor, the girls—and an occasional guy—wanted the truth. He'd told Malory he always engaged straight male student assistants, and always kept one in his office when a coed came calling. "You know, just like a male gynecologist keeps a nurse in the exam room when a patient climbs into the saddle and puts her feet in the stirrups." The Tongue liked westerns. Malory found it cute most of the time.

The buzzer sounded, ending the class. No males dared stand. Behind his desk, Piccolo said, "Class dismissed. Anyone who would care to hear the rest of Ms. Thomas's talk, please come back by one-fifteen."

A few of the girls stood up and milled around. Malory smiled at Art Caliburn, then smiled more broadly as Merilynn Morris approached, hugging her books in front of her breasts like a little girl.

"Hello, Sister," Malory said with as much warmth as she was capable of.

"Hi, Malory."

"Class dismissed!" Piccolo repeated. "All of you, out of here. You can return in fifteen minutes. Shoo!"

Merilynn bestowed her Madonna-like smile. "You gave him an erection," she said softly. "That's why he's still sitting there and telling us to leave."

Malory nodded. "Sweetie, I gave them *all* erections. Look behind you. The boys are all holding their book bags in front of them."

Merilynn looked, turned back to Malory, beaming. "How'd you do that?"

"What?"

"Give them erections. So fast."

"They're college boys. They get erections just from breathing."

"You didn't, ah, *do* anything?"

"Whatever do you mean?"

"Nothing. It just sort of seemed like you wove a spell or something."

Not yet. But I will. "Thank you. That means I gave a good talk. Let's get out of here before the professor throws us out."

They walked outside and down the hall to the water fountain. Merilynn drank, then said, "I wish I could stay for the rest of your talk."

"You can't stay? Really?"

"No, not today. I have to run. I'm sorry."

Malory smiled. "I'm sorry too. I'll see you later, at the house."

"Okay. Good luck."

Merilynn walked quickly down the hall toward the exit. Malory watched her with mixed emotions. All in all, it was probably best that she left; she was too aware of the magic and until she became a Fata Morgana, keeping her in the dark was a good idea.

6

"I'm back," Merilynn said after Kendra opened the door, "and before you say yes, I should tell you I'm kind of weird."

Kendra smiled. "Sometimes weird is good."

"Or not."

Closing the door, Kendra went to the little fridge by her desk and took out two bottles of water. She handed one to Merilynn, who had already flopped onto Eve's desk chair.

"Thank you." Merilynn got the top off in record time and started to drink.

"Did you run all the way back? You sound out of breath."

"And I'm thirsty, too!" She took another drink and set the bottle on the desk. "That's so good. Anyway, I did run. Well, I sort of trotted. The class ran over a little. Malory's in it."

"You're in a class with a senior?"

"It's public speaking. It's totally mixed. Freshmen, seniors, jocks, brains. I'm there because I'm bad at it. I mumble."

"No, you don't."

"Only in front of groups."

"Oh." Kendra took a pull on her own bottle. "Malory is the last person I'd expect to find in a public-speaking class. I mean, what does she need it for?"

Merilynn savored the moment. "She doesn't need it," she said very softly. "She *likes* it. She's an exhibitionist."

"Really?"

"I'm almost positive. She gave a speech on tongues. Every guy in the room had a woody. It was hysterical. She even made simple facts about taste buds sound dirty."

"Tell me more."

"I will. Later, okay? I want to have our talk and confess all my weird shit to you and find out if you'll still have me."

"Confess away."

"Do you remember when they made us all announce our majors and I didn't want to give one?"

"Sure, I remember. I liked that you didn't care what anyone else thought." She hesitated. "And you should know that it helped Eve. She didn't have a major picked out either and was very embarrassed. You made her feel better."

"That's good." Merilynn smiled. "Poor little Evie. She was afraid of everything when she was a kid. I guess she never got over it? Being easily spooked, I mean?"

"She seemed fine," Kendra said after looking toward the ceiling and considering. "Maybe a little on the timid side. I didn't know her very long, but I think she might have been the only person I've ever met who honestly seemed, I don't know . . ."

"Earnestly good? Kind?" Merilynn asked. That's how she remembered her from Applehead.

Kendra nodded. "Exactly. And that worried me at first. Most people that come on that way are seriously *not* good or kind. I like people to have some faults. Makes them human, like me. Know what I mean?"

"Yes, I do." Merilynn had liked Kendra the first time they'd met, but she'd stayed away to spare Eve. She saw now that she'd been right about her— Kendra was a good guy. "I saw how you watched out for Evie. You're just like Sam."

Kendra raised a hand. "Stop! Hold it right there. I don't know if I want to be just like Sam. I admire her, but she's a little scary."

"Sam? Scary?" Merilynn loved Kendra's reaction. It was typical. She'd seen it as a kid in camp and she'd seen it at Greenbriar.

"She's, uh . . ."

"Intense?"

Kendra nodded. "That's it. I hope I don't come off like that."

"No, you're much more approachable." She laughed. "I don't think I'd want you pissed off at me though!"

Kendra laughed. "Can I take that as a compliment?"

"Yes. See, if I'd said that to Sam, she would have just said, 'Thank you,' instead of asking if it was a compliment. You have better social skills. But don't let her scare you. She's all warm and fuzzy inside. She'd never admit it, though. She watched out for Eve like you did."

"Thank you."

"So, do you want to hear my faults?"

"Okay. But why'd you bring up your major? When they pressed you, you said chemistry, right?"

"I think so. Yes. Maybe I said several things. I like to be creative with my answers. But I do like chemistry."

"So, what's your horrible secret? A traveling lab? You're a mad scientist in training?"

Merilynn finished her water, feeling good about coming to Kendra. "I'm taking some normal chemistry classes, but it's a more old-fashioned kind of chemistry I'm *really* interested in. They don't have classes in it. I study on my own and take classes related to it. Like chemistry and botany."

"So, what is it?"

"Well, it's weird. And I don't have a suitcase full of chemicals, but I *do* have a box full of the stuff I study on my own. It's weird." She watched Kendra for a reaction, but got none. "Don't worry, I don't make crack or grow pot in my closet."

Kendra smiled. "So tell me the worst."

"Herbs. I study herbal medicine." She studied more than medicine, but didn't think she should say so. Not yet anyway.

"Well, that's fascinating!" Kendra shook her head. "There always used to be an herbalist in our family. My granny's kind of a half-assed herbalist. She learned a lot when she was young, but never practiced, except for tacking rosemary on doors to keep ghosts out, and things like that. Anyway, I have no problem with your herbs." She paused. "They don't smell gross or anything?"

"Some smell gross, but you'd have to open the containers and stick your nose in to know it."

"Well, then I don't even know why you thought I'd think that was a fault. You know I'm mainly studying folklore-type subjects, right?"

"Yes. That's one of the reasons I thought we might get along. I'm interested in those things too." Merilynn hesitated. "But my herbs and stuff? I have to tell you. Sometimes I do weird things with them."

"Hey, as long as you don't turn 'em into incense and smoke up the room, I'm cool, otherwise. I just hate smoke."

"Even smoke that smells good?"

"Yeah. It messes with my sinuses."

Merilynn loved incense and had to hide her disappointment. "No smoke."

"So what do you do? Mix them? Turn them into powders and mysterious concoctions to cure warts?"

"Yes, pretty much. I can cure a wart. Do you have one?"

Kendra looked confused for a second, then smiled. "No. No warts. What else can you cure?"

"What've you got?"

"A craving for chocolate."

"I can cure that."

"Now?"

"I don't have my lab with me, but if I go get my stuff, I'll cure you quick."

"Okay."

Merilynn walked to the door. "I'll be right back. If it's okay."

"Of course it is. You live here now." Kendra consulted her wristwatch. "I have a class in forty-five minutes, so you'll be on your own moving in."

Merilynn laughed. "You're so nice. I was just going to get the cure for your craving. But if you don't mind, I'm done with classes for the day. I'd love to move in."

"Not a problem."

Merilynn started to open the door.

"Wait. I have one question."

She pushed the door closed. "What?"

"Do you have any other quirks?"

"I sleep in the nude."

"Oh . . . okay . . ."

Seeing Kendra's discomfort, Merilynn quickly said, "Just kidding."

"Good. I'm not sure I'd ever get used to that!"

"Do *you* have any quirks?"

"Me?" Kendra said. "I'm a regular paragon of virtue."

"So you don't keep Limburger cheese in your underwear drawer or anything weird like that?"

Her new roommate chuckled. "No, but now I'm worried. What made you think of such a thing?"

"I have no idea. But I'll be right back with the cure for chocolate craving."

"It doesn't taste nasty or anything, does it?"

"Heck no. There's only one cure for a chocolate craving, and I have a whole shoe box of it in *my* underwear drawer. Cadbury bars. Two dozen of them. Well, four have gone missing in the last two days. That's another reason I want out of the monkey house down the hall. Those two little bitches are going through my stuff and stealing from me! One of them got into my herbs and tried to smoke some. That girl turned green."

"What did she smoke?"

"Mugwort."

Kendra snorted. "If she mistook that for pot . . ." She shook her head, smiling.

"I don't really *know*. She didn't admit it. I could smell it, she was sick, and half my supply was gone."

"People used to burn mugwort to get rid of ghosts," Kendra said, locking eyes with Merilynn.

"They still do." The two studied each other. It felt good.

"Then go, before they steal any more chocolate. Better bring the whole box back just to be safe. I'm not a thief."

Merilynn made her Gollum face and voice. "What's the cheerleader got in its pocketses?"

Merilynn left, closing the door behind her. Kendra's laughter trailed her. As she approached her old room, she wondered how Kendra would react if she knew *everything* she did with her herbs and crystals, and vials of oil, and decided, overall, she felt pretty optimistic.

7

"Tongues are amazing," purred Malory Thomas, pleased that nearly all of Professor Piccolo's public-speaking class had come back and were silently hanging on her every word. "They have no bones, and yet we can make them go stiff." She batted her lashes at Art Caliburn. He might be a pleasant ride. "The tongue and the penis are the only organs capable of this feat—"

"Ms. Thomas, this isn't sex ed."

The protest was weak, at best, and she ignored him. "The feminine equivalent of the penis does share these qualities, but it's such a tiny little thing, you can see why I don't really include it with the larger organs. Of course, ladies, we all know that that's one place where size doesn't matter."

The class was too excited now to giggle. As she spoke aloud, she silently wove little power spells over the room, harnessing the sexual energy that emanated from the students in threads so thick it seemed to ooze from their pores, pulling it all together, male and female energy, into one big psychic jolt waiting to happen. Pulling and pulling, slowly, tenderly, like good foreplay.

"These organs have something else in common. Does anyone know what that might be?"

The room was silent but for the sound of breathing. Students, male and female, stared hard at her. Piccolo said nothing, but she could feel his eyes caressing her ass. "The organs are the most sensitive on our bodies." She glanced at the professor but he was looking at his hands, folded together on his desk, no doubt to keep them from trembling. Smiling, she turned back to the students. "Who wants to take a guess? Of the penis and the tongue, which one's tip is the most sensitive? Art? Do you know?"

The quarterback reddened as she drilled him with her eyes. Nostrils flared, as did his aura. Normally, she purposely paid no attention to auras—she didn't need to see them to know how people felt, and they could be quite annoying—but his grew so strong and spiky that it couldn't be ignored. She wished Meri-lynn had remained. It would be interesting to know if the girl could see the pulsing purple-red colors that surrounded him. She approached his front-row seat and stood close enough to bask in his energy, to feed on it. "Art? Do you know?"

"Know what?" he managed.

"Which is more sensitive? The tip of your tongue or the tip of your penis?"

His jaw worked, but like Piccolo, he seemed to have run out of words. She backed off. "Anyone else?" She scanned faces, noted that there were some new ones mixed in, like Spence Lake, Art's buddy.

"The tongue," a female voice said, "is the most sensitive organ."

"Samantha Penrose," Malory said with delight, spotting the young woman at the rear of the room, mostly hidden behind Frank Steiner, the incredible hulking golden boy of the Green-briar wrestling squad.

"Are you sure?" she asked, walking back to see her up close.

"I'm sure," Sam said.

"Then I'm happy to tell you that you're correct." Up close, she could sense a strong pulse of sensuality emanating from her young sorority sister, but Sam Penrose was holding it close, not letting it escape. It was hard to read, so Malory let herself see Sam's aura. Held tight to her body, it was shades of orange, red, and purple, a narrow silhouette. Her normal aura, golden in tone, shot farther out, surrounding her body like the sun's corona. *A control freak.* Slightly disturbed by the strength and color of the Penrose aura—*I should have looked her over this way before*—Malory reached down and touched Sam's shoulder, weaving a special spell as she did.

Samantha caught her breath as the narrow orangered-purple stripe of sexuality doubled in size. She looked at Malory with sharp eyes muddled with a lust she no doubt didn't know she possessed. Malory quickly withdrew her hand and turned, walking to the front of the class. When she arrived in front of the blackboard and turned around, Sam had already begun to pull the sensual colors back to their former size. *Amazing strength.*

Excited by the brute willpower of the girl, she knew she wouldn't rest until she broke it down. That would come in time. "We use our tongues for many purposes besides taste," she began. "And animals use them for even more things than we do. Cats and dogs use it as a ladle to scoop up water. Watch a cat sometime and you'll see something amazing. Cats don't do this—" She extended her tongue and dipped it down and up, as if she were lapping water. She paused, soaking up the doubled energy in the room, taking it, winding it into a ball of psychic sexual power.

Finally, she continued. "Cats do it a different way. Like this—" Now she slowly pushed her tongue out from between her lips and curled it under, down, and then up into her mouth, like a butterfly sipping nectar from a flower.

At the back of the room, something stirred in the air. Still sensing auras, she followed the feeling and saw brilliant white light flashing around Frank Steiner. His eyes squeezed closed, his mouth in a grimace, his big body was stretched and stiff at his desk. Malory watched his secret orgasm until everyone else turned to see what she was looking at.

Spence Lake started to laugh first. Fearing he'd break the tension in the room, she wrapped his tongue in silent words, silencing him, turning his thoughts—and the other students'—back to their own desires. No one even noticed when Steiner grunted and looked around, his face the color of embarrassment.

"Animals use their tongues to clean their own fur or to groom one another. Cats, again, are the creatures to watch. They excel at it. We humans sometimes lick one another as well, but not to clean, unless it involves sex and food. Who hasn't fantasized about licking whipped cream off a lover?"

Sexual tension flared even higher. She gathered it to her and looked back at Piccolo—his reaction was so strong she could feel it from behind. He was still looking at his hands.

"So, when we lick another person, we are really showing affection or desire. We do this with something as simple as a kiss when we let our tongues twine and dance with our lover's."

The tension was so thick now that the air seemed fogged and she could see the ball she'd accumulated, as big as a basketball, glowing before her. She wondered if Merilynn would have seen it as well. Looking over the faces as she spoke, she saw that a young man with dreadlocks—she couldn't remember his name— appeared to see it, though it probably just looked that way. Most likely he was staring at her—but not at her face, as the others were. "Animals," she continued, dismissing him as she prepared to release the ball, "do the same thing, using their tongues to greet one another or their owners. Dogs are so good at this that sometimes women have been known to encourage them to lick their genitalia." Weaving words of power, weaving a fog around the ball so that no one would remember exactly what happened, she continued to talk. "Of course, dogs' tongues are soft. If you prefer a rougher sensation, you can pour a little tuna oil over your clitoris to get your pussycat to—"

Now! The ball of energy burst like fireworks, shooting up and out and over the students, raining across them. Every student body in the room started to arch. Quickly, Malory stepped among the desks to bask in it.

Men grunted, experiencing orgasms longer than they imagined possible. *Too bad they won't remember why their shorts are soaked.* Some shrieked, regardless of gender. From Piccolo's desk came a hearty "Yeehaw!" a cry familiar to her. One girl, then two, ululated Xena style, and at least half the students invoked deities in true porno film fashion. One student, Diana Peckerwood, had thrown her large head back on her large body and breathlessly cried, "Yes! Yes! Yes!" at least two dozen times in a row, sounding like an ad for shampoo.

She looked at Art Caliburn and Spence Lake, saw grimacing pleasure. She looked at the guy with dreads, amused to see his eyes closed, his wide mouth spread in a huge blissful grin. *He could be fun too.* If she could get past his mellowness, into his animal side, he might be a true tiger.

She walked up to Samantha Penrose, pleased to see the closed eyes. The purples spiked through the golden aura, but they were controlled, as was Sam, who made no sound, but looked to be concentrating intensely. Beneath her lids, her eyes jittered back and forth. Orgasmic blush spread up from her neck, over her cheeks, and as Malory watched, even to her forehead.

And then she opened her eyes and looked into Malory's. Her gaze was straight and sharp with curiosity. In a hoarse voice, she asked, "What did you do?"

"Nothing. What did you do?"

"Yeehaw!" cried Professor Tongue, a second time. Frank Steiner stiffened again.

Sam Penrose started to look around the room. Malory put her hand on top of her shining dark hair, sending her into another orgasm, this one beyond control. Sam screamed like a horror movie queen. Malory put her hand over the girl's mouth, and was nearly bitten before she'd woven her screams into silent ones.

An orgy, she thought as she examined the other students one by one. An orgy with Tongue and Caliburn, with the guy with the dreadlocks, with Brittany, and most of all, with Samantha Penrose, the most controlled and most strongly orgasmic human female she had ever encountered. *Such a strong-willed creature, I should tame her a bit.*

Visions of handcuffs and hot candle wax dancing in her head, Malory strolled from the orgasmic classroom, knowing that as soon as she was gone, the spell would die away, leaving lots of confused but very relaxed and happy people to wonder what had happened.

8

"Puckwudgies," proclaimed Professor Daniel Mc-Cobb. Light chuckles erupted behind him as he wrote the word on the board, and died off as he turned around, his big old lion's head with its mane of white hair limning his face as if a thousand volts had just fed through him.

He smiled at this class, his favorite, Folklore of California. He had learned to smile years ago, after Vera pointed out that his rocky face intimidated students. That was good, of course, but unnecessary most of the time. With his puckish blue eyes and tangled Einsteinian brows, his little St. Nick-pursed mouth, Vera said he was part Santa and part Satan.

The classroom door opened and Jimmy Freeman, of the peaceful smile and wild dreadlocks, came in, looking a little sheepish. Jimmy was a good kid, so McCobb let him slip in without commenting on his tardiness.

"Puckwudgies," he repeated instead, tipping his head back to look at the students from over his reading glasses. "Are any of you familiar with the word?"

Kendra Phillips was the one to raise a hand.

"Yes?"

"It's a native word meaning 'little people of the forest,' and refers to nature elementals. They're a variation on fairies or gnomes."

"Yes, exactly. The word is found throughout the states in various but similar forms. For example, in the Algonquin dialect of the northeastern states, they were Puckwudjinies, which translates into 'little vanishing people.' They considered these beings to be somewhere between this world and the spirit world, usually invisible, but occasionally seen.

"It's interesting to note the resemblance to European words. Shakespeare's Puck in *A Midsummer Night's Dream* is a good example. He's an elf of sorts, a king of the forest. It probably derives from the old Gothic word, Puke, which is a name for minor spirits in Teutonic dialects." The name brought expected giggles. He waited for the students to get it out of their systems, then continued. "There's also the Dutch word, Spook, which translates to ghost, and German's Spuk, which means goblin. The Irish variant is Pooka. All these creatures refer to spirits with the ability to vanish. Perhaps, somehow, in history yet to be figured out, the word traveled between here and there long before Columbus. Perhaps it's a coincidence." He winked at the class. "But there are no coincidences."

As he spoke, he pondered mentioning his sighting of the Greenbriar Ghost. Despite what he'd told his wife and son— that the leafy visage with glowing green eyes was the work of mischievous students—he thought that, perhaps, he'd really seen something supernatural, the face behind the myth. *Or I could just be going senile.*

"Our local Puckwudgies are of the same mint as all of those supernatural beings. Here in America, the natives weren't the only ones who told tales of these creatures. Immigrants brought tales of fairies and elves and gnomes with them, and usually kept those words. There are variations. New England has the Gentry, for example. Do any of you know other names?"

A few variations were given, but not the one he was looking for. "There is a little-known variant on these creatures, one that very closely resembles the natives' Puckwudgies. The Green-jacks. Have you heard the term?"

Silence was his answer.

"Greenjack is a term brought from Scotland to California by immigrants in the nineteenth century. A Greenjack is a nature el-emental, a frightening spook with a penchant for stealing the bodies of humans, but only ones who can see them. They can in-habit nonseers, but then they are forever cut off from their own kind, and they are too social for that."

He paused. "Fortunately for us poor humans, seers are very rare. Greenjacks are of the spirit world far more than the physi-cal. Hence, the story goes, they long for physical sensations, to taste food, to touch, to lust. Like most nature spirits, they are rarely evil in and of themselves, but they *are* hedonists and trick-sters, and body snatchers.

"Their power ebbs in winter, and grows throughout spring and summer, to peak in the fall, on All Hallows Eve. That is the one night of the year that they can do their dirty work. They can steal bodies then and affect the world in other ways. The Green-jacks built a physical being on that night, built it of wood, bark, and leaves. It was called Big Jack, and it could capture the seer for them so that they could steal the body. Big Jack, being phys-ical yet supernatural, is a Green Man form. Green Men range from all plant, like Jack, to blooded gods like Pan, to humans who have qualities that make them one with nature. Robin Hood is a human Green Man."

He looked around the room, seeing rapt attention on most of the faces. Even students who took this course because it was a fairly easy one with no requirements were inevitably drawn into it since it was about California, and that was where they lived. This class and his always overflowing Urban Legends class were fun. He'd told Vera he enjoyed them because they generally made good students out of bad ones. *If you give someone some-thing to study that actually interests them,* he told her whenever he came home pleasantly surprised by an underachiever, *they discover they are capable of more than they ever expected.*

"Professor?" Kendra had her hand up.

"Yes?"

"Are the Greenjack stories still extant?"

"You mean, does anyone believe in Greenjacks anymore?"

"Yes, or at least tell the stories?"

"My son actually lives in a southern California town founded by a family who claimed to have seers in their bloodlines. The stories spread from them, as well as from other Scots immigrants throughout the country. It was a story peculiar to a small area of the Highlands, and it is still told here and there. The family who founded the town still lives there. I expect they tell the tales." He winked at her. "Who knows? Maybe some even see the Greenjacks." He laughed.

"Now, why am I telling you about Greenjacks when I started with the midcoastal Puckwudgies, you ask? Because they are virtually identical. There is really only one difference. The Puckwudgies of the natives didn't build a Big Jack, nor was there a single Green Man form as a nature diety, although there were stories of a dangerous trickster spirit of great power that lived in the woods and had glowing emeralds for eyes. Local natives had multiple spirit gods, one for green growing things, one for the soil, one for rocks, and so forth. But the many became one when Europeans arrived. They became a Green Man form, a mix of Big Jack and a supernatural form that is able to affect our world. This form is not restricted to Halloween night, but it is powerful at that time, as are all Green Men. This form is known for its green glowing eyes and its ability to shriek, a trait perhaps added by those who enjoyed banshee tales.

"You all know this form. Even if you're from somewhere else, you've surely heard the stories of the Greenbriar Ghost by now. He lives in Applehead Forest and is usually called, simply, the Green Ghost. Sometimes, he is the Forest Knight. He is reputed to hold court in the old chapel in the woods—and I *know* you've all heard of that trysting spot by now—and to be seen, as often as not, holding his green head by its tendrils of green hair. And that's extremely interesting to a folklorist because it's an example of European folklore mixing with native stories. The tale from the British Isles may be based in truth, there is no way to be certain, though the Forest Knight is certainly a mythical aspect. Have any of you guessed what I'm talking about? Just speak, no hands necessary."

"It sounds familiar," Kendra said finally.

"If I use another term, then, I think you'll know. Our Green-briar Ghost is occasionally referred to as the Green Knight as well as Forest Knight."

"Sir Gawain and the Green Knight!" Kendra nearly exploded with the words. "I should have known that."

"You did know it, my dear. What Kendra said is the title of a lyric poem about one of King Arthur's knights. It is a story of honor. The Green Knight rides his horse into Arthur's court and demands that a knight fight him, a blow for a blow. Finally the honorable Sir Gawain takes the challenge and ends up behead-ing the Green Knight, who does not avoid the blow. Calmly, the knight picks up his head, and the head speaks, telling Gawain that he must meet him in a year.

"A year passes and Gawain rides out to meet a certain death. Nearing the home of the Green Knight, a chapel in the woods, he meets a minor lord who takes him in until the day arrives for the battle. While staying with the lord and his lady, Gawain is tempted by her each day with a kiss, but he never acts upon the urges she arouses. Each night, the lord and Gawain tell one an-other everything that happened that day. Gawain tells him everything. One day, the lady gives Gawain her scarf to wear into battle with the Green Knight. This, Gawain takes and fails to tell the lord.

"When the day arrives, Gawain meets the Green Knight and stands to take his blow, expecting to die. But the Green Knight, who is allowed three tries, stops short of his neck twice and the third time barely nicks him. Then he lets him go free. Gawain finds out that the Green Knight and the generous lord are one and the same, and that the nick was punishment for keeping the scarf a secret.

"Any questions?"

The usual suspect raised her hand.

"Yes, Kendra?"

"I've only heard of the Greenbriar Ghost being headless because my grandmother told me the old stories. I haven't heard it like that here on campus."

"That's a very good point and an excellent example of how our myths keep evolving. Someone, long ago, came here and told the Arthurian legends. The green-eyed trickster spirit of the natives of this area transformed into the Green Knight, always headless, then slowly began being seen with his head on occasion. Nowadays," he added with a nostalgic yearning, "I'm afraid our trickster usually has his head firmly on his shoulders." He smiled. "I encourage you all, when you have children of your own, to tell the tale with the knight—Forest or Green—holding his head by its leafy hair."

Kendra waved a hand. He nodded.

"Professor McCobb, I thought the trickster was represented as Coyote or Raven by the Chumash and other local tribes."

"Generally speaking, that's true, but there are always variations. The local natives had long been distant from the primary tribes and developed their own trickster form over time."

"Why?" Kendra asked. "Do you think there was a reason for them to change it?"

McCobb loved the question. "I suspect there's usually a reason behind everything. People here still tell of seeing the green eyes, sometimes even a green ghostly form. Perhaps there is something in the woods, maybe some odd refractions of light, or some local birds, that give basis for the stories. Maybe the tradition is now simply carried on by tricksters of flesh and blood, out to scare people just for fun. Yes, Jimmy?"

"All the deaths we have around here," the young man said, "play into the stories, don't they?"

"Yes, they do. We have the serial-killer story, dating back over a century, and that's a mythic form more in line with the Hook and Phantom Hitchhiker stories. Obviously, we occasionally do have bad people lurking in our woods, and that feeds the myths. We are developing the serial-killer myth both separate from the Greenbriar Ghost and *as* the Greenbriar Ghost or Forest Knight. It will be interesting to check in thirty or forty years to see how the stories have grown or died away."

He looked around the room. "Or maybe the Greenbriar Ghost *is* the predator, directly or indirectly. The latter, I think, is far more likely. We've had rumors of human sacrifice since the region was settled. Some may be true, and if so, someone is sacrificing to some form of the ghost." He cleared his throat. "Many someones, I should say, since these stories go back so far. There is another myth that intertwines with our Greenbriar Ghost and may also meld together with the other stories someday. Guesses?"

"The ghost of Holly Gayle?" someone asked timidly.

"That's right. Next time, we'll talk about our most enduring recent ghost story, one barely old enough to be mythic, but it bears all the earmarks. Many of you probably even know people who claim to have seen her. Do any of you ladies happen to be Gamma sisters?"

Kendra raised her hand.

"Holly is often said to roam the halls of her old sorority house. You must be fairly familiar with this ghost story."

"Yes," Kendra said in an uncharacteristically somber voice. "Yes, I'm acquainted with the stories."

Something in her demeanor intrigued him, but he hid it. "We're going to stay on the subject of the Greenbriar Ghost stories today, but next week we'll talk about Holly. Kendra, perhaps you can make an appointment to see me during office hours? I'd like to compare notes so that our class on our own campus ghost is as complete as possible."

Kendra wet her lips and nodded.

"Now then, let's get back to the habits of the Puckwudgies and the King Puck that the early settlers bestowed upon them."

The rest of the session, he kept wondering what a girl like Kendra Phillips was doing in that house. It worried him.

9

"That little stunt you pulled today wasn't very nice," Professor Tongue said, as he stood back and let Malory enter his cottage.

She ignored him, shedding clothes like snakeskin as she crossed his living room and passed through the little dining room. By the time she opened his refrigerator, she was nude. She found a can of whipped cream on the top shelf, then turned and looked at the Tongue. He had closed the drapes, which was rather boring of him, but in these times of sexual politics, she supposed it was necessary. Now he approached, gathering her clothes along the way. At the kitchen threshold, he picked up her black thong.

"Carry it in your mouth," she ordered.

"Why?"

"To turn me on."

"Yes, m'lady." He grabbed the crotch in his teeth and stood there staring at her like a big dumb hound dog.

No, not a hound. A bulldog. Bulldogs always seemed to have their tongues hanging out. "Use your tongue like a hook to carry them."

He even cocked his head like a dog. "What?"

"I want to see your tongue."

He took the panties out of his mouth and grinned. "You've been absolutely nuts about tongues lately."

"I'm always nuts about your tongue, you know that."

"Yes, but you've changed. You don't just want me to use it on you. I think you're developing a fetish."

She turned and grabbed a jar of maraschino cherries from the second shelf, then, hands full, used her ass to close the door. She grinned. He was right, to some extent, but he didn't know the half of it. He had inspired the glamour she had used to frighten Eve

Camlan, the twisted face of the Forest Knight with a tongue Pan himself would kill for. "Well, Professor, if I'm becoming a tongue freak, then it's all your fault."

She passed him and he followed close behind, a puppy waiting for his treat. In the bedroom, she turned and looked at him. "Why aren't those panties on their new hook?"

"Huh? Oh." He stuck his tongue out and snagged them up. "'ow's dis?"

"Fine. Don't talk with your mouth full." She set the canned cream and the cherries on the nightstand and pulled back the boring bedspread—shades of blue in geometric patterns—and blankets, letting them all drop to the carpet at the foot of the bed.

Climbing on, she spread out comfortably and grabbed the jar of cherries. "Get undressed, Professor Piccolo. You're going to practice bobbing for apples." She opened the jar and took out a cherry.

He watched, eyes glazing, pants tenting, as she held it between her fingers and put it in her mouth. She sucked the juice off, then held it up by the stem and showed it to him. "It's almost Halloween, you know." His eyes watched every movement as she put the cherry in the designated receptacle, then took another and another from the jar. "A baker's dozen," she told him as she squeezed the last one in. "Think you can get them all out?"

The panties dropped, forgotten, as he started undressing, his eyes never wavering from the cherries' new home. He removed his shirt and pants, revealing a broad chest covered with curly light brown hair. Unfortunately, his waist was the same width as his chest and his hips had love handles, but it all gave him a pleasant teddy bear or puppy dog—it depended on her mood—appearance. Below a ridiculous bush of nether hair, his little man stood at attention. Too bad, she thought, it was such a modest member. She smiled at him as she shook the can of cream. If he'd been hung below as he was above, he undoubtedly would have been too arrogant to be allowed to live.

She began decorating her body with the cream, running

pearls of it across her neck and making cream pasties for her breasts. She filled her navel, then decorated the cherry pie with the rest of the cream. "What a bad little puppy dog you are today."

"What?"

"Close your mouth. You're drooling." She took a fingerful of cream from the top of the pie and put it in her mouth, sucking it off slowly, never taking her eyes off him, even when she withdrew the finger, then licked the dark crimson nail with the tip of her pointed tongue. "On second thought, don't close your mouth. Just get over here. Now."

The professor of English, fresh out of words, did as she commanded, cleaning her neck first. Malory shivered with pleasure and glanced at the bedroom window as he moved to her breasts. On the open windowsill, a chipmunk watched, bright-eyed, as it nibbled a Peanut M&M. Malory blew it a kiss.

LADIES OF THE LAKE

10

Hidden in forest shadows, crickets scraped their rhythmic mating calls. Night birds called to one another from fragrant pine boughs, and below, deer wandered the carpet of pine needles and the first fallen leaves of the season, nibbling still-growing grasses, tasting leaves. October nights in this hilly forest were colder than those on the coast, but no frosts ever came this early and even in the coldest part of winter, snow was a rarity. Applehead Forest, with its moderate climate and watchful elementals, was prime real estate for beasts and birds, as well as ghosts.

Applehead Lake lay calm under the light of the waning half-moon. As black and shining as polished onyx, it hid its secrets in cold-water silence, though if someone had taken a boat out and rowed into the still waters northwest of Applehead Island, they would have spied glowing amber jewels deep down. Unless they knew the stories, they would assume these were reflections of stars, because the human mind usually finds a way to make sense of things, even if that means ignoring the fact that the sense, when examined closely, makes no sense.

Tonight, a cobweb of ghost lights spread outward from the stained-glass church window at the center of the drowned town. Lights moved along long-gone roads, held by invisible hands, hung from hooks on phantom horse carts.

If a diver could descend undetected to observe the lights up close, he might have caught glimpses of spirits, flashes of long-dead humanity, living their afterlives among roofless, rotting buildings. He might have sensed undines moving among the human spirits, drawing sustenance from the water and the ghosts.

Some of the ghosts inhabiting the long-dead town of Applehead had been there for a century or more, some were new residents. All were prisoners, though few had the wit left to realize it. Most were nothing but afterthoughts, soulless supernatural energies captured when they drowned in these dark waters, but a few were true spirits, nearly all of them feminine, murdered, forever young, their bodies brought to the lake and personally interred within the old church by the queen of the Fata Morgana and her familiar.

If a human diver found his way into the building and knew where to look, he might even see the remains, the bones of the long dead and, if he looked in an old confessional-sized room, he might have spied the untouched bodies of two special young women. One was recently deceased, the other long dead, their beauty preserved somehow by the deep chilled water, their hair, blond and dark chestnut, waving in the currents. Though each had been weighted down and placed in different parts of the church, they were now entwined, like sisters comforting one another during a frightening thunderstorm.

That the perfect corpses had come together was a secret even from Malory Thomas; indeed Malory had never seen the unsullied body of the girl with chestnut curls, and simply assumed that it had turned into one of the nameless piles of bones whose owners were doomed to walk the submerged streets of Applehead for eternity. If she had known, she would have realized that the perfection had something to do with the spirit's ability to escape her watery tomb and torment her, for in all these years, despite many other sacrifices moldering here, Holly Gayle had been the only one able to walk on land.

Now there were two.

Blond hair and chestnut hair blended together in the gentle current. One dead hand seemed to caress the other's cheek, and if the imaginary diver saw the movement, after the initial shock, he would have assumed that the water currents were responsible for the action, because that was the only thing that made sense.

11

Malory Thomas, still enjoying the aftereffects of serving Professor Tongue a few pieces of cherry pie, entered Gamma House with a serene smile on her face. Brittany hurried along beside her, munching down sunflower seeds, shells and all.

"That was great!" the little blonde said for the tenth time since they had left Tongue's cottage. "Malory, what did you do to him?"

They passed the great room and parlor and walked into the kitchen. "I inspired him with a speech this afternoon," Malory said as she peered into the refrigerator. "I inspired an entire class."

"You did that old orgasm spell on your speech class?" Brittany giggled up the scales.

"Yes," Malory told her. She grabbed her private pitcher of unsweetened lemonade and an apple for Brittany, and brought them to the kitchen table where her bright-eyed familiar had stalled out and perched out on a wooden chair. Setting the items down as the little blonde dumped the last of her sunflower seeds into her mouth, Malory took a tall glass from the cupboard, retrieved some ice and a bottle of Absolut from the freezer, then sat down.

"I wish I'd been there," Brittany said before biting into the big green apple.

Malory poured sour lemonade over the ice, followed it with a big splash of vodka. "You would have turned feral and suffocated poor Professor Tongue, right there on his desk."

Chirrupy giggles tripped over the apple into the room. "You think so?"

"I know you, my little nut cruncher. I know you well."

Brittany held her apple out. "Look, Malory. A worm!"

"Half a worm."

She took another bite. "Worm's all gone."

"And you call yourself a vegetarian."

Brittany grinned. "It sure took you a long time to invite me into Tongue's bed tonight. I thought I was going to die of voyeurism."

"Can I help it if he's a slow eater?"

"Next time, take the stems off first. That'll speed him up."

"You know what they say, Britt. Patience is good for the soul." Malory topped off her half-finished drink with icy vodka.

"Who says *that?*"

"They do."

"Who's *they?*"

"Hi, guys." Heather Horner entered the room, pausing near the doorway. "Am I interrupting anything?"

"Who said patience is good for the soul?" Brittany chirped.

"Nobody. I forget what's good for the soul, but patience is a virtue."

Brittany stuck out her tongue at Malory. "You were wrong."

"And you have no virtue."

"Neither do you."

"Be good, or you won't get an invitation the next time I prime Professor Tongue for a marathon. How many orgasms did you have tonight, hmm?"

Brittany's musical chittering filled the room. "I don't know." She turned to Heather. "Do you count your orgasms?"

Heather smiled as she grabbed a glass and filled it with purple energy juice made by Mildred McArthur. She brought it to the table. "I usually have two or three. Once, I had five." She looked at the vodka. "May I, Malory?"

"You add liquor to your buzz juice?"

"Sure. Don't you?"

"Go ahead, but no. You know I don't drink that stuff."

"Why not?"

Because one of the ingredients is Brittany's urine. Why do you think it makes you so peppy? "For the same reason you don't drink my sour lemonade. I don't like it." Heather had been with them for over sixty years now, but that was a drop in the eternal bucket. She wasn't ready yet to know what was in her beloved purple juice. Or maybe she was, but it was more fun not to tell her.

"So, what's up, Heather?" Brittany asked.

"One of our new sisters has changed rooms without asking permission."

"Oh?" Malory considered. Maybe she was just feeling mellow from the evening workout, but the news didn't interest her much. "We do let them choose their own rooms." *Third time's the charm.* She topped her drink with Russian elixir once more.

"I know," Heather said. "I just thought you should know. Merilynn has moved in with Kendra Phillips."

"Oh?" Malory stared into her drink. She rarely imbibed alcohol and already had a definite buzz on. Getting a buzz was rarer than rare. "I didn't realize they were friendly with one another."

"No, but now they're in there jabbering away like long-lost sisters."

"They both like ghost stories," Brittany observed while balancing the apple core on the tip of her nose.

"And there's the Eve Camlan connection," Malory said.

"Kendra was her roommate, but what's the connection with Merilynn?"

"They went to Applehead Cheer Camp together," Malory snapped. "Gods, woman, you're the damned head of the cheerleaders and you don't know that?"

"I remember now. Give me a break. Merilynn isn't on the squad and Eve never said a word about her. It's not exactly big news. It's not like I was a counselor at that camp when they were there."

"Touchy," Brittany said, cocking her head to look at Heather, proudly keeping the apple core precariously balanced. "Why so touchy?"

"Just antsy. Sorry. You know what night it is, don't you?"

"Thursday?" Malory said. She poured more lemon juice, more Absolut. *Absolut sorcery.* She smiled lazily. "Britt, you look like a trained seal. You want some fish as a reward for your balancing act?"

"What else is today?" Heather added a little more booze to her purple juice.

"Two weeks until All Hallows Eve? The day before Professor Piccolo shows up in class with his tongue in traction?" Her laugh was low and easy, her good mood still on the increase. Tonight, her sleep would be perfect. It could be nothing else. Tongue had wrung every orgasm out of her body, left her every cell depleted and her soul complete. Rarely had she ever been so satiated. "Who cares?"

"Oh, shit!" Brittany cried. The apple core fell and rolled across the linoleum.

"It's fifteen days until Halloween. It's the night of the October half-moon, duh!"

Malory regarded Heather. "I wish you wouldn't pick up so many of those tiresome expressions. 'Duh' isn't worthy of a Fata Morgana." She poured more booze.

"You yourself point out that we have to maintain current speech patterns," Heather said, her voice threaded with irritation. "What do you want me to say, 'It's the bee's knees?'"

"Bee's knees!" Brittany repeated happily. "I loved that line. Twenty-three skidoo. The queen's eyes! The butler's balls!" She looked at Malory. "Seriously, Mal, it is *the* night."

"I know. The anniversary of the flooding of Applehead. The ghosts down there are going crazy with their light show."

"A half-moon on this date means we might do some heavy banishing," Brittany reminded her. "It doesn't happen every year."

"There's something I don't understand," Heather said. Done with her purple juice, she poured two fingers of straight vodka in her glass.

"What?"

"Why do the ghosts under the lake act up on the anniversary of the flooding? The town was uninhabited. No one was killed."

"Don't be stupid," Malory drawled. "The spirit of the town is what lights up. It's nothing, just a ghost vision."

"What about your sacrifices?"

"*Our* sacrifices," Brittany corrected. "They're always there, right, Malory?"

"Right, especially that ridiculous dead twat Holly. They all seem to become active on the anniversary. I suppose they pick up on the energy of the phantom town." Reluctantly, she looked at Brittany. "You're right. We don't get a banishing night on the anniversary very often. Maybe we should convene and try to keep that little bitch under the lake where she belongs once and for all."

"You're slurring," Brittany observed. "You know what happens to your spells when you've been drinking."

Both of them burst into laughter.

"What?" Heather demanded, pouring another finger or two. "What happens?"

"You know," Malory said. "You were there once."

"Where once?"

"Here once."

"When you idiots got loaded and tried to cast a glamour on that soldier group," Brittany explained.

"The UFO show recruiter!" Malory said, flashing back to a World War II stint at Greenbriar.

"U S O!" Brittany got up and rifled through a cupboard until she found a can of mixed nuts. She pulled the tab, moaning slightly as the aroma escaped, then poured the delicacies into a bowl and returned to the table. Taking a handful for herself, she nudged the bowl toward the other two Fata Morganas. "Eat."

"You're *sharing?*" Malory teased. She winked at Heather. "She thinks we're drunk. She only shares when she's worried."

"Why are you worried?" Heather picked out some almonds for her very own.

"You don't remember the USO recruiter?"

"Bob Hope?"

Malory laughed. "You don't remember! You had to have been there."

Heather shook her head as she sucked on a nut. Brittany watched hungrily, even though her own cheeks were already fat with peanuts. "It was here?"

"Yes," Brittany said. "Are you ever going to chew that almond, or are you just going to tongue it to death?"

"She's going to tongue it till it climaxes," Malory mumbled. She put a Brazil nut on her long sharp tongue and pointed at it. Brittany smiled and leaned over, using her tongue to draw it into her own mouth.

She crunched. "Big nut."

Malory giggled. She heard herself and thought, *I don't giggle. It's too silly.* Then she giggled some more, realizing she was getting horny again, and put a pecan half on her tongue. Brittany went for it but Malory was quicker, drawing her tongue back, making her familiar go after it.

"Oh, Gods, don't you two ever get enough?" Heather asked, showing boredom. "Tell me about the USO guy."

Mistress and familiar drew apart. Malory, her mouth nutless, told Heather, "It was just a silly little spell. You remember, the guy was handsome and arrogant as hell? We decided to give him a tail?"

Heather laughed. "I wasn't there, I swear. Are you sure it was during that war? When else have you been here?"

"Vietnam," Brittany said. "Early seventies. *That's* when we did the glamour on the USO guy. Time flies, huh, Malory?"

"It does. Like little grains of sand, so fly the days of our lives."

"You're toasted," Heather told Malory.

"You and your slang."

" 'Toasted' means smoking marijuana," Brittany said.

"It does?" Heather asked.

"I think so. I mean, it makes sense. Smoke, toast, it involves heat."

"Brittany's my guiding light," Malory said. *Gods, what a combination. Sex and alcohol. The Greeks really had things down pat.* "She stays with me as the world turns."

"You *are* fucked up!" Brittany giggled. She turned to Heather. "You weren't there?"

"Where were you in seventy-two?" Malory asked. A little

part of her mind, the sober part, was bitching at her to get up, get it together, and go out and try to banish Holly Gayle, who no doubt was dragging her ectoplasmic ass out of the water as they sat here at the table sopping up modern mead. *The Greeks weren't so hot after all. They drank mead. Vodka beats the bee's knees out of mead.*

"In 1972," said Heather, "you had me running the Gamma Eta Pi chapter in Jeremy, Arizona."

Malory laughed. "Oh, I remember that. Jeremy, Arizona. You'd pissed me off. You did something . . ."

"She beat you into JFK's pants during that private party at the White House in 1961," Brittany said. "Malory, I expect humans to get stupid when they're drunk, but *you?*"

"Blame the Tongue. My defenses are toasted."

"That means—"

"Shut up, you little rodent. I know what it means. So, how *was* Jeremy, Arizona, Heather? Or did I ask you that already?"

"It was full of cock, Malory. I rode a lot of bucking broncos. In fact, I wouldn't mind going back to that little college out there again someday. Ever see a guy in chaps, no jeans?"

In response, Malory put another nut on her tongue and looked meaningfully at Brittany.

She took peanuts from the bowl and ate them, looking at Malory's invitation. "You need to get laid," she said. "You're getting too much oral sex. How long since you've ridden a Knight?"

"Too long. How about you, Heather?"

"Yesterday." She poured more vodka, for herself, then for Malory. "So, what's the skinny on Professor Tongue?"

"Never you mind," Malory said. "I don't share." She paused. "You get the best-hung Knight on the team into my bed, maybe I'll tell you a little."

"Maybe she'll let you watch," Brittany offered.

"Maybe," Malory agreed. "Now get your mind out of your vagina and tell Heather what you did to the USO guy."

12

"I'm done," Kendra told her new roommate as she closed her notebook and set down her pen. "No more homework tonight. How about you?"

"Not a drop." Merilynn sat in a cross-legged yoga position on a small round hooked rug she'd placed on the floor near her bed. It was one of the less peculiar of her possessions, if you didn't count the fact that she'd made this rug herself and it depicted a nun and a satyr holding hands as they ran across a field of daisies. Now she stood up and stretched, twisting and turning and reaching for the sky. Then she sat on her bed, again crossing her legs so that her feet looked trapped.

"How do you do that?" Kendra asked.

Merilynn grinned. "Watch this." She untied her legs, parting them and putting the soles of her feet together. Then she tugged her ankles forward until her knees stuck out almost even with her hips.

"Ouch!" Kendra grimaced. "Are you double-jointed?"

"No. I just bend this way. I couldn't do those cheerleader splits to save my soul . . . Sorry, that came out wrong."

Kendra smiled softly. "It's okay. I'm glad you're here, and I'm glad you brought your stuff."

"You like?" Merilynn gestured at the stars-and-moon bedspread she sat on; the flowery one that Eve loved had been returned to Gamma's linen closet.

"I love it. It makes the room happier. It's different. You don't happen to have some funky curtains so we can get rid of those ruffly white things, do you?"

"I'll ask Father to bring some when he comes to visit. I have ones that match my bedspread."

"I love that spread. The brilliant blues and golds are way more my speed than this floral pastel stuff."

"In my room, I had twin beds. There's another spread. Shall I ask him to bring the other one for you?"

Kendra barely hesitated. "Yes! So, did you bring any art for the walls?"

"I have a couple watercolors in a folio I stuck in my closet. They're scenery. I don't know if you'd like them or not."

Kendra nodded toward a small framed print of geese with bonnets that had come with the room. "That's sure not what I like. Let me see."

"Okay."

It took Merilynn about ten seconds to get to the closet and pull out her folio. She opened it and took out a medium-sized watercolor of a forest lake at night.

"That's Applehead Lake." Kendra stood up and moved closer. "It's spooky."

"I didn't think you'd like it," Merilynn said, starting to put it away.

"No, I do like it. It's spooky. Spooky's good."

"You're weird," Merilynn said warmly. "I like you."

Kendra continued to study the painting. It was dark, full of greens and blues, the black lake water reflecting the full moon above. "We have to get a frame and put it up."

"I have poster frames." Merilynn set the painting down and lifted another. "Déjà vu, almost," she announced as she lifted it up.

It was the lake at night again, much like the other painting, but here the view was from the water, not the shore, and the moon was half and partly obscured by clouds. A thin mist hovered on Applehead Island. There was an additional sparkle to the lake. Kendra looked closer. "You've painted in the ghost lights."

"When I saw them, I tried to memorize them so I could draw them. The first time, I drew them in crayon as soon as I got home. There must be a hundred versions of this painting at home. This is the best one."

"Do you take art classes?"

"One now, but it's just a hobby. I took art in high school and the teacher specialized in watercolors. She taught me the tricks, you know, how to do water and light."

"What's that?" Kendra asked. "It looks like a stained-glass window." She paused, looking at the artist. "You said you saw this once?"

Merilynn nodded.

"You saw the window?"

Another nod. "You know about the window?"

Now Kendra nodded. "It's up in the administration building's tower. Are you sure it's the same window?"

Merilynn laughed lightly. "It was way too deep to see details. I like to think it is, though. That's how the story goes, after all."

"I would kill to see it. All of it. The lights."

Merilynn put the painting back in the folio, looking pleased. "You believe me?"

"Why not? I mean, I don't know what it is, but I believe you saw it. Folklore usually has roots in something real, don't you think?"

"Yes. Absolutely." She pulled a much smaller painting from the folio, not showing it to Kendra. "This one, you won't want on the wall."

"Let me be the judge of that."

"*I* don't want it on the wall."

"You painted it and you don't want it up? Is it terrible?"

"No. It's pretty good, if I say so myself. But if you thought the lake pictures were spooky, well, then this is spooky to the tenth power."

"Show me, already!"

Merilynn slowly turned the painting and as she saw it, Kendra's flesh rose in goose bumps. It was a watercolor of a woman's pale face and dark eyes staring up from just beneath the water. She was frightening to look at, eerie, but as she studied her, Kendra discerned a look of pleading in her eyes, not anger, not terror, but sadness and longing. "Holly."

"Yes."

"She's beautiful. So sad."

"She wants something," Merilynn said.

"What?"

"To be found, I think. That night, she almost dragged Sam under. It was like she hypnotized her. I pulled her back—you can't repeat any of this to her."

Kendra nodded. "I remember, you said that before."

A pixie grin. "Can't be too careful!"

"Hypnotizing her . . . That doesn't sound very friendly."

"No, it doesn't, but I'm not sure it means she's wicked or anything. I think she's desperate."

"Sam Penrose doesn't seem like the kind of person who would let herself be hypnotized," Kendra said, wanting to slow things down.

"I agree. She's not now and she wasn't then. But it happened."

"Can we get her to talk about it, do you think?"

Merilynn shrugged. "I'm not sure. You can't tell her I told you anything; sorry, I said it again."

"That's okay. You're worried. Go on."

"We could invite her over for pizza or something. I can talk about what I saw, maybe she'd talk, but don't count on it. Maybe we could start by getting her talking about camp. The adventures. If you let her know you believe in ghosts, she might open up more."

"Let's do it, but not here," Kendra said, unconsciously lowering her voice.

"Okay, but why not?"

"I'm paranoid."

"Yes, well, I can understand that. But we're just telling old kid stories. Who cares if anyone hears?"

"I don't know, but I have a feeling someone might. I think we should be careful."

"If that's how you feel."

"I do."

"Then we should be careful." Merilynn set the portfolio aside. "Kendra? Why do you believe in ghosts?"

"My granny says she saw one and I believe her," Kendra began. "Other women in my family saw them. Perfectly intelligent people see things that can't be explained."

"But why do *you* believe?"

"Why not? I think they're memories and sometimes we can see or hear or smell them." She shivered, remembering Eve's telling of her nightmare shortly before her death. "They come in dreams, conjured up by our minds most of the time, but sometimes they come from outside us. Sometimes they're real. I used to think that ghosts were just mindless shadows drifting around, but maybe some of them can think. Maybe there are actual *spirits* out there once in a while." She stood up and closed the double-hung window over her desk without looking out.

"You've seen one." It was a statement, not a question.

Kendra turned to face Merilynn. "Yes."

"Holly?"

"No." She walked to Merilynn's bed and sat next to her, then bent to her ear and whispered, "I saw Eve."

Merilynn's eyes opened wide and she mouthed one word: *When?*

"After the initiation. That night. It was near dawn."

"We were drugged."

"I know, I know. I've tried to convince myself it was a hallucination, but it wasn't. I wish it were. I *know* she was real. She came to tell me something."

"What?"

Kendra shook her head. "I don't remember. I keep trying, but I just can't figure out what it was. Sometimes I think she asked for help, but like you said, they'd drugged us, so I don't trust my memory."

Merilynn laid her hand over Kendra's. "Let's talk more later. Want to go out for a pizza? If you want, we can invite Sam."

Kendra glanced at her watch. It was barely after eight and all she'd had for dinner was a cup of instant soup. Her stomach growled so loudly that Merilynn could hear it.

"I'll take that as a yes."

They stood and got their bags and shrugged into their jackets.

"Are you a vegan?" Kendra asked as Merilynn paused to tuck the paintings into her closet.

"No. Why?"

"You look like a vegan."

"Gee, thanks. What does a vegan look like?"

"Sorry. I mean, you do the yoga thing and the herb thing. It just kind of seemed to go together."

"Think again. I like my steaks medium rare and my carrots completely cooked. Or completely raw." They left the room and pulled the door closed behind them.

"I hate not having a lock," Kendra said.

"Me too." They walked a short way toward the staircase and stopped at Sam Penrose's door. Merilynn knocked. "Sam? Are you in there?"

"Who is it?"

"Merilynn and Kendra. Are you busy?"

Sam opened the door and looked them up and down. "I'm always busy. Why?"

"We're going for pizza. You want to come?"

Sam glanced back toward her desk, then nodded. "I'm never too busy for pizza." She eyed the pair again. "You two aren't vegans or anything like that, are you?"

"Pepperoni," said Kendra.

"Sausage," said Merilynn.

"And onions," Sam said. "Let me get my coat." She left the door open while she put her computer to sleep and fiddled around.

Merilynn looked at Kendra. "Do you know what tonight is?"

"Thursday?"

"It's the anniversary of the day they flooded out the town of Applehead."

"Oh, heavens, you're right." Kendra smiled. "I should have known that. Granny always said the town comes to life on the day it drowned."

"Yeah." Merilynn's eyes lit up. "When the town lights up, Holly Gayle walks."

"What are you two giggling about?" Sam demanded, joining them.

"Nothing," Merilynn said.

"History," Kendra said simultaneously.

"Funny history? You'll have to tell me all about it while we go into town."

"I thought we'd just go to the cafeteria," Merilynn said.

Sam pulled car keys from her jacket pocket. "You call that mush they serve there pizza? It's a pancake with some tomato sauce smeared on it. If we're going to eat pizza, we're going to do it right."

"It's a weeknight," Kendra said. "Caledonia's pretty far. I don't want to be dead in the morning. Dead tired, I mean."

They started down the grand staircase. "What else would you mean?" Sam asked, her tone teasing. "I found a pizza place in Greenbriar. It's not great, except compared to school food. Then it's sublime."

"Let's go!" Kendra said, her stomach echoing her desire.

13

"The USO guy," Malory said, "wasn't that big of a deal. He was hanging around campus, supposedly looking to discover new talent to take on military show tours. Brit, do you remember his name? Something like Dick Biggs?"

"Peter Long." Brittany giggled.

Heather went to the fridge and found a jug of orange juice. "So what did you do to him?" she asked, sitting down and pouring until her glass was two-thirds full. She added vodka.

"You are going to be sick tomorrow," Malory observed.

"And you're not?"

"I'm not like you. I'm immune to such petty annoyances as hangovers."

"Oh." Heather looked at her glass dubiously. "Can you do a spell to keep me from getting a hangover?"

Brittany cackled with amusement. "Never ask her to do a spell when she's like this. You'll know why in a minute. Tell her what you did, Malory."

Malory decided to sulk and put a fresh peanut on her tongue. Brittany gave her a long-suffering look, then leaned forward and nabbed it with her mouth.

"Ouch! You little bitch, you bit me."

"You needed biting, Mistress. Now, tell her what you did."

"Well, Captain Long—I don't remember if he was a captain, but I liked the sound of it so I called him that—he was a work of art. Chiseled chin with a cleft on a square jaw. One of those blond Nordic warrior types with eyes the color of a clear summer sky." She chuckled. "I'm a poet. Anyway, he knew how good he looked. He had broad shoulders and a six-pack."

"Of beer?" Heather asked.

"Abs," Brittany said.

"One night, the last night he was here, he came to Gamma House. He wanted the cheerleaders to give him an impromptu performance. He said he was thinking of taking them on the tour.

"They did it. That year none of them were Fata Morganas, just Gammas, and they made fools of themselves, falling all over each other, completely in heat. Captain Long had looks and an aura of charisma and sexuality that were really quite interesting." She poured another drink. "Heather, I want to ride a Knight tonight. Make that happen."

"Malory, Heather's going to be lucky to make it upstairs to her own bed," Brittany said.

"Whatever. Then you get me a Knight, Brittany."

"Tell your story first."

"Okay. Captain Long was an ass. I knew it the moment I met him, but he kept it well hidden. He was in the parlor with the squad. One man, eight girls. It was a warm night, not long before school would be out for the summer, and he kept encouraging the girls to remove garments."

"Were they wearing their uniforms?"

"No, no. This was impromptu. I remember lots of bell-bottom jeans and tie-dyed shirts. It was the Age of Aquarius." She paused and started to sing, "This is the dawning of—"

"Tell the story," Brittany ordered, "before Heather passes out."

"Right. Do you know that my mentor, when I was a young girl, before I found immortality, he predicted an Age of Aquarius?" Brittany rolled her eyes, so Malory got back on track. Britt was a pain, but as a familiar she was great at keeping her organized.

"I'm an Aquarius," Heather slurred.

"That's nice," Malory said. "I was born—when was I born, Brittany?"

"You're older than dirt," Brittany said. She rose and went for the jug of purple juice. It would bring Heather back to earth, at least a little.

"Hey! You can't talk to me that way! I'll turn you into a—a rectum!"

Brittany grabbed a fresh glass and patted Malory's head as she returned. "Not just any old rectum, I hope," she said, pouring purple juice. "Here, Heather, drink up—no, no booze. This will wake you up."

"I want more vodka."

"After you drink this." Brittany sat. "So Captain Long was getting the squad to undress."

Malory nodded. "I'd cloaked myself in an invisibility spell so no one would notice me and I sat right there, taking it all in."

"And drinking," Brittany added. "Drinking tequila sunrises. That was the in drink back then. Jimmy Buffet sang about them all the time."

"They were good."

"Your drink was cloaked too?" Heather asked. She'd had half the purple juice and was sharper already.

"Hey, I'm not just any old Sybil, you know. I could have cloaked a roast chicken and eaten it and they wouldn't have known."

"As long as she didn't burp." Brittany giggled. She started in on the bowl of nuts again.

"You whore," Malory said affectionately. "I ought to tie you down and—"

"You were watching the girls and Captain Long," Brittany said. "Was he undressing too?"

"Not yet. He sweet-talked those girls into taking off every iota of clothing. They were drinking too."

"Tequila sunrises," Brittany said.

"Mostly. And Captain Long, he just had a bottle of tequila he was nursing. A bottle and a lime and a salt shaker. It was mescal, the liquor, I mean, the kind with the worm in it, and there wasn't a lot there. He had no intention of getting so drunk he couldn't get it up. It was nauseating to watch. He kept showing the Gammas the worm and threatening to eat it."

"Swallow it," Brittany corrected.

"Oh, how do you know, you little slut? Maybe he was going to chew it up!"

"He was an ass, not a moron."

Malory decided not to push it. She needed some tail and someone to supply it. *Best to keep Brittany smiling.* "I was amazed. The man didn't have a magical bone in his body, but between the charm and the booze, he'd gotten every last one of them to take off their clothes. And then he had them undress him. One item of clothing per girl. They had to use their teeth. Why, he had them all over him, biting his buttons, yanking his belt, unzipping. They were in his thrall. That night, the tequila hit me. It doesn't often, you know. I'm not susceptible ordinarily."

"The story. You were drunk, they were undressing him. Then what happened?"

"I was really starting to get pissed off," Malory admitted. "Those were *my* girls, my handpicked little Gamma sisters, and he was manipulating them! That's *my* job!"

"I know, Mistress. Go on."

Sweet Brittany. Malory loved it when she called her that in front of other sisters. She rarely did it. "Well, then, once he was stripped naked, he stood up and I nearly dropped my drink. He was perfect. Absolutely perfect. I thought of commandeering him for myself. But then he opened his mouth and he commanded—*commanded*—*my* girls to perform fellatio on him. On their *knees.* He had them kneel in a line like they were worshipping the Forest Knight himself, and he began to go from one to another, *bathing* himself in *my girls'* mouths! If I hadn't been so horny, I would have flayed him, then and there."

"Did he have a big cock?" Heather giggled.

"It was a fine specimen," Malory said, the fire in her belly growing stronger. "Fearsomely rampant, so hard you could have hung a coat on it and it would have stayed up."

"What kind of coat?"

"Be quiet, Brittany."

"You can tell a lot about a man by the weight of the coat he wears." The familiar giggled.

Malory pulled the dish of nuts to herself.

"Hey!"

"Apologize."

"I apologize. Now, let me have my nuts."

Malory smiled and pushed them back over to Brittany. "I watched, furious, as my girls obeyed his orders. Finally, I left the room and removed the spell, then walked back in and gave them hell. The cheerleaders were humiliated and ran off shrieking, grabbing their clothes. That was the whoriest bunch of cheerleaders we ever had—"

"Hey," Heather said, back into the vodka again, "my squad isn't slutty."

"Shhh. That wasn't your squad." Brittany pushed the vodka bottle out of Heather's reach. "They were total skanks. But it was the era. Free love. They liked to paint each other in body paint and do cheers. Once—"

"*I'm* telling the stories here!" Malory interrupted. The room was starting to spin a little, so she poured sour lemonade to drink without the booze. "After they ran off, Captain Long just stood there, smiling at me, naked as the day he was born."

"What happened to the coat?" Heather asked.

"What coat?"

"The one on his cock."

"You're an idiot. There was no coat. He was naked. He actually said to me, 'Do you like what you see?' The arrogance of the man was astonishing. Then it got worse. He said, 'You didn't have to send them off. There's enough of me to go around.' He wanted me to call them back so that he could share his magnificent body with *all* of us! That bastard had no intention of giving us any pleasure. He just wanted to *be* pleasured."

"So what did you do?"

"I walked up to him and grabbed his penis. He loved it. He said, 'You want me.' Well, if there was any desire left in me, that killed it completely. I'd been torn before, thinking I'd ride him and see if he was good enough to spare. I thought maybe I'd cast a glamour and give him a tail or turn him into a sex slave for the Fata Morganas. But that was too much. I cast a different glamour. I tried, but I was drunk and it didn't work quite the way I planned."

"Tell me!" Heather squealed.

Malory smiled. "Well, I decided to shorten his penis to a nub that would make Professor Tongue look like a stud. I knew something would happen when I did, it always does, doesn't it, Brittany?"

"It does."

"What do you mean?"

"When you re-form humans, every action causes a reaction of some sort. When I took away his nice big penis, something else on him would grow. I'd done it in years past and it often resulted in long earlobes or nipples, or even a foot-long scrotum. But not this time. The alcohol made me twist something in the spell and his penis grew longer and longer, like Pinnochio's nose. Nothing else changed on him, because it was simply a re-formation of its own mass. It became as slender as my finger and fell past his knees. He just stood there, not believing what he saw."

"And you?" Heather asked. "What did you think?"

"I just laughed. I laughed until Brittany showed up."

"I laughed too. It was like he had this long tube hanging down. You should have seen it. Then Mallory picked up his bottle of tequila."

"What was he doing?"

"Nothing," Malory said. "The man was a statue. He was utterly shocked."

"Malory picked up the tequila," Brittany repeated, "and pointed at the worm floating in it. I knew instantly what she was thinking."

"Of course you did," Malory cooed, thinking about sex again. "You're my little monkey."

"Never call me a monkey. That's degrading. I'd never be a monkey, not even for you!"

"Sorry, little one." She looked at Heather. "Together, Brittany and I cast a major glamour on Captain Long's very long, thin penis."

"We turned it into a worm." Brittany giggled.

"And the worm turned," Malory finished. She drained her juice and started to stand up.

"Wait a minute!" Heather cried. "What does that mean? What happened? You really turned his cock into a worm?"

"A fat white worm. Fat for a worm, not for a penis," Malory said. "The kind in the tequila, with little catepillar legs. Thousands of them."

"It crawled up Captain Long and wrapped itself around his neck. He was strangled by his own dick!" Brittany finished.

"Was that part of the spell?"

Malory shrugged. "I'm horny. Let's go find some Knights. I want to joust with one or two. Ladies?"

"What did you do with the body?" Heather asked. Fortified by the secret ingredients in the purple juice, she was smashed yet ambulatory, and managed to stand up with the others.

"In the lake," Malory said.

"So he's walking tonight? His spirit is trapped?"

"Yes, Heather. I thought you had that all figured out. The spirits of those we kill and dump in the lake stay in the lake for all time."

"What if you don't dump them in the lake?"

"Then they either wander the area, or we banish them. Remember, dear, we banished Mulva's spirit after we got rid of her in the forest? I wouldn't want a traitorous bitch like her hanging around, would you?"

"No. But why does Holly escape the lake? Why only her? None of the others?"

Malory regarded Heather with hooded eyes. "I don't know. A power she possesses, some sort of magic of her own."

"And you've tried to banish her?"

Irritated, Malory pushed her chair in and adjusted her shirt. "Yes, Heather, we've tried. And yes, we should try again tonight, but I'd rather get laid." She traded looks with her familiar, who was as aware as she was that banishing Holly Gayle was so difficult, not because Holly had powers of her own, but because it was just possible she had stolen a power of Malory's.

It was something that only she and Brittany knew about and suspected. *The stone.* Malory's powerful emerald, set in the haft of a small silver dagger, had been lost the night they killed Holly Gayle. *Lost or stolen.* The stone, a gift from the Forest Knight long, long ago, when her brother was still alive, had pulsed with power, glowing green like the eyes of the knight himself. It was a key to her true strength; without it she was powerful in her own right; with it she was invincible. She and Brittany had spent years searching for it, returning to Greenbriar more often than they should, searching the woods, placating the Forest Knight with sacrifices, far more of them than he had demanded when the stone had given her more solid immortality. When she wasn't so in his debt.

The knight had not forgiven the loss or theft of the stone, and would not until she found it again. Until then, she would have to beg with extra sacrifices, to keep her youth. Until then, she would continue to search the woods and the tunnels below

Applehead Island and the old, dead town. She had even gone into the water, into the old church, looking, but so far had found nothing.

Lust and longing grew in her heart at the thought of it. "Maybe," she said softly, "we should go into the woods tonight."

"What for?" Heather asked, oblivious of her mood. "I thought you wanted to get laid."

Malory glanced at her, nodding slightly. There was power in that as well. *You are drunk! Don't be foolish!* "Okay, let's get laid," she said. "Then maybe we'll walk in the woods."

14

Greenbriar Pizza's pizza was about on par with a halfway decent frozen pie, but Merilynn wolfed her pieces down. Seeing she was a slice ahead of Sam and Kendra, she forced herself to slow down. She looked around. "This place is really something," she remarked as she plucked an olive from her new slice and ate it slowly.

"It is," Kendra said. "How did you ever find it?"

Sam smiled. "I looked behind a newspaper rack and, voilà, there it was. Hiding." She reached for a new piece, picking one from the half that had mushrooms along with olives, onions, pepperoni, and red bell peppers.

Merilynn and Kendra had wanted sausage too, but Sam had nixed the idea, declaring it too likely to cause food poisoning. Like a good reporter, she built up a case in about fifteen seconds that neither of them could argue with. Sausage, after all, was always iffy. And in this place . . .

Merilynn gazed at the decor of the long, skinny restaurant. It was primarily a take-out joint, but tables and chairs lined one side of the corridor that led back to the rest rooms. The lighting was low, with little red glass candle holders that held electric lights on each Formica table, and the walls had posters of anything and everything Italian that the management could scavenge. There was a map of the country, travel posters of ruins, a bad painting of a vineyard, a horrendous painting of a man who might have faintly resembled the Godfather if the artist had been more talented. He wore a red-and-white-checked napkin tucked into his collar and stared at a pizza on a table—with a red-and-white-checked tablecloth, of course—before him, an expression that was supposed to be pleasure, but looked more like a gas attack, adorning his face. And no wonder. The high-piled pizza looked as if it were slathered with Play-Doh vegetables and blood. Merilynn nodded at it. "That's a real appetite inducer."

Kendra laughed. "Is that supposed to be Frank Sinatra?"

"I thought it was Marlon Brando," Merilynn said. *The Godfather.*"

"It looks more like John Belushi's last supper," Sam said.

"That's terrible!" Merilynn said. "It's mean." Then she laughed. "But I see the resemblance."

"Really, that's supposed to be Belushi," Sam said. "The owner says he ate here once. It's their claim to fame."

"I guess he didn't pose for the painting," Kendra said.

"The painting was done by the owner's wife. Don't let them hear you dissing it," Sam warned. "He thinks she's a Picasso."

"He's right," Kendra said softly. "Belushi's eyes aren't quite even. And one ear is higher than the other."

"Shhh. When I ordered, I told them I work for the school paper," Sam said quietly. "We'll probably get a discount if you two don't blow it."

"But we already paid."

"Next time. After I write a nice review."

"Oh." Merilynn liked knowing Sam was planning ahead.

"Now," said the journalist sitting across from her and Kendra, "don't make a sound when you see it, but look at the painting hanging behind you, over the next table down."

They turned. The table was occupied by a couple of jocks from school, so their glance at the painting was blessedly brief. When she looked at Sam again, Merilynn was amused by the grin.

"What do you think?" Sam asked.

"Somebody threw up on the canvas?" Kendra asked.

"Come on, you *did* see it, didn't you?" Merilynn chided softly.

"Yes, I saw it," Kendra admitted. "But do those two guys sitting under it realize what's in it?"

"Probably not," Sam said. "It's for the best."

All three giggled. Merilynn tried to steal another glance, but caught the eye of Frank Steiner, the beefy wrestler from the speech class she and Sam were both in.

He grinned. "Hi, girls."

"Uh, hi." Merilynn spoke without enthusiasm. Beefy Boy was an oversexed tub of lard, his aura all disgusting, dirty red with lust, yellowish green with gluttony. The boy was a walking advertisement for several Deadly Sins.

"Hi," said the other guy. He was pudgy-husky. Another wrestler, probably.

Merilynn didn't recognize him, but Sam did. "Hi, Norton."

"Aren't you going to introduce me to your friends?" he asked.

Ewwww. Merilynn thought he was almost creepier than Frank Steiner. She didn't sense as lecherous an aura, but it was peculiar and prickly. He looked like a nerd. And sure enough—

"Merilynn, Kendra, this is Norton Simms. He's a computer systems major."

"And a wrestler!" he added. "I just made second string."

"How nice for you," Kendra said.

"Norton writes the computer column for the paper," Sam said dryly.

"Viruses are my specialty," Norton said.

"Giving them?" Merilynn asked, very turned-off.

"Are you flirting with my man, Merilynn?" Frank asked.

Merilynn rolled her eyes and turned her back on the pair. Kendra did the same.

"Hey, girls, want to join us?" Frank called.

"No," Sam said.

"Ah, come on. We have beer."

"We don't want any beer," Kendra replied. "School night."

"Who cares?" came Norton's voice. "Skip a class. Live a little."

The girls ignored them. Then Frank leaned his chair back, hot garlicky breath oozing over Merilynn's neck. "You're really cute," he said. "I love redheads."

"So, you mean you two aren't gay?" Sam asked, even more dryly, if it was possible.

"What?" Steiner and Simms squawked simultaneously.

"I thought you were a couple," Sam said matter-offactly.

"If we're a couple because we're sitting together, then you three are pussy-licking dykes," Steiner snarled.

"Homophobe," Merilynn said softly to her friends.

"Did you call me a homo?" Steiner asked, turning uglier.

Merilynn turned and fixed him with her eyes. He flinched and looked away, but as soon as she turned back to her food, he was leaving stench on her neck again. "Why don't you let me show you just how much I like chicks?"

She ignored him.

Norton Simms spoke up, showing slightly more intelligence. *Slightly.* "Why did you say that about us? Because we're wrestlers?"

"Not at all," Sam replied nonchalantly. "It's because you chose to sit together at *that* table."

"This table?" Norton asked. "What's wrong with this table?"

Merilynn could feel ill will pouring off Steiner, even though he'd sat back up and was stuffing his face—you couldn't miss the sounds of his chewing. Like a wolf tearing up a deer.

"There's nothing wrong with the table," Sam said. "I thought you chose it because you found the painting above it titillating."

Merilynn and Kendra turned in time to see the boys look up at the antimasterpiece of art on the wall. Merilynn clapped her hand over her mouth to keep in her laughter as the wrestlers realized what they were sitting under.

It was a painting of the statue of David, in brilliant shades of pinkish flesh and no fig leaf. The owner's wife obviously thought highly of David's prowess. The statue showed a David who might have been posing on a very cold day. This David wasn't nearly so unhung. This David could be in a porno movie if he wanted.

"Shit!" said Steiner. He picked up the pizza platter and his mug. "Come on, we're moving away from these dykes. Get the pitcher."

The pair moved down to the table with the map of Italy over it, and the girls laughed so hard it hurt. "Shh," Sam said when she caught her breath. "Not so loud. We have classes with those guys."

"Samantha Penrose," Merilynn said, doffing an imaginary hat, "I salute you."

"Me too." Kendra started on another slice as she spoke. "So, you and Merilynn went to cheerleading camp together?"

Sam rolled her eyes. "That was a long time ago."

"Neither of you seem the type."

"Lord, no," Merilynn said. "I went for the ghost stories. What did you go for, Sam?"

"My parents wanted me to, and I decided to go ahead and do it so that I could write an exposé on cheerleaders."

"Come on," Kendra said. "An exposé? What were you, ten?"

"About that." Sam paused, pizza at her lips. "Why is that so hard to believe?"

"Ten-year-olds play with dolls and—"

"I had a doll once," Sam said tonelessly. "It talked. So I took it apart to see how it worked."

"You must have driven your poor mother crazy," Kendra said, smiling.

Sam's lips crooked up a little. "Probably." She sounded proud.

"That was the only doll you ever had?" Merilynn asked.

"Of course not. That was the last one. I don't remember when I was very small. I'm human, though. I probably played with them."

"You sound disgusted at the idea."

Sam shrugged and chewed, had a Pepsi chaser. "I was a tomboy."

"Not me," Merilynn said. "I loved dolls. I had Barbie and Ken. A couple of each."

"Me too," Kendra said. "They were fun for a while."

"Did you play games with them?" Merilynn asked.

"What do you mean? I guess I did the usual, you know, dressing them up and having little weddings, junk like that. Once I stuck a Ping-Pong ball under Barbie's dress and pretended she was pregnant. My granny thought that was rude." She laughed. "Is that what you mean?"

Merilynn trilled a laugh. "I took it a little further. Father's housekeeper—she lived in—she loved to sew. She made me Barbie and Ken costumes. I had an outfit for Ken that made him look like *The Exorcist*. You know, the priest costume, a black overcoat. She even made a little bag out of felt. So I'd dress him up as Father Damien—I had such a crush on that man, isn't that awful?—and I'd put makeup on Barbie. Not real makeup, but like I'd paint toothpaste on her face to make her look white and rub cayenne pepper on her eyes to make them look red."

Sam laughed so hard she launched a nugget of pizza. "Sorry. Cayenne pepper? I love it!"

"The housekeeper didn't wear makeup, so there wasn't any. Necessity's the mother of invention."

"I'll say."

"So, I'd put Barbie in her nightgown and tie her to her little Barbie bed and play *Exorcist*." She paused. "I ruined a couple of them that way, but Father finally bought me one that bent better."

"He knew what you were doing?"

"Yes. Mostly. He's very open-minded. Heck, I was exorcising evil, how could he disapprove?"

"He let you see the movie that young?" Kendra asked.

"Yes." She cocked her head. "Is that weird?"

"I don't know. My mother and Granny would never let me see things like that. I think that would have given me nightmares, so I'm glad I didn't see it that young."

"Father always explained everything when I wanted to see something scary or weird. He always stayed with me and gave me the remote so I could turn it off if I got freaked out. It was cool. Anyway, he did get mad once and took away my *Exorcist* costume."

"Why?" Sam asked.

"Well, he walked in while I was doing the crucifix scene, you know, where Regan screws herself with the cross?"

"And he disapproved?" Sam's eyebrow Spocked up, her mouth crooked with amusement.

"I was using the cross on his rosary beads. He never would have caught me though if I hadn't gotten so carried away."

"What do you mean?" Kendra asked.

"I was good at doing the possessed-Regan voice and right before he came in, I was saying, 'Fuck me! Fuck me!' just like in the movie."

"So he really came to bawl you out for saying fuck?" Sam said.

"Not bawl me out, but yes, that's what alerted him."

"He didn't bawl you out?" Kendra asked. "I would've gotten a mouthful of soap for saying that!"

"Father's realistic. He'd explain to me that the word was bad and I'd get in trouble for using it." She paused to chew. "That was good, because if he'd stuck soap in my mouth, I would have rebelled and started saying it every five seconds."

"What did you do after he took away your *Exorcist* costume?" Sam asked.

"He gave it back, but I'd made up lots of other games. I had nun costumes for all my Barbies. Old-fashioned costumes. So I liked to put one on Ken and one on Barbie."

"On *Ken?*" Sam asked, grinning.

"Well, he had his priest costume on underneath. I hardly ever made him into a transvestite. Usually, I pretended he was wearing it so that he could get into the nunnery and fool around with the nuns."

"Oh," Sam said wryly. "That's okay then."

"Goose," Merilynn said. "You're being silly."

"Did you ever play ghosts with them?" Kendra asked.

"Did I ever!"

15

The Pi Eta Gamma fraternity house was two stories of Federalist mansion, brick and stone, with a narrow pillared porch running across the front. There was none of the gracefulness of the Gamma's antebellum mansion; rather, it stood sharp and proud in true masculine fashion. Located ten minutes away (on foot), backed up to another part of the forest bordering the college property, it was the House of Jocks, and Malory was out to locate some, the bigger the better. One could only ride Professor Tongue so long before a good rooting became necessary.

Brittany and Heather and Michele, a Gamma officer, cheerleader, and Fata Morgana they'd met up with in the foyer on the way out, were with her. Michele carried a sixer of Michelob, and was killing one as they walked in order to catch up with her inebriated buddies.

Brittany, of course, never drank, but she didn't need to; she seemed to be in a perpetual state of intoxication. *Seemed* being the key word. That was how she liked to be perceived, a little goofy. Even Malory, who knew better, usually fell under the spell and underestimated her.

They entered the house, quietly pushing open one of the unlocked tall green double-entry doors. It wasn't late, only nine-ish, and Brittany found the girls' stealth—including Malory's—amusing. It was the alcohol. It had them, for the moment, in sneaky mode. It pleased them, Brittany knew, because it made them feel wicked in an alcohol-silly sort of way. She watched her mistress. They had spent centuries together. Malory Thomas was a stone-cold killer, but right now she was as giggly as a little girl. Brittany liked that.

She also liked that she was after men tonight. While they were at the kitchen table, she had thought Malory was going to want to use her as a sex toy tonight—which wasn't bad, but it was exhausting, especially after the workout at the professor's. In fact, Brittany was still sated and thought that Malory ought to be as well. It wasn't like her, but then it wasn't like her to drink so much either. *The half-moon. The anniversary. She's nervous. She's avoiding the ghosts. Why?*

They walked down a corridor into the big main living room, and Brittany watched her mistress, growing more ill at ease with each passing moment. Malory was fearless. Always fearless—and with good reason. Tonight, there was a vulnerability. Maybe it was just the alcohol playing tricks. Maybe she truly hadn't thought about the anniversary and the activity in the lake tonight. About Holly Gayle's likeliness to appear on the grounds or in Gamma House.

But that rang false to Brittany too. Malory had spent the day having sex, going at it like a machine, insatiable. In her gut, Brittany believed she was avoiding something. *Holly.* But why? They'd seen her many, many times over the years. Malory didn't fear her; she usually thought of her as an annoying gnat. When Holly had shown up and helped Eve Camlan escape her fate, Malory was furious, not frightened. *But she's had time to think about it. That must be it.*

"Hello, boys," Malory said, approaching some football players who were having a study group at a table near the sofas and chairs. As at Gamma, the furniture they favored was near the fireplace. Tonight, a chill was in the air and they'd lit a fire. It crackled merrily as it licked the logs and made Brittany wish to be at a bonfire in the woods, to commune with the Forest Knight, not these human boys. But what Malory wanted, Malory got.

"Ladies!" Art Caliburn stood up and grinned. Spence Lake, Duane Hieman, and Perry Seville did the same. All varsity boys, all big and reasonably handsome. Perry was smaller and more earnest than the others, and Brittany decided he was the one for her with his haunted blue eyes and black hair. He had a look of innocence, and real or not, she liked that.

"Hi, Perry," she said, claiming her territory. "Studying hard?"

"Hardly studying," he said, a little shy.

"We were just about to take a break," Duane said. He was a big man of African descent. He had a warrior look about him, and Michele eyed him.

"We're tired of studying," she said. "Do you want to do something, Duane?"

He looked surprised. "Sure."

Heather said, "Art?"

Malory cut in. "Art? Would you like to take me for a walk?"

Heather glared; then the captain of the team did something that Malory hated. He said, "Did you want to take a walk, Heather?" He looked at Malory while Heather stood there, obviously wanting to say yes, not daring to. "Malory, Heather started to say something first. I hope you don't mind."

Malory didn't answer. For a moment, Brittany thought she was going to blow up, so she thought *Spence Lake!* at her as hard as she could. Malory glanced at her and gave a slight nod. "Of course I don't mind. I'd rather walk with Spence anyway. Are you up for a little exercise, Mr. Lake?"

Art and Spence exchanged glances, then both smiled. The football players closed their books and left them on the table when they stood. "So what's up?" Spence asked. "Is this a group walk? Or something else?"

Malory looked to Brittany, picked up her thought, and said, "Group. For now, at least. Is that okay with you boys?"

"Just fine," Art said. "Where are we going?"
Malory smiled. "Into the woods."

16

Eve Camlan had lost all track of time, and existence seemed to come and go. Almost always, she felt as if she were on the verge of sleep, though sometimes she walked through an old town, encountering other people. Most were ghosts and never spoke, but some were more. Some were like her. Especially Holly.

Holly Gayle was the one constant. Whether she dozed or walked, Holly was always with her, a comforting presence.

The last thing Eve remembered was walking along the old road, passing amber lights in old houses, passing silent people. Now they were in an old church. The transition was sudden. One moment, she had looked up and seen the beautiful glowing jewels of the stained-glass window above them; the next, they were in this little hidden room, looking at their own physical bodies, bodies that clung together, just as their spirits did. Eve knew she was dead, and had known it from the moment Holly had called her out of the room in the smokehouse. *How long ago?* She didn't know. Now, she stared at the corpses in fascination.

Those bodies are ours! Eve Camlan's silent words were easily heard by her spirit companion.

Yes. I need to show you something. Holly, as plainly visible to Eve as she was to Holly despite the darkness and the water, drifted forward, gently touching her own physical form, pushing chestnut hair from her face. She did the same to Eve's mortal body.

Why are we like this? Unspoiled? The others are all just bones.

I am going to show you why. I am going to show you our salvation. Holly turned to Eve and lifted the ruffles covering the bodice of her white gown. The dress's waist was revealed and with it, a green sash. In the center was a small silver dagger, shaped like a sword, slipped through the material to hold it together like a belt buckle. A large green jewel set into the ornate haft glowed with its own inner light.

Eve gasped and reached out to touch it, but her fingers passed through it and through Holly. It, too, was a ghost.

This was given to the creature we call Malory Thomas by the Forest Knight himself. It wields great power. I took it the night I died. Malory still searches for it.

Does she know you have it?

She only suspects. She doesn't know where it is, nor does she know about my body, or yours. The stone in the little sword is what gives me the power to walk on land, and the power to save you.

I'm the only one you could save?

Yes, and only because you let go of your life before she expected you to. That is why you are here, with me. You share the power with me now. The stone is filled with real magick.

Is the real stone there?

No. No more. I used the power to move it to a safer place. It was difficult to manipulate matter, but I finally learned how. It's exhausting. I will teach you, but it takes time.

Where is it?

They drifted through the closed door, back into the main part of the church. Holly pointed at the stained-glass window. *Up there. Hidden in plain sight.*

How will it help us?

It will free us. It will free the other spirits as well.

How?

Someone will help us, if she can. Someone of the same blood as Malory Thomas.

Confused, Eve stared up at the stained glass. *A sister? A mother?*

No. A daughter. The time is coming. We must help her. Other daughters have failed. Holly watched Eve. *What are you thinking?*

Can we go up and see it? The stone?

No. If Malory or a Fata Morgana were to come along and spy us, they would know and they would take it back.

What do we do?

Tonight is special. Malory may try to banish me, but she cannot. Tonight is a night of power for her, but even more so for you and me.

They were out of the church, drifting toward the surface. *Tonight, we will walk on land and try to make contact.*

With Malory?

Perhaps. But someone else as well.

Who?

Her daughter.

Kendra . . . The name floated into Eve's mind. *My roommate.*

You went to her briefly the night you died. You tried to warn her. Do you remember?

You helped me. She saw me, I scared her. She's Malory's daughter?

No. There is another.

Above the water, the half-moon wavered. Then they broke through the surface and the moon became solid. Eve looked at Holly, perfectly clear in the dark night. She looked at her own hands and saw that they seemed real. Around them, as they moved onto the shore—it felt like walking, but it wasn't, not exactly, for she couldn't feel the earth under her feet— loomed the woods. Behind them, she saw the Applehead Cheerleading Camp. It did not seem to be lit by the moon, as she and Holly were, but she could see more details in the darkness than she ever had been able to with her physical eyes.

Come with me.

Holly guided her forward, into the woods. The leaves of the oaks and *Liquidambar* trees were night-colored but she could see individual needles on the firs, veins in the turning leaves of the deciduous trees.

Where are we going?

To the Knight's Chapel, first. Then we shall decide where next to travel.

17

"*The Shining* game," Merilynn said, sucking the last of her lemonade through her straw, "was sort of about ghosts."

"Good heavens," Kendra said. "Is this another Barbie game, like *Exorcist* Barbie, *Return of the Living Dead* Barbie, and *Alien* Barbie?"

"Yes."

Sam picked a crumb of crust from the platter and popped it in her mouth. "I don't think you can beat *Alien* Barbie, Merilynn. Shaving her head takes the cake."

"Actually, that was *Alien Three* Barbie, but I guess the games all sort of ran together. I really liked *Aliens* Barbie. Putting her in the Transformer toy was fun. Even you would have liked that, Sam."

"Maybe. So what's *The Shining* game?"

"I know," Kendra said. "Barbie is Wendy and Ken is Jack Torrance. Skipper was Danny."

Merilynn smiled happily. "Exactly. I cut Skipper's hair for that too, so she'd look like a boy."

"What did your father think of that?" Kendra picked up her cup and poured some crushed ice in her mouth.

"He didn't care. In fact, he thought it was nice that I turned one of my Skippers into a boy. I made a little Hot Wheels cart for him and everything. Of course, it was more like a wagon, but you know, when you're a kid, every cardboard box looks like a cave or a castle."

"Or a fort," Sam said. "I loved to build forts."

"You would." Merilynn laughed. "Father wasn't too happy with *The Shining* game after I made a miniature bat for Wendy and an ax for Jack." She paused. "But he complimented me on how well I could whittle."

Kendra laughed. "So, did he catch you swearing again?"

"I'll bet you were doing my favorite scene, where Wendy interrupts Jack while he's staring at his typewriter and he goes off on that rant about how when he's at the keyboard, he's working, whether he's typing or not." Sam sounded downright excited. "I love that scene because it's true."

"No, sorry. He didn't like Barbie and Ken beating each other up, but he talked to me, you know, to make sure I knew good people didn't do that stuff. He was okay once he knew I knew. It was the blood in the elevator part that made him forbid that game."

"Blood in the elevator?" Kendra asked.

"You don't want to know. Even I knew I was going too far." Merilynn craned her neck to look at Kendra's watch. "It's going on nine-thirty. We should probably go back."

Sam nodded and all three stood up. Merilynn went to refill her lemonade and Kendra's iced tea while Kendra dug up two ones and dropped them on the table; none of them were sure if this was a place where you left a tip. The two waited by the door for Sam, who was at the counter, talking up the pizza guy. Finally, she joined them and they walked outside.

"So, look what I've got," Sam said. She waved a coupon for a free large pizza in front of them.

Merilynn gave her the eye. "Some reporter you are, getting paid off."

"Hey, we're students. I'm poor, aren't you?"

"Pretty much," Merilynn said. "I'm just surprised you're on the take."

Sam's jaw dropped, then snapped shut again. "I'm giving

them a good review because they're the only game in town, but they don't have to know that," she said defensively. "And they didn't give me the coupon *before* I said they'd get a thumbs-up. They gave it to me after. So, technically, I'm not on the take."

"Would you have told them if you were going to write up a stinker review?" Kendra asked.

"Probably." Sam started toward the car, keys out. "Well, maybe not. But I wouldn't lie and say it was good when it wasn't just to get a freebie."

"I was teasing," Merilynn soothed. "You're so easy to ruffle. *I'd* give it a good review to get a free pizza even if it sucked. Well, not too much sucking. I wouldn't do it for a free pizza if I didn't want another pizza."

"Well, I wouldn't compromise like that," Sam said. She pushed the remote on her key, unlocking her little five-year-old white Camry.

"We know you wouldn't," Kendra said, waiting while Merilynn climbed into the backseat. She sat down and closed the door.

"That's why we love you, Sam. You're honorable."

"Merilynn, don't yank my chain."

"I'm not," Merilynn said. "You're honorable. You really are. I admire you."

"So do I," Kendra said.

Sam started the car. It purred.

"How do you keep this car in such good shape?" Merilynn asked. "It runs like new and it's so clean."

"My parents gave it to me when I left for Greenbriar. It's my mother's old car. She hardly drove it."

"She doesn't like to drive?"

"She loves to drive. She always took my father's SUV, so he bought her one too. She thought this car was boring because it's automatic, not stick." She pulled out onto the quiet main street of the town of Greenbriar.

"It's just so clean."

"My parents kept it that way."

"But you've had it for months. Where's all the trash?"

"Are you serious, Merilynn?" Kendra asked, looking back at her.

"She's serious," said Sam. "I bunked with her. She doesn't know how to put anything away."

"That's a quirk you didn't tell me about when you moved in," Kendra said.

"I'll be good," Merilynn said.

Sam laughed. "Just don't look under her bed, in her drawers, or her closet."

"Okay, I won't look. Merilynn, just don't leave gum on the furniture or clothes on the floor, and I'm cool."

"What if I leave them on my bed?" Merilynn prodded.

"That's fine. I just don't want to walk on them, okay?"

"No problem. Sam, you were one anal-retentive bunkie."

"The odd couple?" Kendra asked.

"We would be if we tried to share a room," Merilynn said.

Sam groaned. "Perish the thought." She halted for a stop sign.

"This place is absolutely dead," Merilynn remarked. "Greenbriar goes to bed early."

"It sure does." Kendra looked out the window. "I don't see anything open."

"There's not much here to *be* open," Sam said, peering in the rearview mirror as she accelerated. "We've got an asshole on our tail."

Merilynn looked around. Something tall with its brights on was coming up on them. "It's a truck or something," she said. "Maybe a Jeep. I think I see a roll bar."

"The wrestlers?" Kendra asked.

"I wouldn't be surprised," Sam said.

The lights were blindingly close, but she ignored them, flipping the nighttime switch on the rearview mirror to kill the glare and slowing down to twenty-five miles an hour.

"Are you trying to get them to pass you?" Merilynn asked.

"The speed limit in town is twenty-five. The place makes half its money ticketing speeding students. They aren't going to bully me into speeding."

"But you were going faster before they came along," Merilynn said.

"That was my choice. I won't let them make a choice for me."

Merilynn saw her smirky smile reflected in the center mirror. "You love this, don't you?"

"Is that wrong?"

"What do you think, roomie? Is she wrong?"

"I don't think so. I'd probably wuss out and pull over to get rid of them."

"I think they're the wrestlers," Sam said. "If we pull over, they will too."

Merilynn squinted back. "I think you're right. Two guys. Big ones. Yeah, I'm sure it's them."

"They'll follow us all the way back to the campus." Kendra sounded worried. "Once we're there, what do we do?"

"Don't be intimidated," Sam said.

"They're huge, they've been drinking, and we razzed them," Merilynn pointed out. "I know you're tough, but unless you have a gun or pepper spray or something, I don't want to mess with them."

"Nonsense. All we have to do is be confident," Sam said. "They won't come near us."

"Merilynn's right. I don't want to take that chance. When we get to the school, let's just pull up in front of the campus cop building. Just until they go away."

"Don't worry—" Sam began. "Damn it."

The wrestlers were flashing their lights at them now.

"I have an idea," Kendra said. "Pull over, but make sure they can't get in front of us or too close behind us. When they get out and walk up to the car, we take off, and leave them in the dust."

"That'd work," Sam said.

"Do you like the idea, Merilynn?" asked Kendra.

Merilynn had closed her eyes. She was concentrating, trying to call up that inner spark Father had helped her uncover.

"Merilynn?"

"Keep going," she said. "Just drive like you are. Give me a minute."

"What are you going to do?" Sam asked. "Moon them?"

"Not exactly. Just drive and don't make any smart-ass remarks when I say something weird, all right?"

"Sure."

Merilynn could feel Sam, could sense her concentration on driving. She also knew Kendra's eyes were on her, fascinated. That was a cool feeling. *I hope this works!*

"Wrestler boys drive wrestler toys. Roll-bar truck, now make a noise!"

Behind them, the vehicle backfired.

Sam laughed heartily. "If I were gullible, I'd think you did that."

"Shh," Kendra said softly. "She's not done."

"Frank Steiner and Norton Simms, your tires pop, you drive on rims!"

Merilynn opened her eyes and turned just in time to hear the *pop!* of a tire blowing out. The truck tilted slightly. Then three more *pops* sounded in quick succession. The vehicle sank and slowed behind them.

"They're on rims," Kendra said, awe in her voice. "Can you hear it, Sam? The metal?"

"I can. Merilynn, you have a lot of explaining to do."

"You mean you don't think that was a coincidence, Sam?"

"That wouldn't be logical," Sam said, sounding grim. "Unless you had it all set up in advance, and I don't believe that for one instant."

"She knows I never plan anything in advance," Merilynn said, pleased as hell.

"Explain," Sam said as they entered the tall wrought-iron campus gates.

"As much as I hate to do it, I'm going to invoke Gamma sister secrecy," Merilynn said. "If I tell you, you can never tell another soul."

Sam snorted. "Nobody'd believe it anyway. I'd lose my credibility before I even start my career. Don't worry. I swear on my honor that I won't talk."

"That's better than swearing on Gamma," Merilynn said.

"Much better."

"I swear on my honor and on Gamma," Kendra said.

"Okay. But, Sam, there's one other thing you have to do if you want me to talk."

"Name it."

"Tell Kendra what you saw in the boat that night on the lake."

"I don't know what you're talking—"

"Swear it or I won't talk until after you do." Merilynn sat forward as they pulled into the parking lot nearest Gamma House. "She already knows what I saw."

Sam pulled into a slot and turned off the engine. "I swear, I swear."

"Okay, I'll tell you later." Merilynn opened her door.

"Later, when?" Sam asked.

"In a little while. Let's go in for a bathroom break. Then we'll meet outside and talk."

"You're worried about being overheard?" Sam asked.

"You bet."

"Good," she said as they crossed the lot. "Me too."

18

Malory wished she had brought along the dregs of the vodka as the four couples walked into the forest. They had crossed the road and were deep in the woods now.

Her arm through Spence Lake's, they led the way along the

path leading to the old chapel. Brittany, behind them with Perry Seville, radiated caution and Malory understood why. Things could happen here, this night, things might be seen that couldn't be explained to the quartet of jocks.

On the other hand, what could go wrong? If anything happened that they didn't want the boys to recall, she and Brittany alone could easily fog their minds. Hell, she didn't even need Brittany for that.

"I wish we had a better flashlight," Art said, shaking the penlight he'd taken out of his pocket when Malory lured them into the forest. She could see the shaky light on the path before her.

"It's okay," she said. "I know the way by heart."

"Me too," chirped Brittany.

"You girls must come here a lot," Duane said, from his position at the rear with Michele.

Malory's laugh hinted at sex. Brittany's giggle did the same.

"We've been here a few times, haven't we, Brittany?"

"I could live in the woods," her familiar answered, quite truthfully. "I love them."

They continued down the dark path. Malory saw well in the dark, Brittany even better, but the men didn't seem to think that was strange. She moved closer to Spence. All the males were thinking about was sex.

Which was all she really wanted to think about too.

They walked on for another ten minutes. The path, well worn, was smooth and she silently wove a spell for speed around them and found it commingling with one that Brittany had made. Her familiar sensed the connection. They traded smiles, never breaking stride.

"We're almost there," Malory announced as the trees began to thin. Soon, they entered a grassy clearing lit by the brilliant half-moon. She heard gasps from the males. Michele and Heather had been here before in moonlight like this and though it was breathtaking, they remained silent.

"The Forest Knight's Chapel," Malory said after they had gathered together.

"Awesome," Art Caliburn said. "I've seen it in the daylight, but this is something else."

What a way with words. Let Heather have him.

"You've never had a nighttime tryst here, Art?" she asked coyly.

"Uh, no, not really."

"What about you, Spence?"

"Just a few daytime ones," he said, putting his arm around her waist.

"Perry?" Brittany asked her jock. "What about you?"

"I hiked out with a few of the guys once and checked it out. No trysts."

"I've been here at night half a dozen times," Duane boasted.

It was a lie. Despite its reputation, no one but the Forest Knight or a Fata Morgana dared stay here after dark. They had woven glamours around it to protect the sacred ground upon which it stood. Upon which they all stood now. The glamours frightened humans away. Heather and Michele would even be uncomfortable here and in fact, Malory could sense Spence's lowering libido, so she grabbed Brittany's hand—they stood side by side—and whispered, "Unlock with me" to her. Silently they said the words in unison.

Sexual tension soared back into Spence's aura. Malory prodded them all with a web of desire, trapping them. Only Brittany knew what she'd done.

"What do you think of the chapel of the Forest Knight?" she asked.

"Far out," Spence said.

Another brilliant one. Oh, well, he'll be fun to mount.

"It's just an old church," Duane said.

"An old church on sacred ground," Malory said. "This land has always been sacred and there have been other altars here, and standing stones. Some of the stones are incorporated into this incarnation of worship. Come on, I'll show you."

They approached the old chapel. Made of stone and mortar and wood, it stood tall in the clearing, its steeple intact, the window glass and doors long gone. Stepping through the doorway, they saw a bed of green grass and all looked up. The roof was gone, and the moon shone directly overhead, granting so much light that even the humans could see the inviting green of the grass.

"Wow," said some oafish male.

Brittany took her aside. "Was it wise to bring them here?"

"I don't know," Malory said, still feeling drunk. "Was it?"

"You want to fuck here?"

"Yes."

Brittany nodded. "Be alert. I'll warn Michele and Heather. We may have to cast a glamour."

"We could let them see Holly Gayle, if she shows up," Malory murmured. "That might be fun."

Brittany studied her. "It might be. But I wasn't thinking about Holly. I was thinking about *him*."

"Tonight?"

"Why not? It is his home."

"He will approve and let us be, if he comes along."

"Don't be so sure. He's hungry. He's waiting for a sacrifice."

"He's always hungry. Sex fills him."

"Caution, Mistress. Caution. Don't let your mind be numbed." Brittany nodded toward Heather, who was wrapped in a kiss with Art Caliburn. "Her mind is numb. She won't be of much use if something happens."

Malory shrugged. "She took what I wanted."

"It's just a man, no different from the one you have waiting. We need her."

"True. Don't worry, little one. Nothing will happen. Go."

As Brittany returned to Perry, Malory felt a slight chill. Brittany's advice was always good, but she often erred on the side of caution. "Spence?" she said, walking up to her tall, broadshouldered man.

"What?"

"Let me have some of your beer."

He smiled and handed it over. She swallowed it in one long gulp, then tossed the bottle in a shadowy corner and took him

by the hand, leading him to the softest, thickest patch of grass in
the shell of the chapel.

Tilting her head up, she kissed him quickly once, then again,
more slowly, letting her tongue work over his lips, teeth and
gums. She sucked his tongue into her mouth and felt his entire
body shudder with desire.

"Undress me," she whispered.

He obeyed.

Out of the corner of her eye, she saw the other couples undressing, kissing, caressing, and the sight filled her full of lust,
cutting through the alcohol, sharp and clear.

Spence laid her on the ground gently and stood over her, undressing. His body was magnificent, brown and clean, with a
hairless chest, broad and muscled, and biceps that bulged. Between his legs, his erection grew into a fine fat sausage, and she
hungered for the taste of it, for the feel of it inside her body. It
had been too long.

"Come here," she said, hoarse with need. She tilted her legs
akimbo. "Kneel here and worship at my altar."

Nearby, that little bitch Brittany giggled. She'd heard the silly
words. Malory glanced her way, saw her rolled into a naked
yin-yang ball with Perry Seville. Brittany wasn't looking, just listening.

As Spence knelt and put his huge hands on her knees, pulling
them farther apart, she saw Heather pleasuring Art Caliburn
and felt lust and anger; she would have that one too. She would
have all of them before the night was over.

Spence's warm hands caressed her legs, pushing gently.
"You're beautiful," he said. "Beautiful."

Malory looked at Michele. Already, the oafish liar Duane
was mating with her, she on all fours, he ramming from behind.
Michele's eyes opened wide with each thrust. Malory felt a
sharp tingle as she realized Duane was using the other entrance.

"Make love to me," she said to Spence.

"Let me taste you first."

She almost laughed, but cut it off before it could escape. "I
need you inside me," she insisted, still watching Michele's face.

"There's no hurry. I love to taste—"

"All right." She clamped her legs around his head and pulled him down. "Taste."

He was good for a man with a normal tongue. She watched the other couples mate as he worked. He built into a frenzy after her first orgasm, and she laughed softly and released his head, realizing she'd nearly suffocated him.

"Now," she said. "Fill me up."

Slowly, deliciously, he pushed toward her, showing a control that was agonizing and delicious. Finally, he filled her, stretched her, hurting her in the best way possible with his size. He began to move.

A banshee scream rent the air.

19

Kendra walked out of Gamma House at twenty past ten, wearing a fleece-lined denim jacket over an olive sweater, jeans, and her old Reeboks. She'd chosen the worn black pair over the new white ones at the last minute for a silly reason—the white ones were bright, easy to see. Why this mattered was a mystery to her, but Granny always said to follow her instincts, so on went the dark pair.

She paused on the veranda, feeling as if she was being watched, then walked casually—*I hope!*—down the steps and along the walk. The reflecting pool looked dark and chill beneath its clusters of lily pads. A frog croaked, another answered from the other side of the pool. A reply, a splash, another, a froggy tryst. All as she strolled toward the end of the pool.

As she approached, she saw a feminine silhouette rise from the bricks and turn. *Sam.* "Hi," she said.

"You're late," Sam said.

"Give me a break. We said around quarter after ten. We didn't synchronize watches."

Sam grinned. "Touché."

"Speaking of late, where's Merilynn?"

"I don't know. I thought she'd come with you."

"She took off before I had my shoes on."

"Pssst," someone whispered. "The cock crows at midnight."

"Merilynn?" Kendra said softly. "What are you doing?"

"Giving you the password. I feel like we're playing *James Bond* Barbie."

"Show yourself," Sam murmured.

She appeared so suddenly that Kendra jumped. "How'd you do that?"

"Where were you?" Sam chimed in.

"Wow, you two are easy to impress. I was just over there." She pointed at a single oak tree on the lawn near the forest edge.

"Bull," Sam said. "You did something."

Merilynn looked like a pixie in the dim light from the street lamp twenty feet away. Her green eyes glinted. "I stood in the shadow of the tree, that's all."

"But how'd you get here so fast?"

"I didn't. Look how far the shadow extends. I was only ten feet from you when I spoke. Almost at the end of the shadow. I just stayed very still. You didn't notice me."

"No magic, huh?" Kendra asked, still a little flustered and wanting to hide it.

"More like spy tricks. Sam, I know you know those tricks. You knew them back at camp. Keeping to shadows, moving slowly."

"Keeping to shadows, sure. That's common sense. I couldn't pull off what you just did though."

"Sure you can. I'll teach you. Both of you. There's nothing to it. So, let's get out of sight."

"No one can hear us here," Sam said. "No one but you could sneak up on us either."

"I want to walk a little ways," Merilynn insisted.

Kendra exchanged glances with Sam. "Okay," Sam said. "Lead on."

Merilynn led them to the sidewalk. They followed it as the lawn grew narrower and narrower, until the house was visible against the woods as glowing windows, nothing more. When the grass was only a two-foot-wide strip separating the sidewalk from the edge of the forest, Merilynn slowed and glanced around. "Follow me," she said and turned off the walkway, heading right into the forest.

They followed her into the shadows of the trees, out of sight, and then Kendra said, "That's far enough, Merilynn. Even James Bond would think this was a safe spot to talk."

"I'll say." Sam looked heavenward, then at Merilynn. "I have a class at eight A.M. I still have some reading to do tonight. Let's get this over with."

"Kendra," Merilynn said amiably, "Sam. What's today?"

"A school night," Sam said.

"Seriously, we talked about it earlier. It's an important one."

The first thing that went through Kendra's mind was that Eve had been dead exactly three weeks, but it wasn't exact. She thought a moment; then it hit her. "Of course! It's the birthday of Applehead Lake."

"And the death of the town of Applehead," Merilynn added somberly.

"The town was already deserted," Sam said. "It was already *dead,* if you really need to use such a dramatic word. Deserted is more accurate."

"The burial of the town, then. The *real* death. Until it was covered with water, it was still alive. People could have moved back in. Samantha Penrose, you saw those lights. You saw—tell Kendra."

Samantha's face cycled through several emotions; then she took on a look of sternness. "You tell us how you did the tire trick first."

"Sam, don't be a twit. Kendra, I told you about the ghost lights and about seeing Holly Gayle under the water reaching up."

"Yes, you did."

Merilynn turned to Sam. "You don't have to describe it. Just verify it. Did you see the ghost lights?"

"I saw something that couldn't have been reflections—I think. They appeared to be lights and *seemed* to emanate from under the water."

"Did you see the stained-glass window?"

"The window is in the administration building."

"You know what I mean."

Sam hesitated, looking as though she wanted to strangle Merilynn. "I saw something that resembled a stained-glass window, yes. But I don't know what it really was."

"That's fine," Merilynn said. "Kendra knows all about ghosts. She doesn't think you're crazy, do you, Kendra?"

"Not at all," she said. Then smiled slightly. "I wouldn't dare!"

Sam's face softened. "You've seen anomalies yourself?"

"Yes."

"Do you have any opinion about what they are?"

"I didn't, but recently I've begun to form some. Only begun. I don't claim to know anything."

"Okay." Sam cleared her throat softly. "I saw something that appeared to be a female ghost. Probably just like Merilynn described."

"I didn't exaggerate at all," she assured her. "It was Holly Gayle."

"That's an assumption," Sam said.

Merilynn's eyes flashed in the darkness and Kendra saw Sam flinch slightly. That amazed her.

"Samantha, it was an apparition. It was Holly Gayle. She matched all the stories."

"The stories assume it was a former student named Holly Gayle. There's no proof."

Now it was Merilynn's turn to roll her eyes. She was good at it, drawing it out, making her point.

"Let's call what you saw Holly Gayle, just for clarity's sake," Kendra said, trying to make peace.

Both the other girls looked relieved. "Maybe it was a hallucination," Sam said.

"Don't start."

"It could have been a shared hallucination, Merilynn. Stranger things have happened."

"You know that alleged hallucination was drawing you overboard. If I hadn't stopped you, you'd be at the bottom of the lake right this minute."

"Bullshit. I know how to swim."

"You wouldn't have had a chance. She was going to pull you down."

"You don't know that."

"Please," Kendra interrupted. "Please don't argue. Whatever it was, you saw it."

"Do you want to see it?" Merilynn asked.

"Me? What are you saying?"

"Tonight is the anniversary. The town always lights up on the night of the anniversary."

"That's just folklore," Sam said.

"There's usually some truth in folklore," Kendra said, trying to sound light to Sam and serious to Merilynn.

"When the town is lit, the ghost of Holly Gayle walks too." Merilynn made a sourpuss face at Sam. "According to legend."

Kendra shivered, remembering Eve, even now trying to recall her words. But all she could remember was the image, the chill, and the smell of the lake. "It's late," she said finally.

"Tell us how you did your trick," Sam said. "Now. A bargain's a bargain."

Merilynn glanced around. "Magick. Magick with a *k*."

Sam looked annoyed. "Magick with a *k*. That's just New Age Wicca hokum."

"You're wrong." Merilynn looked triumphant. "Look it up, Sam. Magic is sleight of hand, tricks of a stage magician. Illusions. *Magick* is the real thing. I can do a little of that."

"A Catholic priest raised you and you think you're a witch?" Sam looked to the sky again, as if praying for release.

"It's not Wicca, I'm not a witch." Merilynn paused. "Well, maybe by some people's definitions I am, but not by mine."

"What do you claim to be, then?"

"Sam, cool it. You're going to burst a vessel."

"Let's hear her out," Kendra said. "Go on, Merilynn. What do you consider yourself to be?"

She shrugged. "Nothing. A little talented in ways we normally don't recognize. Maybe some senses science hasn't decided exist yet are more developed in me."

"What does your father think of it?" Kendra asked.

"He helped me understand it."

"I would think he'd want to have you burned at the stake."

"What's your problem, Samanatha?" Merilynn said sharply. "You should be half as open-minded as Father is."

"He's into religious dogma. How could I possibly be less open-minded than a priest? Less superstitious, yes."

"He's a theologian. If the diocese knew how open to everything he is, they'd kick him out."

"Why does he stay in the priesthood? Isn't that a lapse of faith, being open-minded?"

"Sam," Kendra said.

"It's okay," Merilynn snipped. "She's always been this way. She's got her ideas and she's sticking to them."

"Sorry," Sam managed. "This is all just so, so . . . illogical."

"Sometimes life is like that," Merilynn said gently. "Hey, don't give up your bite, Sam."

"I'm not." Her voice was ferocious.

"Oh, okay. Good. So, you want to see something?"

"Sure," Kendra said quickly. "Some magick with a *k*?"

Merilynn nodded, then eyed Sam. "If you look at me like I'm a bug under a microscope, it's going to be really hard for me to do."

"Sorry. Go ahead."

"Okay." Merilynn shut her eyes. "Be really quiet for a minute while I get it together."

They waited. The sounds of the forest, the crickets, the birds, even the wind gently soughing through the trees seemed to grow softer and softer until silence surrounded them.

"Within this forest live many deer. Send me three, send them near.

"Sorry, that was lame. I'm a little nervous," she said, looking sheepish.

"No," Kendra whispered, feeling as if she might float away. "Look to the right. But just move your eyes."

They looked. Three deer, two does and a spotted fawn, stood under an oak, waiting, sniffing the air, calm.

"Shit!" Sam muttered.

Merilynn turned slowly, then walked to the animals, moving slowly and smoothly, holding out the palms of her hands, murmuring. The deer stayed where they were and let her pet them.

Sam took a step forward. The spell was broken, the deer startled and fled.

Merilynn turned and smiled. Her eyes gleamed green. "You can search me, Sam. I'm not carrying a deer whistle."

"I don't think there is such a thing," she replied, studying the red-haired girl. "Your eyes," she said finally. "Sometimes they're like the ones we saw on the island. The reflections," she added, in a voice that sounded forced.

Merilynn nodded.

"Is that part of why you can do these tricks?"

"Magicks," Kendra said quietly.

Merilynn cast a serene smile her way, then answered, "I don't know. I really don't. Maybe. But probably not. Sometimes Father's eyes do the glowy thing too."

"Really? They're the same color as yours?"

"Not so intense. I've only seen him do the glowy thing a couple of times. Me, I can't help it."

"You have your father's eyes," Kendra said.

"Only he's my uncle." She paused. "Though I'm not sure about that. I think he could be my father."

"Uncle is close enough," Sam said quickly. "Do something else."

"Three times the charm?"

"Yeah."

At that moment a scream tore through the forest, inhuman and horrible. Kendra saw Merilynn and Sam look at one another and knew they'd heard it before.

20

Gliding through the woods, Eve tried to avoid trees out of old habit, but sometimes moved through them as she followed Holly Gayle toward the Forest Knight's Chapel. She felt alive, but not alive, awake, but also in a dream. She could neither smell the air nor feel it against her face in the ways she had while in her body, but now she was just as aware of it. Perhaps more aware of it than she ever had been. She *knew* the smell and feel, *knew* the taste. It was all so clear that it felt like her normal senses, just as her vision seemed to come through her eyes. But while she knew all of these things, nothing touched her, not the ground, not the trees she floated through. It was all separate, another world.

It is another world, Holly told her, reading her thoughts as if they were her own. *We are parallel to it. We live now in the land of spirit and you will see the magical beings you only heard of in fairy tales in your lifetime.*

Are they good? Are they evil?

Nothing is wholly good or evil. Things have leanings, tendencies, Eve. You have a tendency toward good. Malory has a tendency toward evil. But there are no absolutes.

Eve took in her surroundings, basking in her altered senses. *Are there fairies here? Trolls?*

She heard Holly's gentle laughter. *Yes. Though they are known by many names, in this forest you will sometimes see earth elementals called Puckwudgies. They are the servants of the Forest Knight. In the lake, you will see water elementals. Their special name is lost in this land, so the living call them undines, from the Greek myths. They are the same. There are elementals of air and fire as well. But none are so plentiful as the Forest Knight's minions.*

Eve felt delight. *Are Puckwudgies good or evil? I mean, which way do they lean?*

More tinkling laughter, like water in a brook. *They are neither, though their tendency is to be like their king, the Forest Knight.*

What is he like?

Eve sensed humans nearby, felt their life force. And a special place nearby.

A special place, Holly agreed. *The land sacred to the Forest Knight. He is the king in this realm, in this place. There are other kings in other forests, in deserts, in fields, in valleys and seas. Others like him and unlike him, but all are kings. The knight is made of all things green. A desert king is made of sand and blows like a whirlwind.*

Eve felt disquiet, in herself and from Holly. *What's wrong? Something's wrong!*

They defile the sacred land. And the Forest Knight knows.

What is his nature? Vague fear, leavened with excitement, filled her.

In reply, Holly filled her with pictures of trees and bushes, flowers and ferns. Butterflies, bees, a bird feeding its young in a tree. An odd little manlike creature with big eyes and green-gray skin moving among the shadows on the forest floor. And then glowing green eyes in a leafy face.

No! It killed me.

The knight did not kill you. Think, remember. Is the face I'm showing you so hateful as the one you saw? Are the eyes those of devils and demons?

Eve looked inside herself, and saw the picture Holly sent for what it was. A powerful face, frightening in its strength, but the glow of the eyes were not like the demon-slits that had visited her. No fat green tongue lolled. Leaves ran from each side of the knight's mouth, trailing into a beard lushly green and alive. There was humor in the eyes, if fleeting. *Malory killed me. She is like him?*

No. He is far more powerful, a god, the trickster god, and she is partly of his world, partly of the mortal one. She imperson-ated him to frighten you. She is not an elemental, but born human, long ago. She is like a Greek half-god. She buys immor-tality from the Forest Knight.

Then he is mostly evil? Eve thought of the sacrifices, of the bones in the submerged town, the spirits and ghosts that roamed its streets.

No. He is not evil or good. He simply is. He is what others expect. He began with the first green sprout and will last until the end of this place. Perhaps longer. I don't know much except that he is far beyond much concern about the affairs of humans.

Eve tried to understand, but everything Holly told her seemed to be at odds. *Malory gives him human lives. How can something that takes life not be evil?*

Holly laughed gently. *All gods take lives.*

Eve heard voices, saw the chapel, stark in the moonlit clear-ing. *Malory is in there. So is Brittany— Holly, what is she?* Though she couldn't see her, she sensed something unsettling about her, something wrong.

She is of the spirit realm, but able to take material form. Brit-tany is Malory's familiar and has been for many, many years.

She's bad.

She is what she is. She is a being who craves a master or mis-tress who is powerful in the ways of sorcery. She is Malory's creature. A long pause. Tension grew, thickening the air like cold syrup. The crickets and birds silenced. *Without her gem-*

stone, Malory is less powerful than she could be, and without her familiar, her power further decreases. These are things her daughter should know.

Who is her daughter?

You will see later.

Preternatural silence took the forest, but for the sounds of lovemaking within the chapel ruins. Abruptly, an unearthly shriek tore through the woods. It came from Applehead Island, and she remembered it from the day she, Merilynn, and Samantha had rowed to the islet and peered into the black cave. She had seen the eyes, then heard the screams.

It is the knight, Holly affirmed. *He is coming.* The spirit swirled around Eve, and swept her away, into the trees, out of the line of fire.

Another horrible scream tortured the air. Closer. *We should leave.*

There's no need. The knight will not harm us. He holds the spirit sacred. We are of his world. Holly pointed at the chapel as another cry sounded, closer still. *There are some in his chapel he will not deal with so kindly.*

Wind rose, howling, mixing with the screech, becoming one as they tore into the trees, spraying leaves and pine needles, furrowing the ground. In the center of the wind glowed the green orbs Eve remembered so well.

Ride the wind, Holly told her. She had joined with her, and that made Eve less afraid as they buffeted painlessly through the trees. They caught on the knight's wind and Eve thought they would be pulled along, into the chapel. *I don't want to go in there, Holly! I don't want to see!*

Don't worry. Holly surged around her, carrying her high into the sky, above the trees, above the wind.

Eve saw two figures run from the chapel, and come together and vanish. *Magick!*

Yes.

And then the Forest Knight exploded into his chapel, a tornado of screaming rage.

Human voices began to shriek in counterpoint.

21

"Malory!"
Deeply involved in the depths that Spence Lake's varsity eight-incher could reach, Malory vaguely heard her familiar's voice call her name. She nearly answered, but the running back redoubled his drilling efforts and she gasped his name instead.

"Malory!"

Brittany, as delightfully naked as she could be, but stepping into her jeans, stood over them, looking urgently down into Malory's face. Spence made to pause and look up, but she forced his head back down and trapped his ass with her legs, scissoring up and down to make him keep moving.

What? She mouthed the word silently to keep the jock focused on his work.

"You heard him."

"The knight?"

"What?" said Spence.

"Nothing. Don't stop," Malory told him.

He grunted assent.

"I heard him." Brittany pulled her baby tee over her head, flipped it down to cover her breasts. "They heard him." She tilted her head toward the other couples. "They're getting dressed."

"Even Michele?"

"Yeah." Despite her concerned expression, Brittany smirked. "Duane's a quick-draw."

"His kind always are."

"Wha—?"

"Shh, Spence, just pump. Don't stop until I tell you to."

"'Kay." He started nibbling her neck.

"Mmmm. Brittany, I heard it. We've heard it plenty of times. It came from the island lair."

A new banshee shriek resounded through the air, slightly closer.

"He's coming."

"Yeah, yeah," Spence Lake grunted. And he did.

Malory let him finish, then pushed him off of herself. "Damn it, Brittany. I was about to climax."

"You idiot!" the little blonde sputtered. "I'm never going to let you drink again. You're going to get us killed! Now! Get dressed!" She bent and grabbed Malory's jeans and threw them at her.

Malory's sex-and-vodka-soaked brain started to register the alarm in Brittany's voice. Still on the ground, she shook the pants, rolled back, and shoved her legs into them, then moved forward and up, pulling them over her ass. Brittany handed her her Gamma green T-shirt just as another shriek sounded, much closer than the last one.

"What the hell?" Spence said.

"Grab your pants and get out of here!" Malory ordered. The other three jocks stared at her, all of them pantless. "All of you! Out! Michele! Heather! It's him. He's coming."

"Who's coming?" Art Caliburn asked.

"The Greenbriar Ghost," Brittany said. "You guys get out of here."

"We're not leaving you girls alone!" Art yelled as the wind began to howl.

"No way," Spence said.

"You have to come with us!" Perry Seville said as he finished pulling his pants on. He reached for a shoe.

"Leave the shoes. Get out of here!" Brittany yelled as another furious screech rent the wind.

"It's a tornado," Art called. "We need to find cover!" He grabbed Heather's arm and pulled her toward the empty doorway, not bothering to grab her pants.

Brittany started to protest.

"Let him take her. She's too wasted to save herself," Malory told her. She raised her voice. "Get her out of here, Art. Now!

We're right behind you!" Art nodded and picked the cheerleader up as if she weighed nothing and put her over his shoulder, fireman style. They disappeared into the night.

Wind tore needles from nearby trees; they struck Malory's
face like hail. "Michele! Come on!" she screamed. "We need
you."

Duane put his arm around Michele. The two other jocks just
stood there like idiots and stared at the storm of leaves. Malory
knew the humans, even Michele, were strongly affected by the
sound of the Forest Knight's rage. It was the stuff of legends.
"Get out of here!" she ordered, putting a boost of magick in the
words to make them obey.

Art and Perry hesitated, looking dazed as the magick took;
then they started running. Duane Hieman still held on to
Michele. He didn't move, but stared at the sky.

"Look!" Brittany said. She pointed at the sky.

Beyond the swirling leaves, Malory saw the unmistakable
flowing dress of Holly Gayle as the spirit rose above the wind.
But it wasn't just Gayle. She surrounded another spirit. Malory
squinted, saw pink clothing and blond hair.

"Damn it, Malory. It's both of them!"

Malory grabbed Brittany's hand and yanked her out of the
chapel, into the clearing.

"What about Michele?" Brittany yelled in her ear as they embraced.

"No time. Do it. Now!"

They spoke the words that would move them to another
place just as the Forest Knight's eyes became visible. They saw
Malory and Brittany for a split second before the spell took and
they left the place. As the chapel vanished, she saw the Forest
Knight engulf it.

22

Merilynn stood still, listening to the shrieks from childhood grow louder. Part of her wanted to turn tail and run away, back to the safety of the house, as Kendra and Sam were urging, but another part of her wanted to run forward to meet the power behind the voice, to gaze into those eyes she had seen in the cave so many years ago.

Not just the cave. Sitting in the boat, facing Applehead Island that stormy afternoon as Sam and Eve frantically rowed toward camp, she had seen him— the Green Ghost. *The Forest Knight.* She knew it absolutely now, as she listened, ignoring Kendra and Sam, shaking them off when they took her arms, so she could listen to the shrieks.

In the boat, she had seen the glowing eyes watching from the shoreline and had been surprised that they didn't follow them across the water; she knew that the ghost could do such things if it wanted. That day, through the rain, she saw the eyes and thought she saw the tall greenish form that owned them. The light was bad, the rain a torrent, so she had decided it was her imagination. Now she knew it wasn't. If she followed the sounds, she would meet the Forest Knight.

"He's going to the chapel," she said.

"What?" Sam said. The wind was gusting, blowing their voices away before they could be heard.

"It's the Greenbriar Ghost," Merilynn said, remembering that was how Kendra had identified the phantasm. *The elemental. Pan. Puck.* "He's at the chapel."

"Good," Sam said nervously. "Let's get back to the house."

Merilynn turned to look at the others. "The chapel isn't far. Wouldn't you like to see it?"

"No," Sam said.

"Where's your reporter's instinct?"

"Gone with the wind, Merilynn. That's a storm and it's headed this way. It could be a freak tornado."

"We're safe," she said. "It won't come here, across the road. The Green Ghost stays in the forest."

"We're *in* the forest," Kendra said. "Sam's right. It's not safe to stay here."

"He won't cross the road. It's too close to civilization."

"I don't think storms care about roads," Sam said.

"You can't claim you don't recognize the sound. I know you do."

"The island," Sam replied. "Of course I recognize it. There was a storm then too."

"The eyes—"

"Screw the eyes, Merilynn."

"You saw them."

"I did, but that doesn't mean they had anything to do with that shrieking wind."

"It's not just the wind and you know it." Merilynn stood straighter and turned to Kendra. "Do you want to see the stuff folklore is made of?"

Kendra's eyes betrayed fear, but there was temptation too. Finally, she shook her head. "No."

"But you would have gone there before the shrieks. That's where we were going."

"I never agreed to walk all the way to the chapel tonight; did you, Kendra?" Sam asked.

"No," Kendra said apologetically. "I thought you might be leading us there, but I wouldn't have crossed the road."

"Me either," Sam said. "It's a school night."

The shrieks reached fever pitch and then there were more sounds, screams, human ones, very faint and small.

"We are *out* of here!" Kendra took Merilynn's arm and turned her as the screams faded.

Sam took her other arm as silence replaced the shrieks of wind and the Forest Knight. "Let's get back."

"Okay." Merilynn began walking with them. Deep and thick, the quiet felt like a quilt around her body, her ears, muffling everything. It wasn't until they reached Gamma House that the crickets and frogs began to make their night music once again.

They paused on the steps of the mansion and looked back the way they had come. "It's real," Merilynn said. "It's out there."

23

The knight is gone, Holly told Eve when the wind died down. They still hovered above the trees. *Let's go down.*

Are you sure it's safe? Eve resisted Holly's attempt to move into a position over the clearing.

Even if he was still here, we would be safe. You must forget your fears. Come.

Eve let herself be guided over the clearing. Below, she saw bodies in the ruins of the chapel. She and Holly began to descend.

Not so fast.

All right. Slower then.

Eve looked over the entire clearing as they came down just outside the chapel walls. *Where did they go? Malory and Brittany?*

It is a magick they use. It's draining. No matter what we do tonight, they won't be able to stop us now.

They moved along the ground, just above it. Eve moved her legs—*phantom legs*—but knew she didn't really need to. Holly didn't.

If you ever want to scare the living, the girl told Eve, reading her thoughts, *don't walk. Just glide a few inches above the ground. It causes grown athletes to urinate on themselves.* She smiled at Eve. *It's really quite amusing. Now come, let's go in. Don't be afraid.*

All right. Eve was afraid anyway, but she tried to push the fear deep down where Holly wouldn't be so aware of it.

They entered the chapel from a small door space on the side. *Old habits die hard,* Holly said softly. *I still forget to just go through the walls more often than not.*

Two bodies lay in a dark crimson heap near the wider main entry. They seemed puddled in reddish shadow, but Eve knew what the shadow really was— their blood, soaking into the ground. She hesitated.

You may stay here, Holly told her. *I want to see who they are.*

Eve lingered behind as Holly glided to the bodies. She hovered around them, moving to look at them from different angles. Finally, she told Eve, *They are male and female. I think one is a Gamma, but I'm not sure. I don't recognize the boy. Do you think you could look?*

Eve didn't want to but . . . *I'm dead. It can't hurt me to look at death.* Haltingly, she walked forward.

It's an ugly sight, Holly warned, too late. *They've been flayed.*

Flayed?

Their skin is gone, except on the faces. The knight wanted them to be recognized. It's all right. Look.

Looking at blood makes me vomit. Or faint.

It will do neither now. Don't worry.

Eve covered the final few feet and made herself look. *Michele. That's Michele. One of the officers of Gamma.*

Then she is Fata Morgana too. She probably wouldn't have been here with Malory if she wasn't. Do you know the boy?

Eve forced herself to ignore the glistening pink and red meat, the spill of intestines, and just look at the face. *Yes. He's a football player for the Knights. Duane, I think.*

Holly moved closer to Eve and urged her around the bodies and out the main entrance. They saw no one else for a few minutes, then suddenly encountered another pair, male and female.

They were in a small depression surrounded by ferns, still hiding. The man wore only pants and was tending to the unconscious girl, who wore only a green Gamma shirt.

Art Caliburn, she told Holly. *I went on a date with him. He's very nice. The Gamma is the captain of the cheerleading squad—*

Heather. She's the most senior human Fata Morgana member right now. Come.

Holly led her quickly through the woods. They crossed the road and traveled through more forest, finally coming to the smokehouse where Eve had died. They crossed the lawn, moving toward the house.

We're going in?

Absolutely. We have messages to leave.

Behind them, noises. They turned and saw Malory and Brittany emerge from the woods.

Should we hide?

No. They can't make us leave. Malory can't. Brittany will try. Defy her will.

24

"Where are we?" Malory asked Brittany as the world returned. The forest still surrounded them, but it was a place she didn't recognize.

Brittany stepped away from her mistress, looking around before saying, "We should have agreed on a place in advance. Where did you will us?"

"I didn't think about it. Just a secluded place near the mansion. What about you?"

"I tried for your rooms upstairs. Obviously, it didn't work."

"I should have done the same." Malory was exhausted; the transport magick drained her energy. *If I had my stone, it would be nothing.*

"I have a feeling we're close to the house," Brittany said.

Wearily, Malory sank to the ground and put her back against an oak trunk. "I hope so. Do me a favor and scout?"

"Sure," Brittany chirped. She showed virtually no tiredness from their spell. Malory resented her ability to bounce back.

Brittany smiled, picking up Malory's thoughts. "You can't help being tired, Mistress. After all, you're part human. I don't have that problem."

Malory nodded. "I know. Go find out where we are!"

Nodding, Brittany moved away, trotting, sniffing the air, following her nose. Malory watched until the familiar whirled and shifted her shape.

A small striped chipmunk looked her way, chittering, then turned and raced off.

Malory waited, wondering what happened to the others, if they were still alive. She hoped so; she couldn't afford to lose two Fata Morgana members. She closed her eyes.

A few minutes later, she came out of a doze, feeling familiar little feet running up her arm. Groggy, she opened her eyes and stared into those of a chipmunk. "Get off of me," she said, exhausted.

The little bright-eyed creature hopped off, whirled, and became Brittany again. She held her hand out to her mistress. "We're very close. I think you brought us here."

Malory took her hand and sighed as she let herself be pulled to her feet. Hand in hand, Brittany led her through the dark woods.

"The animals and insects are back to normal," Brittany said. "It's over."

"I wonder if we lost anyone. I hope not. I hate messes."

"I'll go look after we get back, if you want."

"No, the knight is furious. I don't want you returning to the chapel alone, even in your other form. Tomorrow, after daybreak, we'll go survey the damage."

"We're going to need to do something about the jocks' memory."

"If any are alive."

"Look." Brittany squeezed her hand. "Can you see the lights?"

Relief swept over Malory as she spied upstairs lights coming from the back of Gamma House. They quickened their pace and came upon the smokehouse thirty seconds later. They walked around it, and came face-to-face with Holly Gayle and Eve Camlan, standing together on the back lawn.

"Damn it," Malory muttered. "I hate ghosts."

"Let's try to banish them."

"I'm out of juice, little one." They continued walking, arriving in front of the spirits, who glared at them.

"Get out of the way," Brittany ordered. Despite her chirpy voice, the command held power. The apparitions wavered slightly, but didn't leave.

25

Merilynn and Kendra lay in their beds and talked softly of the Forest Knight, Eve, and Holly, for twenty minutes, both of them growing more alert despite the lack of ghostly visitors and the late hour.

Finally, Merilynn sat up and switched on her bedside lamp. "It's useless. I can't fall asleep when I know the ghosts are walking."

Kendra stretched and got up, crossed to the little refrigerator. "Want a bottle of water?"

"Let's make hot chocolate," Merilynn said as she walked over to the window and pulled the curtains back.

"Go down to the kitchen at this hour?" Kendra turned, hands on hips. "You just want an excuse to wander around and look for ghosts."

Merilynn laughed softly. "No, but I like the idea." She left the window and went to her closet, pulled a tall square duffle out. "I didn't unpack this yet," she said, putting it on her bed and unzipping it. "If I had, you wouldn't be accusing me of such things." She lifted a mini-microwave from the bag and put it on the dresser. "Plug this in someplace. I've got mugs and tons of packets of Swiss Miss."

"I'd tell you it was too late to be doing this," Kendra said, working, "but it sounds *so* good."

Merilynn placed the mugs—dark blue with gold stars glazed on and in them—on the dresser and Kendra poured bottled water into them then put both in the little oven and tapped it to life. "Four minutes?"

"Probably. It's not the world's speediest."

"You sure have lots of interesting kits. Herbs and stones, and mysterious powders . . . Like chocolate."

"I have my uses," Merilynn said as they returned to the window.

Below, the lawn and gardens were empty, lit by moonlight. "Mind if I crack the window?" Kendra asked.

"I'd love it."

Kendra smiled. "Eve hated the window open, but I like it cracked unless it's really cold out. I thought I was weird."

"If you are, so am I."

The window twist-lock was stuck but just as Kendra was about to give up, Merilynn produced a hammer-shaped silver tool from her herb chest. "It's to tenderize meat," she explained, covering the lock with a towel to dull the noise when she started rapping on it.

"I know what a meat tenderizer is," Kendra said as she went to add the chocolate to the hot water. "What I want to know is why you're carrying one. That's definitely unusual, you have to admit."

"Got it!" Merilynn announced. She opened the window wide. A chill breeze whooshed in as if it had been awaiting admittance. "Cripes, that's cold!" She pushed the glass down until only half an inch of air could seep in, then sat down on the bed and accepted the cup of chocolate from Kendra.

Kendra sat down next to her, cupping the ceramic mug in her hands. She hadn't expected the air to be so cold. "So, tell me about the meat hammer."

"People are tough." Merilynn's eyes twinkled like green Christmas lights. "You have to tenderize them before you eat them."

Kendra made a face.

"It's handy for crushing crystals and things. The pointy ends start the job, then I use the smooth sides to powder the crumbled material."

"Oh." Kendra blew on her chocolate. "I guess I liked the cannibal story better."

"I knew you would."

26

"There, there, Mistress," Brittany soothed as she stroked Malory's forehead. "Everything will be fine."

Malory looked up into her familiar's bright eyes. "Your lap is nice and warm. Rub my temples."

Brittany obeyed. There was much she wanted to say to Malory, but none of it would make the sorceress happy and there was no point in talking to her while the dregs of alcohol still swam in her system. She moved her small fingers in smooth, firm circles over Malory's temples, then worked her way to the sinus cavities below her eyes, her touch always firm but never harsh.

"Ouch. No, don't stop. It's helping." Malory sighed. "Why did I do that tonight of all nights?" She stared hard at Brittany. "Why didn't you stop me?"

"Oh no, you're not going to blame me, Mistress. You chose to drink."

"I didn't remember that tonight was the anniversary."

"Really?"

Malory didn't answer for a long time. "Alcohol almost never hits me."

"I know that." Brittany moved her hands to the tight muscles in Malory's neck and began working them. "And I would have stopped you if I had thought it would. It was a surprise."

"I don't like surprises," Malory told her. She sounded like a petulant little girl.

"I know you don't."

"I don't like that Merilynn moved rooms without asking permission."

"Brittany, you told Heather you didn't care at all. You acted like she was over-reacting by telling you!"

"Well, I didn't mind then. Now I mind."

"Why?"

"Too many surprises. Brittany, I've tried to figure it out, but I can't. What made the alcohol affect me so strongly?"

"I don't know, but I think magick could be involved."

"Who?" Malory came upright so fast that she bumped Brittany's chin.

"Ow! Lay down. Let me rub the tension away or you'll have a hangover."

"I don't get hangovers," Malory replied.

"You don't get drunk either." Brittany pushed her fingers lightly against Malory's forehead and the woman lay back down. "I don't know if anyone put a glamour on you. Probably not. It might just be an effect of the night. The anniversary. Holly's presence."

"That little dead bitch. I'll bet you're right. And now she's dragging Eve around with her. We have to put a stop to it before she gets stronger." She paused. "That's what's happening, isn't it, Britt? Holly Gayle's stronger than she used to be."

"Shhh. Calm down. You're exhausted. You must regain your strength. But yes, I think she's stronger."

"She raised Eve Camlan."

Brittany nodded. "She snatched her soul from us. And kept it with her."

"I'd kill them both a thousand times if they weren't already dead."

"We have to figure out why Holly is stronger."

Malory reached up and ran a finger along the side of her familiar's face. "We know why, don't you think?"

"Tell me."

"Because the Fata Morgana is missing a member? Two, now. Maybe three, if something's happened to Heather."

"Heather's fine. I checked while you were bathing. Art Caliburn brought her back to the house. He thinks they got lost in a windstorm and that Heather drank too much." She smiled. "Which is all true."

"He remembers nothing else?"

"No. I hope you don't mind, but I took it upon myself to cast a mild glamour over him and the other boys that survived. They'll all awaken with hangovers and no memories of being with us. Art won't even remember bringing Heather here."

"You're wonderful," Malory murmured.

"I know. But let's get back to Holly's power. I agree, it's growing. There's another reason."

"She has the amulet. I know it."

"Malory, stop trying to think until the alcohol wears off. We've always known she probably has it. Why else would she still be here, tormenting us?"

"Because she's a bitch."

"We've established that already, dearheart. Think another way. The Forest Knight was denied his sacrifice. He is angry."

"But we'll give him one on All Hallow's Eve." Without thinking, Malory touched her own face, as if feeling for wrinkles.

"He won't deny you your immortality now, don't worry." Brittany leaned down to kiss her mistress's forehead. "He had the blood of one of our own tonight. He is sated for the moment. But we must complete the ritual of the thirty-first to truly please—and appease—him."

"I know. Tomorrow, we'll cover our losses and restock the Fata Morgana."

"Yes, that's a good start. But we must be wary about our choices. There is more to Merilynn than we know."

"You know what she is," Malory hissed. "*Who* she is."

"Of course I know. But the priest has influenced her. She may not be what you want."

"What? Do you know something that I don't?" Malory sat up again, took Brittany's shoulders and held them. "Tell me what you know."

"Mistress, I don't *know* anything. I have a *feeling*. That's all."

Malory ran her hands over Brittany's cheeks, her eyes bright and not entirely focused. "You make such a pretty little girl."

"Thank you."

"Do you really think my little Merilynn has been sullied by her father?"

"I don't know. We must be cautious. If we bring her into Fata Morgana without knowing everything about her, she could harm us."

"Perhaps we should simply pass her by for now. We can choose a couple of the lesser candidates and see what happens with her. We can test her." Malory laid her head against Brittany's shoulder.

"That's a good idea." Brittany stroked Malory's glossy dark hair, felt the warmth of her breath upon her breast. "I think she is powerful," she said softly. "I think she has inherited much from her mother . . . and her fathers." The last, she murmured.

Her mistress had fallen asleep in her arms. Contented, Brittany gently lay back in the big bed and brought Malory with her. They tucked together.

Brittany listened to Malory's soft breathing but could not fall asleep herself. The night wind blew, the drapes billowed like ghosts. Brittany had cast a protection spell upon the house when they had come in, hoping it would be strong enough to deny entry to the ghosts. Now she shivered and silently cast another spell, one to keep their room safe from entry until Holly and her companion returned to the depths of Applehead Lake.

27

"Let's have a séance!" Merilynn announced as she wiped away a chocolate mustache.

"Girl, do you know what time it is?" Kendra was still wide awake and feeling very guilty about it.

"It's late."

"Past one."

"Want some more chocolate?" Merilynn took the empty cups to the dresser.

"No! I mean, I would, but I'll be peeing all night, so no!"

"Okay, you're right." Merilynn set the dirty cups and spoon in the refrigerator then unhooked the microwave and stowed it back in the duffle.

"Okay, why did you do that?"

"The chocolate won't be so hard to wash off."

Kendra nodded. That made sense, though the voice of her granny was having a fit about it inside her head. "Why put away the oven?"

"Are we allowed to have them?" Merilynn asked. "I read the rules, but you know, in one eye and out the other."

"I don't remember seeing anything about them in the rule book. I have the fridge, so I'm sure it's okay."

"Well, I'd rather put it away. Things get stolen around here."

"They do?" This was news to Kendra.

"Yeah. Little Lou, the cheerleader that was one of my old roomies, she had some underwear stolen."

Kendra snickered, feeling evil. "She probably lost it at a frat house."

Merilynn grinned. "Maybe, but she said it still had the sales tags on it. Red thong. Victoria's Secret."

"Thongs," Kendra said. "I tried thongs. Maybe it's just me, but I don't know how anyone can stand them."

Giggles spilled from Merilynn. "I know—and yuck! After a hard day irritating your ass, they must smell like an outhouse."

Kendra caught the giggles. "Maybe we're built wrong."

"Maybe. Do you wear high heels?"

"Not if I can help it," Kendra said. "I have two pairs for dressing up, but I hate them."

"Me too. I have *one* pair. Father got them for me for high school graduation. His idea. I thought I'd die."

"You and I are both abnormal," Kendra said with delight. "You know that, don't you?"

"I treasure it," Merilynn told her as she opened one of her bureau drawers and started digging.

"You're dropping your clothes on the floor."

"They won't go anywhere," she muttered. "Hang on. Got it." She pulled a flat wooden board out of the depths of the drawer. "Ouija." She set it down and bent, grabbing the fallen clothing and stuffing it back in the drawer. Then she opened another drawer and felt around, quickly pulling out a wooden planchette.

"Okay, let's have a séance." She brought the items over near the bed, stopping at her little yoga rug. She placed them on it and sat down cross-legged, looked at Kendra and patted the floor. "Come on."

Despite herself, Kendra moved to the floor. "I can't believe a priest would let you have one of these!"

"Father gave it to me. When they re-released *The Exorcist*, we got like a dozen of them. Parishoners turned them in. They were afraid." She paused. "That new scene of Regan doing the crabwalk on the stairs even scared me."

"Me too. But why did he give you this? I mean, aren't they considered evil by the Catholic church?"

Merilynn shrugged. "Probably. But Father's no ordinary father. Wait'll you meet him. He'd get kicked out of the church if the Popey guys knew what he does."

"Good God, Merilynn," Kendra gasped. "What does he do?" Visions of blood sacrifices danced through her head.

But Merilynn's eyes glinted green with merriment. She whispered, like the kid in *The Sixth Sense,* "He marries gay people."

Kendra stared.

"They generally frown on that. What did you think I was going to say? That he uses real blood for communion?"

"Something like that. That's nice, what he does. But wouldn't he get kicked out for the ouija board too?"

"I don't know. He keeps quiet. He likes his parish. The people. He likes helping them. It's a good job for him because it gives him plenty of time to study."

"He studies folklore?"

Merilynn nodded. "The occult, comparitive religion."

"Isn't that sacreligious or something?"

"Probably, but only if he went around preaching it. The church has nothing against scholars. That's what he is, a scholar. He doesn't talk about it to anybody but me."

"It? The occult?"

"Yes. Pretty much. He has an old friend that's like him, another priest who studies weird stuff. He talks to him sometimes. He's sort of a mentor. Father Tim gets assigned to a lot of traveling jobs though, so he's not around much." She looked down, pushing the planchette around with one finger. "I hope he's around now. Uncle Martin—Father—is probably lonely. He doesn't admit it in his e-mail, but I can tell."

"He sounds nice."

"Wait'll you meet him. You'll love him." She paused. "He has eyes like mine."

"Those are some powerful eyes, Merilynn. On a priest, well, he must be killer at Mass."

She twinkled. "He's not bad. Women are always trying to get him in the sack. Men too. He's a cutie."

"But he resists? Both?"

"He's straight, so guys are easy to resist. He tries not to be alone with women on the make. I don't think he's ever been seduced, but then none of us can stand thinking of our parents having sex, right?"

Laughing, Kendra nodded, then shivered as a trickle of cold wind entered the room. "So, let's do this. We have to get some sleep. At least I do."

"Okay, put your fingertips on the planchette. Very lightly." Merilynn did the same. "Now, we close our eyes and concentrate."

"On what?"

"On calling spirits to visit. I'll talk. You just concentrate."

"Okay." Kendra's spine prickled up with goose bumps, but she hid her nervousness.

"We call to any spirits who are listening," Merilynn murmured. "We call you in peace and kindness and love. We call you to come and talk with us." She was silent for several moments. "Spirits, you are welcome to join us . . ."

The temperature seemed to drop. *I'm just freaking a little.* Kendra ignored the sensation as best she could, but she opened her eyes. Low light filled the room, Merilynn sat before her, as serene as a madonna.

"Spotty," Merilynn said abruptly. She opened her eyes. "Spotty?"

Kendra couldn't speak.

"Does that mean something to you?" Merilynn asked. "I hear a voice saying 'Spotty.'"

"Oh my God, you couldn't know about that!" Kendra

snatched her fingers off the unmoving planchette. It felt ice-cold.

"Wait. What? Tell me! Don't get up!" Merilynn grabbed her wrist, forcing her to stay.

"You couldn't know."

"I *don't* know. Tell me."

"It's a horrible old high school nickname," Kendra said. "I never told anyone but Eve, the day we moved in together. I'm sure she didn't repeat it. I had a little accident. Some cheerleaders nicknamed me 'Spotty.' I told her. You know," she added, trying to shake off her anxiety, "Eve and I were bonding."

"Evie wouldn't repeat that," Merilynn said. "She used it to show you she's here. To make sure you know it's her."

"I don't know. Malory and her Gamma girls could have dug that up when they were checking me out."

"And they told *me?*" Merilynn looked ready to get royally pissed off.

"No, no, of course not. I just mean, somebody could know."

"And what? Send me signals on some freaked-up radio wave?"

"No!"

Finally, the redhead smiled. "I'm giving you a hard time because you're looking for hard answers when there's a simple one you just don't want to accept. Eve is here. We saw her outside. We saw Holly Gayle."

"You're right." Kendra rubbed her arms. "I'm just spooked."

Merilynn studied her. "Spotty, huh?"

"For quite a while."

"Then the Gammas probably know. Some of them probably do."

"Heather," Kendra said. "Head cheerleader. She'd know."

"Want to have some fun?"

"I've had all the fun I can stand. I really don't want to talk to any ghosts tonight."

"No, no. I mean *fun.*"

"Sleep would be fun."

"Yes, but after some real *fun.* Some instant karma. I mean, don't cheerleaders—except you, Eve—" she added, looking up and around, still hoping for contact, "really irritate you?"

"Of course. That's their job."

"High and mighty. All cliquey."

"I'm with you."

Merilynn stood up and ditched the ouija board, much to Kendra's relief. She then opened her chest of herbal medicines, powders, oils, and heaven knew what else, and selected a small pouch of fine reddish power. She brought it and a piece of paper to the rug, placed the paper on the rug and opened the plastic pouch, took a pinch of the reddish powder.

"Concentrate," she said.

"On what?"

"On what I'm about to say."

Kendra nodded.

Merilynn began to slowly let the reddish grains fall to the paper, speaking softly:

"I wearied of my period and sent it off to you

"Gamma cheerleaders wake up red, Aunt Flo's come and stained your bed

"Tampon strings and pantiliners, maxipads without wings

"My spell binds you to all these things!"

Kendra couldn't help it; she started laughing.

"What?" Merilynn asked, her smile sly.

"That was mean."

"I told you, instant karma."

"You really did it?"

"I feel like it worked."

Kendra stifled another laugh; it came out a snort.

"It won't hurt them, will it?"

"Nah. They'll just be surprised. Same old, same old, otherwise. Nothing Midol won't cure. But I did curse their supplies. You noticed?"

"I didn't realize."

"Intent," Merilynn said. "Tampon strings will fail and liner wings won't stick right. They're going to be a little cranky."

Kendra was holding her stomach and rocking, trying to keep her laughter and voice down. "How will we know if it worked?"

"Oh, I think we'll know when they come begging for Midol and tampons that work right." She hesitated. "But just to be sure—I mean, we're lowly freshmen, they probably wouldn't come to us—let's add something they can't hide. And maybe spread it out a little."

"You look like a little devil."

"Thank you. Now concentrate:

"Gamma senior sorority lasses, listen to me now:

"May your asses fill with gasses

"Noxious fumes and evil perfumes

"For twenty-four hours, your farts could kill a cow!"

Kendra held her breath, trying not to laugh. "Just seniors, right?"

"Right. I suggest we skip breakfast."

"You're mean."

"Nah," Merilynn said coyly. "Just a little wicked."

"Raised by a priest and you do this!" Kendra teased.

"Must be my mother's side coming out!"

"Was she evil?"

Merilynn shrugged. "I don't know anything about her. Father didn't know much, there were no grandparents, yada, yada, yada." She rolled her eyes. "I never knew her and she's dead, I guess. Unless she ran off and Father just played the gentleman." She fell silent.

"It's two in the morning," Kendra said, rising. "I have to get some sleep."

"Yeah."

28

Brittany awoke from a fitful doze to the sound of a long, thin whistle that faded away as she listened.

Malory still lay nestled in her arms, breathing softly, regularly, fast asleep. She studied her mistress. A beautiful sorceress, centuries old, milky skin, hair like ravens' wings, lush mouth, sooty eyelashes, arched eyebrows, perfect cheekbones, a nose any woman would want.

Lower, her long neck and shoulders were naked above the covers, the satiny sheets and forest green velvet spread. Perfect flesh but for slight goose bumps from the cold air swirling in from the window.

Brittany lifted the covers to pull them higher just as another long, high whistle filled the air. Gagging, she expelled her breath and clamped the covers down as her mistress's ass sang its dirty tune. Malory didn't move until Brittany tried to ease out of her arms.

"Don't go, my little love," Malory murmured, mostly asleep, oblivious as a fresh whistle rose.

"Bathroom," Brittany murmured, loathe to wake her mistress. "I'll be right back."

"No," Malory muttered in her petulant child tone. "Stay with me." Her grip tightened.

Trapped, Brittany endured, but she'd rather have slept with ghosts taunting her than the foul odors coming from her mistress.

29

"I guess the ghosts aren't going to visit us tonight," Kendra said, slipping between her sheets after a quick trip into the bathroom to be rid of excess chocolate milk. Bed never felt so good.

Merilynn, already in her bed, said, "I guess not."

She sounded so regretful that Kendra felt sorry for her. She also felt guilty about bringing up the girl's missing mother. Making amends, she said, "The idea frightens me, but I'd still like to see them. Eve and Holly."

"There's nothing to be afraid of. Holly and Eve would hate the Fata Morganas, not us. We're Eve's friends. Or at least you are—and I don't think she would come here to scare me, even if she's not too crazy about me." She yawned so hard her eyes watered. "She couldn't scare me anyway."

Kendra chuckled. "I don't think anything could scare you. You're more fearless than Sam. I couldn't believe you wanted to go to the chapel and try to see the knight!"

"Maybe I'm just crazy. I have to warn you—I lack common sense. Nobody's braver than Sam. I mean, how can you compete with that attitude? It's not just show either. You should have seen her back at camp. She's a rock."

"Maybe we could walk out to the chapel tomorrow," Kendra said softly, still feeling regretful. "My last class is at one. I could be ready at two-thirty. We could go then."

"I'd love to."

"It's a date." Kendra closed her eyes.

30

Merilynn listened to Kendra's soft even breathing and felt herself start to drift off, began to see quick flashes of near-sleep dreams.

Then the air pressure changed. It pressed on her ears, so gently she barely felt it at first.

Steadily, it increased, then the hairs on her arms began to stand, the hair on her head to crackle against the pillow.

"Merilynn!" Kendra called out in the dark. "What's happening?"

"It's okay, Kendra," she said, not trying to hide her excitement. "It's just static electricity. Stay still. Leave the light off."

"Meri—"

"Shhhh. Don't be afraid. Keep your voice down."

She barely got the words out before the air in the room grew chill. "Holy crap," she murmured. "I think they're coming after all! To visit—"

Holly Gayle and Eve Camlan glided through the closed door as if it weren't there. The chill grew as they drew closer. The cold odor of the lake filled her nose.

Kendra.

Eve's voice. Merilynn glanced at Kendra. She was staring at the phantom in the pink sweater and jeans. She could hear the voice too, this time.

Kendra. Eve's spirit gazed at her former roommate with fondness.

"Eve," Kendra choked out. "I saw you before."

Yes. I wanted to warn you. They drugged me. They were going to sacrifice me to the Forest Knight. But I died before they could. Holly rescued me.

"They?" Kendra asked.

The sorceress and her familiar. Holly's voice sounded clear and pure, like water, and her eyes locked on Merilynn's. *They are dangerous.*

Holly glided toward her, silently, smoothly. Merilynn felt a shiver of fear. "Kendra?" she whispered.

She didn't answer.

She sleeps now. Holly hovered over her. *This is for you to know: The living daughter of Malory Thomas can release us.* Holly's eyes were dark, hypnotic, like so long ago on the lake.

"Do you want me to find her for you?" Merilynn asked nervously. The ghost did not feel friendly.

You know of whom I speak.

"I don't."

In your heart, you know full well.

Merilynn's mind reeled. "Me?"

You. The sorceress consorted with the Forest Knight then appeared to your father in a dream and used his seed to complete your conception.

"My real father died."

No. Your true father is the priest. You know this in your heart as well. You are as Malory's teacher was: the product of a union between a man of the cloth and a magickal being of evil intent. Her teacher's father was a demon, her mother a nun.

"Does Father know he's my real father?"

Yes. He knows many things. He can help you. The image flickered slightly. *There is more to tell you but we are nearly out of time. There are those who would keep us out of this place. We must go.*

"What do you want me to do?" Merilynn begged.

In response, Holly lifted the ruffled bodice of her white dress to reveal the jewel set in a silver knife that glowed the color of the Forest Knight's eyes.

The color of my eyes sometimes, Malory thought.

Yes. Holly had heard her thought. *You have two fathers and the knight is one. Listen to me. You can release us and all those others trapped under the lake if you can find this dagger and kill your mother. It is the only way she can be killed.*

"Where is it?"

I will show you in your dreams. Holly and Eve floated backward toward the door. *Sleep now.*

Then they were gone.

31

Morning sunlight woke Kendra. She stretched, enjoying the warmth of the covers, still drowsing. Until she remembered their visitors. She sat up instantly. "Merilynn!"

The girl didn't answer. Kendra jumped out of her bed and went to Merilynn's empty one. There was a note, just two sentences:

Kendra, I know where the knife with the stone is and I've gone to get it. Don't tell anyone.

Love, Merilynn

SAMANTHA

Applehead Lake Cheerleading Camp

Eight Years Ago

1

Meteors showered the black velvet night. *The Perseids.* Samantha Penrose lay on her back just inside the tree line not far from the cabins and tried to concentrate on the annual mid-August display.

It wasn't easy. Tree limbs blocked much of the view, but the only other place nearby—*the best place*—to view the meteor shower would be from the shadows of the dock or boathouse. *That's where you should be. What are you, a coward?*

Maybe I'm just smart. She wiggled a little, trying to get more comfortable on the loamy bed of ancient oak leaves and pine needles. After what she and Merilynn had seen under the water two nights ago, she really didn't want to approach the lake or its creaky old structures at night.

By herself.

You're chicken! taunted her inner bully.

No, I'm exercising caution! retorted her inner reporter.

Sam craned her neck as a bright flash fled across the sky and quickly disappeared behind the trees. She knew all about people who weren't cautious; they were the ones who got killed when rock-climbing because they didn't bother to check their ropes, or murdered because they pretended it was safe to walk down a street alone even though everyone knew muggers struck there. If you had to do something risky, you went prepared, alert, confident, but as her father always told her, you darned well better not do it just to show off.

Lurking around the dock and boathouse would have been showing off. Definitely. And just standing out there in plain sight on the beach would be even stupider. *You know you don't want to go near that lake anyway.*

If she had brought anyone with her, she might have been tempted to approach the water, and that was part of the reason she'd slipped out of her cabin at one in the morning all alone. Her father always said that taking stupid chances had to do with your inner bully wanting to get loose and show off—or other people's inner bullies daring you to. He said it was more of a man thing, usually, but that she was a chip off his block, not Mom's, so she should learn from his mistakes.

He'd made lots of them, he told her. He couldn't resist a dare when he was young and ended up breaking his arm twice and his leg once. The worst was the time he'd gone up the stairs of the local abandoned "haunted" house (three stories of peeling white clapboard) while the other boys watched— that was when he broke his leg. It wasn't because of imagined ghosts or guys trying to scare him, but because his foot broke through one of the stairs and he crashed through the rotted wood halfway up his thigh before his leg snapped.

He was full of stories like that. He finally learned his lesson in Vietnam. Despite broken bones, sprains, stitches, and a concussion at the age of ten when he took—and won—a bet that he couldn't make his swing go over its A-frame in a complete circle, he had still believed, at nineteen, that nothing could kill him. He did all sorts of stupid things. Bullets barely missed him as he took chances the others in his squad wouldn't. He loved the feeling it gave him. But finally, shrapnel got him. Even now, Sam wasn't sure what shrapnel looked like, or even what it was, but she pictured hunks of twisted knives. The surgeons had removed pieces from his abdomen—he had shiny scars that were pretty cool looking—but they'd also had to remove his left hand and arm, halfway to his elbow.

That wasn't cool, not at all, and it was why she listened to him. His missing hand gave her nightmares when she was younger. Even now, sometimes. She shivered despite the warmth of the night. *Don't think about it!*

Thinking about things that scared you could get you into

trouble, too. Old dreams about crawling hands climbing her bedspread, moving over her covers, dripping blood as the fingers moved steadily toward her neck, suddenly flashed through her head. The hand never looked like Thing in *The Addams Family*. The one in her dreams had a ragged, bloody stump, meaty, with white bone shards sticking out of it like needles.

Stop thinking about that! I have to be on alert. I can't let anyone catch me out here! Only two more days and this stupid camp is over. No more dumb cheers. But if they catch me, they'll make me practice extra until it's time to go home! Yuck!

The horror that thought stirred was preferable to the kind brought on by thoughts of severed hands. It buoyed her, and she concentrated on the sliver of sky visible between the trees. Soon, she felt no fear at all, just irritation at how little of the sky show she could see.

Quietly, she rose and brushed away the brown leaves sticking to her legs and shorts. Walking to the very edge of the forest, she stood in the shadows of the trees that met the lakefront beach— *don't move, people who move get caught*—and studied the sky. The still air, retaining dregs of daytime warmth, smelled pleasantly of pine and earth. The view here was much better, but it was easy to look at the lake too, and she really didn't want to look at it.

That's as silly as being afraid of a crawling hand.

She made herself look at the lake. It was a good twenty yards distant. It gleamed darkly, a black jewel, unfathomable. Far out, a low mist hung a foot or two above the water. Undoubtedly, it shrouded the island; she couldn't even see its silhouette. The moon hung coyly low, flirting with the tops of the trees, and what light it shed left Applehead Island completely untouched.

Calm now, in control, Samantha returned her gaze to the velvety clear night. Stars twinkled, planets glowed steadily. She picked out constellations; Leo, the Big Dipper. Smaller, more distant, her favorite, the Pleiades. The Seven Sisters. Mythical, magical sisters. She liked mythology, especially Greek stories of gods and demigods.

The still warmth was broken abruptly by a stray breeze. It felt good against her face, holding a hint of coolness, no doubt from the lake, for it brought with it the faint dank cold-water smell. It gave her goose bumps, bringing the image of the ghost of Holly Gayle staring up at her from beneath the lake surface. *Stop it, right now! Maintain your control!*

The breeze continued, strengthened enough to ruffle her bangs, and she thought she heard faint voices come with it. *Singing?* It was too soft for her to be sure, but it made her think of times when the water pipes in her home vibrated just right. Her dad had explained how that worked, dispelling imagination with science, but it still reminded her of distant feminine voices singing, almost chanting. She thought that this was what the Sirens of myth sounded like as they lured sailors to their deaths.

Now, in the woods, the voices grew clearer but remained too faint to be truly recognizable as human. Not birds, no, but probably the wind vibrating leaves the way water sometimes vibrated through the plumbing. She cocked her head, forgetting the sky, enchanted by the music.

It sounded closer as the breezes increased.

Five minutes passed before she decided that what she heard really were voices. *Not too far away* . . . She was drawn to them. *I can walk along the edge of the forest. No one will see me.*

For an instant, she hesitated, wondering if she was being foolish, like the sailors who listened to the Sirens' call. *Maybe.* But as long as she stayed away from the lake and kept to the shadows and paid attention to where she stepped, why not? Reaching in her pocket to make sure the still-packaged lightstick hadn't fallen out—*I probably won't need to break it open, but I have to be prepared!*—she began walking toward the singing.

2

Skirting the lakefront, moving from tree to tree away from the cheerleading camp, toward the voices singing somewhere along the eastern side of the lake, Sam imagined she was a native scout, sneaking up on buffalo killers, then switched to pretending to be Jane Bond, girl spy. By the time she had turned to her favorite game—investigative reporter, about to break open a story—the singing was very clear, though she couldn't understand any words.

Forgetting the games, she paused to look back at Applehead camp, seeing little but the sodium glow of a few tall lamps among the trees, a suggestion of a square building or two, the hulk of the boathouse, and short length of dock. She wasn't sure how far she'd come—*a quarter mile, an eighth?*—but the camp looked small and far away. It lay at the short south end of the oblong lake and she was well away from there now, somewhere on the lower eastern side.

The song of the Sirens. Listening to the a cappella voices, she felt a fresh surge of fear, but it passed quickly. The choral music rose and fell, so beautiful, so foreign. The tone grew more intense, stronger paced, as she listened. It was building to some sort of climax and the beauty and intrigue compelled her to move on despite the danger. *Alleged danger.*

No longer playing pretend, not even thinking of it, but relishing the adrenaline rushing through her, she kept to the shadows, as close to the edge as possible. It seemed darker here. *It is darker. You can't even see the moon from here!* She patted her light-stick, safe and sound in her pocket, but didn't even think of using it yet, not as long as she could see by the dim phosphorescent gleam of the pale beach sand.

The voices rose higher and stronger, flavored with a tinge of ugliness in the foreign words that stained the enchantment of the choir. She moved forward ten more feet and stopped. The music came from within in the forest—directly within.

There was a well-worn path to follow. She turned onto it and faced the trees, thinking that this was the end of the line. If she used the light-stick, someone might see it, but how could she walk into the trees in near blindness? *You can still see the path a little. Just stay on it and go a little ways. Just until you can't make it out anymore. It's what a smart reporter would do.*

Reporters, her father had told her when she asked, usually had much longer life spans than spies, and agreed that journalism would probably be a more rewarding career. When he said that, he was bandaging her magnificently skinned knee. Finished, he told her, *You have to be cautious now so that you can grow up and become what you want to be.*

The path was pale bare dirt, mixed with sand at first, and as long as she walked very slowly, she could make it out. The choral sounded closer, wilder yet still oddly religious. *Just a little ways farther,* she promised herself. *Stay in control, don't take risks.*

As she crept along, a slave to her curiosity, it suddenly occurred to her that these voices might not belong to students from the college or girls from camp, or even counselors. Sure, camps had sing-alongs, but this didn't sound like anything associated with roasting marshmallows.

Telling ghost stories, maybe.

She shivered and stumbled as the all but invisible path jogged. She paused, her eyes on the ground, her ears entranced, her nose full of earth and pine and lake smell. And fire. Just a hint. A campfire, a bonfire, but not a forest fire. Slowly, she became more aware of the trees pressing in on her, of the voices, singing so close—*it's the way the wind is blowing, they can't be that close!*—of the lack of other forest sounds. Nervously, she continued to look down, and could barely see the outline of her shoes, let alone the path. *This is it. Time to turn back.*

And then she looked up.

In the woods, not too distant, she spotted a small square of firelight—*the bonfire*. It was as if she were looking at it through a window, but that didn't make sense, nor did the color of it— the flames, if that's what they were, had a greenish tint.

Sam realized she was trembling. *You can change the color of fire by tossing chemicals on it.* Or maybe it was just the green of the trees casting strange reflections. The chorus lowered, then rose again, frenzied, reminding her of church music, weird church music. And then she realized she was looking at the old chapel.

The haunted chapel.

A few days ago, she would have laughed off the haunted part. Now she wasn't so sure. Voices rose impossibly high and, for the first time, they reminded her of the banshee-howls on Apple-head Island.

They don't sound anything like the howls did, her inner bully challenged.

No, but they still remind me of them, replied the wary investigator within.

She'd come so far that she decided to continue on. Soon the fiery greenish gleam coming from the window threw enough light to let her see the path. Silently, she moved forward and the size of the window grew quickly. She was nearly there. Singing filled the air. A few more steps and the trees ended, encircling a broad clearing the same way they did the lake. In the middle of the clearing stood the ruins of the chapel. *It's a make-out spot.* But it sure didn't sound like anyone was making out in there.

Swallowing, she crouched low and moved fast, covering the space to the window in twenty steps. She stayed slightly hunkered beneath it as she worked up her courage to look in. She took a deep breath, exhaled slowly, and studied what she could see of the building. There were actually two windows; this one, which had been her beacon, at one side of the small chapel, and another, just like it, at the other side. The blank center of the stone building must have once been behind the preacher's pulpit.

Slowly, slowly, she rose, leg muscles tight and tense, and peered into the window.

The fire burned about ten feet away, casting eerie light and shadow on green-robed figures gathered beyond. They were hooded, covered from head to knee—which was as far down as Sam could see. They stood in a circle, their arms raised and hands held. They continued to sing and Sam couldn't see what, if anything, was in the middle of the group. Rising higher, calf muscles trembling, threatening to knot, she saw their feet.

They were all floating a foot above the ground.

Nah, don't be ridiculous. Only half a foot.

Sam nearly laughed, forced herself to maintain control. *No! Don't lose it. It's just a trick.*

She couldn't look away as the girls' song grew soft and they slowly floated to the ground.

They parted into two columns and as they did, Sam held her breath at the sight of a pale, naked woman on the ground between them. She was staked out, roped at wrists and ankles, completely exposed and helpless. A gag of green cloth invaded her mouth. Long blond hair spilled around her head. Her eyes rolled back in her head. *She sees me!*

One of the robed figures stepped forward, holding a long black dagger with a weird wavy blade. It caught the green fire and reflected it. The captive's eyes locked on the weapon.

The high priestess—*that's what she is, she must be some kind of high priestess, what else could she be?*—raised the dagger high, pointed it skyward, and as she did, her robe simply fell off. As if by magic. *Or a button came undone.*

But an instant later, all their robes fell to the ground. *Thirteen,* Sam counted. *There are thirteen of them.* They began their chant once more, and the high priestess, her face made up like an Egyptian queen's, moved forward, stepping between the legs of the captive, lowering herself to her knees.

The blade plunged into the girl's breast. It seemed to move in slow motion. Sam couldn't look away. The chanting crescendoed as the priestess twisted the weapon. Blood spurted across her painted face, gushed up in a geyser. With an animal cry, the priestess rose, holding the captive's heart up for all to see.

She licked blood from her lips. And then her eyes locked with Sam's.

GREENBRIAR UNIVERSITY
TODAY

3

Samantha Penrose moved restlessly, deep in troubled sleep. In her dream, she heard screams and shrieks in the murky forest, but she saw nothing except dark shadowed tree trunks looming everywhere like monstrous prison bars. She tried to run from the horrible sounds, but her feet wouldn't obey, couldn't obey, and she moved in slow motion, fettered by tarry, grasping soil.

Determined, she kept trying to run, just as she had in dream after endless dream, all night long, but the forest floor sprouted fingers, hands that grabbed at her ankles and dug dirty nails into her flesh as the shrieking echoed through the trees. She pulled hard, tearing away from the hand, but it came with her, hanging on, trailing blood. More and more hands pushed up from the earth and tried to stop her, but she wouldn't stop and they pulled out of the ground like clumps of grass with foxtail fingers.

The hands grew among the ferns beneath the trees, everywhere, fields of them, grottoes of them, and the ones that weren't trying to catch her began to clap. The sound grew and grew until it was like thunder pounding all around her, thudding in time with her heartbeat, her pulse, faster and faster.

No! she yelled in the nightmare. *No!* A strong hand caught her, stopped her. She pulled but couldn't get away. Applause rumbled and rattled, filling her head.

"No!" Sam cried out loud, heart pounding as she jolted awake. Something held on to her ankle and she shook her leg hard, frantic to be free, nearly panicking before she realized the sheet had twisted around her leg.

Clapping. More adrenaline shot through her body.

"Sam?" Kendra Phillips called from beyond her door.

It's just knocking, you idiot! Sam saw daylight seeping in from behind her thick curtains. Her alarm clock read 7:10 A.M. It would go off in five minutes.

"Sam?" Kendra's voice was hushed but urgent. She rapped on the door again.

"Just a minute." Sam turned off the alarm and untangled herself from the bedding. *What a mess.* Embarrassed—it was obvious that she'd been flailing around all night—she pulled her plum comforter over the mess, then ran her fingers through her hair and shook her body slightly to straighten the T-shirt and pajama pants she wore. "Come in."

Kendra opened the door, paused in the darkness. "I'm sorry. I woke you up, didn't I?"

"Better you than the alarm clock. The light switch is on your right." Sam crossed to her dresser and picked up her brush as she spoke.

"Sam, I have to show you something."

Sam whipped the brush through her dark hair and turned, alarmed by Kendra's tone. "What's wrong?"

Kendra touched the door, making sure it was latched, then crossed to Sam, holding out a piece of lined yellow paper. "Read this," she said softly.

For a brief instant, as she stared at Merilynn's graceful looping handwriting, Sam imagined she felt a cold disembodied hand grasping her ankle again. "ëKendra, I know where the knife with the stone is and I've gone to get it. Don't tell anyone. Love, Merilynn.'"

"I figured Merilynn wouldn't mind if I showed you," Kendra said as she took the note back, folded it, and put it in the pocket of her jeans. "She's gone."

4

"I don't understand. What's this business about a knife with a stone?"

Sam's room was a single, smaller than Kendra's, and with the dark curtains it felt claustrophobic. Kendra walked to the window and touched the plum-colored cloth. "May I?"

"Sure."

Behind her, Kendra heard Sam moving around, opening drawers, then the closet. Kendra let the morning sun in and stared down at the back garden, shivering slightly at the sight of the morning mist low above the lawn. She imagined spirits swirling within it as she heard Sam's pajamas land on the bed, and the distinctive swish of jeans sliding up legs. *It wasn't a dream,* she told herself, patting her pants pocket, very aware of the note folded inside it.

Sam made a little grunting sound and Kendra heard a bra hook snap closed, a shirt being pulled on, then footsteps as she came to join her at the window.

"So, what does the note mean?"

"I'm not sure, but Merilynn's gone and I've got a bad feeling about it." Kendra watched a crow swoop down and land on the lawn. It poked its beak at the ground. A moment later, two more shiny black birds joined it. The first one cocked its head and seemed to peer up at the window. *At me.* She turned toward Sam. "A *really* bad feeling."

"Why?" Sam was watching the birds now.

"Because something happened last night."

"Tell me."

"If I do, you can't repeat—" Kendra cut herself off, seeing the look on Samantha's face. There was no need to say it. "We were fooling around last night," she began.

Sam cocked her head, not unlike the crow. "Fooling around?" she asked slowly.

"Oh, Lord, no. I mean goofing off. I'm used to hearing my granny use those words. She doesn't mean... that."

"You might want to stop using the expression," Sam said, sounding amused, "unless you want to make some really close friends in this house."

Kendra smiled slightly. "You've noticed them too? Malory and Brittany?"

"Who couldn't notice?" Sam said. "I've tried to keep an eye on them. I'm almost positive they have a ménage à trois going with Professor Piccolo."

"Really?"

"Yeah, but what about Merilynn? What happened?" She paused. "You two didn't go back outside, did you?"

"No. You didn't happen to look out your window a little while after we left you, did you?"

"No. I always close the curtains. Why?"

"We saw them. Holly Gayle and Eve. Out there, on the lawn."

"You're kidding."

Kendra shook her head solemnly. "I swear it."

"Why didn't you come and get me?"

"We didn't think of it." She studied Sam. "Actually, Merilynn decided we should have a séance. I don't think she thought you'd want to join in."

Laughing, Sam shook her head. "I'll bet. So did anything happen? Did you call up something?"

"No. Nothing happened."

Sam's eyebrow went Spocky.

"Not then. Not until after we went to bed."

"And?"

"They came. We felt them first. The air turned cold and electrical—"

"Static electricity?"

Kendra nodded. "Then they just drifted into the room, plain

as day. The lights were out, but I saw them. And there was the smell of water, sort of outdoorsy, know what I mean?"

"Lake water."

"You've smelled them?"

Sam's mouth crooked up slightly. "I don't know, but I do associate the smell of Applehead Lake with Holly Gayle. You know, from the story Merilynn told you about our little boat trip."

"I know. And that's what they smelled like. Eve looked just like she did when she disappeared. She had on that pink sweater and jeans. Holly was in the white dress. She looked wet."

"What happened then?"

"It was surreal. Eve spoke to me, in my head. Does that make sense to you?"

Sam nodded. "What'd she say?"

"She warned me that I was in danger, that they'd killed her. Drugged her. They were going to sacrifice her to the Forest Knight."

"They? Who's they?"

"Holly said, ëThe sorceress and her familiar.' Or something a lot like that. I think. It's a little blurry."

"Wait. Wait a second. Eve said they were *going* to sacrifice her? Not that they *had* sacrificed her?"

"Yes." Understanding dawned. "You're smart, you know that?"

Sam shrugged. "Maybe something went wrong. Maybe not. What else?"

Memories fled in and out of Kendra's mind. "I think Eve told me that Holly rescued her. Do you think she meant from Malory and Brittany?"

"I wouldn't be surprised. You know about the secret society, right?"

"Some, yes."

"I think they may do things like that."

"Sacrifice?"

"Yeah." Sam glanced at her wristwatch. "So, what else did they say?"

"It was weird. I faded out. I didn't want to. I mean I was awake one minute and sort of half asleep the next. Holly talked to Merilynn. I sort of heard it. She said something about the knight's daughter being able to rescue them. All of them." Kendra paused, shivered. "The ones under the lake. The ghosts."

"How?"

She shook her head. "I wish I could tell you. Suddenly, I couldn't keep my eyes open. It was like a dream, but I don't think it was. Holly showed Merilynn something. It was on the bodice of her dress. I didn't see it exactly, but she lifted the ruffles and there was something silver and a green glow."

"Green like the eyes?"

"I think so. But it was just one thing. Maybe a big brooch or something. A piece of jewelry, I'm almost sure. Or maybe a knife?"

"A gemstone set in a miniature sword, maybe?" Sam asked.

"I think that's likely. I wish I could remember more. I think Holly said she'd tell Merilynn where to find it in a dream. It was really important. Damn it. I'm sorry. I should remember more."

"Well, keep thinking about it, but don't tell anyone else anything."

"I wouldn't any more than you would."

"I believe you. Don't write anything down either. There's no privacy here."

"I know."

"What are you going to do with the note?"

"I thought I'd contact her father. The priest?"

Sam nodded.

"I think he's involved in it. There was something said about him too." Kendra searched her memory, came up empty. "Damn it."

"Let's talk about it away from here. Later. I'm going to go get finished in the bathroom; then do you have time for some coffee and a donut or something?"

"Sure. Here?" They walked to the door.

"It's free here," Sam said. "We can go see what everyone's up to."

"What if they ask about Merilynn?"

The pair stepped into the hall. "We know nothing. She must have had an early class."

They paused outside the door, then turned toward the grand staircase, hearing voices coming from the east wing. Malory and Brittany.

"Hi, sisters," chirped the little blonde.

"Hi, Brittany," Sam said. "Hi, Malory."

Kendra echoed the words, and added, "How are you this morning?"

Brittany giggled and Malory glared. Neither replied, but as they reached the staircase and stepped down, a high-pitched *tweeeeeeeoot!* sound came from one of them, followed by a horrible stench.

Kendra backed up, Sam with her. As soon as the president and her VP were out of sight, Sam fanned the air. "No wonder Malory looked so sour."

"Something crawled up her ass and died." Kendra fought back a giggle.

"Yeah. About three days ago."

5

"God, what the hell happened here?" Jenny Goram asked Ginny Hill as they—the least senior pair of Fata Morganas—surveyed the carnage in the ruins of the Forest Knight's Chapel. The shiny skinless bodies twined together in a nest of blood-spattered grass, like food upchucked for gigantic baby birds by their mother. Or an Easter basket for a dragon.

"Brittany said the Forest Knight was angry at them, that *he* did this," Ginny said. "He wants his sacrifice."

Jenny nodded. She'd heard what Brittany had said, too. She just didn't want to believe it. Nor did she want to believe she and Ginny were in charge of getting rid of the remains. Shrugging out of her backpack, she forced herself to keep her eyes on the mangled bodies. "It's *so* gross."

"It is." Ginny opened her own pack and took out a folded camping shovel. "Eww," she added as she flipped it open and locked the joints. "Wow, this is cool. For a shovel, I mean. It's, like, a real shovel."

"Full-sized." Jenny opened her own, doing it carefully and slowly, an excuse not to look at the bodies they were supposed to bury. All too soon, she was ready to work. "So, do you have that map?"

Ginny took a folded piece of graph paper from her pocket and the girls turned from the tangle of bodies to study the diagram. It was a simple drawing of the chapel's interior, graphed off to show square footage. The door and window openings, the altar, and several other fairly permanent items—two piles of rocks, a log, the firepit—were marked. Other groups of squares were filled in as well; many others. Those, Brittany had explained when she awakened them shortly before dawn, were other graves. She had then marked six squares with blue pencil and told them to bury the new bodies strictly within the blue area.

Jenny got out the measuring tape Brittany had sent with them and before too long, the pair figured out where to dig and that they would only have to drag the corpses a little ways. "What a relief." Jenny hadn't even been sure they'd be able to figure out the measurements correctly, but Ginny turned out to be good at that sort of thing.

"We'd better get to work," Ginny said grimly as she stuck her shovel into the grassy earth.

Jenny did the same. "Do you think it's dangerous, burying

them here? I mean, it's so obvious." She paused, turning to look in the direction of a series of squirrelish trills. "Ah, look! How cute!" She pointed at a little reddish brown chipmunk perched on a windowsill. Its brown and white stripes shone, highlighted by morning sunlight that peeped through the trees. In one delicate little paw, it held something bright yellow and slightly nibbled-looking.

"Oh, it's so sweet," Ginny cooed, then pitched her voice up to a squeak. "Hi, little guy!"

The rodent emitted a loud chirp and held its empty paw up at them, making the girls both giggle. "I think he's flipping us off," Ginny said. The rodent made another shrill noise and raised its little paw higher.

"I think *she* doesn't like being called a guy," Jenny said. "Right, sweetie?"

The chipmunk lowered its paw, trilled pleasantly, and set to work gnawing its yellow goodie. "See?" Jenny said, pushing her spade into the loamy earth. "She's a girl. I wonder what she's eating."

Ginny scooped dirt out of the ground, then peered at the chipmunk again. "I'm guessing it's a peanut M&M."

"Maybe she stole it from Brittany."

The chipmunk trilled merrily.

"I think she's laughing," Jenny said.

Ginny pushed her hair out of her face. "I wish I had a scrunchie. Let's get done before Brittany shows up to check on us."

Jenny nodded and worked. "I wonder why Brittany's in charge, not Malory or even Heather."

"Brittany's the only one who didn't look like shit this morning. Didn't you notice?"

"Yeah, you're right. But this seems like something Malory would want to oversee herself. Brittany's not exactly, you know . . ."

"What?" Ginny asked.

"Leadership material? I mean, she's more like, I don't know! Do *you* know what I mean?"

"She's cute," Ginny said. "Malory's more the leader type, but I think there's a lot more to Brittany than meets the eye. That dumb blonde act is just an act."

"Watch out!" Jenny laughed as the little chipmunk, the candy still in its mouth, raced from the window and up Ginny's leg.

Ginny stood still as the little thing hopped up to her shoulder, took the candy from its mouth, and chittered in her ear.

"She likes you," Jenny said.

The chipmunk held the remains of the candy out, pushing it toward Ginny's mouth.

"Ewww," Ginny said, disgusted.

"She's trying to share with you."

"It's a fucking rodent," Ginny said.

The chipmunk screeched, sank its teeth into Ginny's ear, then leaped onto Jenny's shoulder and held out the candy bit. Jenny opened her mouth and let the creature put the morsel on her tongue. It watched her carefully as she chewed and swallowed, then let out a happy series of trills and raced back to the window.

"I wonder if I need a rabies shot," Ginny moaned, holding her ear.

"Let me see. Let go."

"Okay. How bad is it?"

"She didn't even break the skin," Jenny said. "It's barely red, even." She paused. "Those little ground squirrels have incredibly strong jaws. I think she was just teaching you a lesson. She could have taken your earlobe off if she'd wanted to."

Ginny looked over at the chipmunk sunning itself on the window sill. "Maybe. Or maybe it's just a stu—"

"Shh!" Jenny hushed.

"What?"

"Just be quiet and work. Count your blessings."

"But that—"

"That chipmunk is so adorable it's hard to work," Jenny finished quickly, suddenly nervously aware of the little creature's shiny black button eyes. She didn't understand why, but she had the feeling it understood their every word. One of the reasons she'd been accepted into the inner circle of Gamma, the Fata Morgana, was her ability to intuit things, and she knew enough to listen to herself now.

6

Kendra waited for Sam on the upstairs landing, enjoying the morning sunlight that strobed across the gleaming wood risers and the floor below. The old house looked fresh this morning, and the sounds of sorority sisters bustling around downstairs seemed lively and normal. She thought she could smell the rich fragrance of coffee wafting up the stairs, but there was a foul odor beneath it, one that overwhelmed the usual lemony wax smell of the polished wood and the funereal odor of roses.

"Hey," Sam said, joining her. "The bathrooms are zoos. Sorry I was so slow. Petra Mills shares my bathroom. Do you know her?"

"No."

"She's a senior. She's always slow, but today, Lord! And whatever Malory ate, she must have had some too. I had to hold my breath to brush my teeth, and I'll tell you, that's not easy to do."

"Is Petra a cheerleader?"

"No, why?" Sam asked.

Kendra shrugged.

"Gods!" shrieked Heather Horner as she appeared from the recesses of the east wing, the look on her pasty face as nasty as the sound of her voice. "Shit!" she snapped, then saw Sam and Kendra watching her. "Do either of you have a tampon you can lend me?"

"I'll give you one, but I don't want it back." Sam opened her book bag and started digging around the bottom, soon came up with a slender white-wrapped item and handed it Heather, who didn't look amused.

"Thanks."

"Got a surprise visit from Aunt Flo?" Kendra asked in her most sympathetic tone.

Heather rolled her eyes, emphasizing the dark shadows beneath them, then started to shake her head, but stopped abruptly.

Hangover, Kendra thought with a mean little twist of satisfaction.

"I'm way early. I'm always like clockwork. I don't know what happened. Damn it. I had plugs, you know?" she added, using the wrapped one as a pointer as she spoke. "Half a fucking box of the things, but every last one of them fell apart on me."

Kendra tried to appear concerned. "I'm sorry, Heather."

"You should complain to the manufacturer," Sam added in her reporter voice.

More eye rolling commenced. "Yeah, a lot of good that's going to do me right now." She put one hand over her stomach. "I feel awful."

"Cramps?" Kendra asked.

"Not that kind," Heather replied in a pained voice. "I think it's something I ate." A delicate machine gun *tat-tat-tat-tat-tat* burst from her behind.

"Shit, I'm sorry. I've been like this since I woke up. Maybe I just drank too much last night."

Before Kendra could stop her, Sam said, "You and Malory must have had the same drink then."

Kendra stepped back as Heather's nether fragrance bloomed again.

"She's got gas, you mean?"

"Unless someone knows how to throw farts, she does."

Heather gave Sam a dirty look and stuck the tampon in her pocket. "Thanks," she said over her shoulder as she turned on her heel and headed back into the off-limits wing.

"What's so funny, Kendra? I thought you were going to have a fit right in front of her."

Kendra loosed a broad grin. "Merilynn did it," she whispered.

"Did what?"

"Wished twenty-four hours of flatulence on all the senior Gammas."

"*What?*"

"You know, she threw a spell on them the same way she popped the wrestlers' tires and called the deer. She did it."

"Possibly," Sam replied slowly. "Or it could be a coincidence."

"We'll know when we go downstairs, won't we? And, Sam?"

"Yes?"

"I don't think it's a coincidence. She did a period spell too."

"To all the seniors?"

"No. Just the cheerleaders. She gave them all their periods and cursed their hygiene products." She grinned. "Double curses."

Sam snorted. "You're kidding."

"No," she said, smiling. "I thought it was a joke. Evidently, it isn't."

"Well, let's go down and have some breakfast," Sam said, stepping toward the staircase. "We'll do a little investigating on the sly."

"You really have a nose for news," Kendra said, hefting her book bag.

Sam let out a half a chuckle. "I'd say you're not bad at smelling a story yourself."

7

"What are we going to do about Michele?" Heather asked, swilling her second glass of purple juice, alcohol-free, this morning. "We have to do something. There's a game tonight."

Malory barely looked up from her coffee. "You're in charge of the fucking cheerleaders," she muttered as she tilted slightly to let a silent-but-deadly take flight. How could her body betray her like this? She'd tried spells and Gas-X and Pepto Bismol, but nothing would quiet her gut.

"You should have some juice," Heather said. "It'll perk you right up."

Malory shot her a killing look. "That stuff tastes like piss to me."

"Piss? You drink lemon juice without sugar, you're a fine one to talk— Lord, what died in your ass?"

"Don't start on the juice thing, Heather." She paused. "And you don't smell so great yourself. Maybe it was the vodka."

"Maybe. Anyway, I got my period," Heather replied.

Malory ignored her.

"Why do I still have to get a period after all these years?"

"You stopped aging. If you'd stopped aging at sixty, you wouldn't have a period. Haven't we been over this before?"

"Do you still get a period?"

"Don't be an ass. Do I look like I don't?"

Heather let out a percolator-fart. "Sorry. Did you get yours this morning?"

"My what?"

"Your period."

"No."

"Huh."

"What's that supposed to mean?"

"I don't know. Brittany said that when she got Ginny and Jenny up to go do the dirty work, they were both on the rag and complaining about it."

"Good morning, Petra," Malory said, relieved to see the senior Gamma enter the kitchen.

"Good morning," Petra said, heading for the coffee-maker. "Lord, what stinks?"

"Sorry," Heather said, covering for Malory. Heather always did know exactly how to make points with the boss.

"Do you guys have any Midol?" Petra asked, sitting down.

"No."

"No."

"Shit. Nobody does."

"Nobody does what?" Sam Penrose asked as she and Kendra Phillips entered the huge kitchen.

"Has Midol," Heather replied. "Do you?"

"No."

"Sorry," added Kendra.

Malory let out another silent-but-deadly as the freshmen girls got themselves coffee and day-old donuts. She watched as the pair approached the table, smiled as Kendra's nose wrinkled.

Samantha's didn't twitch. "Where is everyone this morning?"

"It's early," Malory replied, sitting up straighter, curious about Samantha's thoughts.

"True," Sam said. "Usually Jenny and Ginny are down here before I am. And Julie and Jeannie and Michele." She smiled at Heather. "I've noticed that you cheerleaders are early risers."

Heather looked at Malory for guidance, but didn't get any. "I guess we usually are."

"Even Brittany's missing," Sam said lightly.

"She's off on her morning jog," Malory said, watching Sam. "She always goes out in the morning." She eyed the girl. "Surely, you've noticed that, being so into investigative reporting and all."

Sam looked her in the eye. "Yes, I have. But don't call me ëShirley.'"

Kendra and Petra both snickered, but Sam never cracked a smile.

Malory gave her a little nod of approval.

"Oh, sorry!" Heather said as she ripped off another percolator imitation.

"How do you feel?" Malory asked, looking from Petra to the freshmen. "Before you arrived, Heather and I were comparing notes on what we ate last night. We think we may have a little food poisoning. Upset stomachs. Did any of you eat here last night?"

"I had a Lean Cuisine," Petra said. "Nothing else. I'm fine."

"We went out for pizza," Kendra said.

Malory nodded. She'd been told by other Fatas that they'd been out; Merilynn and Sam were two girls she liked to keep a special eye on. "Did Merilynn go with you?"

"Yes," Kendra replied after the briefest hesitation.

Sam never blinked, but Malory felt suddenly suspicious. "Where is she this morning? I take it she's all right?"

There was no mistaking the brief flare of nostrils and constriction of pupils on Kendra, and even Sam wasn't able to completely hide a reaction. She was so good, though, that Malory thought Heather was probably fooled. But she could tell something was up.

"Merilynn's fine," Kendra said. "She took off so early that I hardly remember hearing her leave."

I'll bet you don't. "Early class?"

"I guess," Kendra replied, a shade too quickly this time.

Sam briefly laid her hand on Kendra's forearm. "No, it wasn't a class, not exactly, remember, Kendra?"

Kendra opened her mouth but Sam spoke again, touched her again. "Of course you don't remember. You were in the rest room. She had an early class, but not *that* early," she said, turning her steady gaze on Malory. "She wanted to go sky-watching. There was some sort of planetary alignment she was interested in."

Kendra's smile and nod seemed genuine. "She loves astronomy. Or maybe astrology. Her bedspread is blue with stars and moons," she added, her own eyes surprisingly steady as they met Malory's. "I don't know her all that well yet."

Very nicely done. So nice, Malory thought, that she might even be telling the truth. "Merilynn just moved in with you, didn't she?"

"Yes, she did."

"I was surprised. I didn't know you even knew one another."

Kendra didn't reply, but half smiled and half shrugged, then took a bite of donut.

"How did you meet?" Heather asked, ignoring Kendra's full mouth.

"They're Gamma sisters, initiated together," Sam said serenely. "How could they *not* meet?"

Heather looked annoyed, but maybe that was just the gas.

Malory smiled warmly. "Well, I'm glad Merilynn is all right. We wouldn't want you to get a reputation, Kendra."

"A reputation?"

"You know what I mean, sweetie," she replied, all silk and sugar.

"No, I don't. A reputation?"

"As a jinx," Heather said.

Malory chuckled softly. "That's too strong a term. I just mean that when a girl goes through a lot of roommates, sometimes people get nervous about rooming with her."

Kendra studied Malory carefully, revealing little but a flash of well-tethered anger in her eyes. "You're speaking as though Merilynn has disappeared. I don't appreciate that, and neither would Merilynn."

Bravo! Kendra Phillips had never been retiring, but the courage she displayed now was new. *Most likely, Samantha's influence.* "I'm sorry," Malory told her. "That came out wrong. I didn't mean to imply anything. It's just that I don't feel quite myself this morning. Neither does Heather."

Heather nodded peevishly.

"Any of you guys have some Pepto Bismol or Maalox?" Teri

Knolls moaned as she entered the kitchen. She was dressed in a Gamma megaphone sweater and jeans, and was holding her abdomen. "I don't feel so good." She went for the coffee, muttering, "And Midol. I need Midol."

8

"**Y**ou bitch!" Nancy Mayhew squawked at her roommate, Diane Jespam. Actually, she squawked at Diane the Spam's big fat ass, which was all she could see of her since the Anna Nicoleñwanna-be had her torso hidden in the recesses of Nancy's closet. She was rooting through her clothes like a pig roots for truffles. Nancy heard an audible snort as Diane pulled out of the depths and looked at her with smeared lipstick.

No doubt smeared all over my clothes.

The Spam blinked her false eyelashes, all breathy like Marilyn Monroe force-fed Crisco for a month. "What did you call me, Nancy? A witch?"

"A bitch," Nancy said evenly. "With a b. I called you a *bitch.*"

"That's not very nice."

"I don't *feel* very nice." Nancy had awakened to find her period had come early and her sheets were stained. She was out of tampons and the stick-um on the emergency pads she dug out of the recesses of her bureau didn't stick. She'd ended up using masking tape on the damned things. *That's real attractive.* As usual, she had cramps, and there was a football game tonight. And now her asshole of a roommate was scrounging through her closet—like she'd even *fit* into anything Nancy owned.

She took a deep breath and counted to three, trying to push the fury she felt back down into stomach. Rarely had she felt such anger. *Super PMS?* "What are you doing in *my* closet, Diane?"

"You're wearing your cheerleading clothes tonight, right?"

"So?"

"So, I have a date tonight and I wanted to borrow your sweater set."

"Oh?"

"The baby blue?" The Spam fluttered her polyester lashes. "It's really more appropriate for my skin tone than yours, you know."

"And the fact that you weigh fifty pounds more than I do?"

"Hey! That's mean!"

"Did you factor that in?" Nancy persisted. "All that flab? Do you really think you could squeeze *your* pork into *my* sweater set without ripping it?"

Diane's too-red lower lip pooched out. "You're mean! Sweaters stretch, you know." She turned back to the open closet. "For those of us with feminine bustlines, anyway."

"They. Only. Stretch. So. Far." Nancy took another deep breath. "Get out of my closet, you walking cellulite factory."

Diane Jespam didn't even turn to look at her. "I'll be done in a minute."

Nancy saw red filtering into her vision, coloring everything she saw, especially Diane the Spam's lardy ass. Her cottage cheese cheeks billowed white, then pink, then seemed to turn as red as roses around a black thong that struggled against strangulation in her ass-crack. "You're done *now*," Nancy announced.

Diane turned, did her pout. "Come on, Nanny. Don't be so *mean*. We're *sisters!* And roommates. What's mine is yours and what's yours is mine. You know that, Nanny."

"I warned you not to call me that." Nancy stepped forward and yanked Diane's wrist, pulling her away from the closet.

"Hey—"

"I *don't* want anything of yours and you *can't* have anything of mine. Now take your filthy hands off my stuff or I'm going to knock that little piggy nose right off your face."

"Hey, my daddy paid seven thousand dollars for this nose! It's *perfect!*"

Nancy's world was suddenly awash in red, drenched in crimson tones of blood. Diane Jespam's blood. It felt hot and it felt good as she flattened her free hand and rammed it as hard as she could, up against the Spam's nose.

The girl's eyes widened, her face exploding in blood. The crunching sounds were very, *very* loud.

Diane Jespam dropped like a two-hundred-pound sack of potatoes. Blood ran into her open eyes. Her dead, staring eyes.

Her vision no longer infused with scarlet, Nancy bent and wiped her hand clean on the Spam's ass cheek, then went into the adjoining bathroom and washed properly before returning to the bedroom. Stepping over the body, marveling at how it was true—that you really could kill someone by squashing their nose up into their brain—she rifled through Jespam's drawers until she came up with a brand-new box of tampons.

Feeling triumphant, she decided that as soon as she finished dressing, she should talk to Heather. As the newest member of the squad—edging Little Lou out for Eve Camlan's vacated position—she knew that the head of the squad would be her best friend and advisor now.

9

"I think Malory knows something," Kendra told Sam Penrose when they met for lunch in a quiet corner of the cafeteria. It was still half an hour before noon, but the place was filling up fast.

Sam had picked the table for the view it gave of the entire eatery, and she'd picked her chair because it put her back to the wall. It was something her father had taught her when she was a kid. *Always be on the lookout, Sam. Keep your back to the wall and no one can sneak up on you.* She lifted her ham on wheat. "She knows something about Merilynn, you mean?"

Kendra nodded as she chewed the first bite of her hamburger, then set it on the plate and opened it. "Yes, about Merilynn." She removed half the onion and a thick spine of lettuce, then put it all back together again. "What do you think?"

"I *think* she was fishing," Sam told her. "I also think she was trying to get reactions out of us."

"Did she? Get a reaction out of me, I mean? You were a complete rock." She tried the burger again.

"Thanks, but I wasn't a complete rock. I'm not that good, but I tried. And, yes, I think she was able to get some reaction out of you, but not enough to really put her on to anything." She waved a Frito at Kendra. "You're really pretty smooth."

"Thank you. I wish I were as smooth as you."

Sam felt her eyebrow go up. It was an old movement she'd picked up as a kid watching Sean Connery in James Bond movies. When she was seven or eight, she spent hours pretending to be the master spy, and that eyebrow thing was part of the play. Now, she couldn't help it. Her father had explained to her when she was fourteen and worried about scaring off a junior nerd she liked, that the lift was a learned motion and very hard to get rid of. He said she could, but it would take concentration. Then he told her he liked it because it made her look smart.

Well, then she really tried to get rid of it for a while—no fourteen-year-old girl, not even she, wanted to look too smart. It would scare off boys. Fortunately, she'd soon met one that was as smart as she was and was also compelled to try to prove that he was not her equal but her better. She played along at first, keeping her eyebrow at bay, but being dumb wasn't her style and before long her competitive streak won out and she trumped the guy. Put him in his place. Raised her eyebrow. Robby, that was his name, liked the eyebrow and told her she was as hot as a female Vulcan. He called her Ms. Spock. *God, I loved that. Thank heaven I can take that fact to my grave!*

At the time, the Trekiness didn't seem geeky; it felt cool. And being smart and logical was great; Robby respected her for it. He backed off for a time, but after a while, he just had to prove how smart he was again. She egged him on, and then she trumped him again, twice. He fought back, trumped her. Three times. For a few brief, wonderful weeks, it was all-out war with mad necking sessions stolen in remote corners of the campus, under bleachers, behind trees, between the battles. They were both part-nerd, not quite outcasts, but never popular either, and between them they brought zero romantic or sexual experience to their hot little war.

Sam couldn't tell her father what was happen-ing—she was too embarrassed. She couldn't tell her mother, because she would have gone all fluttery and weird on her. But the thing was, Sam knew herself, she always had known herself, and so she knew she would go all the way with him soon—just think-ing about the intellectual battles left her with soggy underwear. She knew she would be the aggressor, too, and it was just too humiliating. She didn't want to go all the way—there were too many risks she wasn't prepared for, but that wasn't the big thing. She could figure that out if she had to. No, the *really* big thing she couldn't quite comprehend, the thing she couldn't bring herself to ask her father about, was why using her brain like that—to spar, to compete—was the one thing that she knew would make her lose control of herself physically.

It was just too illogical. Why would using her brain make her want to have sex? She should be able, she thought, to use her brain to make herself *not* want to have sex.

So, she stopped it herself by relentlessly ramming Robby into the ground. She hated doing it because she cheated, making things up, twisting facts, whatever she had to do, to win. Finally, she succeeded in driving him away.

"Sam? Earth to Sam?"

"Sorry. What?"

"You raised your eyebrow. I asked why."

"Oh, just an old *Star Trek* habit," she fibbed. "I can't break it," she added truthfully. "I try to raise the other one, but it won't cooperate."

Kendra laughed. "You're blushing. I didn't know anything could make *you* blush."

Flustered, Sam gulped Pepsi.

"I wasn't asking about your eyebrow, Sam. I was asking why you raised it when I said you were smooth."

It was the James Bond thing. James Bond was smooth. Why didn't I just tell her that? Why did I blame it on the Vulcans? "I don't know why; maybe because I don't feel all that smooth. Or maybe I wondered why you paid me a compliment."

Kendra didn't hide her irritation. "I'm no butt-kisser. If I say something, I mean it."

"I know. I wouldn't be sitting here with you if I thought that. My words just didn't come out quite right." She smiled slightly. "That's one of the reasons I'd rather write than talk. It's easier to edit myself that way."

Kendra nodded. "I bet Merilynn drove you nuts the way she'd just say whatever she was thinking."

Sam grinned broadly. "I've enjoyed her lately, but that summer at the cheer camp, I totally wanted to strangle her every five minutes or so. But she was also sort of refreshing. She could make me laugh, and she was tough, even if she was a nutcase half the time. She never worried..." She studied Kendra and wondered if her stomach had started flopping like her own. "I'm talking about her like she's gone."

"She is." Kendra paused. "But I know what you mean. Like she's gone for good."

"She's just taken off on one of her adventures."

"Yeah."

Kendra looked pale despite her mocha complexion, and this brought Sam's mind back to the point she wanted to make. "I thought Malory probably read a little from your reactions this morning."

"Yes?"

"There was one thing in particular that you reacted to, and if Malory's as bad as I think she is, she'll keep using it. She senses weakness and goes for it every time. I've seen her do it lots of times, usually in small ways."

"For Christ's sake, spit it out! What's my weakness?"

"She played dirty."

"Just tell me. I can take it."

Sam felt her eyebrow lift of its own accord. "I believe you can."

"So?"

"Malory suggested that you could be considered a jinx as a roommate."

"Suggested it? Girl, she said it outright."

"And you reacted."

"No. I mean, inside, but I kept it inside. That was a nasty thing to say."

"You *almost* hid it. You hid your reaction better than ninety-five percent of people could, I think. But she startled you. You have to learn to control every tiny eye movement, even the flare of your nostrils. I can't do that." She paused. "Of course, I can't control my eyebrow either."

"I bet you can if you have to. *Really* have to."

Sam nodded. "But nostrils flare to get more oxygen when you're upset. Eyes widen—or squint, depending. There all these little tiny responses that neither you nor I can truly control.

Only a really great actor or a sociopath can control things like that. You have to completely turn off emotionally to be completely armored."

"But if you do that, you don't pick up on everything around you."

"Exactly," Sam said.

"So, what do you think my reaction told Malory?"

"Not enough. I think she was trying to find out if we knew anything worth keeping secret. That jab at you was meant to elicit a big reaction—she was getting desperate. You did react, but it wasn't big—it was a normal reaction to an obnoxious, rude comment." Sam finished off her soda. "I'm getting a refill. You want one?"

Kendra nodded. "Iced tea. No sugar."

Sam took the cups and rose. "When I get back, I want you to tell me every detail about what you two did last night."

"Deal."

10

"This is quite a mess you've made," Malory Thomas told Nancy Mayhew as she, Heather, and Brittany stood in the freshman cheerleader's room and looked at the pudgy blond mess that had been the fairly unbeloved legacy sister, Diane Jespam, before Nancy, also a legacy but much more desirable, had flattened her face.

Nancy, clad in navy pants and a baby-blue sweater set, stared at her toes and nodded wordlessly.

Heather had been collared by Nancy shortly after breakfast and Malory, having gone back to bed with a hot water bottle, forgot all about them both until Heather knocked on the door to her room and told her what their impetuous little sister had done.

It had really improved Malory's mood. After discussing everything again with Brittany, they had gone back to the room, where Nancy obediently sat waiting at her desk, not a dozen feet from her victim's body.

Now Malory said, "Nancy?"

"Yes?" she mumbled.

"Look at me."

Slowly the girl raised her head. Her eyes were red-rimmed and puffy from crying. "Wipe your nose." Malory handed her a tissue and waited while the girl did as ordered.

"Nancy, why did you kill your roommate?" she asked in her best Elementary School Teacher voice.

"I'm sorry."

"I didn't ask you if you're sorry, Nancy. I asked why you did it. No, no. Look at me." She gently but firmly put her finger under Nancy's chin and forced her head back up.

"I was mad. I'm sorry. I got my period and I get really cranky when I get it and I just lost my temper."

"What did she do that made you angry?"

Nancy's lower lip trembled and a tear escaped one eye. Malory wiped it away with her finger. Nancy kept her chin up. "She was going through my closet." More tears leaked.

Malory gave her a fresh tissue. "I'll bet she was doing it without your permission. Am I right?"

"Yes!" Finally, Nancy's spirit flashed in her eyes, betraying the anger. "That cow wanted to borrow my—this." She touched the finely knit tank and matching sweater. "It's silk! And she didn't ask, she never asks, she just takes things, and she ruins them because she's a big fucking fat cow."

Nancy's shoulder shook seismically and she began sobbing out loud. Malory gathered her into her arms and let her get mucus and tears all over her own shoulder. It was disgusting, but part of the job. She murmured and stroked Nancy's hair soothingly until she calmed down. Fortunately, she had already had several hours to cry and it didn't take long before she dried up.

"Malory?" she asked. "What's going to happen to me now? Are you going to call the police?"

"You really shouldn't have killed her, Nancy," she said reprovingly.

"I know. I didn't mean to."

"We probably should turn you in. I think you're just a tiny bit insane."

"I'd rather be in a crazy house than in jail," the murderess said hopefully.

Malory slipped her arm around Nancy's shoulders and turned her away from the body. Together, they looked out the window that opened over the front of the house, giving a long view of the reflecting pond. "Nancy, you're a sister of Gamma Eta Pi. You're one of our own. You took vows."

Nancy nodded and wiped her nose.

"The sisters of Gamma Eta Pi protect one another within the limits of the law. Sometimes beyond. But murder, that's a little further beyond than we're willing to go...."

Nancy took a deep breath, expelled it with a shudder. "I understand."

"No, sweetie, I don't think you do. Within Gamma, there is a secret core, the very heart of the sorority. We of the society of Fata Morgana protect one another from everything but doing harm to one another." She paused, letting her words sink in but resisting the impulse to weave a spell around the girl. To be a Fata Morgana, she had to go in with her eyes open.

"A Fata Morgana is a special Gamma, one who is able to do things far beyond the realm of a normal sister. She is required to make sacrifices. And I don't mean silly things like burning your bra—"

"Huh?"

"Sorry, wrong decade. I don't mean silly things like getting your breast implants removed. I mean *real* sacrifices. Blood sacrifices. Like what you did here. Can you do that again?"

"What?" Nancy's eyes had turned to saucers. Bloodshot

saucers, but Visine would clear that up before tonight's football game.

"Was Diane the first person you ever killed? Don't answer yet. If you have any desire to join our society, you must tell the absolute truth and, trust me, I'll know it if you're lying. Now, was she your first?"

"You mean human? Chickens don't count?"

"Chickens?"

"I tried voodoo, but my grandmother caught me in her henhouse and that was that."

Malory smiled. "What about humans?"

"Well, I'm not sure."

"Why don't you tell me about it?"

"Not a really long time after she caught me killing a chicken, my grandmother asked me to bring her her pills and a glass of water. She was sitting in the dark—she had a migraine and was really miserable—and I brought her some pills. She took them without looking. She died."

"What did you bring her?"

"I don't know," Nancy admitted. "Just sort of a pupu platter. One of these, two of those."

"So you weren't trying to kill her?"

She shrugged. "I don't know. I mean, she took all these vitamins and supplements too, so it was a lot of pills. All she had to do was turn on the light and she would have known I didn't bring any vitamins, just heart medications and migraine pills and tranquilizers. Lots of those. They felt just like her vitamin C capsules."

"So you did it on purpose?"

"No, well, yes. I was just testing her. She didn't pass the test."

"And what happened next?"

"She got all strange and funky and told me to call 911."

"And did you?"

"Well, yes. But first I sat down at the kitchen table and played solitaire until I won three games in a row. Then I called."

"How many games did you play before you won three times running?"

Nancy looked at her, a trembling smile on her lips. "Only twenty-three."

"Nancy, dear, you aren't a nut. You're an entire basketful of nuts."

"Is that good?"

"It's just fine, as long as you want to become a Fata Morgana."

"Can I ask one question?"

"Of course."

"What does ëFata' mean? It sounds fat. I hate fat."

"It has nothing to do with fat. Fata Morgana is Italian for Morgan LeFay. It also is a type of mirage."

"A mirage?"

"You know, something that appears to be something else?"

Nancy nodded. "I like that a lot. Who's Morgan LeFay? Is he the president of your society?"

"*She* is your new goddess, and yes, you could say she is president. She is a great sorceress, immortal, just as you shall be if you are loyal to her."

"I have to worship a goddess?"

"Yes, but you'll enjoy it. You'll have a god as well. It is he that we make sacrifices to in order to maintain our youth and beauty."

"Who is he?"

Malory gestured toward the woods, dark and forbidding even at midday. "The Forest Knight is your new god. Now, come, we will prepare you."

They turned. Under her arm, Nancy flinched slightly at the sight of Diane. "What about her?"

"Don't you worry a bit about her. We have ways to dispose of bodies. Many ways. This one, though, looks especially nice and tender, so I think, Brittany, if you'll give the good sisters down in Moonfall a call and see if they're in the market, we'll let them turn her into their famous mincemeat pies."

"Sisters in Moonfall? Is there a Fata Morgana society there?"

"No, they're another sort of sisterhood, but they're lots of fun."

"Will I meet them?"

"Not unless we need to turn you into mincemeat. And that won't happen, will it, Nancy?"

"Never!"

11

Sam finished her afternoon classes with her mind barely in attendance. All she could think about was Merilynn Morris. There were Kendra's stories about their seeing the ghosts to ponder, and Merilynn's spell-casting at the Gammas' expense to mull over, but what consumed most of her ability to concentrate were her own memories of the previous night. Because of them, she could not deny Merilynn's powers—she had seen them used twice last night and try as she might, she couldn't write off everything as coincidence. She wished that she could. Despite the fact that she trusted Kendra was telling her the truth as she interpreted it, she still would have been able to dismiss those tales if she hadn't seen Merilynn in action herself.

Yet it was the unearthly shrieks and screams that had come from deep within the dark forest the previous night that her mind wandered back to over and over again.

The sounds and Merilynn's reaction to them. The reaction was all wrong. Abnormally wrong. Sam's own instinct had been to run, as far and as fast as possible, and she trusted her instincts; they had never been wrong.

That Merilynn practically tried to pull them deeper into the woods was aberrant behavior. Sure, she lacked caution and possessed enough curiosity to damn a hundred cats, but that didn't explain her stunning lack of fear.

Kendra had felt it; they spoke of it at lunch. Merilynn insisted it was the cry of the Greenbriar Ghost, the Forest Knight himself. Certainly, it was the sort of feeling that legends were made of, a terror felt cold and deep inside your bones, something that could not be understood if it hadn't already been experienced. It was like a new color of fear, a new scent of terror. *A green face,* Sam thought. *The face of the forest, fear in shades of green and gold, scented with earth and pine and black lake water.*

Stop that. You're thinking like Merilynn!

Sam turned her mind, trying to consider the terror she had experienced logically, unemotionally. She knew she had felt it several other times, long ago. The first time had been while fleeing the island in the rain, after she saw those green-glowing eyes, when she heard that never-to-be-forgotten banshee wailing.

The second was in the boat with Merilynn, not when she saw the beautiful ghostly town, nor even when she first encountered Holly Gayle's white face staring up at her from just beneath the lake's surface, but when Merilynn had yanked her away from the phantom hand that was about to pull her below. The instant she had come out of the fugue state or trance or whatever the hell had hypnotized her into unthinking fearlessness, she felt the terror and knew how close to death she had come.

Is that how Merilynn felt last night? Was she in a trance, unable to even feel fear?

She reached the sidewalk that led to Gamma House and turned, barely glancing at the oblong reflecting pool, only vaguely aware of the beauty of the sparkling sunlight bouncing off the dark water and dancing over the lily pads. *Was Merilynn entranced? Hypnotized?* But certainly the shrieks hadn't caused her own trance; there had been no cries that night. Her instincts told her that she had been held spellbound by the eyes of Holly Gayle.

Now, as she approached the steps, Sam cruised rapidly through her memories, knowing she had felt the terror at least one other time. *Worse, worse terror than the other times.* The memory resisted her search momentarily, but then she captured it. *It was the night I went out to watch the Perseids meteor showers.* The stark remembrance stirred goose bumps up on her neck and arms as she mounted the stairs and stepped onto the veranda. *I heard it that night. The shrieks of the Greenbriar Ghost.*

There was more. She had wandered, gotten lost. *There was singing. The Sirens' song! Samantha!*

Sam whirled at the voice, just behind her, but saw no one.

Samantha!

She opened her mouth to call, *Merrilynn!* but caught herself. *I'm going to give her holy hell for scaring me like this.* Sam looked over the edge of the veranda, but the redhead wasn't there. She let her gaze travel over the lawn, across the reflecting pond, and to the forest's edge. Nothing.

Samantha!

Sam thought she caught a flash of movement among the trees. Shading her eyes, she squinted at the shadowy borderland. Yes, something flickered red, a stray sunbeam. And there, suddenly, pale against the forest, she saw a faint, lithe figure, saw brilliant coppery hair blowing in a phantom breeze. She could almost see the green of her eyes. The figure, dressed in some sort of flowing lavender cloak or gown—it was too far away to be sure—raised one arm and waved.

"Merilynn," she murmured, and waved back. The figure faded away like smoke borne away on a breeze.

12

"Okay," Heather Horner said, startling Sam. "I got here in time to see you wave, but I don't see anyone."

The cheerleader, dressed in her two-piece bare-midriff uniform, must have come out of the house, but Sam hadn't heard her. *You were too busy seeing ghosts to hear her.* The thought sank in an instant after it passed through her mind. *Merilynn? A ghost?*

"What's wrong, Sam?" Heather asked, joining her at the railing. "I've never seen you at a loss for words before."

"Oh, sorry. I was lost in thought. What did you say?"

"I asked who you were waving at," Heather said, the friendly tone disappearing. "You couldn't have been too lost in thought if you could think to wave at someone."

Sam tried a subtle smile. Actually, I'm not sure who I waved at. I thought someone waved at me, but now I think it was a tree limb moving in the breeze."

"What breeze?"

"The one over there." Sam indicated a sweep of forest. "It was strong for a moment. It fooled me." She hesitated, seeing suspicion in Heather's eyes and wondering why it was there. "Or maybe it really was someone."

"What were they wearing?"

"Something greenish," Sam said, doing her best to sound bored. "If it was a real person, that is."

"Male or female?"

Sam shrugged. "Who knows? Probably it wasn't a person at all." She paused, grinned. "Maybe it was the Greenbriar Ghost."

Heather's eyes widened, then hardened back down as she scanned the forest boundaries.

"I was joking," Sam chided. "You don't believe that ghost nonsense, do you?"

"The Forest Knight isn't something to joke about."

"You call it the Forest Knight? That's sort of an old-fashioned term."

Heather eyed her. That wasn't a pleasant sensation. "It's not old-fashioned. It's respectful." Now she paused and plastered on a grimace of a smile. "The Forest Knight is part of Greenbriar University history and lore, and that makes him part of Gamma history. That deserves some respect, don't you think?"

"Sure," Sam agreed. "I'm sorry if I offended you."

"You didn't. I should apologize for being so bitchy."

"Is your stomach virus still bothering you?"

"Yes," Heather said, a faint foul scent rising to agree. "Several of the squad members have it." She eyed Sam.

"I'm so sorry. It must be miserable, especially with a game tonight." Sam exuded all the pity she could muster. "Did you ask Mildred about it? Is it food poisoning?"

"Probably. Mildred threw out all the leftovers in the fridge just to be safe." She paused, her eyes hard on Sam's. "We all got the curse this morning too."

Knowing she was looking for a reaction, unsure why, Sam nodded and spoke blandly. "I think that's common, isn't it? Women who live together often cycle together. Or so I've read."

Heather, her eyes scanning the forest, nodded dismissively.

Sam walked into the house, knowing she'd passed some sort of test, unsure of what it was. Then, as she started up the grand staircase, her own thoughts came back to haunt her. *Is Merilynn dead? Did I see her ghost?*

THE STONE IN THE SWORD

13

In the forest, or perhaps in the lake, drifting along the dappled sunlit paths, Merilynn thought she might be dreaming. She hoped she was still in the dream that had begun so many hours ago. *Has it really been that long?*

Dreamtime was not the same thing as waking time. Not the same thing at all. That could very well mean she had been asleep for endless minutes, not hours.

Or maybe I'm awake.

Maybe I'm dead.

That thought panicked her and she tried to push to the surface, to emerge into wakefulness and feel her bed beneath her body, her head nestled safely into her soft down pillow, which was covered with a cobalt case printed with golden stars and silver moons.

Kendra! she thought as hard as she could. *Help me wake up!*

Slowly, as if swimming through thick, cool water, she felt herself moving forward. In the distance, she saw a spot of light. *Swim to it,* she told herself. She stroked her arms forward and back and kicked her feet, hoping the movement would translate into thrashing that would wake up Kendra, who would, in turn, help her to awaken, to find her way back from the long, long dream.

Kendra!

The light grew brighter and she became more aware of the woods than the lake. She recognized Applehead Forest as she moved through it, faster and faster. Suddenly, full daylight shone on her. She saw the road beneath her, just for an instant, and then she was back in the forest again, still heading in the same direction. Toward Gamma House.

Kendra! She concentrated on the word, willing herself to say it aloud so that her roommate would hear her. The forest flashed by, more daylight gleamed ahead of her, growing quickly. I'm almost awake! *I'm almost out of the woods!*

She laughed as she sped toward the forest's edge, delighting in the dream for an instant, then worrying again. *What if I just keep going?*

Nearing the last few trees, she forced herself to slow down and step out from among them as if she were awake. *Kendra?* she called. *Where are you?*

There was Gamma House. As she emerged into daylight and stepped onto the lawn, she could see it with the clarity of a dream, all the details, even some peeling paint she had never noticed before, on the lower left side of the veranda railing.

There was one girl visible. Merilynn tried to move across the lawn, to see who it was, but she couldn't move out of the forest. *Great. Just great. Sleep paralysis. Come on, wake up!*

Her body wouldn't obey, so she concentrated her energy on seeing the lone woman on the veranda. The figure turned slightly and Merilynn knew her.

Samantha! she called as loud as she could. *Samantha.*

Sam turned and looked. Merilynn called again and raised her hand, waving at her.

Samantha saw her. She waved back.

Then another figure came out of the house and saw Sam's raised hand, started to follow Sam's gaze.

Merilynn, all instinct, instantly let herself be drawn back among the trees, out of sight. *Out of danger.*

14

Kendra!

"Merilynn!" Kendra awoke abruptly from her catnap, positive she'd heard her roommate calling her, not just once, but several times. *She was trying to wake me up!*

Kendra sat up so rapidly that the room briefly spun, but an instant later she was on her feet, searching the room. "Merilynn?" she asked, before opening a closet door. "I know you're here. You can't scare me by popping out and saying boo!" She yanked open the closet door, knowing the girl would be there.

But she wasn't. *Maybe I dreamed it.*

Kendra!

This time, she knew it was no dream. "Where the heck are you?" she said, checking inside the other closet without fanfare. Merilynn was in the room; she could tell by the closeness of her voice. "I've been so worried about you," Kendra said as she looked under one bed, then the other. Under the desks.

Kendra!

The voice was in her ear, right in her ear! Kendra stood still, listening, waiting, and for one or two seconds, fear prickled across her belly and down her back. Then she realized that her roommate had to be outside the door, in the hall.

Smiling to herself, Kendra tiptoed to the door, paused, then yanked it open.

Sam Penrose, hand raised in a fist, stared at her, goggle-eyed.

"What are you doing?" they both asked in panicked voices.

Sam recovered first. "I was about to knock."

"Christ, get *in* here." Kendra stood back to allow Sam inside, then shut the door firmly and turned to look at her. "I swear, I thought you were about to punch me. You scared the hell out of me!"

"How?"

"I thought you were Merilynn. I swear, Sam, I heard her. I heard her *in this room*. In my ear. Not more than a minute ago."

"You did?" Sam shook her head. "I heard her too."

"Was she calling my name?"

"No. She called *my* name. Outside. Hey, are you sure this room is clean?"

"Why? Do you smell something?"

Sam rolled her eyes. "I mean *clean*. No bugs?"

"Bugs? I hope not. Why are you asking about that when Merilynn needs—"

"*Electronic* bugs," Sam interrupted, almost whispering.

Kendra felt foolish. *I should have known that.* Instead of speaking, she shrugged in reply, then watched as Sam went over the room, peering at every inch of it, running her fingers beneath the desks and beds.

"I think we're okay," she said finally, still speaking very softly. She sat down on Kendra's bed and patted the spot next to her.

"How could you have heard her outside when I heard her in here?" Kendra asked quietly as soon as she was seated.

Sam shook her head. "I don't know. Maybe it's a trick."

"Merilynn's trick, or someone else's?"

"I don't know." Sam paused. "There's more."

"What?"

Sam leaned closer and whispered, "I saw her."

"Where?" Kendra controlled her excitement. "When?"

"Just a couple minutes ago, by the woods."

"We should go get her. She's probably using telepathy to call us."

Sam touched her hand. "Listen, it might be bad."

"What do you mean? What did you see?"

"I saw her, but she was too far away to hear."

"Then it had to be telepathy."

"Maybe. I hope so. Kendra, she may be dead. I saw an apparition."

"How do you know?"

"She vanished right in front of my eyes." Sam looked at the

ceiling. "I heard her first. I looked around, thinking she was on the porch, hiding—"

"Like I thought she was in this room with me."

"Yes. But when I finally saw her, she was way across the lawn. I think she knew that I saw her—that's when she waved. I waved back and she just sort of dematerialized or something. I don't know how to describe it."

"You're sure she didn't just step back behind a tree?"

Sam made a face. "I know what I saw, even if I don't know what it really was, and Merilynn's image disappeared as soon as Heather came up behind me."

Kendra nodded. "That makes sense."

"It does?"

"Of course." She leaned to Sam's ear and whispered, "You asked me before if I knew about the secret society?"

Sam nodded. "How much do you know?"

"I know that it's real. I know it's existed since the sorority was founded. I know there's a whole lot more going on in that east wing than drinking and sex."

"Do you know the name?"

This time, Kendra nodded. "Do you?"

"Yes."

"Don't say it."

"I won't."

The girls looked at each other and embarrassed smiles appeared. "If we say the name three times," Kendra said, "the society will appear in front of us and we won't be able to get rid of them."

Sam smiled. "You think Heather's one of them?"

"Undoubtedly. There should be thirteen altogether."

"Your source?"

"My family. Generations. What's yours?"

"Research." Sam hesitated. "So what do you think? Is Merilynn alive? Or did I see a ghost?"

Kendra thought a moment, then asked, "What was she wearing?"

"Something long and lavender."

"That's not what she wore to bed. Did she look . . . well, wet or anything?"

"Like Holly, you mean?"

Kendra nodded. "When we saw Holly last night, she was just like you described. Long white dress, all wet, her hair was wet. And Eve was wearing what she had on the last time I saw her."

"Well, that's interesting, but it's not proof she's alive," Sam said. She could have been put into other clothes and then . . ."

"Killed?"

Sam nodded.

"How did she look? I mean, what was your general impression of her?"

"I don't understand."

"Well, when you saw Holly, what was your reaction?"

"I thought she was dead."

"She looked pretty dead to me last night too, even when I heard her voice. Eve didn't have the same— I don't know—energy? Yes. Energy. Her energy wasn't the same as it was when she was alive. It was subdued, a little sad." She rubbed her chin. "Very sad. Not like Evie at all." Kendra fell silent and waited for Sam to speak.

"She was very far away, but my impression was that it was her. Her energy. That sounds peculiar."

"Don't analyze. I know what you mean, and you know I know."

Sam's mouth crooked in a shadow of a one-sided smile. "Yeah. Well, then, I'll go out on a limb. This is just feelings though, no facts."

Kendra rolled her eyes. "I know. Now tell me what you felt."

"There was a sort of fairy-tale feel to her. I think it was because of what she was wearing. I don't know if it was a long dress or a cloak, it was much too far away to tell, but it had kind of a ëGlenda, Good Witch of the West' feel. From *The Wizard of Oz*. But less lace."

"I know."

"If I had to guess—this is so illogical."

"Don't Spock me, Sam. Just say what you felt."

"I think you were right about the telepathy. I think maybe I saw her as she wanted to be seen."

"A purple cloak," Kendra said thoughtfully.

"Lavender. And I'm not sure it was a cloak."

"Shhh. It doesn't matter. Purple, and lavender is a shade of purple, is a sorcerer's color. It's associated with magic and wizards and witches. Merilynn has an entire set of herbs and potions and crystals. She's into magic. Did you know that?"

"Well, I'm not surprised. After that performance with the tires and calling the deer..."

"And every cheerleader is on the rag," Kendra said. "I checked. Except Michele. She's not here at all, as far as I can tell. Sam," she said after a moment of silence, "I wish I could remember better what I heard last night, but I think maybe Merilynn is all right. That she went off on her own."

"An adventure," Sam said. "Like we talked about in the first place."

"Yeah, but I think something's gone wrong. She's trying to call us."

"Any idea where she might be?"

Kendra nodded, her heart thudding. "Out there. In the forest. Maybe at the chapel."

"She wanted to go last night."

"I said I'd go with her today and she was fine with that," Kendra said. "But maybe she went alone anyway. And something happened. Something to do with what Holly Gayle said." She paused, trying to sort jumbled memories of the night before. There was the warning about the sorceress and her familiar—Kendra was pretty sure that had to be Malory and, most likely, Brittany, and reminded Sam. "But," she added, "I still don't think they're involved in Merilynn's disappearance."

"Why?"

"It just doesn't *feel* like they are. Sam, I really think she went off on her own to help Holly and Eve. Damn it, I wish I could remember more. The thing is, I think Merilynn might be trapped somewhere out there. Maybe the chapel, maybe even on the island."

"Holly almost lured me into the water." Sam stood up and looked out the window. "There's not much daylight left. I don't think we could even get to the chapel and back before dark. I'm sure we couldn't. And the island is impossible."

"We have to go to the chapel." Kendra stood next to Sam and watched shiny crows working the back lawn for their supper. She shivered.

"Too dangerous," Sam declared.

"I think it's safe tonight."

"You do? Why?"

"Most of the—society—will be at the football game. Cheering and popping Midol. Malory's been dragging herself around all afternoon moaning about food poisoning. And she's not the only one. Most of them are miserable. Brittany's the only one who's not looking a little green." Kendra studied Sam. "You know what that means, don't you?"

"Tell me."

"If Merilynn can put hexes on *them,* she's one powerful little sorceress herself."

15

"**W**here the hell is my football player?"

Coach Max Choad, accompanied by a small but voluptuous Latina coed, appeared in the kitchen doorway of Gamma House, full of piss and bluster, and stared furiously at Heather, Malory, Brittany, and several of the J-clones. The cheerleaders all held glasses of freshly made purple pick-me-up, having a well-needed jolt before the game.

"I asked you girls a question." The girl with him hovered just behind him, looking anxious, but exuding anger as well. Heather didn't recognize her. "Answer me." Choad adjusted his stance to a wide-legged immovable-soldier look, hands on hips, in an imitation of a peacock showing its colors. It worked pretty well, with his military haircut and heavy ridge of brow. The gray sweats weren't as effective as cammie fatigues might have been, but all in all, Heather thought, not too shabby.

Mildred McArthur appeared from the recesses of the kitchen, a new pitcher of her magic potion in hand. Like a big gray army tank, she rolled toward the table where her girls sat, put down the pitcher, and folded her arms across her chest. She was every inch as macho as Coach Choad and while he didn't back down under her steely tight-bunned stare, he did look a little more respectful. The coed gave off noticeably less anger.

Mildred placed herself behind Heather Horner, like a loyal mastiff. You could almost hear her snarling, though she didn't say a word.

Heather, who had felt like absolute, total crap all day, appreciated the housekeeper's presence. They all did, of course, but Heather was Mildred's pet, and she knew it. Between the housekeeper's wonderful purple juice, which she'd added something extra to to help ease the gas problems and female problems— she wouldn't say what, but who cared?— and her huge rock-slab presence, Heather felt some of her spunk returning. She could handle this, just like the Fatas had agreed she would, earlier in the day.

She stood up, knowing how good her body looked in the uniform, using it, and met Choad's beady gaze. "*Your* football player took *our* best cheerleader and ran off," she told him. "You know Malory Thomas, our president?" she added. Without waiting for a reply, she held her hand out and Malory produced a pale pink envelope, took out a folded note on matching stationery, and silently handed it to Heather. "If you think you're any more upset than we are," she said, "you're wrong. Duane Hieman took advantage of Michele. And now they're gone." She unfolded the note.

"Duane and I are engaged," the dark-haired coed with Choad said. "He wouldn't cheat on me."

"If you believe that," Brittany chirped, "you don't know men."

" 'Dear Sisters,' " Heather read, ignoring the girl, " 'I'm sorry I won't be there for the game tonight, but Duane Hieman and I are in love. He's the most wonderful man I've ever met and he's asked me to go away with him. I'm carrying his child and we want to keep it. Please don't look for us. Once we're settled, I'll be in touch. Gamma rules! Love, Your Sister, Michele Marano.' " She held the note out.

Choad snatched it, glanced at it, passed it to the football jock's wronged fiancée. "My boys said they went drinking with some of you last night," he grumbled. "Duane was with them. They said you and some of your sluts here seduced them."

Malory laughed. Not a nice sound. Then she locked her gaze on Choad. "Your boys can't resist pussy, so they're blaming their lack of control on *my* girls?"

Silence filled the room. Heather could see the concentration on Malory's face. She was doing something to the coach, whose look of resolve began to crumble.

"Don't your boys have any discipline?" Malory asked softly.

Choad looked slightly befuddled. Heather zoomed in. "Look, Coach, a few of us did have a couple beers with a few of your players, but that's all. We weren't out long."

"Where did you go to get drunk?" the coed asked.

"Just out on the lawn, not far from here. We took a blanket and sat on the ground. It was cold, so we weren't even out long—and we certainly didn't get drunk." She paused. "Michele and Duane were with us. They stayed behind when the rest of us returned to our houses."

"*We* returned to Gamma," Malory added. "Heather, Brittany, and I returned. We assume that your star quarterback and—who were the other ones?"

"Spencer Lake and Perry Seville," Heather said.

Malory nodded. "I'll vouch for what Heather just told you." She put her chin up. "I assure you, one of your jocks is not what I'd look for if I wanted to get laid."

Brittany wrinkled her nose. "Me either.'"

"We just wanted to relax," Heather finished. Being a cheer-leader, she didn't dare claim disinterest in laying jocks. It wouldn't have rung true. "Maybe we can figure this out. What did your boys tell you?"

"Not much. They were drunk off their asses and full of non-sense about getting lost in the woods."

"It wasn't with us," Heather said, glancing at Brittany, who gave her a tiny nod of approval. "We were sitting near the woods, but none of us would ever go into them at night."

"Bull," Choad said. "You kids go into the woods to make out."

"Talk about an urban legend," Malory said. "That's the real bull. One of our cheerleaders died in the woods just before school started. All they found was bones. Surely you remember that, Coach Choad?"

"Of course I do. What's that got to do with it?"

"We like our skins," Brittany said. "We wouldn't risk losing them."

"Look," Heather said, "I don't know what your boys did. They *said* they were going back to their house. They took off and so did we. Only Michele and Duane stayed behind."

"If I had to guess," Malory said, sounding bored, "I'd say your boys got some more beer, got shitfaced, and maybe really did get lost in the woods."

Heather nodded. She barely remembered what happened, but she did remember that Art Caliburn had rescued her and brought her back to Gamma before Brittany messed up the players' memories. Choad didn't say anything about Art in par-ticular, so Brittany's spell must have done what it was supposed to. Art was sweet; Heather was sorry he didn't remember his heroic deeds.

"Duane and I are getting married," the coed reminded them.

"I doubt it, sweetie," Malory said dismissively. "He's been planting his seeds in another garden. Why don't you try to snatch yourself another jock? You know how to snatch, don't you?"

The coed stared at her.

"You just open your lips and blow."

The coed and the coach turned and stomped off. Instantly Malory laughed. "Did you see the look on that girl's face?"

"Malory, you shouldn't have said that," Brittany said. "It made you sound slutty."

"Oh, who cares?"

"Sit, Heather," Mildred rumbled. "I'll pour you all some more juice."

Heather gratefully did as she was told. Mildred filled her glass first and she drank greedily, made a slight face. "It's a little tart," she said.

"Just like you," Malory drawled, waving Mildred off. "No, thanks, Mildred. I'll stick to lemon juice."

"This will fix your stomach."

"No, I'll be fine."

"It really works," Heather said, halfway through her glass.

Brittany giggled, and pushed away from the table. "Excuse me, ladies. I have to pee."

16

The cheerleaders, full of juice and moaning less about their periodic problems, took off for the football stadium half an hour later. Malory and Brittany left the kitchen and walked out onto the veranda to enjoy the last of the daylight. The woods cast early pretwilight shadows that beckoned to Brittany. She longed for a romp.

"Thank you for overseeing the burial this morning," Malory said, sounding relaxed for the first time that day.

"Jenny and Ginny did just fine."

"No cases of vapors?"

"No freaking out," Brittany corrected. "Keep your language up to date."

"Don't be bitchy. You know what I mean."

"Ginny freaked out once."

Malory turned. "Tell me."

"It wasn't about the bodies. She doesn't like chipmunks."

"What did you do?"

"Offered her a piece of candy. The bitch said I was a disgusting rodent. So I bit her."

"You bit her?" Mal laughed.

"No blood. I was careful. Jenny's much nicer." Brittany, leaning against the veranda railing, stared at the woods. "They're the real thing. Real Fata Morgana material. Jenny for sure. Ginny, probably."

"That's good. We've had so few that last lately. They either get themselves killed or they prove unworthy." Malory paused. "So, what do you think of Nancy? Do you think we're rushing things, initiating her tonight?"

"I think she's a good temporary answer to our problem," Brittany said. "We may have to do a little binding spell on her temper though. We can't have her running around killing people every time she's got PMS."

"I agree." Malory paused. "Sorry."

A stench wafted into Brittany's pert nose. "I hope you're not going to take that ass over to Professor Tongue's tonight. You'd kill him."

Malory smiled. "I could test his love for me."

"He'd pass out. Why don't you break down and have some of Mildred's juice? I noticed a distinct lessening of stink after that last batch."

"You and your magical urine. Sorry, love, I don't drink pee. Not even yours."

"Why not? You'll drink anything else."

"Back when my brother was still alive and I was just a sorcerer's apprentice—" She paused. "Actually, I was a quick study.

I was at journeyman level. In fact, it was only a year or two before I trapped my old teacher and took his power and added it to my own."

"I know the story. Tell me why you won't drink urine."

"My mentor gave me a potion once, when I became ill after eating some bad rabbit. It was food poisoning and I was much sicker than I've been today, vomiting, shitting blood, you know, the whole E-coli thing."

Brittany nodded, pleased to hear a new story, no matter how crude.

"Myrddin was a great teacher and sorceror, but he made his share of mistakes. Once, he tried to create a strange creature—"

"The platypus. You've told me that story hundreds, maybe thousands of times."

Malory laughed. "Very well. My mentor created a concoction to cure me, but it nearly killed me. I thought I'd vomit my innards out before it wore off. The ingredient was the urine of one of Myrddin's familiars."

"Anyone I know?"

"I doubt it; this was in the old country."

"We travel."

"Do you know any badgers?"

"No. I know a raccoon from Bavaria. He's famous. He inspired a Beatles song."

"You're such a name-dropper."

Brittany took a packet of sunflower seeds from the change pocket on her jeans and ripped it open with her teeth. "Are you allergic to badger urine?"

"The urine of a familiar is an old cure and energizer for humans. But I was like Myrrdin. My mother was human, but my father was the Wild Man of the Woods." She paused. "That's what we called the local nature diety back then."

"I know all that."

"Those such as Myrrdin and I cannot drink the urine of a familiar. I lived only because of my human nature."

"I thought you just had a thing about drinking urine."

"No."

"Why have you never told me this before?"

"It never came up."

"And why didn't Myrrdin know this?"

"Our kind are few and his teacher did not know. So how could he? It's rare for one of us to become ill. Very rare. There was no reason for him to know it until, experimenting to find out what had happened, he ingested a tiny amount himself and had the same reaction, though milder. He'd taken in less and he was more powerful than I was then, so it only took him a few days to recover. It took me months."

"You're easily as strong as your teacher was."

"Yes. But I still wouldn't want to experience even a fraction of that agony again." She paused. "If I had my athame, it probably couldn't touch me at all."

They silently watched distant figures of students moving about the campus. A breeze full of autumn promise and chimney smoke beguiled Brittany's nose. "All Hallow's Eve draws near. We need to decide on a sacrifice worthy of the Forest Knight. And we must find more women worthy of becoming Fata Morgana before then."

"Merilynn," Malory said softly, "will be the sacrifice. I've decided."

"She's missing."

"I know. Of all the daughters I've born over the centuries, she is the finest. I believe she has great power and I hoped we could make her one of our own. But her will is too strong and she's under the influence of Holly Gayle. I believe she does her bidding."

"We should find her as quickly as we can."

"Yes. But we have to watch her. I suspect she knows about the athame."

"Why do you believe that?"

"I think Holly Gayle was here for her last night. She already has Eve Camlan. She's after Merilynn. She's gathering souls who can help her get free. If Merilynn is looking for my stone, she may have enough power to use it on Holly's behalf. Against me."

"Why do you think she has so much power? You've seen no

proof. I think you're just swayed by her eyes. They're her father's eyes."

"They're the eyes of *both* her fathers. No other daughter has had so much of the Forest Knight in her."

"The priest is not entirely human?"

"No. He carries the blood of the Forest Knight. His mother was a student here many years ago. We were here part of the time she was here—a beauty, entirely human, but with a fey quality that appealed to me. To us. Do you remember her?"

Brittany shook her head. "No."

"She had auburn hair like Merilynn's and blue eyes. We tried to interest her in Gamma but she didn't take the bait."

Brittany searched her memory. "There have been so many."

"Her name was Gwen Aldan."

"I remember that one. She left school. She was pregnant."

"Um-hmm. She was dating a frat boy that I was interested in trying out. I don't even remember his name, just that he was faithful to her. It was very annoying." She smiled like a contented cat. "He didn't marry her though. He didn't know about the baby. I had him a year later, but he was a Johnny-comeearly. Not worth much in bed."

"I don't remember much about him. Other than he existed."

"He wasn't worth remembering. I only tried him once and you weren't there. I doubt I even mentioned him to you."

"How did her baby come to have the knight's blood in him?"

"You don't remember that?" Mal rubbed her chin. "I think you were off on that lesbian kick at the time. I was pretty annoyed about that."

"Sure." Brittany smiled as visions of a tall Nordic blond student with long legs and full lips came into her mind. "I remember that pissed you off, so I didn't tell you, but Gretchen was a cross-dresser. She was a he."

"You little twat. Why did you want to anger me?"

"It made me feel loved. I knew you needed me. And you're an incredible lover when you're jealous."

"That's sweet. Remind me to spank you later."

Brittany grinned. "I will, just as soon as you stop stinking up the place."

"Bitch," Malory said affectionately. "One night, during your fling, Gwen Aldan and her quick-draw boyfriend decided to go into the woods. I followed them, primarily because there was a full moon and spring had come early. The sap was running and the Green Knight was very active that year, just before the equinox. I was horny, nearly as much as he, I think. I had some vague plan to cast a glamour and join them in a threesome.

"They wandered farther into the woods than I expected, across Applehead Road, and straight for the Knight's Chapel. That excited me even more. Humans don't venture there on their own, no matter the stories—"

"Don't tell me what I already know. Tell me what happened."

"You are so impatient, one would think you didn't have all the time in the world." Malory leaned forward and took a deep breath. "I love autumn." She looked at Brittany, smiled at her instant of patience, then continued. "Gwen and her beau made it to the clearing, then hesitated. I knew they felt the power there. Not to mention our protection spells. They had to be frightened. The boy certainly was. I heard him telling her they should go elsewhere. He said others might catch them in the act.

"But Gwen was adamant. I think his fear just turned her on. I also think she could sense the influence of the knight and it excited her. She began kissing and fondling the boy as they stood in the clearing. He started to respond. I sensed the knight's presence and kept hidden in the trees.

"Gwen undressed and stood naked in the moonlight in the clearing. The grass was new and tender, the oak leaves bright and fresh. She was beautiful, irresistible to the human and to the knight. The boy undressed and lay on top of her." She paused. "I should have known he was boring then, just going straight for the missionary position."

"Did they hear the knight?"

"He wasn't like he was last night. The humans were in love,

even if they were bad at lovemaking. The knight approves of love, the old softie."

"And they weren't actually defiling his chapel," Brittany added.

"Even if they'd been in there, it was not defilement. It was nothing like the idiotic orgy we had last night. *That* was defiling the chapel."

"Tell me about it. I can't believe I let you do that."

"You couldn't stop me. You indulge me, little one. You know that."

Brittany let her hand move onto Malory's, squeezed it.

"The knight arrived that night in a gentle whirlwind that whistled softly through the trees and bushes. Just as the boy entered Gwen, the knight took form—I could see him, though they couldn't, of course. But from the sounds Gwen made as the knight entered the boy's body, I'd say she sensed the passion.

"Oh, Britt, it was a sight to see. No wonder I assumed the boy was worth fucking. Once the knight possessed him, he became more lover than Gwen had ever imagined. He was magnificent, and his excitement spread in waves through the clearing, entering the forest. His passion was so great that I was overcome with orgasms and fell to the ground, unable to stand. But I watched. Finally, it was over. The Forest Knight, having sown his seed, departed.

"The couple slept deeply. I walked around them, sat by them, touched them. They never knew. But I knew the knight had impregnated Gwen, so I kept track of her and then her child."

"But it was a boy."

"It was the priest, one-third elemental, two-thirds human. Males partly fathered by forest gods are rarely born, and if they are, they rarely live long. But this one thrived. Gwen married Douglas Morris, a schoolteacher, before the child was born, so the infant was christened Martin Morris. He showed no signs of his elemental roots, except for his eyes, but I had the Fatas here keep an eye on him anyway. They told me he was handsome and charismatic but lacked any traits of the Forest Knight."

"That's to be expected," Brittany said.

"So it is. I still thought to make him my lover to help sire my next daughter, just to see what would happen, but I didn't get around to it until the Fatas reported that he'd become a priest, denying the lust that had to be in his nature."

"You and priests," Brittany chided.

"Forbidden fruit is always the tastiest."

Brittany grinned. "So Martin Morris must have been the cherry on your sundae."

"Mmmm. That man was delicious and he resisted me as no mere human male ever could. I'd never admit this to anyone but you, but I actually had to cast a glamour to get him to make love to me."

"Mal, you do that all the time."

"To speed things up. When I want a real lover, a father for my child, I prefer to seduce him the old-fashioned way. I brought him to the chapel without magick; the priest wanted to see it. In fact, he'd been there before. Quite the scholar on the occult."

"A natural interest."

Mal smiled. "Yes. I impressed him with stories of the Forest Knight and when I saw desire in his eyes, I tried to seduce him. I nearly had him, but the damned Papist had a will of iron. Finally, I cast a little light glamour and his will of iron turned into a willy of iron." She laughed like a young girl.

"Once I had him where I wanted him, I removed the spell. He couldn't deny me at that point. From that union, I created Merilynn. That is why I believe she's so powerful. Not as powerful as I am, of course."

"Malory," Brittany ventured, "you had him impregnate you at the chapel."

"I enjoy it more that way."

"I know. May I ask you something?"

"Of course."

"Did you sense the Forest Knight?"

"I always sense the knight."

"I know, but I mean in the same way you did when you peeped the priest's conception."

"Peeped?"

"You know what I mean."

Malory hesitated. "As the daughter of a Green Man myself, I have a similar degree of lust. Making love in the chapel makes me one with the Forest Knight. I am the same."

"*Almost* the same. I just want to know if he manifested. If he rode you or the priest."

"He didn't possess the priest," Malory said. "I would have known if he had."

"Could he have been in you?"

"My lust is the same as his."

"Mal, what I'm saying is, if he rode with you, Merilynn might be more elemental than you think.

She could be *as powerful as you.*"

"Nonsense."

"I hope so."

"Why would you think that?"

"You've been too ill to think about it, but somebody is behind everything that happened today. The gas. Did you notice, every senior sister had gas? No juniors, sophomores, or freshman. Just seniors."

"Coincidence," Malory said without too much certainty.

"No. Because the girls who all got their periods this morning? Every single one was a cheerleader. Every one of them had problems with stickless wings or broken tampon strings. I asked around. *Every single one.* No exceptions. And the senior cheerleaders like Heather have *all* the problems." She squeezed her mistress's hand. "That's why *I* think you're right about Merilynn. Especially now that you've told me this story. She must have done it."

"Not bad, huh?" Malory said with pride.

"Not bad? She even got *you!* You yourself said you don't get sick easily. If she's strong enough to cast a glamour over you, then she may be your equal or more."

"No, that's just ridiculous. I wasn't on my guard. I had too much to drink and my human nature got the upper hand, that's all."

"I hope so."

"Besides, even if it were true, she was raised by a priest with more morals than an inner-directed atheist."

"That's a lot of morals. Religious nuts are usually so easily bought and sold."

"The priest is no religious nut. He may not even be into dogma, but he has the spiritual streak. I suspect he thrives on the discipline of his profession. And he's a scholar."

"A martyr?"

"I'd say no, judging by Merilynn's behavior."

"Then why did you let him raise her?"

"Honestly? I almost always leave the girls with their fathers. You know I've used men of various cloths plenty of times. Not the average preacher, mind you, but the fiery ones. I choose them for their dogmatic attitudes, the stronger the better." She chuckled. "They're *so* easy to seduce. And they make lousy parents because they're usually too strict and shove so much religion down the girls' throats that they're primed to rebel."

Whenever Malory decided to produce a new daughter, Brittany bore it without pointing out that the daughters rarely lived long after Malory brought them into the sisterhood. She didn't point it out now. Instead, she said, "So, you overlooked this priest's morals and intellect because of his heritage?"

"Wouldn't you?"

"Yes. Now. What are we going to do about your daughter?"

"We have to find out where she is and watch her until she leads us to my stone. Then...we lock her up tight and save her for All Hallow's Eve."

Behind them, someone pushed one of the front doors open. Brittany turned, then Malory. "Hi, Samantha, Kendra."

"Hello," they both said.

"Off to the game?" Brittany asked, looking at the knapsacks both carried.

"No," Sam said, boldly swinging hers around and patting it. "We're off to study."

"On a Friday night?" Mal asked.

"We're nerds," Kendra said, smiling. "What can we say?"

"I may come by the library later myself," Malory replied. "See you there?"

"No," Sam said. "We're actually going down to Caledonia to study."

"We're going to my granny's house," Kendra added. "She's making us a home-cooked dinner. We're going to study there."

"That's a strange place to study," Brittany chirped around a sunflower seed.

"Not really," Sam said without a trace of defensiveness. "We're working a report together for Professor McCobb's cultural iconography class. We're doing a paper on local lore, and Kendra's grandmother is an expert."

"She worked here, didn't she?"

Kendra smiled. "Malory, I'm surprised you'd remember that. Yes, she did, but that's not really important. It's the stories that were handed down to her about the Greenbriar Ghost and the Puckwudgies that we're interested in."

"That sounds like something your roommate, Merilynn, would be interested in," Malory replied. "Why isn't she with you?"

"She's not in the class," Sam said.

"But it seems strange she wouldn't tag along. I know how much she likes that kind of thing."

"She's busy," Sam said.

"Oh? Big date?"

"I don't know for sure. Maybe she's going to her father's. Maybe to see friends. I didn't ask, she didn't tell me."

"When was this?" Malory asked casually. "I've been in the house all day and I haven't run into her once."

"I saw her earlier this afternoon, but just for a moment. She was in a hurry to take off."

Malory nodded. "Well, have fun, you guys."

"Don't drink and drive," Brittany called after them.

Exchanging glances, they both turned to watch the duo walk quickly toward the nearest parking lot. A moment later, they exchanged glances when Sam Penrose's white Camry drove slowly by. Sam waved, Kendra too.

Brittany raised her hand. "Well, I didn't really think we'd see a car. I didn't think they were really going to Caledonia, at least not to eat dinner with an old lady."

"I still don't think they are," Malory said. "If they're really going down to Granny's house, who cares?"

"Maybe they're pumping her for information."

"Britt, they *admitted* that. And who cares? Now, be a love and race over to the woods. To the chapel. Make sure nothing's been disturbed, just in case that's where they're really headed."

"We need to go there together to do the quick-rot spell on those corpses Jenny and Ginny buried. If we transport ourselves via aport, we can get it done before they get there, even if they're on their way."

"Brittany, that takes energy I don't have today. That's why I want you to go by yourself. If they show up, watch them. Follow them. They might be looking for her, or they might know where she is. I wouldn't be surprised if they're taking her food."

"Okay." Brittany stood straight and stretched. "When Samantha claimed she saw Merilynn today, did you think it was a lie?"

"I—no. But I still don't believe it. The girl is gone. Samantha is an amazingly accomplished liar."

"I think she was telling the truth," Brittany said firmly. "Granted, she's difficult to read most of the time, but when humans make an absolute statement, I can tell if they're lying or not. I don't believe she was."

Malory nodded. "Okay, she saw her. Now scoot! You need to get to the chapel quickly."

Brittany handed Malory the almost-empty sunflower seed bag, glanced around, saw no one, transformed into her elemental form, and joyously sped into the forest.

17

Father Martin Morris sat alone on the comfortable old couch in the cozy living room of the California bungalow-style house he'd lived in ever since he'd taken over Caledonia's little parish more than twenty years ago. The room was lit by only by one lamp on a side table and the television, which was airing the 7:00 P.M. rerun of the previous night's *Conan O'Brien,* one of Martin's favorite guilty pleasures.

Merilynn's too. Before the show had started rerunning, before Merilynn had gone off to college, they had taped it nearly every night and watched it during supper.

Tonight, he was all alone, except for Pio, his aging fat tabby who was snoring away on the back of the couch. Delores, his live-in housekeeper and Merilynn's mother substitute, had been living-in less and less lately. After all these years, at fifty-two, she had finally found romance. Of course, she'd never gone looking when Merilynn was home. Now, Martin expected Delores would announce wedding plans soon, and he was happy for her, but very sorry for himself. He would miss her company, though not half as much as he already missed Merilynn's. *A priest suffering from empty nest syndrome. There's something novel.*

In a perfect world, Merilynn would be here beside him, watching Conan dismember politicians and going off on ridiculous tangents like a big Irish Robin Williams whenever a guest turned into a snore-fest. *Snorefest.* That was Merilynn's term. *Good God, how I miss her!*

Tonight, if she were here, and Delores was out, he would have zapped two Hungry Man Salisbury Steak TV dinners instead of one, and they would have eaten every last bite (except for the generous pieces of meat they always cut up for Pio). They'd bond over the damned dinners, telling one another how disapproving Delores would be if she knew. And that simple thing, a silly secret kept, had seemed grand to little Merilynn, and truth be told, to him as well.

Instead, there was one empty-compartmented TV dinner tray and a fork, on the coffee table. Thanks to Pio, there wasn't a drop of evidence left (or there wouldn't be, once he tossed the dinner tray and rinsed the fork). He smiled. The cardboard tray was clean enough to put in the recycle bin, but he'd bury it in the trash so that Delores wouldn't be so likely to deliver a lecture about chemical preservatives or look hurt that he hadn't eaten the bland little shepherd's pie she'd made for him. The pie, more evidence, would disappear soon too, chopped up and put out on old plastic plates, a special treat for the small colony of feral cats he cared for.

Settling back, he put his feet on the table. Pio opened one sleepy eye, then oozed his gray and black tiger-stripes down the back of the couch and across the seat, then onto Martin's lap. The feline began purring and pressing his paws up and down on the priest's thigh. Martin endured the sharp claws—Merilynn liked to say that their Pio caused stigmata, instead of enduring them like his holy namesake.

And she was right.

Merilynn, I wish you'd call me. Absently, he stroked the cat and tried to concentrate on Conan, but found himself glancing at the Regulator pendulum wall clock and wondering what his little girl was up to. He did that a lot, but more than usual since this noon or so. Generally she phoned for a moment or two every day, and usually warned him when she wouldn't be able to, but he hadn't heard from her since Wednesday. It hadn't been long, and it was a Friday night. *Maybe she went to a football game.*

The thought amused him so much that he chuckled. Pio gave him a disapproving glare.

On-screen, Conan was making throaty meows and raising his eyebrows suggestively to cover for a boring starlet whose breasts were engineering marvels and probably had higher IQs than her brain. He studied her. *Is she drunk? High? Simply stu-*

pid or terribly nervous? Who cares? What's Merilynn doing? He smiled again. He knew his girl; she wouldn't be at a football game, but otherwise, all bets were off.

Conan smoothed his eyebrows, cutting up the actress's drone with manic double entendres, but Martin barely heard them. Merilynn was smart, but she was impulsive too, and he could never completely stop worrying about her. She needed someone to ground her and he had been relieved when she told him that she had reconnected with a down-to-earth girl named Sam whom she'd met at camp and never forgotten. Back then, she'd called the girl "the funnest party pooper" she'd ever met. He had sensed a little bit of idol worship and thought it was probably a good thing.

Martin hadn't wanted Merilynn to choose Greenbriar, but it was his own fault that she had. He had fostered her interest in the occult, telling her stories of the Greenbriar Ghost and the legend of Holly Gayle any time she asked. And he had allowed her to go to that cheerleading camp even though he knew full well she had no interest in cheerleading—*Thank you, Lord!*—but was only there to scout for ghosts.

And now, she had entered the sorority that Holly Gayle had been in. Joining Gamma was no different than Merilynn's reason for wanting to go to the cheerleading camp years ago. She simply wanted to live in a house that had ghost stories attached to it. She'd dismissed his generalized warnings about the cult within the sorority as speculation and assured him that he'd done a fine job of raising her, that she could take care of herself.

She had him trapped with that argument and they both knew it. He didn't really know much about the sorority itself—he only held some suspicions based on vague stories. As for the ghosts, well, ghosts couldn't hurt her.

Or could they? He remembered all too clearly the stories she had brought back from Applehead Lake. She'd told him about the island, the eyes, the shrieks, and she'd told him about seeing the ghostly lights of the long dead town, and the apparition that had beckoned to her friend, Sam. They had seen Holly Gayle, seemingly in the flesh.

He believed her stories; Merilynn was blessed with a rich imagination, but fortunately, she knew fantasy from reality and always went to pains to keep the line between them clear, a habit that probably explained why his hair hadn't started to gray yet.

After the camp experience, she took up art, drawing endless pictures of the lake, the ghost, the town, even the eyes. He still had the old drawings; first crayon, then charcoals, a year of pen and ink sketches, and then sheaves of high school-era art. When she turned fourteen, he had given her a set of professional watercolor paints, and that turned out to be her chosen media. By the time she'd gone off to Greenbriar, her work was professional-looking and verged on bursting into a magnificent style. He hoped she wouldn't give up painting, even if what she created disturbed him.

Although she occasionally painted other sorts of pictures, nearly all of them displayed the eerie themes she had fallen in love with at the camp. If she painted a field of wildflowers, there would still be something ghostly about it. It was simply her style and he doubted it would ever change. She loved the supernatural, and there was nothing wrong with that; he loved the study as well.

He had brought her up as honestly as he could, answering questions about life and death, about sex and ghosts and war. The only thing he hadn't been entirely honest with her about was the old chapel in the woods. When she was a child, he had played it down in the stories, and he thanked God or Synchronicity or Chance that she hadn't stumbled on it as a child at camp. Later, when she was in high school, especially when she became interested in attending Greenbriar University, she did some reading of her own and asked him about the old structure. He told her what he knew of it from his books and from stories handed down to him from older folks, but said nothing of his own experiences there, of her tie to the place, and his, and he prayed she would never ask, just as he had always prayed that she wouldn't press him for details about her mother.

Amazingly, she didn't. *Not just amazing, but astonishing.*

The girl was born curious, but she asked virtually nothing about her roots. Martin had no living relatives by the time she arrived, but he had had a brother who died young. Fearing for his job if his superiors found out he had a child of his own, he wove a fictional life and marriage for his brother, and then a fictional death.

Later, when Merilynn was old enough to ask questions, he stuck to the story. It was the only thing he could do when she was a child, partly to protect his position but mainly because he couldn't bear to tell her what little he knew about her real mother or about his suspicions about her. Now that Merilynn was grown, when she decided to ask, he would have to tell her the truth. The thought terrified him now almost as much as he'd worried about her mother, in the early years, suddenly showing up and stealing the child back.

The concern faded considerably over the years, rising when she went to the camp so near the chapel, fading more, then rising again when she left for Greenbriar. What if she went to the chapel and encountered... something? *Her mother?*

How do you tell your own child that her mother is a demon?

Pio meowed loudly and Martin automatically started to scratch the cat behind his ears, but the animal hissed at his touch and stiffened in his lap. Claws began to dig into his legs.

"Hey, Pio, what's wrong?" He moved his hands away from the cat, who meowed again and then began to purr too loudly and frantically, his body stiff and trembling. Panic seized Martin; Pio had purred like this only twice before, once when he broke his leg as a kitten, and a couple of years later when his hide got caught on the protruding point of a drawer handle shaped like an arrow and frantically tried to get loose before Martin could reach him. There had been little blood, but the six-inch-long gash in his hide had been horribly, obviously painful for many days even though the vet provided pain medication.

During the week that Pio had been barely able to move, Martin changed the drawer handles and Merilynn spent all her free time soothing the feline. That was when she had developed her interest in herbal medicine and in learning to heal with her hands. While he knew the old herbal poultices wouldn't hurt (he had checked with the vet just to make sure) and actually seemed to soothe the cat—since Merilynn added catnip to everything, it wasn't terribly surprising—Martin had never seen any hands-on healing that wasn't of the snake oil variety.

But Merilynn, barely twelve years old, brought home a library book and studied. Within an hour, she was working on the technique, holding her hands just an inch above the wound, her eyes closed, her lips moving silently. And Pio would begin to purr contentedly. When Martin asked what she was doing, Merilynn looked at him as if he were an imbecile, then explained that she was channeling energy from the earth through herself and sending it into Pio to help him get better faster. She invited him to pass his own hand beneath hers when she was working on the cat. Astonishment overcame skepticism when he felt the unnatural heat pouring from her palms. Pio stopped purring and glared at him until he stopped blocking Merilynn's energy. As soon as he moved away, the cat relaxed and purred like a kitten. Martin's hand had felt warm and slightly tingly for an hour after the experience and the vet had proclaimed Pio to have healed faster than he thought possible.

But now, Pio's purr was distressed, not contented. Martin, realizing he was likely to be bitten and clawed if he touched him again, studied his pet, assuming he was in pain.

But Pio's fur had prickled up and he was staring intently at the television screen. Martin looked, saw O'Brien introducing a comic, but nothing else. "Pio?" he murmured.

The cat ignored him. Martin carefully placed one hand on the animal's back, ready to pull away fast, but Pio didn't react. His body trembled with the harsh purrs and nervous energy. "Pio, are you okay?" He put his other hand on the cat's flank and there was still no reaction. Carefully, he began touching the cat, looking for a sign of pain, fully expecting to be shredded when he felt the animal's abdomen, but Pio didn't respond or even move. He was like a statue, a trembling one. And he continued to stare at the screen. Martin did too.

Suddenly he saw something, just a waver in the air in front of the television. It was gone in an instant, but the short hairs on Martin's neck rose on end. "Pio? What do you see?"

As he spoke, he saw it again, the wavering in the air, like heat rising from the black asphalt on a desert highway. If it was possible, Pio became even stiffer under Martin's hands.

The wavering clearness slowly lengthened and began to look like a misty, translucent human form. Martin and Pio watched. As the mist took on a light purplish color, the cat's frantic purring ceased, but he remained tight and stiff. Martin felt fear but also fascination. He watched. He waited.

Seconds slowed and seemed like long minutes as the form grew clearer.

Father!

"Merilynn? Merilynn? Is that you?"

The figure clarified as he spoke, and his daughter stood before him hidden in the rich folds of a velvety deep lavender cloak, except for her coppery hair, longer and fuller than he remembered, falling over her shoulders. Her face looked pale and pure, her Madonna smile exactly as he remembered, and her green eyes . . . They startled him. He had seen them flash with emerald brilliance at times, but now they glowed.

Father!

He saw her lips form the word, but heard her voice inside his head. "Merilynn. What?"

I see you, Father. And Pio. Hi, kitty!

The cat relaxed the instant she said his name. He meowed softly, then stood up and jumped onto the coffee table.

Good kitty, Pio. I miss you.

Pio trilled at her and sat down, his head cocked up to look at her face. *He hears her. He sees her. I'm not losing my mind.*

"Merilynn," he said, "are you all right? Are you . . . " He couldn't say it.

Dead?

He nodded.

I don't think so. I think I'm dreaming, but I'm not sure. Are you real?

"Yes. You are too. You're not dreaming. I see you and so does Pio."

I hope you're right.

"Where are you?"

I'm not sure. It's cold. Very cold. It's dark, too. I had a dream. Maybe I'm still having it. Or maybe it wasn't a dream. I don't know.

"It's okay, honey. We'll figure it out. What did you dream?"

Holly Gayle came to my room. She asked me to help her and the others.

"Others?"

Under the lake. There are so many ghosts trapped there.

"What did she ask you to do?"

I have to find something and then I can set them free. But I'm scared. I can't think. It was clear, but I lost it. I'm lost. Please help me!

"I'll find you, Merilynn."

Even as he said the words, her image faded away. Conan O'Brien was saying good night. Pio turned and hopped back into Martin's lap. "I'm sure glad you saw her too."

Pio pushed his head up hard under Martin's chin and purred.

"I love you, too," the priest said as he stood up and set the feline on the couch. Pio instantly curled up in the warm spot Martin had vacated and was sleeping by the time Merilynn's cell phone rang six times and her voice mail came on.

Damn it! Martin went to his writing desk and opened the drawer, stared at the jumble of papers, of bills and receipts. The last time he'd talked to his daughter, she had given him her new roommate's cell number. He'd written it down and put it in the desk. The first thing he had to do was find it.

18

"You passed it," Kendra said as Sam cruised by a mile marker located near the narrow trailhead that led to the chapel ruins an eighth of a mile deeper into the woods.

"We can't park in plain sight." Sam drove on another five hundred feet, then slowed to a crawl and put on her brights. "There's a great place to hide the car right about here."

"You've been here before?"

"I scoped out a parking place when I first came here."

"Why?" Kendra looked at the girl, at the odd expression on her face.

"I intended to check the place out eventually. I like to be prepared."

"What aren't you telling me?"

Sam stared at the road, driving slowly. "I would think you'd be happy I'm prepared. We'd never find a hiding place for the car otherwise."

"I appreciate it, but you seem a little freaked. Why won't you answer my question?"

"There it is." Sam nudged the Camry off the road and eased forward into a grove of pine trees. The space was barely wider than the car itself, but she kept moving forward.

"The ground looks smooth, but the pine needles are really thick. They could be filling a hole." She paused. "You aren't worried about getting stuck?"

"No. I checked it out already, remember?"

Twilight dimmed into near darkness as the car was swallowed by the trees. Sam, looking confident and satisfied once more, cut the engine and pulled the parking brake, then looked at Kendra. "We're her-re," she sang softly and killed the headlights.

"We sure are."

Sam made no move to get out. "Are you sure you want to do this?"

"I'm sure I *don't* want to do this," Kendra said.

"But we have to."

"Exactly." With the headlights off, she could still make out the sky, and only ten feet away, bits of the road were visible between the trees. "It's not all that dark."

"Kendra, it's pretty dark and it's going to be totally dark in maybe twenty minutes. But we won't know it because it will seem that way to us in about five minutes, just as soon as we're farther into the forest, away from the road."

"Maybe we should have brought some large men," she joked.

"You're kidding. The large men are all at the football game living up to their IQs. They'd be useless here."

"They're not the brightest bulbs, but they'd be nice to have along in case we run into the local serial killer."

"Okay, that's true. And if we run into any ghosts, it would be fun to watch them run off, screaming." Sam stared at her. "If you want to do this, let's do this."

Kendra nodded. "How do you feel about it?"

"I feel like I'm the idiot girl in a horror movie who walks up the stairs by herself. My feeling is that this is too stupid of an idea to even consider. But I also feel like we need to do it."

She released the trunk latch, opened her door, and stepped out, went to the rear of the car. Kendra did the same. By the little courtesy light in the trunk they opened their backpacks and removed the books they'd piled in to hide their flashlights and light-sticks.

"What else have you got in there?" Sam asked.

"Water, some Band-Aids, and aspirin. And pepper spray." She took the small canister out and clipped it to a belt loop on her jeans. "And this," she said, showing Sam her sharp silver letter opener. "It's sort of an heirloom and it could pass for a knife."

"No, no. Don't put it back in your bag. Put it where you can get at it quickly."

Kendra's heart raced as she carefully slipped it into the long pocket inside her denim jacket.

"I've got this." Sam showed her a metal rod, less than an inch in diameter and only about six inches long.

"That's a weapon?"

"Uh-huh."

"Is it a martial arts thing?"

"No. It's a billy club."

"Don't you think it's a little short?"

Sam smiled and hefted the metal rod, pointing it away from Kendra. She flipped her wrist and Kendra heard a disturbing metallic sound and saw the rod shoot out a full eighteen inches. "Okay, I believe you. That's a billy club."

Sam tapped it, releasing the springs, and the rod slipped back down and became an unimpressive six inches again. "I like it," she said. "I wish I'd thought of pepper spray too, though." She put the rod in her pants pocket, shut the trunk, and said, "Let's go."

"Wait." Kendra searched for the right words, then decided to be as blunt as Sam. "You never answered my question."

"Which was what?"

"Have you been to the chapel before?"

Sam didn't answer for a long moment. Finally, she said, "Yes. When I was at camp."

"You and Merilynn went there?"

"No. Just me."

"Something happened."

Sam nodded. "I don't remember much about it and it's not pertinent to why we're going now. I'll tell you some day."

"All right." Kendra swallowed and squared her shoulders. "I'm ready. Let's go find Merilynn."

19

Father and Pio faded away like phantoms as Merilynn began to notice the smell of old, damp wood. Next, she recognized the cold scent of the lake and the sound of water lapping and sloshing below her and the unmistakable muted knock-knocking of small boats moored and gently sloshing against the dock.

Am I awake? Or am I dreaming?

She opened her eyes but the view didn't change; there was only darkness. Wanting, needing to know if she was awake or dreaming, even if she was alive or dead, Merilynn searched for clues by calling upon her other senses. She lay on her back on an uncomfortably hard, ridgy surface and realized it had to be the old damp wood she was smelling. Her body, which she hadn't even been aware of until now, felt chilled to the bone, stiff and achy. She welcomed the pain.

I'm alive and I'm awake!

She decided to sit up and did so without mental effort—further proof she was truly awake at last. Rubbing her hands together so fast and hard it ought to have started a fire brought only a bare hint of tingly warmth, but it was enough for the time being.

Her mind was beginning to function better as well. Endless dreams of being lost, wandering in Applehead Forest, trying to contact her friends and, last, Father for help, still muddied her mind. It had seemed so real. She still felt lost and she had no idea where she was.

That's not true. You're sitting on a dock at the lake. You're inside a boathouse.

There were several little docks with boathouses scattered around the lake, so what she didn't know was which one she might be in. Or how she'd gotten there, but the cobwebs were clearing. It would come back to her. It had to.

Cautiously, she got on her knees, then felt around to determine the width of the dock. *At least five feet.* Satisfied, she started to rise, then lowered herself back down as she realized she had no sense of direction. It was safe to bet the planks ran across the width of the dock. . . Wasn't that how all docks and piers were built? Suddenly, she wasn't so sure. But even if she was right, standing up to walk would be foolish; she might walk straight off the end of the pier, right into the lake.

And judging by the damp feeling of the Levis she wore, she'd already taken a dip. With a sigh, she put her hands flat on the wood and began to crawl, hoping she'd chosen the right direction.

20

The forest was quiet but not silent, and for that little bit of normalcy, Sam was grateful. A light wind stirred the leaves of the oaks studded among the pines, and their sounds reminded her of sheets flapping on a faraway clothesline. Every so often, a stronger gust caused a flurry of golden leaves to let go of their branches and sprinkle down on them in gentle waves.

Night birds called. Now and then some small creature would scuttle through the underbrush, making sounds too small to cause alarm. Kendra's flashlight lit the narrow worn path, and while the trees loomed tall and close, Sam felt none of the claustrophobic heaviness that she had felt long ago and expected now.

"Any idea how much farther we have to go?" Kendra asked in library tones.

"I've never been on this path before but it's supposed to be only a little over an eighth of a mile to the ruins from the road. It can't be much farther."

They walked another ten feet before Kendra remarked, "This isn't so bad. I'm not getting goose bumps, or anything. I thought I'd be terrified. Instead, I'm just a little nervous."

"I know what you mean. When I was in here as a kid, the atmosphere was different. Heavy. Nasty-feeling. You know what I think?"

"What?"

"I think the weather must have a lot to do with how people perceive this place."

"You mean like when the barometer rises or falls?"

"That's exactly what I mean. Tonight, the air is dry and the wind feels light. Does that make sense?"

"Yes," Kendra said. "The wind feels playful. More kid-Halloween-spooky fun than seriously scary."

"It does." Sam squinted into the darkness ahead and thought it seemed less dark. "Hey, raise your light a little—I think the clearing is ahead."

Kendra lifted the lantern higher and pointed the beam ahead. The beam wasn't terribly strong, but it was enough to show that the trees lining the path gave way, letting some dusky twilight in another hundred feet or so. Something skittered through the bushes to their right and Kendra swung the flashlight around, looking for the source of the sound. And found it.

"What's a chipmunk doing out at night?" Sam asked. The cute little creature sat up on its haunches, sniffing the air and staring at them.

"For all I know, they come out at night. Don't they?"

The chipmunk chattered, then raised its striped tail and scampered down the path, disappearing in seconds. "Maybe there are nocturnal types."

Kendra shrugged. "Shall we?"

They began walking to the end of the path and a moment later, came to the clearing. They paused there, still sheltered by the trees, and silently studied the black outline of the ruins, still vaguely visible despite imminent nightfall. Sam looked up at the sky. The waning moon was up; that had to be helping.

After several silent moments, Kendra said, "I don't think anyone's here."

"Neither do I." Sam stepped into the clearing, gesturing to Kendra to follow.

Turning on the lantern, Kendra joined her, playing the light around the boundaries of the round meadow, then over the ruins. Nothing moved. She illuminated the broad empty doorway, saw only grass inside. Then she put the light back down, angled over the ground. There was slight evidence of a path, but it was overgrown with grasses. She glanced at Sam, who nodded.

Keeping the lamp pointed just ahead of them, Kendra and Sam crossed the meadow and stood in the doorway of the chapel. Kendra used the light to check the interior for dangers. "Safe," she said softly.

They entered, walked to the end, where grass gave way to dirt and ashy wood remnants in a thick circle of smooth, smoke-blackened stones. A faint odor of burnt wood hung around the firepit. Sam squatted, examining the bonfire leavings more closely. Her nose twitched at the strong scent. "This was used recently."

"Today?"

Touching the stones, then a chunk of wood, mostly burned, she said, "No. At least not for a couple of hours. I'd guess this is leftovers from last night, or even two nights ago. I don't know enough to be sure." She rose and they walked around in the small building. Above, the slice of moon was bright enough to make her squint, and when she looked away, she saw its after-image.

"This is interesting," Kendra said, taking a few steps toward a large vague rectangle where the grass was sparser and shorter.

Sam stepped onto the area. "It's softer. But if it was a grave or something, it's been here long enough for the grass to start growing again. I'm sure Merilynn's not down there."

"It's peculiar though."

"Definitely. But it's not what we're looking for."

Kendra cast the light around. "The grass looks trampled."

"Sure. There were people here having a bonfire."

The girls in dark hooded cloaks. They stood around someone who was tied to the ground. One of the cult members had a knife.

"Oh, my God," she said softly. Her voice trembled, her heart pounded as details cleared.

"What's wrong?"

"I saw someone killed here when I was a kid."

"The serial killer? You saw him kill someone."

Sam shook her head. "I wish. No, it was a coven. I heard singing and followed it from the camp. I thought it was beautiful. Then I stood right outside that window"—she pointed—"and saw them. There was a fire roaring. They were in a circle around a naked girl. Then their robes came off and they were nude underneath. They stood back—that's when I saw the girl tied down on the ground. The priestess had Cleopatra makeup on. She had a black knife." Sam paused, trembling.

"Are you okay?" Kendra murmured.

Sam sucked it up. "I'm fine. The victim saw me. Her eyes—she was terrified. Then the high priestess kneeled over her, raised the knife, and plunged it in. The sounds were horrible. I think the cult was singing, but I'm not sure. Then the priestess pulled the girl's heart out of her chest and held it up." Sam hesitated. "And she saw me."

Angry chittering made them both jump. Sam swung the light around. The little chipmunk sat, not five feet away, staring at them, cursing in Squirrel.

"Let's get out of here," Sam said.

"Let's."

They moved rapidly toward the exit.

21

The chipmunk watched them go, then raced around the interior of the chapel, examining everything. It had already done so before the girls arrived, and been satisfied that nothing damning was obvious. The grass, helped with a touch of magick to grow rapidly early that morning, after Jenny and Ginny were done burying the bodies, was not yet as long as the surrounding growth—even her spells couldn't do that, not without the help of the Puckwudgies, who were disinclined to cooperate with her. In the dark, the lack of length was barely noticeable, yet the Gamma freshmen *had* noticed.

Disconcerted, the elemental decided it didn't matter—Brittany and Malory would return together in a few hours to cast a spell that would instantly disintegrate the bodies, making them indistinguishable from the soil unless someone knew to take samples for microscopic examination. But no one would, and the grass would be look no different from the older greens by morning; the short patch would be gone.

Everything was fine, except, perhaps, for one little thing.

When Samantha Penrose had said she remembered seeing a sacrifice here years ago, the little elemental had been shocked. Although Malory and Brittany hadn't attended Greenbriar University as sorority sisters that year, they had come for the sacrifice, as they always did. The Greenbriar Wood—it had only become Applehead Forest in the nineteenth century—was the elemental's natural home and so the Forest Knight of Greenbriar had become Malory's personal patron when she took Brittany as her familiar. (That was how Malory saw it, but the truth was that Brittany had chosen Malory.)

The elemental's rapid-fire thoughts returned to the words of Samantha Penrose. Malory had worn ornate makeup, as she always did for the summer sacrifices, so there was little chance Samantha would know it was her.

And only Malory had seen her; Brittany herself had stood opposite her, her back to the window, and had barely sensed something amiss before Malory, full of power instantly after the sacrifice, wiped the little girl's memory clean. The Fata Morganas hurried out of the chapel before the knight's arrival, and Brittany never even thought of the incident again until, later, Malory spoke of it.

The little girl had grown and now lived in the sorority house among them. Worried, the chipmunk took off, racing through the woods, back to her mistress.

22

"You said what happened to you at the chapel when you were a kid at camp wasn't pertinent to our trip tonight," Kendra said after Sam backed the Camry out of the grove and pulled onto Applehead Road. "Where are we going?"

"The road's too narrow here; we'll have to go a ways before we can turn around." Sam turned her brights on, illuminating trees that seemed to lean forward, looming over the car, edging the curving road, old and evil. "As for pertinence, I said that because I honestly couldn't remember what I'd seen. All I knew was that the place frightened me and I thought there was probably a reason."

"So, the sacrifice . . ."

"Remembered it while we were standing there." She laughed nervously. "I'll tell you, I about wet myself. Suddenly, I could see that girl spread out on the ground, and that face that looked like Cleopatra, you know, in that ancient Liz Taylor movie?"

"I remember."

"Only this priestess or whatever she was, she wore even more makeup. Her face was white—too white. It was makeup, I think, not a mask. I remember noticing that the whiteness blended away into normal pale skin at the base of her neck."

"Her hair?"

"Black, Cleo-style. I think. I was fixed on her eyes. They were all edged in black. I swear, when she looked at me, my mind just filled up with those eyes, and then—nothing."

"What happened after that?"

"I don't know. I wandered in the woods and finally found my way back to the camp." She paused. "I've always known that part though. I think I got lost. I sneaked into my cabin not very long before dawn."

"So you have some missing time."

"Maybe, maybe not. It was really late when I went out."

"But the priestess saw you. She didn't just let you go, did she?"

"Kendra, if she didn't, would I be here? That has to be how I got lost—running away in a blind panic."

"We've seen things, Sam. Like what Merilynn did. Maybe she made you forget."

"Oh, please. Spell-casting? I doubt it. I know what Merilynn can do and I don't deny what I've seen, but there was nothing supernatural going on in that chapel. Just some sick satanic cult getting their jollies. I was a kid. I repressed the memory." She slowed for a hairpin curve, laughed once, a bitter sound. "After that, I was decidedly uninterested in going into the woods. Merilynn and Eve were going to walk this little nature trail that loops up behind the camp the next day and I made up some excuse so I wouldn't have to go with them. The truth is, I was terrified."

"Are you still?"

"Hey, I walked to the chapel in the dark with you, didn't I?"

She slowed as they approached a wide spot in the road, nosed into it to make a U-turn. She pulled forward, letting the engine idle, the high beams lighting the road and the other side of the woods. "I don't really like Applehead Forest, though," she admitted. "I don't really like any forests. Maybe that will change now that I remember what happened."

"Well, I've got to hand it to you, Sam. I couldn't have gone into that forest tonight if I felt like that to begin with. You're the bravest woman I've ever met."

"No, I'm not. I never would have done it on my own."

"Sure you would."

"No, not alone. I only managed to walk in there because I had you there to watch my heroic act." She looked Kendra in the eye, embarrassment showing. "By myself, quivering jelly. I'm just a show-off."

Kendra smiled and patted her knee. "Hey, whatever works. Some day, when I write a book about the history and legends of Applehead Forest, you'll go down as the warrior maiden who dared enter the chapel at night despite the horror she'd seen there as a child."

Sam snorted. "And who will you go down as?"

"The narrator." She grinned and said archly, "I shall be your humble Boswell."

Sam laughed, all traces of anxiety vanishing. "You're full of it. I'm no warrior maiden."

"Hey, it works for me."

"Okay, but change my name. And don't tell the story for at least twenty years, when those cultists are too old to track me down."

"Deal."

23

Merilynn's hand touched empty air and she knew she had crawled the wrong way along the dock. Exhausted, she lay down flat on her stomach, hand still extended over the water below, turned her face to one side, and pillowed her cheek with her other hand. Almost too tired to shiver, but not quite, she rested and remembered.

The room at Gamma came back to her; she recalled how they'd seen the ghosts of Holly and Eve on the lawn below, and that Malory and Brittany had encountered them. She remembered sitting on the floor playing the Ouija board unsuccessfully with Kendra, trying to call the ghosts. And then they had gone to bed—and the phantoms came into the room, just as she was drifting off.

They spoke to Kendra, but mainly to her. *How much did Kendra hear?*

If she hadn't run off so quickly, if she'd compared notes with her roommate, at least, then she'd know if help might be on the way. Her impression was that Kendra had heard little before falling asleep. *They made her fall asleep. I think.* Why hadn't she at least left a note that would help Kendra locate her? *That was really, really stupid, Merilynn!*

Sleepy and cold, hunger a gnawing ache in her middle, she thought through what she had heard, her heart skipping a beat as Holly Gayle's words came back to her. *The living daughter of Malory Thomas can release us.*

Merilynn's mind had reeled. If she hadn't been lying down, she might have fainted. She dared not believe what had popped into her mind, not until Holly answered her question:

You know I am speaking about you. You. The sorceress ap-

peared to your father and used his seed to conceive you. Your father is the priest.

Does Father know he's my real father? Merilynn had asked.

Yes. He knows many things. He can help you.

On some level, she knew it was true. She had always suspected that Uncle Martin was her true father, but had sensed from earliest childhood that it was not a question she should ask; instead, she called him Father. And she had never dared ask about her mother, not because Martin gave off a don't-ask vibe, but because she knew it was better not to know. Instead, she embraced Delores, her nanny, Martin's housekeeper, as her mother and pushed her questions down into a deep, dark place inside herself.

Deep and dark, like her mother.

But how can I be Malory Thomas's daughter? She's not old enough to have a daughter my age.

It made no sense, but it was true. She remembered Holly's words: *the sorceress and her familiar. They are dangerous.*

Her mother was a sorceress. She might be any age. She might be an old crone who cast a spell to appear young and beautiful. She might be able to shape-shift. And Brittany . . . *a familiar?* Merilynn had never thought of familiars as more than companion animals. When she was younger, she'd called Pio her familiar. Father had laughed and told her not to say that in front of clergy or parishioners. It had never been more than that, but now, she realized, there could be. *What is Brittany?*

She's an elemental. Puckwudgies were elementals, but not the same kind as a familiar would be. They were fairy folk; familiars were animal elementals. Different. *But how?* Her drowsy mind clawed for answers. Familiars would be stronger, she thought, more dangerous to humans because they could be seen by anyone, if they wanted. *What is Brittany?* she wondered again. *A raven? A wolf? A cat? Something else?* She thought of the girl's bright eyes and her penchant for nuts and sunflower seeds. An image emerged in her inner eye. *An elephant.*

If she hadn't been so tired, she would have smiled. In truth, she was probably a bird or maybe a squirrel. *Or a monkey.*

I have to get out of here. She used that thought to attempt to chase away the nonsense, but her mind refused to cooperate, returning instead to Holly, and how she had revealed the silver athame with the glowing green stone in its haft. She had told her, *You can release us and all those others trapped under the lake if you can find this dagger and kill your mother. It is the only way she can be killed.*

Where is it? Merilynn had asked.

I will show you in your dreams.

The apparitions disappeared and Merilynn tried to talk to Kendra, wanting to know what she had heard, but she couldn't get any words out, couldn't even make her muscles obey her orders to sit up. Sleep took her.

And, later, just before dawn, the dream had come.

24

"She *what?*" Malory demanded.

Brittany sat on a stool behind the big claw-foot tub and rubbed her mistress's bare shoulders. "She remembered seeing the sacrifice," she repeated. "But that's all. She told Kendra that it had to be a satanic coven. Relax, your shoulders are like steel."

"*Exactly* what did she say?"

Brittany told her what she'd heard in the knight's chapel, massaging as she spoke. "There's no need to worry. She specifically said she saw no magick."

"And why did she say that?" Malory twisted her neck to look at her familiar.

"Kendra suggested her memory had been removed by a spell."

"She *what?*" Malory demanded again.

"Relax. Give me the soap. Thanks." She lathered her hands in the oatmeal-coconut foam from the bar, then slicked the fragrant bubbles over Malory's neck and back. "You know Kendra's into the folklore stuff. And she's experienced your daughter. It's no surprise. Do you think she hasn't figured out that Merilynn caused the 'food poisoning' and the periods? Hell, she was probably there with her. But I doubt that Samantha was, because she laughed off the suggestion of a spell to erase her memory. She said she'd simply blocked a horrible memory and shamed Kendra for thinking otherwise."

"Is Kendra going to be a problem, do you think?"

"Perhaps. You know," she added, squeezing water over Malory's back, washing away the soap, "she might make a decent sacrifice."

"No." Malory spoke flatly, without hesitation.

"Why not?"

"I've known her family for generations. So have you, remember?"

"Oh. She's the one descended from all those housekeepers. They lived in Applehead before it was drowned."

"Right. And then in Greenbriar. They're coastal now, but Kendra's grandmother is still alive. She worked here for a short time. She saw Holly once. And I'm sure Kendra's mother knows the stories. And Kendra. With her interest in folklore, it's not surprising she's here, although I heard her admit her family isn't pleased. Harming her or letting her find out too much would bring us too many problems."

"Why did you decide to let her in then?"

"For fun. Or maybe tradition. Her ancestors were canny women, worthy of respect. She is as well, unless I'm very much mistaken. We won't be at this campus after this year, and she might make an excellent leader for the Gammas."

"But not the Fata Morganas."

"Of course not. You realize she suspects we exist."

"Does she?"

"Of course." Malory's shoulder muscles finally began to loosen. "She has to suspect because of her family history. The whole mystery surrounding Gamma intrigues her. But she's safe."

"What makes her safe?"

"She's content with legends and folklore. She's far more interested in stories than in truth. In fact, I'm sure she would rather have the mystery than the facts, so in her own way she will protect Gamma, even though she's not a Fata."

"Maybe she should become one of the inner circle then."

"No. Brittany, surely you can sense her true spirit."

"She'd never go along with the sacrifices."

"Never. Brush my hair, please. I can imagine Merilynn or Samantha coming to our side if we had devised the right methods of manipulation." She shook her head. "I had such high hopes for Merilynn. She's full of power and she's attracted to her roots. Ah, well."

"What about Samantha?"

"She is ruled by her need for knowledge and power. We'd just have to shut off her interest in telling secrets to bring her in. In her own way, she would make a superb Fata Morgana. Alas, I doubt we can turn her."

"Why not?"

"She has an annoying streak of morality that I fear we can't undo. It's too bad we didn't procure her years ago, in one of our high school programs. Then we have the fact that she's the girl who saw our rites, happened to join *our* sorority, and has overcome the spell of forgetfulness I cast. *No one* can resist that spell. But she did. Subconsciously, she has probably never entirely forgotten; that's what brought her to us." She smiled. "It's too bad we can't use her tenacity."

"She's our sacrifice, then," Brittany said. "Oops." The brush clattered to the tile floor. She picked it up and continued brushing. "You have such beautiful hair. It's like silk."

Malory made a purring sound in her throat, but a column of bubbles from her rear accompanied it, bursting to the surface like little blossoms of nuclear waste. The mild sexual excitement that had begun building in Brittany's loins was abruptly fumigated.

"Sorry," her mistress said.

"Your problem is no better?"

"I think it's less frequent now."

"But no less fragrant." The brush slipped out of her hand, hitting the floor. "Oops, I did it again." She bent and picked it up.

"You're clumsy tonight."

Brittany didn't answer, but concentrated on relaxing her mistress before she told her the rest. Finally, when Malory started making little sounds of contentment, she told her, "I was so worried about getting back and telling you that Samantha is the girl who saw us performing the chapel rites that I didn't tell you the rest."

"Mmmm. Well, it could be no worse than what you've already said. What is it?"

"Remember the reason you asked me to follow them in the first place?"

"Of course." Malory sat up, stiffening again. "Of course I remember." She sounded defensive, which meant she had forgotten. She only forgot things when a sacrifice was missed and the Forest Knight's gift of continuing immortality became overdue.

Malory could go far longer than this without making a blood sacrifice before any real deterioration showed, but the others, the purely human members of the sisterhood of Fata Morgana, would exhibit symptoms much sooner. Their smaller powers would wane quickly, skin would loosen, hairs turn grayer and grayer until the sacrifice was made. It was really rather fun, as far as Brittany was concerned. Especially when certain girls— *Heather Horner*—who had become a little too full of themelves experienced a taste of mortality.

"What did you learn?"

"As you thought, mistress, they were looking for Merilynn. They said very little, but they obviously didn't know where she is. I'd guess they were simply looking in a place they thought was logical."

"Dry me." Malory pulled the plug on the tub and rose, her body dripping. She held her arms out as Brittany wrapped a thick sage-green bath towel around her. Malory tucked it over between her breasts and stepped out of the tub. "The chapel is a logical place," she said as Brittany took a smaller towel and began drying her arms. "At least if Holly asked for Merilynn's help to find my stone. Where did they go from there?"

Brittany laughed. "Back the way they had come. Something frightened them."

"The knight?" Malory asked sharply.

"No, I didn't sense the knight. I believe it was simply Samantha's memory of the sacrifice that stampeded them."

Malory smiled. "Stampeded?"

"Yes." Brittany moved to her mistress's legs, not bothering to tell her that she had scared them herself. Malory would be displeased by that.

"It took much bravery for them to even enter the chapel," Malory said. "The wards we set around it scare off all but the most determined humans."

"Or the most insensitive." As she spoke, Brittany worked her way up under the towel, dabbing away water droplets from Malory's inner thighs, praying to the Forest Knight that her mistress wouldn't emit any gases as she worked to distract her from her worries. "Tell me, mistress. What are your plans for this evening?"

"I've decided to give Professor Tongue the night off, due to this problem." She punctuated the comment with a nasty little poot.

Brittany leaned back on her knees too fast and tumbled onto her back. Malory laughed. "I just wanted to see if you were paying attention, little one."

"Very funny."

Malory let the bath towel drop from her body. "Finish me off, will you?"

"I'll finish *drying* you if you promise no more surprises. I won't finish *you* off. Not until this noxiousness passes." Brittany, back on her knees, resumed drying the sorceress.

"Come on, Britt," Malory said, pushing the blonde's head crotchward. "I need more than drying. The good professor has earned a reprieve. But you are my servant." She pushed harder. "Give your mistress a little kiss."

Brittany rarely minded playing the subservient role; that's how it worked between a sorcerer and a familiar. But she would brook no humiliation. "No. Let go."

Malory laughed, low and throaty. "Do as you're told."

Brittany, hiding her fury, bent her head to her mistress's private triangle and gently bit a lip.

"That's it." Malory pushed her head closer, urging her to get to work.

Brittany, still holding Malory's sensitive flesh between her teeth, willed herself to change form. Suddenly, there was a faint stirring in the air; then Malory shrieked.

"Let go of me, you little bitch!"

The chipmunk sank its teeth in as Malory tried to pull it away.

"Ouch! Stop it!"

Brittany didn't stop, even though she could taste that she had broken the skin.

She heard the door slam open and a feminine voice shriek, "Oh, my God, Malory, you've got a chipmunk on your pussy!"

"Don't you think I know that?" Malory screeched, yanking the rodent off.

The elemental recognized the voice as not belonging to any of the officers—the only Fatas senior enough to know what she really was—and let go of Malory as the other sister approached. Malory loosened her hold and the chipmunk dropped to the floor, then scurried across the room and out the open window.

Hiding just out of sight, she chittered madly when the other Fata, Helen Bach, an infant of eighty-some years who still looked eighteen, cried, "I've heard of perverts putting gerbils up their asses, but what on earth were you trying to do to that poor little squirrel?"

25

"You can come out now," Malory said. "Helen's gone. The door is locked."

Her familiar hopped onto the open windowsill, chattering madly.

"I won't try to force myself on you again. I promise."

The chipmunk swore eloquently, wanting more than a promise.

Finally, Malory caved. "I apologize, okay? I'm sorry. You're my familiar. You always do things like that for me. You're supposed to take care of me."

The chipmunk crossed its tiny arms and glared at her.

"I apologize. I love you. What more can I say?"

The creature hopped into the room and the air wavered. Brittany stood before her mistress, arms still crossed. "You know what you have to say."

"I'm your mistress. I don't have to say anything, except that I'm sorry if I somehow offended you."

Brittany let her true nature burn through her blue human eyes, turning them dark as night and as sparkling as diamonds. "How soon you forget that this is all a convenient game. A tradition among your kind and mine." She stepped forward and Malory backpedaled. "Have you forgotten, *mistress,* the true nature of our relationship?"

Malory didn't reply, but looked at her defiantly. Brittany could sense a silent glamour being hastily woven.

"That won't work. Remember the last time that your pride forced me to remind you of the truth? You tried to cast a spell on me then, as well. You cannot."

"I can."

"Not without the Forest Knight's gift. And even then, it won't hold." Brittany pinned her like an insect under glass. "Don't forget which of us is his favorite."

Defiant, chin tilted up, Malory glared at Brittany.

"We have work to do, sorceress. Admit your place and it shall be done. Refuse, and suffer the consequences. The knight is already displeased with you."

"And you," Malory said softly.

"No. I am pure. I am part of his world. You are half human. Your mistakes are not mine. I *help* you perform magicks and glamours. I *help* you with the sacrificial rites that keep your beauty and immortality intact. I need no such rites. I am forever."

"A familiar is a minor elemental, nothing without a mistress or master."

"Not so, *mistress*. You merely wish to believe that, and while it's true that my kind benefits from a relationship like this, yours benefits much more."

"You are bound to me."

"Of my own will. Familiars are loyal folk or I would have deserted you long ago. You're not the only maker of magick in this land, you know." Brittany let her elemental soul continue to shine through her eyes to hold Malory in place, but now she smiled as well. "I am fond of you, Malory. I was fond of you from the moment we met, when you were still Morgana, only a few centuries old, a mere babe barely out of her mentor's arms, so quickly into mine.

"Remember how I helped you attain the favor of the Forest Knight so that you no longer had to travel back to the old world to appease a much harsher Green Master? You told me all about him. What he did to you, to your body, ripping you apart with his lust, then rewarding you as you lay dying, with healing and renewed beauty? Do you want to go back to that cruel master? If I tell the Forest Knight you've fallen from my favor, he will not look kindly on you anymore. He already watches you closely. You have lost the precious gift he gave you, so now you must make many more sacrifices to atone. You failed to deliver your most recent sacrifice, a very important one, as you know, and judging by his actions last night, I dare say he's very angry and *very* hungry." She paused for effect. "I don't think you should anger me, either, *little one.*" She spat the words, advancing on Malory, backing her into the wall. "What say you?"

"I say—"

Brittany grabbed her roughly by the shoulders and lifted her from the ground as if she weighed nothing. It was a move she knew Malory despised.

"I say that you are dear to me."

Brittany let her drop, adding a mental push that threw Malory to her knees. "What else have you to say?"

"You are, in truth, my mistress and I am your loyal servant." She bowed her head, cheeks flushed with humiliation and, most assuredly, her own fury.

Brittany had to fight to keep from giggling her delight as power shot through her, her own and Malory's, and satisfaction, too. Years of frustration melted away, as they always did when it was necessary to put her sorceress in her place.

Sexual energy filled Brittany. She began to undress, knowing the power the mere sight of her human body had over true humans, wanting to do to Malory what she had tried to force her to do. Looking down at her humbled mistress, Brittany decided that Malory could do with a bit more discipline, so she indulged herself. Continuing to undress, she dropped her Gamma T-shirt on the floor, unzipped her jeans, and stepped out of them. Finally, she stripped off her red thong, the one she had stolen from the drawer of a new sister a month ago.

Naked and perfect, oozing sexuality from every pore, she put her fingers beneath Malory's chin and made her look up. The sorceress trembled, not with fear, but excitement. She craned her neck forward, licking her lips in anticipation, salivating at the sight of the elemental in human form—no human could resist such a thing, not when there was no clothing to dull the auric emanations.

"No," Brittany told her firmly. She laid her hand against Malory's forehead and pushed her away.

"Why not?" Malory's whisper was strangled with desire. "Let me apologize. I know you want me to."

"You've already apologized. Now you shall pay penance by looking at what you cannot have. Now, it is time for us to work." She turned and crossed the suite, intending to sit down at a small round table covered with green silk, then noticed Malory hadn't moved, but stood, statuelike, drinking in her body. "Come here! You're no goggle-eyed human. You should not be so entranced that you can't move!"

Malory approached, her gaze unwavering.

Brittany pointed at her own face, as she let her eyes blend back down from diamond-black to their usual shades of blue. "Eyes up here, sorceress."

Slowly, Malory managed to meet her gaze. There was such desire and longing evident in her face that Brittany, who did love the magickal old bitch after all, took pity and pulled a green cloak from a wall hook and drew it around herself. She sat down. "Get the black mirror and bring it here. Sit down and we shall scry until we find your wayward daughter."

26

Sam gripped the steering wheel tightly to keep her hands from trembling as she and Kendra approached the turnoff for Greenbriar University. Although she had admitted that she'd been frightened, Kendra couldn't possibly know just how bad the scare had been, and Sam wasn't about to tell her. Pride, plus a very real fear that admission would make what courage she did possess blow away like a dandelion puff on the wind, kept her quiet.

"We're almost back," Kendra said.

"Yeah, we are."

"The game probably isn't over yet. If we go back to the house, it'll be pretty empty."

"Malory will be there. And Brittany. They didn't look like they were going anywhere."

"True. That's a good reason not to go back yet." A car turned onto Applehead Road from the Greenbriar turnoff up ahead. Sam dimmed the high beams. "It's early. Do you want to do something? Get something to eat? Pizza?" She paused. "Maybe we should stop at the house and see if Merilynn's back."

"She's not."

"How do you know?"

"I have my cell." Kendra patted her jacket's breast pocket. "Merilynn left hers in our room and she already put my number in her phone's memory. She'd call if she were back."

"I'm convinced. We won't stop," Sam said. "So, shall I cut through the campus toward town or stay on Applehead and go around it?"

"Bypass," Kendra decided. "I hate crawling through all those stop signs and drunken frat boys."

"I agree."

They passed the college turnoff and continued along the long loop of road. The forest narrowed quickly on the campus side, disappearing completely when the road turned east. To their right, the forest looked impenetrable; on the left, the stadium came into view, brilliantly lit and full of people. Even with the windows up, Sam could hear the muffled roar of the crowd. Something in the sound chilled her.

27

The sorceress and her familiar sat bent over the round oak-framed mirror that covered a good portion of their small table. Together, they murmured words of a language spoken only by those with intimate knowledge of the ancient ways of the otherworld, a place few humans experienced for more than a fleeting instant during their little lives. If they experienced it at all.

Their differences forgotten, their palms lay flat on the green silk cloth, fingers touching, their bodies exchanging energy, the two building more together than either could hope to alone. The symbiotic bond, forged throughout centuries upon centuries, served them quickly and well now, despite Malory's still feeling slightly weakened.

Minutes after they began reciting the words of power, the shiny black surface of the scrying mirror appeared to waver and shift, rivulets of black on black shimmered with metallic ores within its depths, sifting like desert sands. Before long, the mirror took on form and depth that even a simple human might have been able to see.

"Show us where Merilynn is. Show us my daughter," Malory said in the strange lilting tongue. Brittany asked the same.

And waves appeared on the mirror's surface, small and whitecapped. A mound appeared in the center of the mirror, ugly, not unlike a monstrous head rising from the black water. Applehead Island.

Malory studied the water, looking for the gleam of ghost lights beneath the lake, but saw none, at least at this distance.

The edges of the lake became clearer as more power words were spoken and although the aerial view was of the night, details became fairly easy for Malory's eyes to discern and even easier for Brittany's. There, on the northern shore, were little squares and rectangles; that was the boys' summer sports camp.

On the southern shore lay the cheerleading camp, looking much like the boys' camp. It had smaller cabins, and more of them, and the dock jutting from the boathouse at the lake's edge was slightly longer than the one at the other camp or either of the smaller ones dotting the eastern and western shores not far from the boys' camp.

At one edge, the clearing bearing the knight's chapel was partially visible, the outlines of the ruins stark black and white shadows. They could discern the faintest green glow coming from within and around the roofless building; it told them their wards were intact, ready to frighten off trespassers. It was the color of magick, the color of the Forest Knight.

The roads and school were not visible. Brittany and Malory exchanged glances. Merilynn Morris was somewhere within this view. "Closer," Malory commanded. "Show me the island."

The mirror shimmered, dissolving and resolving in the space of fifteen seconds. Now only the island was in view. They examined it, looking for signs of Merilynn, for signs of magick. The only thing there emanated from the black pit on the island's center, a bare green mist that phosphoresced from the frequent presence of the Forest Knight, who often dwelt within the caverns below.

Strange words poured from Malory's mouth. They commanded a closer look at the cheerleading camp. Again, everything shifted and shimmered as the psychic telescope adjusted itself. The flagpole, flagless, appeared. The white spotlight was off. Below it, a few tall sodium lamps glowed among the trees.

"Closer," Brittany murmured.

Again, the vision shifted. They seemed to hover just above the buildings now. Electricity sparked between the pair's fingers as they moved, as one mind, around the buildings, seeing nothing, but sensing something. Without speaking, they examined the edges of the buildings, swooping down for a new view, looking into black windows that were fiercely and suddenly unshuttered by the force of their will.

"She's not there," Malory said.

"The boathouse," Brittany murmured. "We haven't looked there yet!"

The view now was one that they would have if they were watching the feed from someone walking through the camp with a minicam rolling. They approached the lake's edge. The visible dock was boatless and lonely, and the boathouse, built on a doublewide platform that was part foundation and part dock, looked deserted.

There was a single door on the dock that led inside, plus wide garage-size doors at either end. The building had no windows.

Malory examined the edges of the doors, thought she saw a faint glow from within. She glanced at Brittany, who nodded; she saw it as well.

"She's in there," the familiar said.

"We have to be sure. Quietly, the door on the dock."

"It's locked. If we rip it, she'll know we've found her."

"She had to get in there. The big doors are padlocked."

As Brittany spoke, their view returned to the single door. A padlock gleamed in a hasp there as well. "I still say she's in there," she told Malory.

"Inside a building locked from the outside."

"This one, yes."

"She swam under the door."

"Of course."

"Shall we?"

"No." Malory disliked the water; it was the home of Holly Gayle, and the prison of many, many more. While she did not fear the dead, she preferred not to encounter them. She pointed at the old-fashioned rusty doorknob with a large skeleton keyhole. "Look through here. Close now!"

"Damn it!" Blackness filled her vision. "It's blocked."

"I can see that," Brittany said in the soothing voice that Malory hated because it meant she expected her to lose her temper or act impulsively.

"Don't speak to me that way!"

Brittany ignored her outburst. "We have to go under the water to see in." She paused. "Would you like me to look?"

"Don't be ridiculous," Malory said sharply. "We aren't actually there. I'm not afraid of getting wet."

"What are you afraid of?" the elemental asked in the same soothing voice.

"Nothing, you little bitch!" Red filled her vision, staining the blackness of the mirror's view of the boathouse.

"Calm down!"

"Fuck you! Sometimes I think you provoke me on purpose!"

The vision shimmered. Brittany looked impish and innocent.

Malory cursed, drawing the image back to the mirror, clarifying it before it could escape. Ignoring Brittany, she moved to view the the wide double doors on the shore end of the little boathouse. She drew a great surge of energy from Brittany and from within herself, and the doors burst open. Looking past the boats, Malory saw what she wanted at the very end of the boathouse's platform.

"There she is! Let's go get her!"

The image swirled and disappeared, leaving the mirror's surface shining smooth and black.

Brittany stood up and shed the robe. Malory averted her eyes; now was not the time to let desire overcome her.

"How do you want to get there?" Brittany asked. "Are you strong enough to open an aport?"

"Yes."

Brittany leaned over and began tying her shoelaces as Malory got up and found a black sweater and jeans, dressing as quickly as she could.

"I thought you wanted to follow her," Brittany said as she pulled a black hooded jacket over her own dark shirt. "What happened to your plan to have her lead us to the gem?"

"We'll still do that."

"You weren't subtle, Mal. She probably sensed us when you destroyed the door."

Malory slipped on laceless black running shoes. "You think so?" she asked, dripping sarcasm. "I'm altering our plans. With Samantha and Kendra searching for her, we can't just let her run free. We'll bind her and force her to talk."

"Bind her?" Brittany's eyes gleamed, darkness coming into them. "In the caverns?"

"Where else?"

Brittany grinned approval. Grabbing a handful of peanut M&Ms from a bowl on her dresser, she walked up to Malory and held out her hands. "Ready to transport?"

"No. Let's go outside. The less matter we have to travel through, the happier I'll be."

"How's your stomach?"

"It's getting better, I think. The cramps are less intense."

"I noticed you haven't been perfuming the air quite so much."

"That means we'd better hurry. If Merilynn's spell is weakening, she may be dying. We can't let that happen again."

"Again?"

"We need her to find the stone. And perhaps as a sacrifice. I think she would please the Forest Knight, don't you?"

Brittany smiled and popped candied nuts into her mouth, then held the door open and locked it behind them. "Where do you want to transport?"

"The back lawn."

"Someone might see."

"Behind the smokehouse then. Let's just get the hell out of here!"

28

Merilynn was having the dream again. She knew it was a dream, knew she was resting on a boathouse dock in reality, and flying with Holly and Eve on the astral plane.

Not flying. Swimming. In the lake.

Holly smiled at her. *Do you remember what you did after I showed you this last night?*

Yes.

That was how she'd gotten wet. She had gone to the boathouse at the old cheer camp and was looking for a way to break a lock so that she could steal a boat that would take her out to the site of the old town of Applehead. There, she intended to dive—she was an excellent swimmer—and retrieve the stone in its daggerlike casing. It hadn't gone quite as she expected.

It was daylight when she arrived, and the camp was locked up tight. She was searching for something, anything, to use to break into the boathouse, when she heard the rumble of an approaching vehicle. She moved to the far end of the boathouse and stood in the shadows, hoping she wouldn't be spotted by whoever was coming.

A dark green custodial pickup truck came into view. Merilynn clung to the edge of the shadows, desperate not to be seen as the driver pulled up to park right next to the dock. She took one too many steps backward and, with a splash, fell into the water.

Crap! Afraid the custodian would investigate the splash, she did the only thing she could think of: she dived down and swam into the boathouse.

Freezing cold, she had waited for the men—she could hear them talking to each other, shooting the shit about cranky wives and ungrateful children. What they were doing there for so long, she didn't know. What little she'd seen appeared immaculate.

But they wouldn't leave. Eventually, she recognized the sound of aluminum lawn chairs opening, the slide of a tray being set up, even the hiss of beer bottles being opened. The men were having a leisurely morning of man-gossip and beer and, finally, lunch. It was endless.

Hey, Joe, look what Carla packed for me. Pepperoni and onions on a torpedo roll. All thin sliced, must be half an inch of meat on there. And just the right amount of mustard. And look, I got a big kosher dill! No wonder I put up with her shit. She knows how to feed her man.

As foul as the sandwich normally would have sounded, Merilynn's empty stomach yearned for it.

Nice out for this time of year, huh, Earl? Sunny and warm. Though I sure wouldn't want to go swimming. My nuts'd shrivel up into little raisins and drop right off and Shirley wouldn't be real pleased about that. Man, that woman can go down like the Titanic *when she wants something.*

That's how come she's always got those nice new clothes?

Yuck, yuck, yucks all around. Yeah, that's how she gets her clothes. Keeps me broke, but who the fuck gives a rat's ass? The woman's a Hoover.

Carla's always bitching about Shirley's clothes.

So feed her a meat sandwich and buy her some.

I got kids to put through college.

Fuck that. Let 'em earn scholarships. Hey, I got cards. You wanna play some poker?

Shivering cold, exhausted, starving, and just generally miserable, Merilynn waited for them to leave. The thought of using a spell to get rid of them hadn't even occurred to her. *Idiot!*

Now, gliding down through the water, guided by ghosts, Merilynn realized she hadn't thought of it because she was meant to wait here. For this moment.

I wish I remembered the dream.

Holly sent a good feeling to her, a sort of warmth. *Dreams fade. Your first plan was too hasty to work. If you had tried it, you might have drowned. Do you remember where you were going? Where the gemstone in the sword is?*

In the town.

Yes.

Amber lights began winking on below them. Delighted, Merilynn watched the picture she had painted so many times come closer and closer. She felt as if she were gliding among the stars.

It is beautiful, isn't it?

The message had come from Eve. Merilynn smiled at her.

The gemstone is very powerful, a gift to your mother from the Forest Knight. I took it when she killed me, greatly diminishing her power. But she is very dangerous even without it. She wants it back. It is safe from her here, hidden in plain sight, but we are trapped here with it.

Merilynn watched the lights grow, but turned her thoughts to Holly. *What do you want me to do? Hide it somewhere else so you don't have to guard it anymore?*

Holy smiled sadly. *If only it were that easy. We are trapped here with or without the stone in the sword. That's what it is, a miniature broadsword, not a dagger or any other blade. We are trapped here until Malory Thomas is destroyed. No one but blood can do that.*

Suddenly, very close, the stained glass steeple in the old church burst to life. Merilynn stared at the beauty of it, a beacon in the watery night. The colors, ruby, emerald, sapphire, and sunlight, were clear and perfect. She strained to make out the design.

Only you can destroy her and you need the stone and the sword to do that. The blade holding it is strong, full of magic. The stone and the sword are objects, without allegiance, and you will be able to turn the blade against her. You must kill her.

Where is it? Merilynn gazed, awestruck, at the beauty of the stained glass. It was a picture of the forest and Applehead, the tiny town in a green valley full of orchards, green leaves, red apples. It was a picture of the past.

Here! Look here and you will see it!

* * *

An explosion of wood as the double doors came off their hinges yanked Merilynn back to her sleeping body. She sat up, saw the pale sand that seemed to glow in the dark, saw the flagpole, some camp buildings dabbed with sodium lights. The doors were gone, only a few shards remained, a jagged black frame for the beach beyond.

Water sloshed, boats jostled for space, the building creaked. Merilynn shivered, still damp after a day in this dank place, and started to rise, then felt her back pelted with lake water. She turned, and peering at her, her head just above the dock, was Holly Gayle, white with death and cold, all the friendliness and warmth hidden in her haunted eyes.

Run! She knows you're here. Run!

29

"Have you ever tried Thai Gonzales?" Kendra asked as Sam slowed the car to a meek twenty-five miles an hour as they entered the quaint little speed trap named Greenbriar.

"I haven't," Sam admitted. "I thought about it, but I don't have much spare cash, so I hate to take a chance on wasting it on food I'll end up throwing away." She smiled. "Or throwing up. So, have you tried it?"

"No, but Eve did." Kendra hesitated, when the dead girl's name popped out of her mouth, then pushed on. "She said it wasn't half bad. She advised against getting any dishes that were Thai-Mexican mutations though."

"Smart girl." Now Sam felt the discomfort. "I wonder which half isn't bad."

"I'm guessing the half that isn't mutant food."

"Do you want to try it?"

"Do you?" Kendra countered.

"I love satay. Did she say anything about that?"

"Not that I recall. It's so hard to find a place with good peanut sauce for satay. Most sauces suck. But I'll probably try it anyway. When it's good, it's to die for."

Sam snorted. "Too bad Brittany isn't here. I'll bet she could give us a rundown on the quality of the peanut sauce. I've never seen anyone down so many nuts."

"She's always eating. But it's not just nuts. She loves chocolate too."

"So she's normal?" Sam grinned, feeling the best she had all day.

"I wouldn't call her normal. She should be a lard-ass, the way she eats. Oh, turn right here."

Sam turned. "She goes for all those early morning runs. That must be her secret." She paused. "You know, I've watched her. She doesn't run around the campus like the rest of the joggers."

"No? Where's she go? There's the restaurant." Kendra pointed at the modest THAI GONZALES sign glowing like a big postage stamp above the door of a building a little ways down the street.

"Evidently, she runs in the woods."

"Really?"

"Yeah." Sam pulled past the restaurant, skipping perfect curbside parking in favor of the last slot on the block.

"Why down here?"

"In case we want to make a fast getaway. Remember last night?"

"God, that seems like weeks ago. You never stop thinking, do you?"

"I try not to."

They got out and locked the car, both stuffing wallets into their pockets instead of carrying bags. "Hey," Kendra said. "Wait a second. Unlock, please?"

Sam did. Kendra opened the door and moved her long, sharp

letter opener from the seat to the floor, pushing it out of sight, under the seat.

"You sure you don't want to carry that?" Sam smiled, but she meant it.

"No, I'll stab myself." She patted a pocket. "I've got my pepper spray, though. What about you? Are you packing heat?"

Sam snorted again, knowing it was two too many times for one evening, but feeling comfortable enough to give in to the old kid-habit. "I've got my little friend Roddy right here."

"Good. If we run into those wrestlers without Merilynn along to do her tricks . . ." Her expression changed instantly.

Sam locked the car again and stepped onto the sidewalk, touched Kendra's shoulder. "Hey, don't worry. Merilynn can take care of herself. She's fine."

"Yeah. I'll keep thinking good thoughts."

"Really, Kendra," Sam said. "It's going to be okay."

"How do you know?"

"I just feel it."

"Reporter's instincts?"

"No, just my feeling. Come on."

They walked a short half block to Thai Gonzales and looked in the big glass-front windows.

"This place looks suspiciously like a dive," Sam said.

It was bigger and brighter than Greenbriar Pizza, a simple place, the walls lined with red leatherette booths, the center cluttered with tables and chairs that looked like refugees from a 1970s kitchen. The tables had avocado-green metal legs, as did the dinette chairs. The chairs seats and backs had been recovered with the same red leatherette material as the booths, and red and green lights were strung along the ceiling, giving the place a distinct run-down trailer-park Christmas aura.

Ceiling fans turned slowly and a bored-looking girl stood behind a cash register, staring at them without seeming to see them.

Still the place was half full. "It couldn't be too bad, with this much business," Sam said.

Kendra was perusing the menu in one corner of the window.

"It's affordable. I think we're safe as long as we don't order anything with mystery meat ground up in it."

Sam opened the glass door. "After you, madam."

30

The moment Malory and Brittany hugged themselves together in the shadows of the smokehouse and began reciting the spell to open the aport to take them to the Applehead Cheerleading Camp, Brittany could tell her sorceress was still handicapped by Merilynn's spells and, probably, her own overindulgence the night before. Generally speaking, creatures who belonged in the sorcerer category had iron constitutions, but now and then one could be thrown out of kilter by the tiniest things. It all had to do with gravity and weather and body chemistry, along with at least a dozen other boring subjects. It simply happened, and that was that, end of story as far as Brittany was concerned. Whatever spell Merilynn had cast would be stopped the moment they bound her.

The aport wasn't opening. "Mal, concentrate," she said, not admitting she had let her own mind wander off. "I can't do this all by myself."

"I'm trying."

"You're very trying." Brittany gave her a soft, moist kiss to boost her energy and her spirits. "Now, again."

They repeated the words, and this time the aport opened, surrounding them, carrying them toward the camp. She hoped. Aports and deports were peculiar anomalies. In the last few decades, she had been amused by the science fiction shows that unknowingly dealt with them, calling them wormholes and who could remember what else? And then there was *Star Trek*. For a time—several times, actually, as the series' popularity would peak yet again, evidently blessed with more lives than a cat—senior Fatas, even Malory herself, the queen of all Fata Morganas everywhere, had taken to calling transporting or teleporting "beaming." Brittany hated it so much that she had beseeched her lord, the knight, to stop her mistress from using the term. Offering up a trio of greasy disco boys she'd picked up at a club in Caledonia, she begged for help. The knight, pleased with her offering, stripped the white polyester suits from the young men, then stripped them of their skin, spitting out the fake gold chains and medallions.

The knight liked skin. Brittany thought of it as his version of an appetizer. After he had flayed the disco boys, he granted her wish, giving her the power to cast a spell of her choosing to stop her mistress. And ever since, whenever anyone said, "Beam me up, Scotty," Malory was afflicted with burning nipples. Not literal burning, of course, Brittany had no desire to harm her sorceress, but the sensation of fire, white-hot heat, engulfing them. It happened so rarely that Malory had never caught on, and even if she had, what good would it have done? She wouldn't have suspected her little Brittany, not in a thousand years. Or even two thousand. Once, right after the spell was cast, Malory said the fateful words herself in a restaurant in Seattle. Instantly, her expression had changed from pleasure to horror and she'd grabbed her glass of iced tea and Brittany's glass of iced water and sunk her tits in them, sighing with relief, ignoring the staring customers. The spell only lasted for thirty seconds at a time, and when the half minute had passed, she had Brittany help her cast a glamour over the patrons to make them forget what they'd seen. And to humiliate them a bit as well.

But it was a nice kind of humiliation. Malory did love that group orgasm spell of hers. She did it often enough that she packed a wallop all by herself. When Brittany joined in, if there were more than a dozen people present, it was a sure bet that at least one would suffer a heart attack.

Reality wavered around her within the realm of the aport. It wasn't like *Star Trek,* not at all like *The Time Machine.* Instead, it was a place outside of time, where even she had no sense of time passing. It was eternity and a billionth of a trillionth of the blink of an eye at the same time. How you experienced it pretty much depended on your mood.

Now, it seemed endless. Brittany put her effort back into concentrating on the trip. This was a place like the eye of a hurricane, where nothing was stable, and to move out of the eye of the storm at the wrong time could be disastrous, even deadly. Especially for part humans like Malory. They could get lost if they traveled without their familiars to guide them, and even with a familiar along, many a sorcerer had lost a limb when he or she wasn't cautious enough about keeping appendages tight against the body. They never knew it until they reached the deport, either. One familiar, a crow named Shalkinaw, a nice enough elemental despite its penchant for fireworks at inopportune moments, had a master, an old white-beard like Malory's had been, who tilted his head back to yawn and lost the entire top of his head. When they reached the deport, Shalkinaw said that the old wizard looked puzzled, reached up to scratch his pate, and stirred what was left of his brain into mush.

We mustn't let that happen to Malory, even if she deserves it. Brittany tightened her hold, again forcing herself to concentrate. Familiars who took on animal forms always suffered the effects of the animal's true nature. Brittany had a yen for nuts and seeds, and for sex, and a tendency to pack away bags and cans of nuts in her home, a trait that grew as the weather turned cold. Her biggest problem, however, was keeping her mind on one thing for very long. It moved rapidly, taking in everything, remembering the important things, forgetting the rest. Transporting was difficult for her when it felt like eternity instead of fractions of instants.

Concentrate!

Out of time and space, she planted her lips on Malory's, bringing both of their minds into focus.

Instantly, they arrived at their destination, or close to it, she thought. Trees surrounded them.

"Where are we?" Malory asked, sounding out of breath. Transporting was hard work.

Brittany scanned, finally spotting a cabin. "We're here. The camp. Come with me." She took Malory's hand and led her toward the cabin. There, the rest of the camp was revealed, and it really was the right camp. Beyond the cabins, the lake glistened darkly. "Are your eyes adjusted?" Brittany asked. "Can you see well enough to run?"

"Yes."

"Let's go, then."

They raced out of the woods and down to the boathouse. She was slightly surprised to see that the doors really had been blown off their hinges. That rarely happened.

"Look what we did," Malory murmured, pride in her voice.

"A little showy, don't you think?" Brittany asked, thinking of her old friend, the grandstanding Shalkinaw.

"Definitely not subtle. But I think—yes. See her aura? She's still in there. We've got her!"

31

No sooner had Holly Gayle told her to run than Merilynn had turned to do so—but silhouetted in the gaping doorway were two figures, one tall, one short. Both bitches.

"Why, if it isn't Mommy dearest and her little dog, Toto," Merilynn said, knowing she was already dead. None of her piddley spells could get her past these two.

Malory stepped toward her, Brittany at her side. "Come here, Merilynn. We've been looking for you all day. Kendra and Samantha told us they were worried."

"You lie quite well," Merilynn said agreeably. Her eyes darted, seeking escape.

"They're looking for you, too. They'll be so relieved that we've found you."

Brittany spoke those words and they sounded truthful. Merilynn paused, taken in for just a moment. She wanted to believe them, wanted to be taken home and dressed in warm clothes, placed in front of a fire, and fed hot chicken noodle soup. *No, they'll feed me to the fire!*

"You're an even better liar, Toto," Merilynn told Toto.

"Don't call me that, you little—"

"Hush, Brittany," Malory said, snakey-soothey. "This is my daughter, my only child. My heir. Merilynn, please come to your mother."

Something icy cold touched Merilynn's ankle. She barely refrained from jumping, then managed to look down with only her eyes. A white hand had emerged from the water. Fingers tapped her ankle.

Dive into the water, Holly Gayle said. *It's the only way out.*

"Merilynn," Malory said, moving slowly forward, "please come to me."

Something in her voice mesmerized Merilynn. Something in her eyes drew her.

Look away! Holly cried in her head. *Look away! She's hypnotizing you.*

"Merilynn, darling. All these years separated from you, I've been miserable. And I was afraid to tell you who I really am." Malory's voice broke, right on cue. "I was afraid you would reject me. But now you know. Please, please love me as I love you."

"You don't know the meaning of the word!" Merilynn turned and leaped into the lake.

Holly and Eve were waiting. They pulled her down, away from the surface, away from the shore.

Deeper and deeper they went, and Merilynn began to struggle against them. *I need to breathe! Let go! I need air.*

Trust Holly, Eve murmured.

Merilynn's lungs burned as she looked into Eve's ghostly face. *I'm dying! Please, let me go!*

You'll truly die up there. Holly stared into her eyes, her face a bare inch away. *She will take your soul.*

Merilynn saw lights twinkling to life in the depths before them. *Applehead!*

Yes. Holly's face seemed to engulf hers. Then everything winked out.

32

"Crap," Kendra said, a forkful of fragrant jasmine rice poised before her lips.

"The food's not all that bad," Sam replied, swirling a thin piece of chicken in peanut sauce. "And at least it's bright enough in here to see the cockroaches before they can walk onto your plate."

"I'm not talking about the food," Kendra said dryly.

"What are you talking about?"

"Look up."

Sam raised her eyes. "Crap," she agreed. "How'd you know they were coming in? Do you have eyes in the back of your head?"

"There's one of those giant spot mirrors mounted near the ceiling behind you."

"I knew that." She made a face to show she *should* have known that. "Cheerleaders. They're traveling in a pack. Not a single jock among them. That's odd."

"Do you think so? Eve said they do a lot of group bonding, even more than the sorority sisters do." Kendra sipped her Pepsi.

"On a Friday night?" Sam asked. "That's a date night, isn't it?"

"I don't know. I haven't had a date since I've been here."

"I haven't either. What about that guy I've seen you talking to? Jimmy? Johnny? He's in my public speaking class. And he's in at least one of McCobb's classes."

"I'm not sure . . ."

"He has dreadlocks. Sensitive type but he shows up plain as day on my straight-dar."

"Jimmy, sure." Kendra grinned. "He's pretty cute, isn't he?"

Sam chewed. "I've seen worse."

"He's smart, too."

"In that case, I've seen *a lot* worse."

"He asked if I wanted to do a study date with him for McCobb's class."

"And you said?"

"Yes. But I don't know when it'll happen. Everything's so messed up." Kendra raised her voice as the din of cheerleaders started to drown her out.

"Listen to them," Sam said. "No wonder there aren't any guys with them."

Kendra and Sam had chosen a small booth at the rear of the restaurant, looking for peace and quiet. The music playing on the loudspeakers wasn't too soft or too loud, but just right to cover the low murmurs of conversation in the place. Until now.

"They're coming our way," Sam said.

"I can hear them."

"And see them. Are they nice and distorted, all round in the middle?"

Kendra chuckled and checked the mirror. "They are. Lord, listen to them. I'm embarrassed to be female. They really do sound like clucking hens. Do you suppose we sound like that too?"

"We? You mean us studious types?"

"Sure. I meant nerds, but studious types sounds better."

"We can't sound like that. Our voices don't go that high and our lips don't flap that fast. Shit, they sound like they're all doing speed."

"It's that purple juice they swill. You know about that? Eve said Frau Blucher passes it out to them before games. It's a real pick-me-up."

"Frau Blucher? That sounds familiar."

"Cloris Leachman in *Young Frankenstein*. The horses went nuts any time her name was spoken."

"An apt name for Mildred McArthur, then." Sam picked through her rice, looking for things that didn't belong in it. "I've seen them drinking that juice," she said. "It's always in the refrigerator."

Kendra nodded. "In the jug labeled 'cheerleaders only.'"

"I might take a sample and get it analyzed sometime."

"Why doesn't that surprise me?" Kendra's good mood grew a little despite the clucking girls in green and gold. "Listen to them. Can you tell what they're saying?"

"I guess I could if I zoned in on one conversation. All I get is pissed off and bitchy in general."

"We must have lost the game." She paused. "Wait. I know what it is."

"What?"

"Merilynn's spell. They're all on the rag."

Sam laughed. "Let's hope we get out of here alive, then."

"Hi, girls. Where's Merilynn tonight?"

Heather Horner planted herself by their table, her tanned midriff at Kendra's eye level. A couple of the J-clones flanked her.

"She's around," Sam said, looking her straight in the eye. "Do you feel okay, Heather?"

"Of course I do. Why?"

"You look, I don't know, unwell."

"What do you mean?"

"A little puffy." She smiled sweetly. "That time of the month?"

Kendra couldn't help it. She giggled.

Heather glared daggers at her. "What's so funny?"

"Oh, I'm sorry. It has nothing to do with you. Sam told me a joke just before you came up and I just got it."

"Tell it to us," Heather said. The clones agreed.

"You wouldn't like it," Sam said, shooting Kendra a confused look.

"Sam's right, you wouldn't like it."

"Why not? You think it's funny." The three cheerleaders moved closer, bullies in short skirts and sports bras.

"Well, since you insist." Kendra smiled low and slow. "Do you want to tell them, Sam, or shall I?"

"You go right ahead. You're good at telling jokes."

"Okay. Well, there's a woman, and she walks into a drugstore to buy tampons. She sees a display of tampon boxes stacked on the end of an aisle with a sign on them that says 'Five boxes for a dollar.'

"Well, she just can't believe the price is that low, so she asks the clerk if it's correct.

"He says, 'Oh, yes, five boxes for a dollar.'

"She replies, 'That can't be right!'

"The clerk says, 'Lady, the sign's right. Five boxes for a dollar, no strings attached.'"

Sam shook with laughter and Kendra burst with it. The cheerleaders simply glared at them.

33

"She's dead," Brittany said, scanning the lake. "She's never come up and she's not hiding under the pier."

"She can't be dead. I need her." Malory's lower lip stuck out.

"Mistress, no one can hold their breath this long. I spent half an hour alone watching under the pier while you watched the water. If she was there, I would have seen her come up for air."

"Damn it. Damn it. Damn it. Brittany, maybe she already has the gem. If she does, with her bloodlines, she might be able to do just about anything I can do."

"But you've been doing what you do for centuries. She's new. She wouldn't know how to work the stone."

Malory crossed her arms. "She's drowned. But she's a swimmer. I remember that from her application. She was asked to be on her high school swim team repeatedly. How could she drown?"

"Holly took her," Brittany explained. Seeing the look of understanding bloom on Malory's face, she added, "Holly, two. Malory, zero."

"Shut up." Malory paced ten feet of shoreline, paced back, did it again. "That dead bitch is going to pay. I'm going to squeeze her until I get her soul; then I'm going to put it in the bottom of a pit toilet on Pike's Peak. We'll just see how she likes that."

"Grow up, Malory. Think about it. She's building her army. She's got two souls, plus a few more and all the half-wit ghosts down there. This is war."

Malory paced some more. "It sure is. Where's my cell phone?"

"I'm not your secretary. I didn't bring it." Brittany dipped into her pocket and produced peanut M&Ms, crunched them up. "I'm your chipmunk. I brought what I like." She stuck her tongue out, covered with chocolate that was busy melting in her hands.

Malory stalked up to her and embraced her. "Let's go."

"Go where?"

"Back to the house. To my suite. I need to do the voice-shifting trick and make a couple of phone calls so no one will worry about Merilynn. Now, put your arms around me and start chanting."

34

Merilynn left her body when its heart stopped. Suddenly, she was free, swimming along with Eve, trailing Holly, who had somehow morphed around Merilynn's head and upper body, engulfing it in her own.

What's happening? Where are we going? Frantically, Merilynn looked around with eyes that could see far more clearly underwater than ever before. The lights of Applehead were behind them. Ahead lay only darkness.

We're going to the island, Eve told her. *Holly's taking you there. It's safe.*

Excuse me if I'm wrong, but if I'm dead, isn't everything pretty much safe?

Eve reached out to her, twined her phantom fingers in hers. She felt real. She felt alive, not icy cold. *Hurry! We have to keep up.*

Merilynn surged forward without effort. *Holly?*

She can't answer you. Not right now. Eve squeezed her hand. *You're amazing. So powerful. Holly couldn't have done this before.*

Confused, Merilynn asked, *Done what? What are you talking about?*

Your body. She's using your power to save it. You don't think a spirit could move a body on her own like that? She can save you because of who you are. And with your help . . .

I know. I can set you free. The island loomed. Holly swam down and around the earth, leading them into a watery cavern, then straight up. Merilynn surfaced, treading water, blowing water from her mouth, taking deep breaths. Only she wasn't doing any of those things. It just felt as if she were.

We have to help her now. Eve half swam and half glided toward Holly, who had unwound, returning to her normal form.

She held Merilynn's head above the water just below a smooth scoop of rock.

Help me lift her.

It was a peculiar sensation, trying to lift her own body. Merilynn's hands kept going through the physical form. Eve had only slightly better luck.

Holly smiled softly. *We have the power to do this. All you need is intent. Know, beyond all doubt, that you can lift this body. You can. Once it's out of the water, it will be in the knight's care.*

Merilynn and Eve tried again. Eve succeeded quickly, and soon Merilynn got the hang of it. They pushed her body—*so white, so thin*—onto the ledge, then moved back. Holly began to sing an old song, "Greensleeves," in a high pure voice.

Why? Merilynn wondered.

She's calling the Forest Knight. He usually comes to her when she sings this melody. It's beautiful, isn't it?

It was. Merilynn listened, waiting, watching, wanting to ask so many questions, knowing she couldn't, not now.

And then she felt him. The Forest Knight, lord of this land, one of her fathers. His presence filled the chamber before she even saw the green glow of his eyes.

When she did see them, she knew them. This was the bottom of the cave she had leaned over to peer into so long ago. The eyes had met hers. She was frightened then, but not now. Now, she was awestruck. The eyes neared, a dark form becoming visible as it descended to the ledge.

Heal her, sir, Holly asked. *This is your daughter, of your own blood. She wields great power. We need her.*

Merilynn made out a suggestion of a leafy face behind the eyes. They traveled from Holly to Eve and finally came to rest on Merilynn, on her spirit. He held out a hand.

She swam to him.

He embraced her spirit and, overcome, she clung to him. Her body lay dead at her feet but she had never felt so full of life, so wonderful and rich. She dared not look at him, not yet, but pressed against him, melding with him.

Drink of me, daughter. I am your strength.

Merilynn looked up and saw the eyes, not human, nor inhuman, not cruel but firm and full of love. He had leafy vines for hair and beard and when he smiled his green smile, she relaxed against him, content.

Merilynn.

Holly's voice brought her back to the world—whatever this world was—and she saw the two phantoms waving. *Don't forget us,* Eve called.

We shall see you again.

Holly's words faded like an old echo and the spirits disappeared beneath the black water.

The Green Man cradled her spirit in one hand and scooped up her physical body in the other. Then he began to climb, humming some strange but lovely lullaby.

Rest, daughter.

35

Heather and her clones continued to loom over Sam and Kendra. Sam was about to say something rude, but Kendra's phone shrilled in her pocket.

She pulled it out and punched it on. "Hello?"

Sam watched her face; first seeing open mouthed surprise, then a slow smile that turned into a grin capable of lighting up the whole room. Kendra had a finger pressed in her free ear to block noise, so Sam turned her attention to Heather. "Did you want something?"

Heather shrugged, her eyes on Kendra's animated face.

"Hell, yes, you had us scared half to death!" She looked up at Sam and mouthed *Merilynn*. "You're sure you're okay? When will you be back? Uh-huh."

Sam gestured at the phone and said, "Let me talk to her."

"Just a sec. Sam wants to bawl you out for running off without telling us. *Yes*, you deserve it." She laughed. "Here's Sam."

Sam grabbed the phone. "Merilynn?"

"In the flesh." It was Merilynn's voice, all right, with her distinctive lilt that made her sound happy even when she wasn't.

"What happened to you?"

"I was just doing my thing, you know, trying to find Holly Gayle. I told Kendra the details."

"*Details?* You were on the phone for two minutes, three tops."

"I just went out to the lake and looked around. Then I decided I was getting way too into this stuff, you know, obsessive, and I decided to take off for a while."

"Where are you?"

"Up north, staying with an old friend, right near Big Sur."

"What's your number there?"

"I'm calling from the general store. Rebecca doesn't have a

phone in her cabin. Isn't it quaint? She's elderly. You know how *they* can be."

"Quaint is one way of putting it. So how do we get in touch with you?"

"I'll have to get in touch with you." She paused. "I have to get some downtime, you know, away from the school. It's been getting to me, all the ghost stuff."

"I thought you loved that stuff."

"Well, I do, but I mean, *really*, I hiked to the lake in the dark, by myself. Even I know that's a dumb thing to do. Rebecca is a witch. A wiccan, you know, a white witch. She's going to tutor me in herbs and potions and I'm going to stay away for a while. I need a rest."

"What about your classes?"

"No biggie. I'll drop out for a while, then drop back in. Maybe."

"Maybe?" Sam asked. "What do you mean, maybe?"

"I might not come back. You know, the whole place is just sort of creepy."

"Did something happen to you?" Sam asked sharply, instincts up.

"No, why?"

Sam paused. "No reason. Is your uncle coming for your things?"

"No. I told him it was just for a couple weeks. He understood." She cleared her throat and Sam thought, for just an instant, she heard giggles in the background. "Honestly, I probably *will* be back in a week or two. Or three."

She heard laughter again. "Is that Rebecca laughing?"

"Uh-huh."

"I didn't know witches were silly. They seem serious."

"I'm a witch of a sort, and you *know* I'm silly, Sammy."

Sammy? Merilynn never called her that; no one did, and lived. Ignoring it, she said, "I hope you enjoy your vacation. Is there anything you want me to tell Jimmy?" She drew the name from the air, thinking of the boy with dreadlocks.

"Jimmy?" the voice lilted.

"Come on, Merilynn. You told us all about him already, so don't be coy."

She laughed a little too quickly. "I know I told you about him, Sammy, and thank you, but I'll call him myself. If you see him, tell him I'll be inviting him up to the redwoods for some sexual magic."

"Will do," Sam said. "Listen, Merilynn. Keep in touch."

"I will. 'Bye."

Giggles speckled the background until the connection cut out. Sam handed the phone back to Kendra, who kept up her smile for the looming cheerleaders.

Sam looked up and gave Heather a Mona Lisa smile. "That was Merilynn."

"Oh?"

"She's said to tell everyone hello. And then to tell you good-bye for a few weeks while she takes a little trip."

A skeptical look from Heather. "In the middle of the term?"

"You know Merilynn," Sam said breezily. "She's a free spirit. Hey, I see some jocks coming in. Maybe you'd better go cheer them up."

Heather turned and stepped away, the Js following, then she threw Sam a dirty look when she saw a decided lack of jocks.

"Just keep going," Sam urged, barely loud enough for Kendra to hear.

The cheerleaders kept going, over to a table of their own kind.

"So?" Kendra asked, sitting forward. "What was all that about?"

"Whoever it was, it wasn't Merilynn."

"Are you sure? It sure sounded like her."

"Yeah, well, *this* Merilynn says she's going to call Jimmy and invite him up north for some enchanted loving."

"Who's Jimmy?"

"I made him up. A test. She failed."

"So what do we do?"

"We stay very quiet. I think we're up against some nasty people."

"Malory and Brittany?"

Sam nodded. "And probably the rest of the secret sisterhood. The voice imitation was absolutely uncanny."

"What put you on to her?"

"Giggling in the background. Somehow an old lady who practices witchcraft and lives like a hermit in a forest doesn't seem like a giggly type to me."

"What do we do now?"

"We act normal and we go back to your room and go through her notes and things. We need to find out what's coming up, occultwise."

"Halloween," Kendra said promptly.

"That would be a big night for sacrifices."

"The biggest."

"Anything before that?"

"Not unless it's something special to the society. I'd say Halloween's a safe bet."

36

"They bought it," Malory told Brittany, purring like a contented lioness. "Merilynn's priest father bought it and her brilliant friends bought it."

"They couldn't help buying it. You shift voices like a true elemental."

Malory beamed. "Do you think so?"

"I do." Brittany flopped back on the bed and held out her arms.

Malory slid into them. "There's so much to do. We need a sacrifice. We need to initiate our new Fata Morganas. We need—"

"Each other," Brittany interrupted. "We need each other for now. Mistress, you performed so well tonight. I'm sorry you had to lose your daughter, though."

"I lost my sacrifice." Malory nuzzled Brittany's neck, kissing and nibbling. "She was only good as a sacrifice. But what a grand one she would have been."

Brittany stroked her hair, lost in thought. Malory was wrong to assume the Forest Knight would want his own daughter for a sacrifice. Malory was rarely wrong, and never so wrong as this. It was disturbing. Very disturbing.

"Britt?" murmured the sorceress.

"What, love?"

"Make love to me."

"I shall."

"Now."

"Patience, mistress." She rolled away and rose, her eyes on Malory, questioning her motives, her reasoning. It made no sense. Or perhaps it just appeared that way. "I'll be in the shower for five minutes. Be undressed when I return," she said, blowing her a kiss.

Even Malory couldn't tell that her smile was false.

ALL HALLOW'S EVE

37

The final two weeks of October passed in a flurry of fiery colors as orange, red, and yellow leaves dropped from the *Liquidambar* trees on the Greenbriar campus. The forest turned from green with dabs of gold to a mix as the oaks were finally overrun by their aging gold coin leaves that chattered on the chill breeze.

Pumpkins sprouted on porches. Professor Tongue had three on his and replaced them each time they were smashed by drunken frat boys. By night, he gave tongue lashings to the president of Gamma Eta Pi. She wore him out and often brought along luscious little Brittany to double his pleasure. Tongue knew that he would never be honest with Malory about his preference for her bubbly blond sidekick, because if he told her she would never bring her to him again. Malory was a breathtaking bitch and somehow, when she was around, he could refuse her nothing. He was happily whipped. Relatively happily, at least.

The days passed and pumpkins appeared and reappeared on his porch and two insatiable females did the same in his bed. All was right with the world.

Almost.

Almost because Malory had him too whipped. She was more than an insatiable bed partner; she had become a problem in his public speaking class. She disrupted everything with her bizarre—granted, very entertaining, but still bizarre—talks, and he didn't know what to do about it.

He couldn't take her to task like a normal student; as often as not, he wore her scent to class, just a subliminal suggestion, the rest washed from his upper lip with water but no soap, so as not to totally destroy the memory. He couldn't help it; he was that smitten.

And in private? He didn't even dare to bring up the subject of her disruptive speeches. He dreaded her anger though he'd never seen it, and as Halloween drew near he realized that he was afraid of her, of what she might do to him or to his class.

That turned him on. And since he could never quite remember how the classes ended, it couldn't be all bad. He kept telling himself that.

The Monday before Halloween, Malory had soared to new heights with a speech she called, "You Are What You Eat." After announcing the title, she proceeded to give an excellent and fascinating talk on the ways men could improve the taste of their bodies, their sperm in particular. No one's attention wandered as she waxed eloquent on avoiding dairy, caffeine, and smoking "if you want your honey to be more willing to provide oral pleasure."

When he made his weak protest about content, as he always did, she merely smiled and explained that even some presidents of the United States didn't consider this act to be sex, so hers certainly couldn't be considered an obscene speech. She then went right back to her speech, adding that even worse for fragrance and flavor than dairy products, which putrified and befouled the "natural masculine nectar," was the lowly asparagus stalk. No one, she said forcefully, cared to taste semen laced with that particular thistle.

She had lightened her tone then and suggested that women should feed their men sweet fruits to give them a "pleasant sugary flavor."

Tongue didn't remember much about the speech after that, but she deserved an A. No one held the class's interest like she did. Quite possibly, no one even dared to try.

And so, Halloween arrived for Professor Tongue. Alone in his snug office in his cottage, he worried about Malory, pondered grades, and smiled at the little chipmunk that so often came to sit on his windowsill. Lately, the tiny creature had worked up the courage to come indoors. He'd discovered she loved toasted almonds, so he kept a bowl handy. He christened his wild friend "Li'l Darlin'" and spoke to her—it had to be a her—in soft low tones. Now, she abruptly hopped from the sill into the house and scampered across the floor, appearing on his desk, just out of reach, in the blink of an eye. He nudged the little bowl of almonds toward her. Sitting on her haunches, she picked one up and daintily began to nibble as she watched him work.

38

As the comforting scent of woodsmoke from fireplaces began to fill the air more often every day and night, as green grass began to fade toward yellow or brown, Kendra and Samantha became close friends. They pored over Merilynn's journals and notes and endlessly studied her watercolors of the haunted town beneath Apple-head Lake.

There had been no sign of Merilynn since the night the ghosts had come into their room—the phone call didn't count; both knew it was false. Still, Sam and Kendra chose to believe she was alive, that there was a chance of rescue, at least through Halloween night.

Between classes, they spent time in the library studying old newspaper articles and police reports, trying to glean clues from decades-old articles about missing or murdered students. They found that, often, girls went missing around certain dates; the solstices and equinoxes. May first and mid-August. And the last night of October.

"Halloween is the next time the ghost town is supposed to come to life," Kendra mused. "That's good because when the town is alive, Holly Gayle walks. She and Eve will be among us."

"That's good," Sam murmured.

"They're on our side."

"They may be able to help us find Merilynn before it's too late."

"What if you're wrong?" Kendra asked suddenly. "What if Merilynn is already dead?"

"It's a chance worth taking, don't you think?"

"Yes." Tears formed in Kendra's eyes but she willed them away. It was a frustrating time; they had searched everywhere they could, looking for traces of their missing friend. On the weekend before Halloween, they even drove down into the Applehead Cheerleading Camp.

"Dear Lord," Kendra had said, seeing the shattered boathouse doors. The broken wood had been stacked near the dock and plywood had hastily been nailed up to cover the entrance, keeping the boats safe from mischievous college students and drunken fishermen.

They had examined the sand for footprints, but if there had been any left under the workmen's prints, the October zephyrs had erased them. Later that day, around noon, they had hiked to the knight's chapel, taking the route Sam remembered from so long ago, peering in the same window through which she had watched the sacrifice.

"Do you think they'll do it here?" Kendra asked, shivering with terror.

"Perform the sacrifice?" Sam walked boldly into the place that Kendra knew squeezed her heart and throat. She followed. All the grass looked the same; they couldn't even find the place that had looked so sparse the time they came here during the night. "Yes," Sam finally said. "I think it's likely this is where they'll perform the sacrifice."

She spoke strongly, but Kendra could hear a faint tremble in her voice. "Let's get out of here, Sam. I don't think it's teaching us anything."

Kendra felt strange comfort in knowing that Sam hated this place as much as she did. Quickly, they left the building, but the terror didn't fade until they left the clearing as well. Both looked back at the chapel ruins, then at each other; they both knew they would be back soon but neither could voice it.

Instead, they went to Professor McCobb's office. He gently chastised Kendra for taking so long to visit him to have their chat about the Greenbriar Ghost. Over hot chocolate with marshmallows in the comfort of his book-lined office, they retraced the lore, comparing what they knew and what they read, looking for a truth. Eventually, charmed by the old man's white tangle of eyebrows, his lion's mane of wild white hair, and his cherubic lips, they even told him their theories.

None of it had seemed terribly real until he said he thought they might be right. Sitting in chairs opposite the old professor, Sam and Kendra took each other's hands. Both trembled almost uncontrollably.

39

The day faded. As All Hallow's Eve arrived in Greenbriar. As twilight wrapped the campus in darkness, fraternity and sorority houses lit up, decorated with black and orange streamers, black cats, and ghosts. Jack-o'-lanterns sat plump and orange on the steps of the houses, carved faces grinning, fire in their eyes.

Gamma House had the most jack-o'-lanterns. They lined the veranda railing, smiling, frowning, roaring, inscrutable, lusting. They sat one above the other on the steps to the house, gleaming and grinning their blazing eyes and smiles.

Most of the regular Gamma sisters would attend parties on campus or in town. Nearly all of them were currently at the small, relatively quiet celebration in Gamma House's great room, where sprays of dried roses no longer filled the fireplace. Instead, the huge maw was filled with blazing flames that licked hungrily at logs piled on the grate. On the marble fronting the huge fireplace, more carved pumpkins watched the festivities. Punch was poured. Sisters giggled. Young men laughed and spiked the punch.

Some partiers wore costumes, others did not, at least not yet. Parties in Gamma House were mild affairs; no one wanted to harm the furniture or the wallpaper, or knock over an antique lamp. After a warm up here, most of the girls would head out for the serious frat house parties.

At the moment, nearly all the Gamma sisters were in the great room. Obviously missing were most of the cheerleaders and the officers. *The Fata Morgana.* Thirteen.

And two more were out too, though they're lack of attendance wasn't noticed. Long before dark, Samantha and Kendra had slipped away, carrying bookbags filled with flashlights and weapons, water and first aid supplies.

McCobb had offered to help them in some way that none of the three had quite figured out. He warned them of the danger, told them that he had seen Malory before, had confirmed suspicions too absurd for Sam to even voice. But Sam listened as he and Kendra spoke, and knew there would be no help. The Fata Morgana had Greenbriar University sewn up tight.

And the day before Halloween, Professor McCobb stumbled and fractured his leg right after Sam and Kendra left his office after a long conversation. McCobb's secretary explained that he would be in the hospital for a few days because they had to put a pin in his thigh. Then he would be recovering at home for a few weeks. Both girls suspected some sort of foul play—they had seen Malory watching them talk one day outside his classroom.

So, Sam and Kendra were all alone as they headed for the

chapel well before twilight. They spoke little, but exchanged lots of glances. Nervous ones.

There was still light in the sky when they reached the chapel's clearing. Keeping to the trees, they skirted it entirely, moving quietly until they reached the far side of the ruins, the side with the windows, not the wide doorway.

"We really ought to have more of a plan," Sam said as they examined a copse of close-set pines as a possible hiding place. "Or at least some machine guns."

"Remember what McCobb said. The Forest Knight isn't our enemy. Or Merilynn's. We take our cues from her." Kendra paused, fingering the long letter opener in her pocket. "I sure wouldn't mind having one of those guns of Rambo's though."

"Me either. So, what do you think?" Sam snapped her wrist, causing Roddy, her tiny billy club, to grow with a reassuringly harsh metal-on-metal sliding sound. "We need to be able to see what's going on without being seen. This looks good to me."

"Me too."

Sam nodded and slipped off her backpack, pushing it up against some winter-burned ferns. Kendra followed suit. Soon, they were quietly settled on the forest floor, backs against the trees, puny weapons at hand and nearly no notion about what they were going to do.

"I can't believe we're doing this," Sam murmured.

"We have to."

"I know, but we're not prepared."

"You know what McCobb said. If Merilynn is what we think she is, she's prepared. We just need to be here to help her."

"Kendra, I hope you're right. If you're not, I'm afraid we're about to become just a couple more missing students in a long line of them."

Twilight settled in, shrouding them with dread as dark as their clothing. Time passed. A long time, agonizingly slow.

And then they heard voices on the other side of the chapel. Feminine voices, first just a couple; Malory and Heather. A bonfire crackled to life within the chapel walls. Alert, they listened, but the trees and snapping fire muffled the words. All they could be sure of was that the duo was lugging something heavy. Heather's curses rose over the other noises, and silenced the birds.

Merilynn? Kendra asked silently.

Sam could barely see her in the gloom. She shrugged, then whispered, "Maybe we should . . ."

She silenced as more voices neared. The Fata Morgana had arrived.

Holding a finger to her lips, she stood and peered through the trees, caught sight of dark-robed figures silhouetted in the flames.

40

Brittany arrived at the chapel late, infuriating her mistress, who threw her forest-colored cloak at her with barely a glance. Brittany stripped and pulled on the robe, discreetly wiping away signs of the sex she'd just had with Professor Tongue.

She had started seeing Tongue secretly nearly ten days ago. How could she possibly resist a man who was so kind to animals and to women. She'd spent hours sitting on his desk, watching his hands—nice artistic fingers, not terribly long, but strong and graceful—and finding herself more and more fascinated by the human. Drawn to him.

It began with an impulse blindly followed. After he had hand-fed her a honey-roasted almond, she skittered from the room, out the window, and not a minute later, knocked on his front door.

He'd opened it and simply stared at her.

"I'd do anything for some nuts," she said, unbuttoning her shirt to reveal her cleavage.

"I have nuts," he said hoarsely, then invited her in.

It was such fun, having him to herself, having a secret with him; she had told him Malory couldn't know about their secret affair, but he was smart enough to know that on his own. Thereafter, she began to visit him when she knew Malory was attending a class or riding a football player.

She felt affection for Tongue, the kind he probably felt for her chipmunk self, and that and the sex were gratifying, but she couldn't lie to herself; taking Malory's lover behind her back was equally gratifying. Especially now that she wasn't sure about Malory's suitability as a sorceress.

Brittany's dalliances with Tongue were heaven on earth, whatever the reasons behind them. Or at least they had been until an hour before when she had gotten carried away and suffocated the poor man with an extended orgasm the likes of which only an elemental could experience.

It was humiliating. It was embarrassing. And it had happened before. That was one of the reasons Malory wouldn't let her sample her human lovers in her absence. She knew Brittany could sexually murder a human male any number of ways. Usually, their hearts gave out. Tongue's lungs had burst because Brittany had stayed too long in the saddle, and by the time she realized her error, the man had been dead too long to bother reviving. He'd be nothing but a vegetable.

And Malory would be furious.

Brittany had dawdled after realizing her error, trying to decide what to do with the body. Malory would recognize magick. She finally decided to set fire to the cottage, then realized it would have to be done later; dusk was falling and Malory and the Fata Morgana were waiting for her at the chapel. Professor Tongue would have to wait.

What would happen if she told Malory the truth? Fury, wrath, some nasty electrical bolts zapped her way. Brittany didn't need any of it, but she didn't fear it either. Especially now. Normally, a familiar didn't cross her sorcerer overtly, but times were changing. Tonight, if Malory pulled off the sacrifice, if Merilynn was truly out of the picture, things would probably go back to normal—or nearly normal. As long as Malory clung to the idea of sacrificing this particular daughter—more than half elemental, a truly special creature—Brittany couldn't trust her completely.

Now, she watched her mistress as she and her minions prepared for the sacrificial rites of All Hallow's Eve. Her eyes flashed dark and wild; even her movements were odd and jerky. Perhaps it was side effects from missing the last sacrifice, but Malory had grown more unstable and unrealistic over the last ten days. She was becoming an unsuitable mistress.

Something that most alarmed Brittany was the haphazard way her mistress had conducted the initiations of the new Fata Morganas. They were hurried and half-assed. Malory not only didn't teach them what they needed to know, but she chose her initiates badly. One she chose for her psychotic nature, for her willingness to kill her roommate over closet space. She was not Fata material; she was prison material. And the others? Simply warm bodies to fill slots. Brittany couldn't fault Malory too much there; there was no time to really choose. But those neophytes had no idea what was about to happen.

They didn't know they were about to take part in a sacrifice of any sort, let alone a human one, one of their lesser sisters. Malory's plan was to use magick to make them forget what they'd seen if they reacted badly, and her back-up plan was to kill them if magick didn't work. It was not how these things were done. It was wrong. *Wrong!*

Suddenly, Brittany itched for freedom for the first time in hundreds of years. She burned with desire for a new master or mistress. One who respected the Forest Knight. One who respected *her.*

41

Deep in the caverns on Applehead Island, Merilynn's body had lain, not dead, but in stasis, on a soft bed of living ferns by an underground brook, tended and healed by the Forest Knight until it was whole again and ready for her spirit to reenter.

Merilynn didn't want to return to the physical world. Here, with the Forest Knight, she had spent time in the Otherworld learning so much about the things she'd rarely even glimpsed while in her body, knowing things she'd only suspected. Here, she could see as she had never seen before. Here, her forest father schooled her in her power, *his* power, for it was born of him.

I don't want to leave you.

He looked at her with eyes similar to her own, and similar to those of her priestly father, who was also truly a son of the knight. The knight rarely spoke, but showed her pictures, and now he did both. Showing her an image of the ghostlights beneath the lake, of the amber lanterns in ghost houses and the brilliant stained glass of the old church, he told her, *You are always with me.*

I made a promise.

Yes.

May I return to you after?

You will know what to do. We are never apart. Go now. The fate of the living lies in your hands as well as the fate of the dead.

He sent her an image of Samantha and Kendra hiding behind the chapel, where a bonfire blazed. Where a victim waited for a sacrifice that the Forest Knight did not truly want. The knight had made this bargain long ago, and he would not dishonor it, Merilynn knew. But he would, in his own way, be glad to end it.

That night, Holly told me only I could stop Malory.

Then stop her now, before she snuffs out any more humans.

Merilynn slipped into her renewed body, felt blood pump, breathed in the air, felt it cool in her lungs, smelled its green scent, savored the babble of the brook. Sitting up, she cupped her hand in the fresh water and drank deeply.

"I'm alive!"

"Are you ready?" her father asked in a rumbly voice, part oak, part man.

"Yes."

"You will be able to hold your breath long enough to accomplish your task. Go now. Go and kill. Go and be free."

42

The ceremony began and Brittany, as always, stepped forward at Malory's signal and uncovered the sacrifice. Little Lou, the newest cheerleader, had been her mistress's pick despite the fact that she had many relatives that would inquire and cause problems for them.

It was just another example of Malory's lack of judgment. She didn't care about the problems that would arise, no more than she cared about the current Fata Morganas. As cold as Malory had always been, she had still been loyal to her Fata Morganas, taking care of them, nurturing them, teaching them what they needed to know.

But when Brittany made a remark about her lack of thought about the Fatas, Malory shook off the comment like it was a gnat, telling her familiar that they didn't matter since she and Brittany would be leaving Greenbriar soon.

They had left this place many times before, but she had always cared. She always put this, her favorite of all the Fata Morgana groups, in the hands of her most trusted lieutenants. But only months from leaving Gamma House, she hadn't even discussed replacements with Brittany.

Bound and gagged, Lou's eyes betrayed her terror as she stared up into Brittany's own.

Though she didn't truly care about Lou any more than she would about a wounded bird—less actually—Brittany found herself unable to meet the victim's gaze as she fastened her to the spikes driven into the ground and secured by a small spell when Malory first arrived.

She went about her business, her heart cold, making sure that Lou could not roll out of the way of Malory's black onyx ceremonial dagger.

The chanting began, led by Heather while Malory sang an eerie counterpoint spell. Brittany joined in because that was what a familiar did, but she watched the new Fata Morganas, the initiates, seeing anxiety and fear on the faces of all but the psychotic one. That bitch licked her lips as she stared at the naked, helpless girl laid out before her.

The chanting continued.

43

Merilynn dived into the underground pool of water, swimming like a fish, quickly clearing the cavern and island to glide rapidly deeper and deeper, heading for the ghost town beneath the black water.

She flashed through the water, holding her breath without any effort, seeing as she saw only when in spirit form. Before her, Applehead began to wink to life, more and more lights blossoming amber as she approached.

They're welcoming me. She reached the town, moving quickly among the buildings, seeing near-mindless ghosts holding their lanterns, seeing others, spirits, not just ghosts, gathering before her, lighting her way. In some of the old buildings, ghosts seemed to go through the motions of dining or reading. One stoked an amber fire under a cookpot.

She found the church and swam inside, looking sadly at the scattering of bones from Malory's victims. *So many.* Had Malory willed them here through magick because of some perversely twisted sense of humor? Had Holly used the currents to pull them into the sanctuary? Merilynn saw a closed door behind the altar and pulled it open, exposing a small room. The perfect bodies of Holly Gayle and Eve Camlan sat together, arms and hair entwined, Eve's head upon Holly's breast. Merilynn hesitated, then moved closer.

No. Come to the steeple.

Holly's voice.

Leave them. Close the door. They are safe there.

Merilynn glided back into the church and found the staircase to the steeple. She swam upward toward the gleaming jewels of stained glass that depicted the village of Applehead before it was covered by the lake.

Holly and Eve waited for her beside it. Merilynn smiled at them, then Holly pointed at a rectangle of emerald glass. Merilynn saw the small sword, fitted along the rectangle to look like one more piece of leading. But the sword shown silver and as she grasped the hilt, the green gemstone bloomed under her touch. Wonderingly, she turned the sword in her hand. The blade was long enough to stop a heart's beat, and the stone was so large that it had the same faceted brilliance on each side of the hasp. Nothing filtered its brilliance.

Hurry! There's no time!

Merilynn looked at Holly and Eve and nodded. Then, using the sword to light her way, she swam across the lake more swiftly than any human could even imagine.

44

Chants rose to fever pitch. Magick sparked the air, filled it until it crackled like the fire itself. Malory began to lift off the ground, feet dangling. Brittany was swept up as well, and their robes fell away. The experienced Fatas levitated next, boosted by Malory and Brittany, and as they rose, their robes swept off their gleaming bodies as if taken by the wind. The initiates, all but untrained, stayed earthbound, but even their robes fell away, caught in the magick, obeying the power of all.

Brittany loved the feeling of the electricity in the atmosphere. She tasted the air, but felt no sign of the Forest Knight's presence, realizing she had yet to hear his cry.

But she sensed something else nearby.

Something different. Something powerful. Something exciting. It was almost here. Eagerly she scanned, but she saw nothing.

Yet.

45

Merilynn burst out of the lake, running onto the sand, pausing to take deep breaths of fresh air. She smelled the lake and the forest, and a bonfire. She smelled magick too.

From the time spent with the knight in spirit form, she knew the forest intimately. She could see unnaturally well, too. So, hiding the brilliance of the green gem and silvery sword beneath her wet jacket, she ran, as fleet as her father, toward the chapel.

She silently came to rest in the shadows of the chapel, just outside one of the windows at the rear. Crouching, she cautiously peered inside and watched the circle of thirteen robed figures. A bonfire burned.

"Merilynn!"

She whipped her head around, saw Sam and Kendra in nearby shadows, just as the knight had shown her. She put her finger to her lips. *Silence!*

46

As Malory Thomas floated to the ground and stepped forward to kneel beside her sacrifice, Merilynn began to murmur the old words of power that the Forest Knight had taught her. They were words older than Malory's, older than any human's language. As she said them, she unsheathed the sword and the stone.

Green brilliance lit up the night. The chanting stopped. Behind her, she heard Sam and Kendra gasp, but she paid no attention. Instead, she threw her head back and yelled the banshee cry her father had taught her. The sound shook the ground, made the wind blow, brought birds out of nests.

Merilynn leaped through the window, ran through the bonfire, untouched, holding the sword high.

Malory, her onyx dagger raised to take the heart from her victim, looked up just as Merilynn landed on her, toppling her backward and plunging the sword deeply into her mother's breast.

Into her heart.

Malory flailed and cried for her familiar, but no help came.

Green brilliance flared as the weapon claimed Malory's life and power and fed it into the Forest Knight's own daughter.

Merilynn pushed Malory's body to the ground, withdrawing the sword, then rising and holding it up into the night, she called. "Father! Here is your sacrifice!"

She let out another earth-shattering cry then yanked up Malory Thomas's head and sliced her head off as if it were a wing off a fly. Holding it by the hair, she turned, displaying it to all of Malory's followers. "Your queen is dead. Morgana is gone from this world!"

Sam and Kendra moved in, untying Lou and giving her a robe. Merilynn barely noticed. She threw a binding spell to keep all of the Fata Morganas within the chapel until she could deal with them. Then she smiled at Sam and Kendra and little Lou.

She touched Lou's forehead and murmured, "Forget." The girl, dazed to begin with, looked like she was asleep on her feet.

Then Merilynn threw her head back and gave a shout of triumph, frightening in its strength, but not its tone. Silence followed. One second, two, three. Then she smiled as her father's great answer of triumph sounded from his island.

She basked in power and pleasure for one long moment, then turned to see Kendra and Sam staring at her. Behind them, Fata Morganas sat or stumbled, dazed and confused, unable to leave.

"Hey, guys," she said to her friends. "How are things in the real world?"

Before either could reply, a chipmunk suddenly raced up to her and stood on its hind legs, little paws clasped as if in prayer.

"Hello, little one." Merilynn bent and extended her hand to the animal. It ran up her arm and perched on her shoulder, nuzzling her. She smiled at Sam and Kendra. "It looks like I've just made a new friend."

DECEMBER

47

A fire crackled merrily in the great room of Gamma House, and before the windows that looked out over the night-shrouded back lawn, a huge Monterey pine stood ten feet tall, majestic in its raiment of twinkling white lights and globes that looked like the most delicate confections of spun silver and gold. Topping the Yule tree was a sparkling shooting star.

Most of the sisters of Gamma House were here this Sunday night, gathered together and apart, deep in books, outlining, highlighting, taking notes for the exams that would plague them during the coming week.

Kendra, curled in the corner of a love seat, notebook in hand, looked around the room. The house felt different now, homier, more comfortable and welcoming. The departure of Malory Thomas and Brittany was the reason. Without them here, things actually felt sisterly. She smiled, jotted down a stray thought, and fell into reverie once more.

Things had changed, but remained much the same. Merilynn had taken instant and unquestioned charge of the Fata Morganas. All of them had obeyed her on All Hallow's Eve, and continued to do so now, even though she was rarely here.

Merilynn had changed in her time on the island with the Forest Knight. *Her father.* She roamed the woods at all hours, long and lithe, red hair flying as she moved among the trees, the little chipmunk nearly always riding her shoulder or frolicking at her heels.

One day Kendra asked her about the friendly striped creature, if it was really a chipmunk or something more, something very familiar. Merilynn had only smiled in her fey way, giving an answer with her eyes that Kendra could not translate.

Merilynn's slightly flaky personality had changed very much. She was still friendly but far away. No one feared her, except perhaps the Fata Morganas that she hadn't sent away.

Sent away. How she had sent them, and where, were two questions that, for now, Kendra didn't want an answer for. Merilynn was the daughter of a good priest, a powerful forest god, and what had to be one of the wickedest mothers of all time. Kendra studied her friend often, seeing the calm power behind her smile. She wondered how she used the power. How she would use it in years to come.

Some day I'll write a book about a forest queen.

Kendra had the room to herself; Merilynn had moved into Malory's suite, and was less easy to know now. Although she invited her friends to her lush room to watch movies and eat popcorn or down the occasional margarita, she was . . . *What is she?* Kendra stared at the ceiling a moment, then wrote down the answer: *A force of nature.* She also had a handsome boyfriend now, most often seen after he was already in the house, walking with her down the halls, disappearing into her rooms for hours. Handsome, tanned, with thick blond hair and deep blue eyes, Brandon was hard-muscled and compact, standing an inch shorter than Merilynn herself. Neither seemed to notice. When he was around, which was more and more, Merilynn's smile sparkled even brighter than usual. They were a match made, if not in heaven, then someplace very similar, but greener.

Kendra heard the entry door being opened—holiday bells jingled arrivals and departures. A little thrill ran through her.

"Kendra," a soft male voice said from the doorway.

She closed her notebook and stood, then turned and beamed at Jimmy Freeman. Merilynn wasn't the only one who had found a friend of the opposite sex. She walked to the threshold and tilted her head up for a quick meeting of the lips.

"So, are you going to tell me what your big surprise is?" he asked.

"No. I'm going to show you. Let me go get my coat and flash-lights."

His face split in a broad, mellow smile that melted her. They had yet to consummate the relationship and the tension was constantly tight, constantly delicious. He called it foreplay and seemed to relish waiting for the right time and place.

"I'll be right back." Kendra trotted up the stairs and unlocked her room. She shrugged on her warmest coat and grabbed her knapsack, pulled out her flashlight and checked the batteries. They looked strong, but she dropped an extra set in the bottom of the bag and placed the light itself in a pocket on the jacket. To the backpack, she added two bottles of water and a pair of ruby-red apples, wrapped in a towel to keep them from bruis-ing. *No.* Smiling to herself, picturing Jimmy waiting for her at the foot of the stairs, she plucked the velvety blanket throw from the foot of her bed, folded it again and put it in the bag, then placed the apples in the deep fold and tucked the blanket in around them.

She closed the pack and clicked the latch, then swung it around and shrugged it on. Jimmy would insist on carrying it and be pleasantly surprised when he found out how little it weighed. Kendra glanced around the room, ready to leave, then paused, returned to her desk, and took the letter opener from it, slipping it into the long inner pocket of her coat, where it joined her pepper spray.

Satisfied now, she turned off the light and flipped the lock on the knob and left the room. Seeing Jimmy, she took the stairs two at a time.

Eyeing the bulging pack, he asked, "Are we going camping?"

"In December?" She laughed.

"Hey, it's California, after all. No snow."

"California. Not Hawaii." She grinned at him. "You still have a lot to learn about this place."

Jimmy, from Vermont, returned the grin. "Feels like Hawaii to me."

They walked outside. The cold wind washed over Kendra's face. "Jimmy, trust me, this isn't Hawaii. They grow apples up here. Apples need a cold winter. And for your information, once in a while it really does snow here."

"Don't try to one-up me on snow, Kendra. I've got you beat on that and you know it."

They walked down the paving beside the reflecting pool, and down to the roadside in front of the house, where his weird little motor-scooter—*more guts than a scooter, but not a good statement about penis size,* he'd told her—waited. He handed her a helmet and donned his own. He got on first; then she tucked in behind him, moving up close, putting her arms around him, hanging on tight just because she wanted to.

"Where to?"

"The lake."

His head swiveled. "The *what?*"

"Applehead Lake, by way of the old chapel. It's not a bad hike, just a quarter mile in."

"That's a dangerous spot. It's haunted."

"I know, Jimmy. I was the one who told you all the stories, remember?"

"You and Professor McCobb. What are you doing, taking us there? You want to see some ghosts, or maybe a serial killer?"

"No serial killer, but I'd be happy to see some ghosts."

"What about the Greenbriar Ghost?"

"He prefers to be called the Forest Knight. Merilynn told me."

"The funny red-haired girl?"

"That's her."

"So she's tight with the knight?"

"Very. If we run into him, be respectful. And don't leave litter in his chapel. Merilynn says he hates that."

"You're nuts," he said, trying to catch her kiss. It landed on his helmet.

"I'm just messing with you, Jimmy. We're meeting some friends and we're going to see a show."

"Okay. As long as you protect me from the ghosts, I'll follow you to the ends of the earth. And even to that haunted lake." He paused. "Hey, we aren't going out in a boat, are we?"

"Too cold. We'll do that some other time."

"You're the boss." The engine didn't roar as he turned it on, but it purred pretty impressively. "Hang on tight."

"I will."

48

Samantha Penrose walked alone, the greenish gleam of a light-stick and a brilliant half-moon giving her enough light to travel the path to the Knight's chapel.

Since All Hallow's Eve, she had taken this path many times, by night and by day, relishing what she once feared, hoping to see the knight as he was now. Not as he had been when she witnessed the sacrifice nearly a decade ago.

That was what she had forgotten. Merilynn, new and improved, had helped her remember. She knew now that the Fata Morganas had fled after the sacrifice, leaving the chapel even before the knight's angry shriek filled the air and shook the trees. The high priestess—Malory—took the dead girl's heart with her as she hurried away. A moment later, the banshee howl came again, closer, arriving in a hurricane wind that came crashing down into the chapel.

Sam had cringed in the shadows, but still peered through the window. The wind had spun around a greenish figure that covered the girl's body for a minute, maybe less, then rose. She'd seen the flash of the knight's green eyes as they spotted her.

And she expected to die.

Now, she stepped into the clearing onto the remains of last spring's grass. The wards had been lifted, Merilynn had explained shortly after Halloween. It was a holy place, not a forbidden place. Her eyes had darkened as she spoke, saying that anyone thickheaded enough to defile the place would likely pay a price.

Sam didn't question her. She understood. She had seen what Merilynn had metamorphosed into in the chapel on the last night of October. It wasn't a story that Sam would ever report in *Time* magazine, or *Newsweek*. It was a story meant for Kendra to tell. It was folklore in the making. *An urban legend now, folklore later. It has to age.*

Kendra had been horrified that night, traumatized, but she and Merilynn had spent many hours talking about it with her. And Merilynn had done something, laying her hands on Kendra's head, speaking softly as she moved her fingers in small circles over her forehead and cheeks. Kendra had relaxed—Sam had relaxed just watching and listening, for that matter—and then fallen asleep. When she awoke half an hour later, the terror had drained away. She was her old self again.

Now, at the chapel's threshold, Samantha hesitated only an instant, then stepped inside. The air seemed warmer, tingling with electricity.

"Forest Knight," Sam whispered, as she always did when she came here. "Please, show yourself to me."

The air wavered, warming around her, filled with the scent of summer pine and ferny grottoes. It nearly overwhelmed her. Her ears felt pressure and popped and the air seemed gone from her lungs. And then a whirlwind grew before her, twirling up from the ground itself, growing taller, until it towered over her. The scent of the forest filled her senses, but the wind didn't touch her. Suddenly green eyes blinked to brilliant life only inches from her own. The wind vanished and before her stood the Forest Knight, at least seven feet tall, even though he held his head in his big hands, dangling it in front of her nose by its leafy hair.

Frightened, she said meekly, "Hello."

The green face spread into a grin; then the mouth opened and hearty laughter blew hot desert air into her face.

"For you," rumbled the mouth in the severed head. His other hand held out a bright sprig of holly with brilliant red berries.

Then he was gone. Just. Like. That.

Gathering her nerves, she walked out of the chapel and straight into the beam of a flashlight. Instinctively, her hand drew the metal nightstick from her pocket.

"It's me."

"Kendra! I'm so glad to see you! Hi Jimmy." She tried to control herself, but it was impossible. "I saw him!"

"*Him?*" Kendra asked.

"Him." Sam showed her the holly spring. "And now I know where Merilynn got her sense of humor. Come on, let's get to the lake; then I'll tell you the rest."

49

The trio saw flashes of light between the trees as they neared the lake, but when they emerged from the forest and saw the city on the water, they were speechless.

Sam took in the city of castles and towers, spirals and pillars, arches, balconies, vast mullioned windows of colored glass lit like jewels. Amber lights glowed from within the pale whites and tans, misty blues and delicate rose-tinted structures. "What is it?" she murmured.

"I don't know, but it's sure not Applehead, risen from the bottom of the lake," Kendra told her.

"It's amazing," Jimmy said. "Is this what you brought me to see?"

Kendra chuckled. "No. I brought you here to watch a meteor shower."

The three glanced up at the velvet dark sky.

"The knight told me to tell you that you're very brave."

Sam's heart lurched and she whirled. "Merilynn, I *hate* it when you do that."

Merilynn's laughter lilted. She was dressed in dark green and her chipmunk was perched on her shoulder nibbling a nut. "I'm sorry." She took the arm of the fiftyish man standing next to her. "You remember my father, Martin, don't you?"

"Of course," Kendra said. She stepped forward and hugged the man.

Sam shook his hand. "I'm glad to see you again."

Martin smiled. "And you."

"Jimmy, this is Merilynn's daddy, Martin. Merilynn, you've met Jimmy?"

"No, actually." She clasped his hand and said, "I hear we were pretty hot and heavy though."

"What?"

"Relax, Jimmy," Kendra said. "She's pulling your leg."

"Not entirely," Sam said.

"What are you talking about?" Jimmy asked.

"Nothing important," Sam told him.

But he no longer looked at Merilynn. Now his eyes were fixed on Martin's neck. On the collar visible just in the V of his jacket. "That doesn't look like a white T-shirt," he ventured.

"It's not."

"He's a priest."

"Not all priests are pedophiles," Martin said gently. "And some aren't even gay. Not that there's anything wrong with that." He smiled and looked at the lake. "I always knew my little girl was an artist."

Sam turned, horrified that she had forgotten about the ghostly castles sitting on the water, seeming to cast their reflection down into the depths of the lake. "It's amazing, Merilynn. Astonishing."

"What is it?" Kendra asked.

"My other father taught me the trick. It's a real but rare phenomenon I thought you two would be interested in, so I whipped it up. It's a mirage."

"The Fata Morgana mirage?"

"Yes, Sam. I thought you'd like to see one while you can."

They gazed at it for long moments, no one speaking. Finally, Kendra spoke. "It's beautiful."

"As Malory was long ago. It's named for her. Morgana, sister to Arthur. Betrayer of the king and her mentor. She had a long reign." Merilynn fell silent.

"Why did you say you wanted us to see the mirage while we can?"

Merilynn smiled. "I wondered how long it would take you to ask. It's because I won't be able to make such a huge glamour again after tonight. Power turned Malory into a demon. I don't want that. Perhaps some day I'll feel capable of handling power wisely, but for now . . ." She paused, unzipping her jacket and pulling the small broadsword with its brilliant gleaming stone. "For now, I'm returning this to a safe place. Look at the water."

Slowly, Holly Gayle emerged from the water, not walking toward them but moving straight up until she seemed to stand on it. In her long white gown, she looked like a lady from the castles far beyond.

Sam gasped as the spirit glided toward them. Merilynn stepped to the water's edge, holding the gleaming blade across her palms. The jewel sent out a light of its own.

Sam hesitated, them moved to Merilynn's side. The others followed. Holly looked from person to person, her eyes radiating happiness. Out of the corner of her eye, Sam saw movement and then Eve stood there with them, smiling, happy again.

"Take this back to the church for safekeeping for me, Holly. Will you do this for me?"

Of course.

Holly put her hands out and Merilynn put the miniature sword in them. Power filtered from her and into the spirit. "You are all free now," she said. "I was afraid you might have gone already."

We don't wish to leave now that Malory is gone.

We're staying, Eve said inside Sam's head. *As long as you are here, we will be.*

Merilynn's smile was radiant. "But why?"

We're no longer bound to the lake. We can do as we please. And it is our pleasure to guard you. And to keep this safe for you. She gazed at the sword. Holly bowed her head to Merilynn, then slowly glided backward and then down into the lake.

Sam watched the light of the gemstone until it was lost. She looked back up at the mirage, but it was rapidly fading away. "It was so beautiful."

"It was," Merilynn said. "But so are other things. Look up!"

Meteors burst like distant fireworks above them and a deep rumbling vibrated the ground, then raised in pitch. It was the Forest Knight's jolly laughter.